# ANYTHING FOR YOU

## ALSO BY SAUL BLACK

*The Killing Lessons*
*LoveMurder*

# ANYTHING FOR YOU

## SAUL BLACK

ST. MARTIN'S PRESS ≈ NEW YORK

First published in the United States by St. Martin's Press,
an imprint of St. Martin's Publishing Group

ANYTHING FOR YOU. Copyright © 2019 by Saul Black.
All rights reserved. Printed in Canada. For information, address
St. Martin's Publishing Group, 120 Broadway, New York, NY 10271.

www.stmartins.com

The Library of Congress Cataloging-in-Publication Data is available upon request.

ISBN 978-1-250-19991-1 (hardcover)
ISBN 978-1-250-19992-8 (ebook)

Our books may be purchased in bulk for promotional, educational,
or business use. Please contact your local bookseller or the Macmillan Corporate
and Premium Sales Department at 1-800-221-7945, extension 5442,
or by email at MacmillanSpecialMarkets@macmillan.com.

First Edition: November 2019

10 9 8 7 6 5 4 3 2 1

*For the peerless JGs:*
*Jonny Geller and Jane Gelfman*

# ACKNOWLEDGMENTS

Thanks to: Louise Maker, Mark Duncan, Marina Hardiman, Annalisa Ferrarotto, Stephen Coates, Nicola Stewart, Jonathan Field, Vicky Hutchinson, Peter Sollett, Eva Vives, Mike Loteryman, Anna Baker-Jones, Alice Naylor, Susanna Moore, Charles Spicer, and Deborah Schneider.

# PART
# ONE

# 1

## *July 31, 2017*

He'd never been enslaved by a woman before, but he was sure as shit enslaved by this one. Ever since he'd met her two months ago he'd been moving through his days in a state of erotic shock, appalled at the hold she had over him and powerless to do anything about it. Some mornings he looked in the mirror and just shook his head, baffled. He was, he had to admit, worried about himself. He'd had his share of females—dumb, dirty, damaged, depressing, demanding, desperate, occasionally even madly devoted—but he'd never, in the whole gaudy carnival of his unpredictable life, had a Class-A velvet-blond clairvoyant super-bitch like Sophia. The woman was soft as mink and smart as the Devil. The woman read his mind. And he didn't even know her last name.

"So how come?" he said to her.

"How come what?"

"How come I get the chauffeur treatment?"

It was just after sundown and they were heading north out of the city in her car, a top-of-the-line Volvo that smelled as if it had just rolled off the production line. Sophia was wearing a gray cashmere dress and tan suede knee boots he knew (with a little detonation of rage in his teeth and armpits) would've retailed at about five times his monthly salary. All her gear looked kosher. She dressed like the sort of hooker with rates so high you'd never know she was a hooker. Sort who could live like a queen on three tricks a year, jetted out to bored Russian billionaires or kinky Saudi royals.

"I told you," she said. "It's a surprise."

"A dirty surprise?"

She didn't answer. Just smiled and kept her eyes on the road. He took it as confirmation, but to remove any doubt he said: "I ain't forgotten what you said last time."

Sophia kept looking straight ahead. Her eyes had a cold glittery power he knew could spook him if she decided to turn them on him and really look.

"You hear me?" he said.

"Yes, I hear you. I haven't forgotten, either."

"And?"

"And I keep my promises."

His cock stirred. The last time they'd been together, in yet another hotel (she always chose the meeting places, it was one of her many Rules) she'd said to him: I know what you want. At the time he'd been fucking her, slowly and with relished contempt, in the ass. She'd been on her elbows and knees, back arched, blond hair spread on the pillow in a soft explosion.

You know what I want?

Of course I do.

Prove it.

Not this time.

Yeah, this time.

No, not this time. I told you. You've got to earn it.

You're pretty sure of yourself, princess.

At which point she'd turned and looked over her shoulder at him and said:

I know I'm worth it. And so do you.

That, he thought now, as she eased the Volvo out past an eighteen-wheeler lit up like a Christmas tree, was the problem. She *was* worth it. It wasn't that she did everything. Plenty of crazy women did everything. It was the *way* she did everything, with that calm look of knowing every filthy secret you had stashed in your miserable soul. In the sack Sophia looked at him like a scientist getting exactly the results she expected. It was the look that made him come, every time.

He moved his hand to her knee, slid it under her dress and up the long muscle of her thigh until he could feel the tender heat of her cunt. Her perfume smelled of vanilla.

"Not yet, please," she said. "I need to concentrate."

The new strap on his grandpa's wristwatch itched. When they'd given it back to him the old strap had been all but rotted away. He'd felt weird buying the new one. Handing over money. Getting a product. A legitimate, harmless action. This was the other world.

"I need to concentrate," she repeated.

He squeezed her thigh anyway. Then, with the strange obedience her witchcraft demanded, removed it, settled back in his seat, scratched his wrist under the new strap, and closed his eyes.

"Holy shit," he said. "This place yours?"

"No. It belongs to a friend. She lets me use it when she's away."

They'd left I-5 half an hour ago. Since then back roads, scrub, woodland, signs to places he'd never heard of. Now they'd pulled up at the white-graveled front of a country house in a clearing surrounded by evergreens. Not a huge place, but solid and well kept. The kind of civilized home he'd never set foot inside. The kind that made a mockery of his life of other people's couches and roachy one-room shit-holes—not to mention the years in his stinking cell. It gave him a sly thrill to think of fucking her in this house, surrounded by snug furnishings and top-dollar appliances. I ain't forgotten what you said last time. Damn right he hadn't. He was going to make a total pig of himself, whether she liked it or not. In fact he'd make sure she didn't like it. That was what he wanted. Witchcraft or not, he'd bet she didn't know *that*.

They got out of the car. The summer night was quiet around them. He looked up. Black sky crammed with stars. He thought of drifting alone out there, toward some final freezing edge where even the stars ran out. Shut the thought down.

"Help me with this stuff," Sophia said, popping the Volvo's trunk.

She reached in and pulled out a small cooler bag, slung it over her shoulder. "Grab that," she said, indicating a rolled-up tarp and blanket.

"What?"

"The bedding."

"We're not going inside? You're crazy."

"Indulge me. I like it outdoors."

"For Christ's sake."

"We'll go inside afterward," she said. She kissed him, pushed her tongue into his mouth. Then pulled back and looked at him. "You want to get what you want, don't you?"

"Your rules, huh?"

"My rules. Come on."

He reached in and picked up the bedding roll. My rules. It had been that way from the start. When she'd taken his cell phone number she'd said: I'll call you on this when I'm available. You won't be able to call me. Your number will be blocked from my phone. That's how this is going to work. After their first time together, when all she'd put out was a hand job (just a hand job, for Christ's sake—and he was hooked!) she'd made him get an HIV test. He'd laughed when she'd told him. Are you fucking kidding? No, I'm not fucking kidding. Thanks to the force of her witchcraft he'd gone and got the test. Incredibly, it was negative. After that the sexual sky was the limit with her, every spin a porno jackpot. Her only prohibition (she was very specific about it) was that he mustn't pull her hair. He figured a fat-cat husband, ivory tower, bored trophy wife looking for a little action on the dark side. Well, he could give her plenty of that. Enough so she'd wish she'd never been born.

He followed her across the lawn and down a narrow footpath that wound between the trees. The air smelled of dry ground and pine needles. It was a long time since he'd been anywhere like this. You forgot about it, nature, the earth, that darkness like something you could bathe in. It had a strange effect on him, as if his childhood had rushed up after all these years. He didn't like it.

"Can't see a goddamned thing," he said.

"It's okay. We're here."

He felt the air thin ahead of him. The trees gave onto an open space. Ten paces brought him up alongside her, looking out over a small lake, maybe fifty meters wide and not much longer. The woods on the far bank were a wall of blackness. His skin shrank at the thought of the dark water.

"I ain't going swimming," he said. "Rules or no rules."

"Relax," Sophia said. "We're not here for swimming. Would you lay that down for us?"

He dropped the bedding and rolled it out with his foot. She set the cooler bag down and unzipped it. Then she turned to him, kissed him again, touched his cock through his jeans. In spite of his determination to go slow, his hands went under her dress and grabbed her ass.

"Wait," she said. "Lie down."

He had the clear thought that he was going to kill her. It was the thought he always had with women. Their cunts were supposed to tighten when you choked them. Some hilarious reflex. Designed by God. God had a dirty mind.

"Please, lie down," Sophia said. Then she leaned close again and whispered in his ear: "Slow. You want this to last, don't you?"

He moved back from her and lay down on the blanket, propped up on his elbows. He took off his wristwatch and set it by the edge of the tarp. The strap had given him a slight rash.

Sophia slipped her arms from their sleeves and pulled the dress off over her head. No bra. Her bare flesh pale in the darkness. She stood over him.

"Unzip my boots," she said, smiling.

Jesus Christ, Jesus Christ, Jesus Christ . . . His hands trembled. Each boot came off with a soft suck. It made him think of her life of quality clothes and restaurants and bubble baths and twinkling lights and money. Her toenails were perfectly manicured, painted the same deep red as her fingernails. He didn't know how he was stopping himself from grabbing her and fucking her and choking her to death right there and then. Every second it seemed a certainty he would do just that. But he didn't. He waited.

Sophia stepped away again. She turned her back to him and slid her panties down, sticking her ass out a little to get them over her hips. Slender ankles. His flesh was dense and sensitive, his throat dry. She bent and reached into the cooler.

"Do you want champagne or beer?" she said. "You should have champagne, because I won't drink the whole bottle myself."

"I don't give a fuck," he said. "We can drink whatever you want. Just get over here."

It was when she straightened up and turned and he saw she was holding neither champagne nor beer that he realized he'd been wrong about her.

He'd been wrong about Sophia in a way he'd never been wrong about anyone in his life.

# 2

She'd watched it happen as if from outside her body. But the second it was over she'd been yanked back into herself with a force like a roller-coaster drop.

Now the gun was a hot weight in her hand. Her wrist thrummed from the silencered kick. It had felt like being stomped on by a hoof. She let the weapon fall to the ground. Her legs were heavy. She staggered to the water's edge, dropped to her hands and knees, and vomited.

For a few moments she stayed there, spitting out bile, eyes stinging. She had an image of herself, a naked goosefleshed woman groveling in the darkness. Primitive, an animal. The water lapped the shingle's edge. She was grateful for it. Nature didn't judge. The black lake, the pebbles, the trees, they shared a sentience that observed but didn't care. Nature was amoral, self-involved, indifferent to the whole human show. It was there before us and would be there when we were gone. That thought, too, comforted her.

No time. Get up. It's not over. Get up. Now.

But she couldn't, in fact, get up. She crawled further into the water until it covered her knees, calves, feet, arms up to the elbows. She bathed her hands and face, teeth chattering. Her remote Catholicism offered itself. Water to wash away Original Sin. She'd made her First Confession at St. Theresa's when she was eight years old. In the weeks leading up to it everyone in class had been fascinated by the idea that even if you confessed to murdering someone, the priest couldn't report you to the police. Father Arbuthnot had grown weary of being quizzed about it. How many of you are planning on murdering someone? he'd asked, exasperated. One of her classmates, a highly strung girl named Veronica Miller, wouldn't let it go. She was obsessed with the idea that God could forgive a murderer. Father Arbuthnot had spelled it out: There is *nothing*—literally nothing—God cannot find room in His heart to forgive, because God's love is *infinite*. ("Infinite" was a tricky word, but it conjured a notion of God's heart like a dark, star-filled warehouse that went on forever.) *But*, Father Arbuthnot continued, with a raised index finger, God's forgiveness is only for those who are *truly sorry for what they have done*. And you prove that by accepting your penance. ("Penance," they all knew, was something like five Hail Marys or ten Our Fathers.) So if one of you murdered someone and confessed it to me, I would tell you what any priest would tell you: that your penance would be to *hand yourself* in to the police. Do you understand? God would forgive you if you were truly sorry, but you could only prove that you were truly sorry by turning yourself in and owning up to what you had done. All right? Are you satisfied now? Can we stop, please, all this wretched talk about murder?

She got, by degrees, to her feet. The cold water had refreshed her. She didn't want to look at him. She didn't want to do any of the things she had to do.

So she made herself do them.

The first two shots had struck him in the stomach and chest. After firing twice she'd walked over (surreally aware of the grass tickling her bare toes) and put a third shot in his head. It had hit him just above his left eyebrow.

Glistening blood pooled under his skull. His white T-shirt was dark and wet around the other wounds. She thought of all the movies in which someone got shot. All the gallons of Hollywood blood. Fake.

Real.

The big stones and garbage bags were where she'd left them, a yard or two behind the tree line, along with the oxygen bleach. The rope was coiled on the spare wheel in the cavity under the floor of the Volvo's trunk. Four rolls of waterproof duct tape beneath the driver's seat, folded scrubs under the passenger. You do it right next to the lake so there's less ground to cross. You drag him.

Can you drag that weight? And if the stones work loose? The body fills with its own gasses. Floats up. Hi, everyone! Look at me—a corpse! The lake's forty feet deep. How long before ropes rot in water? She'd looked nothing up online. No such thing as an erased search history. Even idiots knew that. Check for blood under the tarp if the bullets have gone through. Dig out the bullets if they have. Remove the turf. Shell casings. Shoes.

She went over to the cooler bag. The air had already half dried her skin. She had a profane sensitivity to her nakedness: nipples, belly, thighs, ankles. It was as if the summer night caressed her, like a cat, with its mind on something else.

Ice. Freezer bags. Hacksaw. Sabatier meat knife.

Meat.

Knife.

The words floated free of their objects.

A bat whirred past her head, startling her.

It occurred to her that she hadn't thought to check no one else was here.

Well, it was too late now. It was too late for anything except going on.

She took the roll of freezer bags, the knife, and the hacksaw and knelt down beside his body.

By the time she was finished she knew the lake was a bad idea. She also knew (remembered hearing, or reading, or seeing on TV) that there was nothing more likely to get a criminal caught than changing his plan in the middle of the crime.

Changing *her* plan, rather. *Her* crime.

She sat back on her heels, took a deep breath—and considered her options.

# 3

## *August 5, 2017*

When the intruder triggered the motion-sensitive security lights in his son and daughter-in-law's backyard just after 2:00 A.M., seventy-four-year-old insomniac Vincent Lyle was doing what he was always doing at that unforgiving hour; namely, sitting in the conservatory trying and failing to read Jonathan Franzen's novel *The Corrections*. It wasn't this author in particular who defeated him. It was the entire project of Reading Books Allegedly Worth Reading.

For a moment, Vincent and the intruder looked at each other. Vincent was in his favored spot: the pink velour wingbacked chair next to the potted asparagus fern that poured down from its stand to the parquet with a delicate joie de vivre. The intruder, in black gear and ski mask with white-rimmed eyeholes, was picking himself up from the turf, where, apparently, he had tripped over the lawn roller in the dark. The white-rimmed eyeholes made Vincent think—in spite of the adrenaline—of a raccoon.

Vincent had been a Reader all his life, as a child, a student, a teacher, a professor, a dean of faculty. Reading had, in fact, been no less his life than his real life. *Ulysses,* he used to say with only slight exaggeration, had affected him easily as much as had falling in love for the first time. (Which he had done at eighteen, with Millie Doyle, a gymnastic Irish girl with corkscrewy blond hair and an appetite for books even more voracious than his own. She had broken his heart. They had both known she would, sooner or later.) Other loves and other books had followed, of course. For Vincent they were the twin sources that deepened the human mysteries and his own vital immersion in them. Eventually he had met Elsa Wheaton, a Classics professor who joined Stanford two years after him. They had both, in their late thirties, sufficient luck, imagination, and character to fall in love in the way that lasted, with a rare mix of sexual passion and the subtlety of appetite that kept it alive despite monogamy and the domestic grind. By forty-five they were both tenured, had two children (Helen and Lucas) enough money in the bank, a pleasant (book-filled, naturally) house on Peter Coutts Circle, and the grace to acknowledge at least from time to time that they were in the tiny minority of human beings who had actually ended up with the life they'd always wanted.

Then, ten years ago, Elsa had been hit by a drunk driver on Divisadero and killed. She was sixty-two. Vincent had stopped reading books after that. After that the quiet understanding the reading life had yielded seemed nothing but a vicious joke. The reading life hoodwinked you into thinking it was seasoning you, schooling you gently in the paradoxes and pratfalls of the human lot. The reading life, you thought, helped you cope with being alive.

But it turned out there were things that couldn't be coped with. For eight years after Elsa's death Vincent couldn't go near an allegedly worthwhile book. He tried. It made him physically sick. The little truths were still there, the humble epiphanies, the metaphors and similes that opened like time-lapse flowers—but they disgusted him. They disgusted him because they weren't enough. Without Elsa, without love, nothing was enough. Continuing teaching—Literature—was, obviously, impossible, so he quit. Instead he watched inane television, read the newspaper in blank indifference, spent hours staring out of the window, seeing nothing. Eventually, his son, Lucas, had persuaded him to move in with him, his wife, Jen, and their twin daughters at their large home in Pacific Heights. They gave Vincent a room on the ground floor and surrounded him with what they knew he needed: active life. Gradually, Lucas had worn away his father's refusal to even try to read. Vincent had agreed to reacquaint himself with Serious Contemporary Fiction. But it still felt to him like a dog returning to its vomit. Pointlessly.

*The Corrections* slid from Vincent's grasp and dropped to the floor. The intruder appeared to be frozen by the sudden glare of the security lights. He stood with one knee bent, arms slightly out.

Then he turned, ran to the back of the yard, trampled through the raised flowerbed, and disappeared behind the colossal and softly crashing bamboo.

Vincent lurched to his feet and stumbled through the conservatory back into the house. He took the stairs two at a time. His thighs labored. His face felt blood-packed. He was aware of the loudness of his own breathing.

"Lucas!" he hissed, pushing open his son and daughter-in-law's bedroom door. "Jesus Christ, Lucas!" The security lights were still on outside, and by their illumination Vincent found his way across the room to his son's side. He shook him. Lucas woke with a start.

"Jesus . . . Dad?"

"There's someone in the yard!"

"What?"

"There's a goddamned burglar!"

Lucas leaped out of bed and fumbled for his pants.

Jen woke up. "What the fuck?" she said.

"Stay here," Lucas said. "Let me check the girls."

"What is it? What *is* it?"

"Dad says there's someone in the yard."

"Oh my God."

It took Lucas a moment to establish his daughters were safe and sleeping soundly. Jen, in her underwear and T-shirt, was right behind him. Twenty-first-century reflex had armed her with her cell phone, grabbed from the nightstand.

"Stay in here with them," Lucas whispered. "Lock the door and call the cops."

The men waited at the top of the stairs until they heard Jen on the line. Then they went down, quickly.

The dark house was an awakened intelligence now, alert and powerless. The smell of the evening's lasagna hadn't quite faded. Lucas plucked a golf club from his bag in the back hall.

"Give me one of those," Vincent said.

"Don't be a moron, Dad. How many?"

"What?"

"How many of them were there?"

"Just one guy. I only saw one guy. Don't try anything. Wait for the cops."

"I'm just going to look. Stay here."

Vincent ignored the instruction and followed his son through the kitchen to the conservatory. Together they peered out through the glass.

The backyard was, not surprisingly, empty.

# 4

Less than twenty minutes later a squad car arrived. SFPD Officers Dean Gershon and Maria Lopez. Gershon was tall and blond, with a look of heavy softness to his limbs and a profile that evoked Winnie-the-Pooh. Lopez couldn't have been more than five seven, with a small, hard-pretty face and liquid black eyes. Her dark hair was scraped back into a short ponytail. For Vincent their presence brought Elsa's death back, those first hours and days in which the police had stopped being something on TV and started being something in his real life. To him the smell of their uniforms and gear was one of the odors of grief. The arrival of the police gave you the brutal truth: that you were never safe from random evil. No one, anywhere, was safe from that.

"Well," Officer Gershon said, coming back into the hall from his sweep of the grounds, "there's no one out there now. We'll notify the neighbors, but at the moment there's not much more we can do."

"Everything's secure," Officer Lopez said. She'd been round the interior with Lucas, checking doors and windows. Redundantly, she knew, since like all the homes in Pacific Heights, this one was intruder alarmed up the wazoo, and the alarm, clearly, had not been tripped.

"Looks like your yard adjoins your neighbor's at the back there, right?" Gershon said.

"More or less," Lucas said. "There's a stupid little overgrown alley between them that comes out between the two *front* yards. We put a padlocked iron gate in there a couple of years back, but it's easy enough to climb over, I guess."

"He's most likely gone," Lopez said. "The lights coming on will have spooked him. I'm guessing we're not dealing with a genius here. Break-ins in this part of town would need to be a lot higher-tech." She turned to Vincent. "You see any gear on him? A bag or a rucksack or anything?"

"No, nothing like that."

"Okay, well, we have your statement. Best thing we can do right now is check with your neighbors. If I were you I'd just reset the alarm codes when we're out of here, then go back to bed and get some sleep. We'll write you an incident reference in case you need to get back in touch. But for now—"

Her walkie clicked and a female voice came through: "Unit Twelve, Code One. Unit Twelve, Code One."

Some instinct or protocol, Vincent assumed, made Lopez leave the room as she responded: "Unit Twelve. Go ahead, Dispatch . . ."

Vincent expected a shift in Gershon's demeanor (though he had no idea what "Code One" might mean) but the officer remained where he was, leaning against the wall with his left hand in his pocket. To Vincent the posture was deflating: It was simply human. The police were human beings. Not omniscient. Not omnipotent. Only occasionally the dispensers of inadequate justice. When something happened to you—when *crime* happened to you—that wasn't what you wanted. You wanted deadly infallible machines who suffered neither fatigue nor ambivalence. That, and the power to raise victims from the dead, to reverse the math that had subtracted the meaning from your life.

Lopez rejoined them in the hall. Her alertness had been dialed up. Now Gershon *did* straighten. His hand left its pocket.

"We've got a two-four-five and possible one-eight-seven," Lopez said to her partner, heading toward the door. "Right now."

"Where?" Gershon said.

"What's going on?" Vincent said.

"Stay inside and lock up," Lopez called over her shoulder. "Don't let anyone in except us. We'll be back."

"What the hell?" Vincent said—but the officers were gone and the door slammed shut behind them.

# 5

Outside, Lopez was running to the squad car.

"*Qué pasa?*" Gershon said.

"It's here," Lopez said, popping the trunk.

"What?"

"It's right next door."

"Shit. Our guy?"

"Home intrusion, double stabbing, husband and wife. Wife made the call. Husband might have bought it already. Here, take the Halligan."

"Perp still here?"

"Apparently not, but we're not taking any chances. Ambulance is five minutes away. Another unit's en route."

They sprinted across the front lawn of the property next door to the Lyles'. Big maple trees, pale flowers like little faces in the dark, the scent of orange blossom and warm, sprinkler-rinsed travertine. Suburbia at night smelled of America at peace, Lopez thought. The old illusion.

At the door to 2088, Gershon worked the Halligan into the jamb. His face had a martial focus. He was sweating.

"Come on," Lopez said.

"It's coming . . . Got it. Chain'll go with a shove. Ready?"

"Ready."

Gershon extracted the Halligan from the second busted lock, drew his Luger, took a step back, and kicked the door as hard as he could.

The chain, as predicted, snapped—and the door flew open. Gershon pulled on gloves and hit the light switch. A large white hallway faced them, doors leading off. Gray stone floor tiles. One huge abstract canvas in streaks of purple and gold. A copper chandelier presiding. Twenty paces to the floating glass staircase.

"She's upstairs," Lopez said. She had her own weapon drawn. Between her and Gershon now was the familiar current, the fear and death and excitement. Years of training force-woven into their DNA. And still there remained the human margins the training didn't cover. That was the thrill, Lopez knew, the gap where you had to trust your imperfections.

"We need to clear."

"I'm going up."

"Don't be stupid."

"She could be bleeding out."

Gershon spoke into his walkie. "Gimmie an ETA on the medics."

"Two minutes."

He looked at Lopez. Two minutes? If there was hemorrhaging . . . He nodded: Okay.

Lopez moved across the hall and went up the stairs. Her hand was wet around the Smith & Wesson's grip. The landing's ceiling light was on, an opalescent glass globe the size of a beach ball. A bronze sculpture of an elongated female figure stood on a white plinth beneath it. The house was filled with judiciously dispensed wealth. How the other half live, Lopez thought. How the other half die, too. Death didn't discriminate. Death was politically correct.

The doors to the five upstairs rooms were all ajar.

The first was unmistakably a teenage girl's, unoccupied. Unmade bed, music posters, strewn clothes, a dressing table cluttered with cosmetics and goth jewelry, an odor of patchouli and denim. A Hello Kitty shoulder bag lay open on the floor.

Don't let it be her, Lopez thought. Rape, kidnapping, murder. Hello Kitty. For God's sake don't let it be her.

The next two doors revealed en suite guest rooms done in white, each with an abstract canvas similar to the one in the downstairs hall, but the second with two walls filled with books. Both rooms empty.

The fourth was a big family bathroom with a blue mosaic floor, walk-in shower, and sunken bath.

The fifth (as Lopez's soul already knew) was *not* empty.

Master bedroom. Polished oak floor and a white bed splashed with blood. Pastel silk scatter cushions, nightstand knocked over, lamp on the floor, its amber glass shade smashed, bare bulb exposed. One wall was occupied almost entirely by arty black-and-white photographs. A door led off to an en suite bathroom.

The first victim was naked on his back on the ivory rug at the foot of the bed. White male, late thirties. Dark lustrous hair and a lean body that was no stranger to the gym. His left arm was twisted under his spine and he was covered in blood. Eyes fixed and staring. Not breathing, as far as Lopez could see.

The second victim lay on her side by the open French windows that led out onto a balcony. White female, maybe early thirties, with short, stylishly chopped red hair. Her green silk nightdress was torn just above the knee, and she was bleeding from wounds in her left shoulder and side. She was struggling for breath—but she was breathing. An iPhone lay by her head. The operator's voice came through:

"Ma'am, stay with me . . . The officers are *right there* . . . Ma'am? The medics are coming . . ."

"Unit Twelve," Lopez said into her walkie. "Ten ninety-seven. She's alive. Give me her name again."

"Caller ID is Rachel Grant. Repeat: Rachel Grant."

"Copy that."

Lopez crossed to where the woman lay, poked her head out the French windows to check the balcony. Empty. Just the night's warm exhalation and San Francisco's lights twinkling prettily in the darkness.

Check the bathroom.

But the woman's hand came up and grabbed her calf.

"Adam . . ." the woman gasped. "Please . . . Adam?"

"Rachel, you're okay. Help's on the way. Is it just you and your husband here?"

The woman's eyes flirted with unconsciousness. Lopez got down on one knee—avoid the blood, don't mess with the scene—and took her hand. "The girl's room down the hall. Your daughter?"

The word "daughter" hauled Rachel Grant back, widened her eyes. "She's . . . at a friend's . . . Is Adam—"

"Just lie still," Lopez said. "The medics will be here any second. Don't try to move."

Rachel Grant released her hand. Her eyelids fluttered, then closed.

Lopez went to the male victim and checked for a pulse. Nothing. She ran to the bathroom and plucked a hand towel from the rail. Returned and did her best with it to apply pressure to the wound in Rachel Grant's side. There was a lot of blood. "Hang in there, Rachel. Open your eyes. Tell me your daughter's name."

"Elspeth," Rachel Grant whispered, but her eyes didn't open.

A siren, close. A vehicle pulled up, doors opened. Revolving blue light splashed the landing. Lopez hoped a vital organ hadn't been punctured. And thanked the God she no longer believed in that the daughter wasn't home. That would be the cold consolation once Rachel Grant learned her husband was dead: Be grateful your daughter was somewhere else. Be grateful for that, even though your life will never be the same again.

# 6

Homicide detectives Valerie Hart and Will Fraser arrived at the Grants'
house just after the CSI team had begun their work. It was getting light out.
The open French windows framed a curdled blue-and-pink San Francisco
sunrise over the bay, thin swirls of cloud it looked to Valerie like God had
stirred in a languid doodle before moving on to other things.

Rachel Grant had been rushed to the ER at California Pacific. She was
just out of surgery, but word was she'd live. Her husband's body was exactly
as Officer Maria Lopez had found it.

The medical examiner, Ricky Santayana, pulled off his gloves. Twenty
years ago he might have greeted the detectives with a jaded quip. But their
professions burned their share of levity fast. Superfluity lasted maybe a year.
After that you were stripped to the essentials. Even hellos and good-byes
were left behind.

"What's the story?" Valerie said, then, glancing at the corpse's face, did
a double take. "Jesus Christ."

"Yeah," Ricky said. "It's *that* Adam Grant."

"Holy moly," Will said. Both he and Valerie recognized the attorney. Until three years ago he'd been a star prosecutor in the DA's office. Then, to
the vocal disappointment of his employers, he'd made the switch to private
practice.

Valerie felt the chorus of assumptions rising. Silenced them. Homicide Lesson One: Take nothing for granted.

Homicide Lesson Two: Don't investigate the murder of anyone you've slept with.

Fuck.

Heat filled her face. Stars of sweat came out in her palms. She had an image of herself as if she were looking down from above: She was on her bed, blouse open, jeans off. She was lifting her hips to make it easier for Adam Grant to get her panties down.

Ricky massaged his left shoulder. Arthritis. He'd grown a plump beard recently. To Valerie, its gray streaks gave him the look of a badger. "Maybe two hours, no more," he said. "At least a dozen stab wounds, one almost certainly through the heart. Multiple deep skull fractures. Claw hammer. Rebecca's already bagged it. Officer Lopez over there was first on the scene."

Valerie and Will skirted the cordoned area (CSI went about their delicate business like large, gentle insects) to where Officer Maria Lopez stood waiting to give her report. Her face made it clear this wasn't her first murder scene, but a microclimate of spent adrenaline still surrounded her. Valerie had seen her around the station, but as far as she recalled they'd never spoken.

"Detectives," Lopez said.

"Maria—right?" Will said. Valerie registered: There wasn't a pretty female officer under forty whose first name Will didn't know.

"Right," Lopez said.

"Talk us through," Valerie said.

Lopez had her notepad open. She'd had time to draft the basics since arriving, but Valerie knew not all her colleagues would have used it. Good. She liked competent cops—but she liked competent *female* cops the best.

"We got here around two thirty A.M. in response to a possible two-five-nine in progress at the house next door. That's Lucas and Jennifer Lyle, their twin daughters, and Lucas's father, Vincent Lyle. Lyle Senior was in the conservatory at the rear of the house when the security lights came on and he saw a guy in black gear and a ski mask on the back lawn. Suspect ran, and by the time we got here there was no sign of him. The two houses' backyards are separated by a narrow alleyway, so presumably he just went over."

"What was Lyle Senior doing in the conservatory at two in the morning?" Valerie asked.

"Insomnia," Lopez said. "Reading. Doesn't sleep much since he lost his wife. He'll tell you all about it. Anyway, we were wrapping up when Dispatch called *this* one in. We were the nearest unit, obviously. My partner forced entry and I came up to find Mr. Grant over there, and his wife, Rachel Grant, with two knife wounds, lying over by the French windows. I applied a compress to what looked to me the more serious injury until the paramedics arrived a few minutes later. Rachel Grant was unconscious by then. They took her straight to the ER."

"I know you didn't touch anything," Will said.

"Aside from checking Mr. Grant's pulse and taking a towel from the en suite, no, I didn't touch anything."

"No one else home?" Valerie asked. "I saw a girl's room back there."

"The daughter. Elspeth. All I got from Mrs. Grant was that she's staying over at a friend's place."

"Teenager?"

"You'd figure, from the room."

"The wife get a look at the guy?" Will asked.

"Unknown. But if it's the same guy he was wearing a ski mask."

"The alarm didn't trip when you forced entry?" Valerie said.

"No, ma'am. From what I can see, they've got a top-of-the-line system here. Guess he knew what he was doing. Or it malfunctioned."

"She say anything else before she lost consciousness?"

"No."

"No blood-prints on the stairs," Valerie said. "Either he was extremely careful or he got out another way. Hang on a second."

She moved around the team and out through the French windows onto the balcony. Black stone-tiled floor with a glass surround. Half a dozen potted plants. As she'd hoped, a brushed-steel drainpipe ran within reach from the gutter above all the way down to the lawn. If he'd bothered with a ski mask then he'd bothered with gloves, but she went over to CSI team leader Rebecca Beitner anyway.

"Check the balcony glass and drainpipe for prints," she said to Rebecca. "Maybe scuff marks on the wall."

"Really?" Rebecca said. "Gosh, why didn't I think of that?" Rebecca looked, as always, sleep-deprived. Frizzy hair and skin so pale you could see the capillary webbing in the orbits of her eyes. *I looked completely fucking exhausted even when I was a kid,* she'd told Valerie, years ago. *Seriously, people used to think my parents had adopted a little Jewish vampire girl. So when I grew up I just chose a job that rationalized the look. It's like becoming a hopscotch specialist if you've only got one leg.*

"Apparently he was in next door's backyard," Valerie said. "So you'll need a cordon and sweep there. The alleyway, too."

"Ex-con with a grudge?" Rebecca said.

"Only if it's a *dumb* ex-con with a grudge."

"Well, they're not in short supply."

Valerie returned to Will and Lopez. "Okay," she said. "I'm going to the hospital to talk to the mother. The daughter's number's got to be in the cell phone but Rebecca'll rip your face off if you try'n go near it. Meantime see what these guys turn up here. Call Counseling and have them get in touch with me. I don't want the kid being picked up in a squad car—" Then to Lopez, "No offense."

"None taken," Lopez said. "It's not a job I'd be volunteering for."

And this isn't a job I should even be doing, Valerie thought.

# 7

Valerie got into her Taurus and took a deep breath. Which was nowhere near as pacifying as a cigarette would have been at that moment. It had been four months. The cravings had diminished but they knew a weak moment when they saw one. It was supposed to be a relief to have quit. In fact it annoyed her. Most of her self-improvements, it turned out, got on her nerves. She took a stick of gum from her purse and folded it into her mouth.

On the one hand, it was straightforward. Four years ago she'd slept with Adam Grant. Ergo, pass the case to a colleague. On the other hand, she'd slept with him *literally*. Both of them had been drunk, and halfway through the blurred preliminaries he'd had a change of heart. He'd told her he'd never cheated on his wife, and despite him and Valerie having boozily made out and gotten half-naked in her bed, it turned out he couldn't bring himself to *start* cheating on his wife right then, either. At the time Valerie had wondered if it was just that he couldn't get it up. Their foreplay had proceeded through a numb haze, but she was aware that he was much more interested in touching her than he was in her touching him—and she didn't find him hard when she did touch him. Given the phase she'd been in—a trawl of love-is-dead one-night stands, labored through with detached self-disgust— it hadn't been a big deal to her.

They'd spent a few strange minutes lying side by side, discussing whether he was going to leave—then both of them had rather absurdly fallen asleep. Valerie had been woken later by the sound of him falling over as he was trying to step into his pants. They'd laughed, and the laughter was the first truly sympathetic moment in the whole encounter. He'd finished dressing, sat on the edge of the bed, and held her hand for a moment, apologized for being a waste of time—then left. Valerie had found herself liking him. But liking him had reminded her of how little she liked herself, and she'd spent the last hour of darkness after he'd gone lying on her bed wondering how much longer she was going to carry on living like this, in empty self-loathing, while the window paled from twilight to dawn and the alcohol in her blood resolved itself into yet another a thudding hangover.

She and Adam Grant had glimpsed each other a couple of times since then, professionally, shared a smile, conceded the moment had passed—and that was all. It had been more than a year since she'd last seen him.

Now he was dead. And she was going to break the news to his widow.

Wonderful. Her history was a swarm of flies, never far away. Always close enough to resettle on her skin. To remind her of what she'd been.

She sat with her hands on the Taurus's wheel, chewing her gum joylessly. Option one was simple: Call Captain Deerholt, explain through clenched teeth that she had a personal history with the victim (and by shameful extension, victim*s*) get him to turn the case over to another team, and, for the ensuing investigation, *stay the fuck out of it.*

Option two . . . Well. Option two was to just keep her mouth shut and carry on. There was absolutely no reason to think that an abortive one-night stand from four years ago would have any bearing on Adam Grant's murder. The overwhelming likelihood was that the investigation would reach its end without it ever surfacing.

But the trouble with *absolutely no reason to think* and *overwhelming likelihood* was that the universe had no respect for such things. The universe was perverse.

There was, of course, Nick to consider. Valerie and her husband had drawn a line under the past (*her* past, since his was infuriatingly innocent) because to do otherwise would have made their shared present at best drearily haunted and at worst simply untenable. Nick knew what she'd been like in the years between their breaking up and getting back together. He knew, because Valerie had told him, that there had been plenty of guys. He knew that she had been, in the words of her own choosing, "a robotic alcoholic slut." In theory, Adam Grant having been *one* of the guys shouldn't matter.

But *in theory* and *shouldn't matter* were treated by the perverse universe with the same contempt as *absolutely no reason to think* and *overwhelming likelihood*. Aside from the professional view Nick would take—namely that personal history disqualified her from the job—his heart wasn't immune: It was one thing to know there had been plenty of guys. It was another to have one of them brought back to center stage, even as a corpse.

Fuck it, she thought. Do one interview with the wife and see how you feel after that. If you don't like it you can pass it on. You can always say you didn't recognize Adam Grant at the scene. Deerholt will believe you because Deerholt (along with everyone else at the Shop) knows the fucking mess you were back in the days of robotic alcoholic sluttery.

More because she was irritated by her uncertainty than because she'd really decided anything, Valerie started the car, reached again for the cigarettes that weren't there, sighed, then pulled away into the deceptive dawn quietude of Pacific Heights.

# 8

"Barring infection, yeah, she'll survive," Dr. Sheila Tabor told Valerie thirty minutes later in the corridor outside Rachel Grant's room at California Pacific. "The abdominal wound just missed the liver but punctured the stomach. We repaired that. The shoulder . . . That's a little more ambiguous. It's possible there'll be lasting nerve damage there. Aside from that, she's stable."

"Conscious? I need to talk to her."

"She's only just out of recovery, so she'll still be groggy. Pain meds, too, obviously."

"So that's a yes."

"It's a yes, with the caveat that she's not exactly sharp. You planning on telling her her husband's dead?"

"Someone has to."

"Do me a favor," Tabor said. "Hold off as long as you can. Shock isn't on the list of things she needs right now."

"I'll do my best," Valerie said. The two women exchanged a look: the prosaic ugliness their jobs entailed.

"One other thing," Valerie said. "I'm going to get an officer here on watch. Your patient's the eyewitness to a homicide, and for all we know this was a targeted hit rather than a break-in gone wrong. There's no guarantee he won't try again. No visitors without my clearance, and the officer'll need a photo

ID checklist of all hospital personnel likely to be entering the room. Who do I talk to to arrange that?"

"Actually I'm not sure. I guess Harold Yang. He's the chief medical exec, but I doubt he'll be in this early. Meantime you can talk to Mike Langley. Ask at the desk and they'll page him when you're ready. Right now I'm due back in theater."

Dr. Tabor walked away, orange Day-Glo Crocs squeaking on the gleaming floor.

Valerie entered Rachel Grant's room and took a seat by the bed, where the woman lay with her eyes closed and her arms outside the covers. Apart from the whisper of medical technology the place was silent.

Rachel Grant was slender but with a look of supple athleticism. A face of elegant prettiness complemented by short dark copper hair niftily chopped to yield a tousled effect. Even bereft of makeup and denuded by trauma an attractive woman. An IV fed into the back of her left hand, the index finger of which was clamped with the standard monitor peg. No jewelry, apart from a wedding band.

Wedding band.

Your husband is dead. But look on the bright side: He loved you enough not to fuck me when he had the chance.

Before opening her mouth Valerie made a final mental check that she really did want to go ahead with this, got the same ambivalence (and irritation) as before—and made the same decision.

"Rachel?" she said.

No response.

Valerie placed her hand over Rachel Grant's. Gave it a slight shake. "Rachel?" she repeated, a little louder.

The eyes opened. Green, intelligent—but for the moment, uncertain.

"Rachel, can you hear me? I'm Detective Valerie Hart, San Francisco—" She stopped herself just before "Homicide," adjusted. "San Francisco Police Department. Rachel?"

Rachel turned her head on the pillow. The green eyes found Valerie's.

Focused. Valerie watched her reconstructing her history, her identity—and the bad dream of what had happened.

Then the recognition that it hadn't been a dream at all.

"My husband," Rachel said.

*I'll do my best.* So much for that. It wasn't the first time Valerie had had to break the worst news. Every time it was the same: You searched for a way to soften the blow. And in the end there was nothing but the violent fact. The violent fact was the gentlest thing you had to offer.

"I'm sorry, Rachel. Adam was dead by the time the medics arrived. I'm so sorry."

For several seconds Rachel Grant just stared at her. Valerie had seen this before, too: the recipient of the worst news trying desperately to make the truth a lie, a trick, an illusion, a joke in the most hideous taste. Anything but what it was. Anything but the truth. The only honorable thing the bearer of the worst news could do was not look away. So Valerie didn't.

Rachel Grant's face burned through the last of its disbelief, lost its composure, seemed, by degrees, to collapse. Tears welled. The calm mouth wobbled. To Valerie it was as if the features were struggling to find a different logic, one that would accommodate this new deformed reality. Another person's grief was ugly. And to the detached part of you, the ugliness was fascinating. This was Being Police: You looked at horror and didn't hate yourself for not being horrified. If you couldn't do that you couldn't *be* Police. It was a necessary condition of the job.

Rachel Grant closed her eyes. Swallowed. Valerie continued holding her hand. It felt hot.

"Elspeth," Rachel Grant said. "My daughter . . ."

"If you give me the number I can call her."

"She's at . . ." But Rachel Grant couldn't, for a moment, continue. With her free hand she covered her face. Her body shook with sobs. "Oh, God. Oh, God . . ."

"Take your time," Valerie said.

"My phone . . ."

"Your phone's with the CSI team for now. Does Elspeth have a cell phone?" Valerie took out her own phone. "She's probably still sleeping, right? But if you have the number for where she's staying . . . Or the address?"

Valerie observed as Rachel Grant's motherhood kicked in. It was extraordinary, and, at the species level, simply impressive. The woman's husband was dead—*murdered*—but that horror had to be shunted aside to establish that her daughter was safe. The maternal priorities, even in moments of extremis, endured.

"She's at her friend Julia's. Let me call her."

"Absolutely," Valerie said. "If you give me the address I'm going to have officers and a counselor go over there and collect her."

Elspeth, not surprisingly, didn't answer her cell. It was only just eight thirty and she was a teenager. Valerie imagined the girl's world of playlists and gossip and crushes and tweets, her inability to imagine anything beyond it—and the new beyond it she was about to meet.

Calling Julia's parents wasn't straightforward, since the number was in Rachel's absent phone. Valerie had to get it from Rebecca. Awkward minutes. Elspeth was woken and put on the line. Valerie watched as Rachel forced herself to hold back the tears.

"Honey, listen . . . Something's happened. I'm hurt and in the hospital . . . No, no, I'm fine. I'm going to be absolutely fine. The police are going to come to Julia's and bring you to see me . . ." Her jaws tightened at what Valerie knew must be the obvious question. "No, Dad's . . . Dad's not here. Just get dressed and wait for the officers. No, no, don't worry, sweetheart. Just wait for the officers. They'll bring you. Everything's . . . everything's going to be okay."

Rachel hung up the phone and handed it back to Valerie.

"I'll be just a moment," Valerie said, getting to her feet. Best not to make the call in Rachel's presence: *Listen, be gentle with this kid. Her dad's been stabbed to death and her mom's a fucking wreck . . .*

She'd just got off the phone with the duty officer at the station when Rebecca Beitner called.

"We found the knife."

"Where?"

"Flowerbeds under the balcony. Looks like he took a tumble getting down. We may actually be looking for Forrest Gump."

Valerie went back into Rachel's room and resumed her seat. Tears still hurried from Rachel's eyes. Valerie handed her the box of tissues from the nightstand. Small gestures. Superficially worthless gestures, which in fact performed the humble miracle of forcing a person to keep going, through the seconds, the minutes, the hours, the days.

"I have to ask you a few questions," Valerie said, taking out her notepad.

Rachel didn't answer.

"I know this is the last thing you feel like doing right now. I'm sorry. I'll be as quick as I can."

Still no reply. Rachel just lay there, clutching the tissue. Her nostrils were raw.

"Could you tell me what happened? Could you tell me what you remember?"

It took a long time. Rachel kept breaking down. There were short periods when she seemed to get herself under control, or when the act of retelling exerted a numbing self-mesmerism, as if she were recounting a story that belonged to someone else—then she'd realize that it wasn't someone else, it had really happened to *her*—and she'd fall apart again, unable to continue. Valerie made the notes when there were notes to make, waited when there was only Rachel Grant's silence.

In spite of how long it took, the story was straightforward. In the late afternoon Rachel had driven Elspeth over to her friend Julia Klein's home about fifteen minutes away for a sleepover. She'd had coffee with Dina Klein, Julia's mother, then picked up groceries for dinner with Adam, gone home, opened a bottle of wine, and started preparing the meal. She'd watched TV until he came home around 7:00 P.M., earlier than usual, since a child-free evening was a precious commodity. They'd had dinner (Adam had drunk the bulk of the first bottle and the better part of a second), watched half a movie, then retired around 11:00 P.M. (Rachel didn't say so, but Valerie inferred—this was one of the moments of breakdown—that they'd had sex.) Adam fell asleep. Rachel read for an hour or so, then she, too, fell asleep. She got up in the small hours to use the bathroom—and when she came out, the intruder, armed with a knife and a hammer, was in the bedroom. (Valerie pressed for a description, but it was the usual helpless blur. Aside from the observation that he was wearing dark clothes—black running gear was how Rachel described it, a zip-up top with a roll-neck—sneakers, and a black ski mask with white around the eyeholes, the physical details were useless. A guess at around six feet tall and slender build. Oddly—to Valerie's mind—he wasn't wearing gloves. Which at least yielded a racial elimination: He was white.)

"He hit him," Rachel said. "He hit him with . . ." She swallowed; fresh tears welled. The words wouldn't come.

"Take your time," Valerie said. "I know how hard this is for you."

Rachel shook her head. Partly a denial of the memory itself—*willing* it not to be true—but partly, Valerie understood, a denial of what she, Valerie, had just said. *I know how hard this is for you.* How could she know?

Rachel closed her eyes again. Opened them. She was forcing herself through. The grief was plain, but there was rage, too, that it had happened right in front of her, in her own beautiful warm familiar home filled with their history and love and life—and there had been nothing she could do to stop it.

"He hit him with the . . . hammer . . ." Her mouth contorted. "He hit him so hard . . . Oh God . . . What am I going to say to Elspeth? What am I going to *say*?"

Valerie waited again. Longer this time. Rachel Grant just kept shaking her head. Swallowing, swallowing, as the images played on a loop from which she would never, now, escape, the movie that would run and run.

"I must have screamed," she said eventually. "He . . . I ran at him. I ran at him but he . . . I don't even remember feeling it. And then he just kept . . . He just . . ."

"He stabbed Adam?"

"Yes."

Pause.

"He kept on . . . He just kept *on* . . ." Rachel trembled. "I tried to get up. I tried to."

"You did everything you could," Valerie said. "More than many people would have done. Please remember that."

Rachel shook her head again. They were all just words to her. She'd watched her husband dying and been powerless to stop it. By definition nothing she'd done was enough.

"I guess I passed out," she said. "He must have thought I was dead."

A note of coldness here. Rachel Grant's delayed realization that her own life had almost been taken. What that would have done to her daughter.

"When I opened my eyes he was gone. Adam wasn't moving. I went to him but I couldn't feel anything. I couldn't feel anything . . . He was just . . ."

She had crawled to her purse by the French windows. Cell phone. Nine-one-one. While the blood hurried out of her body, dragging her senses with it.

"The French windows weren't open when you went to bed?" Valerie asked.

"No."

"And the alarm?"

"What?"

"The alarm wasn't tripped?"

"No. I don't . . . I went up before Adam. He set the alarm."

"You know that he set it?"

"Why wouldn't he set it? He . . ."

"Is it possible he forgot?"

"No . . . No. He wouldn't forget."

"But you didn't see him do it?"

Rachel stirred with helpless impatience. "I didn't see him do it but why wouldn't he do it? What the fuck—"

"We have to learn everything we can about the perpetrator. It'll help us catch him. If he had the ability to deal with a sophisticated alarm system, that's relevant information. It means we're not looking for an amateur, and probably not an opportunist. It means this is someone who planned this ahead. It means it's more than likely someone who's been watching your place for a while. It's possible someone in the neighborhood might have seen him. I promise you, I'm only asking these questions to maximize our chances of getting him."

Rachel turned away. With contempt, Valerie knew. Not just at what had happened, but at the inevitability of all that had to happen, all that had to go on happening, in spite of it. For the survivors of horror, the most sickening thing *was* their survival. Rachel Grant would either get past that—reassemble some new mangled version of herself from the wreckage of the old—or she wouldn't, and instead live the rest of her life like a violently broken machine, one that remembered its functions but could no longer perform them.

"I don't know for a fact that he set the alarm," Rachel said, her face still turned away. "I just don't know why he wouldn't."

There was a knock at the door. Valerie got up and opened it to Riordan, a uniformed officer in her midtwenties she recognized from the station.

"We have Elspeth Grant here with us," Riordan said.

Valerie stepped out into the corridor. Elspeth Grant, in blue jeans and a white cheesecloth hippie shirt, looked about thirteen. Thick, long dark hair and large eyes that made Valerie think of an exquisitely realistic puppet. "Pretty" wasn't quite the word. The girl had a petite dramatic glamor that at just the wrong angle might be ugly. The remnants of last night's heavily applied eyeliner (illicit, Valerie imagined, but indulged in for the sleepover) were still visible. Maybe as recently as six months ago she would have been described as a child. Now the accents of young womanhood were insinuating themselves. At the moment, however, she looked taut and bright with fear.

Standing next to her was an officer from Victim Support, a tall, fair-haired woman in pastel Gap casuals.

"Carrie Wheeler," she said, shaking hands with Valerie.

"Valerie Hart." Again Valerie edited out "Homicide," this time for Elspeth Grant's benefit. "SFPD. Could I speak with you for a moment?"

The two women stepped a few paces away and lowered their voices.

"You know the story?" Valerie asked.

"Home intrusion, father dead, mother just about alive. Nothing more than that. And the kid's still in the dark."

"You'll go in with her? It'll steady the mother."

"That's Mrs. Grant's call, but yeah, I'll go in to start with."

Valerie glanced back at Elspeth. The girl was tracking the exchange. It was familiarly dismal to Valerie to know what was coming to her. And a relief to know that this time it didn't fall to her to break the news. She remembered kissing Adam Grant, their mouths sour from the evening's booze and chili olives. The first touch of his hand between her legs. Lifting her hips to make it easier for him to pull her panties off. She remembered not being sure if it was going to be any good between them. She remembered not caring. The images put a connection between her and Elspeth Grant, as if a phantom umbilicus joined them. Valerie resisted the urge to put her hand over her abdomen.

"Okay," she said to Carrie Wheeler. "I'll leave you to it. I've got to go talk to the exec on duty. Meantime tell the officer no one goes in or out of the room except you and the girl. I'll be back shortly."

Valerie watched Carrie Wheeler say a few quiet words to Elspeth, who absorbed them with a look of incomprehension.

At the door, Elspeth glanced back at her.

As if she felt the connection, too.

# 9

## *July 31, 2017*

There was nothing wrong with the Volvo's air-conditioning, but she killed it and rolled the windows down instead, let the in-rushing night air love her up like an incubus, her hair, her skin, her sweat-damp clothes. The cooling of her underarms was particularly delicious. Post-murder one craved elemental molestation, apparently, the cold water of the lake, the darkness of the evergreens—and now the desert's mineral breath. Childhood came back, with its sensual certainties. She thought of the stones and pebbles out here revolving their shadows through the blazing afternoons. Mute planetary clockwork, without witness.

Without witness.

You better hope. Pray. Not bother to care.

That, bizarrely, was easy. Pure liberty was pure levity, at least in its first hours.

She eased off the gas. The innocent don't rush. Remember that.

Deep down she'd known it would be the desert in the end. Even driving to the lake house she'd taken a mental inventory of the yard tools. Only two mattered: Shovel. Wheelbarrow. The image of the body floating up wouldn't give her peace. She'd played it out according to plan, but the shift at the end had seemed inevitable. Inevitable because it was harder. For the murderer, she intuited now, the hardest option was always the best. An ironically punitive inversion of Occam's razor. She'd gone back to education, after Larry, after the bad years, after her rescue. Opening books again after having drifted so far from them had filled her with frail joy. Now her education was like leftover foreign currency she knew she'd never bother changing back. Murder, it turned out, closed certain doors. She wasn't complaining. It opened others. Oddly, not into godlessness. If anything, the Divine page had been refreshed, albeit with an identity the priests and teachers of her childhood would find abhorrent. God was neither benevolent nor malign. In fact he had only two characteristics: infinite creativity and insatiable detached interest in its products. Auschwitz and the Sistine Chapel. Mandela and the gulags. Love and hatred. Cruelty and compassion. Birth and death.

She took a swig from the bottle she'd opened and turned hard right off the empty road straight into the scrub. She found herself smiling as the alcohol went into her and warmed her empty belly. Superficially because the tequila was Don Julio Real (around $350 a bottle) and she remembered a vestige of political guilt the first time she'd bought it. *Not* superficially because after all the meticulous planning this felt like a crazy trip off-piste, absurdly high risk. She knew where she was—no one owned the land, it wasn't an area of natural beauty, it wasn't protected, *no one bothered coming here*—but it still felt like a red rag to the contingency bull.

And while we're on the subject, missy, how about you quit it with the fucking tequila? All you need is to be pulled over for drunk driving.

Not likely. As far as her eye could see there was nothing but empty Californian scrub, pale dust and creosote bush and desert mallow. Black sky and the stars coming all the way down to the ground. She was well off the road—and the road had been empty.

Without witness. She thought of the bat whirring past her head as she'd stared down at his body. The world insisted life went on.

It's okay. It's going to be okay.

She wanted to drive farther but the Volvo didn't like the terrain. Hit soft sand or lose a tire to some rogue thorn and then what? You'd think that if you could kill a man you could change a tire, but the prospect filled her knees and wrists with urgent weakness. She stopped the car, turned off the engine, and got out.

Into silence. Silence with a remote masculine personality. It was as if she were in the presence of one of the Olympian gods. For a few moments she just stood there, limbs humming with their recently added-to history, newly enriched by all these things it turned out they'd been able to do. *Make a clean, deep incision with the scalpel. You don't want a serrated blade going through anything but bone.* Not that it mattered in this case, of course. The guidelines were for those trying to save life and minimize damage. Whereas, hilariously, the amputative world was her oyster. Buzz saw, guillotine, piano wire, hatchet. She could have gnawed them off if she'd been that way inclined.

You're unspooling. The tequila. Shit. Okay. Get a grip.

She opened the trunk and took out the shovel. She put on the scrubs with a bristling sensation of television and reality intersecting. All the cop shows. CSI.

Thirsty. Goddammit, should have stopped for water. This is, genius, the desert.

She found a half-empty Evian in the driver's door well, drank that, knew it was enough, would have to be enough. The constellations observed. Her grandmother told her once when she was small that the stars were pins holding down God's diagram of Eternal Truth.

She walked a few paces from the car to a spot where there was room between the low bushes.

Then, thinking of beautiful Paul Newman in *Cool Hand Luke*, she put her foot on the shovel and began to dig.

# 10

*August 6, 2017*

"You okay?" Nick said to Valerie.

"Sorry," Valerie said. "Just ignore me."

It was late. They were in bed together. Nick had been kissing his way up her legs, from the tips of her toes to the tendons between her parted thighs. He knew her well enough to sense a wrong note.

"In that case, fine," he said. "Turn over, bitch."

She tugged his hair, acknowledging the joke, though even a cursory laugh was beyond her.

"I need to tell you something," she said.

No matter the circumstances, these were never good words. Valerie felt Nick's first (and given their history, entirely natural) thought. A small electric current went through him. She sensed him checking it, forcing himself not to jump to conclusions, although (again, given their history) the conclusions needed a lot less than a jump to get him there.

"I shouldn't be on the Adam Grant case," she said.

Which was enough information. She felt his body slacken, letting the dull understanding in. He waited a few moments before speaking.

"You're right," he said. "You shouldn't be on the case."

He moved up the bed. (Yeah, away from my cunt, Valerie thought. Now that we've added another name to the list of guys I let into it. Except I didn't, in this instance.)

"I didn't fuck him," she said. "I took him home, but it didn't fly."

Nick waited again. Not, she knew, because he didn't believe her, but because he was trying to decide whether technical non-consummation made a difference, professionally.

"We both know that doesn't make a difference," he said.

"It was four years ago and it was nothing. He might as well have slept on the couch."

"If that were really true you wouldn't be telling me this."

A pause. More Nick cogitation.

"You're not telling me this because you want my opinion on whether you should work the case," he said. "You're telling me this because you've already decided to work the case."

"I'm telling you because I want you to be okay with it."

They lay in silence. Their apartment was a friendly intelligence around them, not wanting anything to go wrong.

Nick put his hand back between her legs. Rested it there, gently.

"Okay," he said. "Here's what I think. It's a bad idea professionally for all the reasons you know. But it's your career, so it's your call. As far as being okay with the fact that you fooled around with this guy . . . That depends."

"On what?"

Nick moved his hand against her. She was, in spite of the conversation, wet. Their desire for each other was sly and more or less reliable.

"On how enthusiastically you fuck my brains out right now."

Valerie got into the station just after 8 A.M., sipping her regulation cappuccino. Will Fraser was already at their shared desk. The office windows showed a clear turquoise sky.

"Look," Will said. "What you get up to in the privacy of your own home is your business, but I know I speak for everyone here when I say we'd all really appreciate it if you didn't advertise it quite so obviously."

"What the fuck are you talking about?"

"You. Glowing. It's obscene."

"It's hair conditioner."

"It's deep sexual satisfaction. And no one likes to see it. I'm just saying. For your own good, dial it down."

Valerie took her seat and woke the snoozing desktop. Laura Flynn came in, holding a file.

"She's been at it again," Will said to Laura. "In my opinion less than two hours ago."

"And now she gets even happier," Laura said, dropping the file in front of Valerie. "We got the forensics back on the Adam Grant murder. It's a no-brainer. Take a look."

Will joined Valerie as she opened the file. The first page was a rap sheet for "Dwight Jenner, aka DJ, aka Shiner," mug shots showing a white guy in his late twenties with short, dark greasy hair and three-day stubble.

"Got your Mr. Bowie's thing going on there with his eyes," Valerie said, having noted that they appeared to be of different colors. Laura was a big Bowie fan.

"Same look, different cause," Laura said. "This is complete heterochromia, one blue, one green, caused by a melanin deficiency inherited at birth. Bowie's—God rest his lady-grinning soul—was anisocoria, which is when one pupil is bigger than the other. Allegedly caused by a fight with a friend when he was fifteen that left the pupil permanently dilated."

"I always thought he looked like Glenda Jackson," Will said.

"That's not a problem for me," Laura said. "I'd fuck her, too."

Valerie speed-read the sheet. A string of burglary and assault charges, culminating in six of a seven-year stint in San Quentin for his part in an armed robbery that left a gas station cashier dead, though Jenner hadn't, himself, pulled the trigger.

"Adam Grant put him away," Valerie said.

"Yeah. Jenner got out eighteen months ago. Prints and DNA slam dunk. All over the scene. Including Rachel's nightdress. The knife, the hammer. And the body of Adam Grant."

"So he's a moron."

"Christ knows. But not a sharp tool, I'm guessing."

"Sharp enough to get past the Grants' security gizmos?"

"They weren't set," Valerie said. "I checked. The alarm keeps a forty-eight-hour data record. They hadn't *been* set since the night before. According to Rachel it was her husband's job. For whatever reason, he didn't do it. He'd drunk quite a bit. It's possible he just forgot." She checked the release papers. "Okay, we've got a parole officer and an address as of six months back. Let's go talk to Mr. Jenner."

According to parole officer Mario Difalco, Dwight Jenner had been playing it straight since his release. He'd shown up for every fortnightly face-to-face for the first twelve months and for every monthly since then. All the requisite community hours had been logged, and since the start of the year he'd been washing cars at a valet service on Guerrero. He was, not surprisingly, pissed at having spent six years inside, but in Difalco's opinion not so pissed he'd be dumb enough to do anything that would send him back. They'd had their last meeting two weeks ago and Jenner had seemed perky. He'd been asking, in fact, about the procedures for changing addresses and getting his own room in state-approved accommodation. "I'm not saying he's turning into a model citizen," Difalco told Valerie. "But he's holding down a job and keeping his nose clean, which in my experience is about as close to a miracle as you can get with cons who've done anything more than a two-year stretch, especially in San Q."

Jenner was not at work. The manager at Gold Star Valet ("You Love Your Car—We Love Cleaning It!") was Genevieve Welch, a bulky bottle-blond in her midforties who'd taken over the family business when her father retired. Her office had a no-frills orderliness to it and even at a glance Valerie's impression of the all-male minimum-wage cleaning crew was of worker bees doing whatever the fuck it took not to get stung by the queen.

"He booked six days off," Genevieve told them. "The only six days he's entitled to, in fact, based on how long he's been here. He's due back in tomorrow."

"Did he say what his plans were?" Valerie asked.

"Not to me. But word in the sewing circle is he's got a girlfriend."

"You have any qualms about hiring a con?"

Genevieve sat back in her swivel chair. She held a ballpoint between the fingertips of both plump hands. In so large a woman the gesture looked disproportionately delicate. Her smile was one of tired righteousness. "My old man got a second chance a long time back," she said. "We pay it forward."

The "sewing circle" confirmed that according to Jenner he was definitely seeing someone, but beyond the fact that she was, by report, blond and the hottest woman he'd ever been with, there was nothing more to know. No one had ever seen her and no one knew her name. Most of the car wash crew had been frankly skeptical of her existence.

Jenner's home address was a small two-bedroom ground-floor apartment in the Mission. He wasn't there. His younger half brother (same mother, different father) was. Thirty-two-year-old Kyle Cornell had light green eyes with showgirl lashes and a complexion that said his father wasn't white. Collar-length dreds and a glossy musculature that made Valerie imagine him pumping iron with suppressed fury. Two small horizontal scars on his left cheek and visible gang tats on his bare forearms. So much for the ex-con's rehabilitative environment, she thought.

But her expectations were confounded. Kyle didn't like cops but he'd left gang life behind. The young-man rage had gone into agonizing self-improvement. Ten years back, to his astonishment, he'd inherited a dilapidated one-story in Viz Valley when his estranged father died. The timing was good. The new T Third Street Muni Metro line had just opened and the immigrant Chinese business influx that had been going on since the coke crackdown in the late nineties had started a little real estate price hike. Kyle had sold to a landlord and made enough for a down payment on the Mission apartment just when the district was trading its ID of high crime for one of gritty hip. He started tending bar. Thanks to an aspirational girlfriend, he contorted himself through a half-dozen community college courses, incrementally got his shit together. He was still tending bar, but the drinks were fancy and the white-collar clientele generous with their tips. The apartment, now that Valerie looked properly, was shabby, but tidy. There were books. A battered copy of Mailer's *An American Dream* lay on the arm of the couch. Kyle Cornell had—everything about his demeanor said—a Life.

"That's admirable," Valerie said. "But why, given that you've *got* a life, would you want to put it in jeopardy by having a convicted felon living with you?"

Kyle smiled. In a way that made plain he regarded them as inferior souls. "It's all black and white to you," he said. Then to emphasize the happy fusion of literal and figurative: "Black"—he looked at Will—"and white"—then at Valerie. "For those of us who don't have that advantage, the world's got plenty of shades in between."

"Bartender or philosopher?" Will asked.

"You don't need to be a philosopher to know blood's thicker than water. Me and Dwight spent half our childhood together."

This was the guy, Valerie thought, who crossed the road in headphones at his own leisurely roll, daring you to run him over.

"What about this girl he's been seeing?" she asked.

"I don't know anything about her."

"Not even her name? Where she lives?"

"Not even her name. Not even where she lives. Contrary to appearances I'm not my brother's keeper."

"And you have no idea where Dwight might be? You haven't spoken to him on the phone?"

"I spoke to him a week ago. Said he was going to her place for a few days."

"And naturally you don't know where her place is?"

"Naturally. I try not to interrogate him. I'd make a lousy cop."

"But a great lawyer," Will said. "You should consider retraining."

"Do you mind if we take a look at his room?"

"Yes, I mind." Kyle grinned at her. "And yes, I know you'll come back with a warrant."

"Actually we don't need a warrant," Valerie said. "Dwight is still under correctional custody in the community. One of the conditions of parole in the state of California is that law enforcement officers have the right to search either the parolee or his or her home without a warrant. Without suspicion, in fact. So let me put it another way: Sit there and talk to my partner while I take a look in Dwight's room."

"She get you hard when she talks like that?" Kyle asked Will, elongating his pretty smile.

Valerie checked herself. A little impatience had crept in. Partly thanks to Kyle's labored pose of nirvanic superiority and partly thanks to his being extraordinarily good-looking. *She get you hard?* Words were lawless, imprinted their images whether you liked it or not. She thought of getting Kyle Cornell hard, knew exactly how she'd do it, staring into his eyes while very lightly running her fingertips up his thigh, touching him everywhere except his cock. She loved Nick. Infidelity was out of the question. But her sexual self was still stubbornly alive. Some men, the basic female in you just fucking *responded,* whether you liked it or not. It was beyond reason. It was a pain in the ass. She wondered if she'd ever grow out of it.

Dwight Jenner's room was shabby and *not* tidy. Orange curtains still drawn against the day's hot light. Unmade bed, loaded ashtray, clothes that had never known the joys of a hanger. She pulled on gloves and went slowly through the available pants pockets and the contents of the dresser. She wasn't expecting anything incriminating (ski mask, bloodstained joggers) and she didn't find it, unless she counted a half-dozen gonzo porn DVDs, which proved absolutely nothing. Thirty-six hours had passed since the murder. Kyle could be lying, of course, but it was equally possible Jenner had come back here when his half brother wasn't home. They'd have to interview the neighbors. In any case she didn't have the requisite kit or skill to conduct a full sweep right now.

"We're going to seal the room and send a team here later today," she told Kyle when she returned to the living room. "You don't have to be here, but I'm sure you'd rather be."

"I can tell you really love your job," Kyle said.

Will went out to get the tape from the car.

"Just for the record," Kyle said, "so, you know, I can say I did actually *ask*: Who is it you think he's killed?"

"Who says he's killed anyone?"

Kyle smiled again, looked Valerie in the eye. Contemptuous flirtation. "Well, last time I checked, homicide detectives don't look for stolen bicycles."

"It's just a line of inquiry," Valerie said. "I can't discuss the details at this stage."

"You don't need to talk like a TV cop. We already get each other."

While Will sealed the room, Valerie asked Kyle for a list of people Dwight Jenner knew, anyone who might have a clue to his whereabouts. It didn't take long. Mother in Union City. Sister in Reno. One former San Quentin inmate, Salvador Jimenez, released the year before Jenner got out, currently living in the Tenderloin.

"Do you have a recent picture of Dwight?" Valerie asked.

She watched Kyle thinking about saying he didn't. Then deciding it wasn't worth it. "Only on my phone," he said.

Valerie looked. A selfie taken by Kyle of him and his half brother, leaning against the hood of a red Ford in bright sunlight, both grinning. Jenner hadn't changed much in six years, apart from dropping a few pounds. The stubble was gone, but the chopped dark hair was pretty much the same. Still greasy.

"That's almost two years ago," Kyle said, as Valerie texted it to her own phone. "The day he got out. I've got better ones of me if that's what you're really interested in."

Valerie ignored him. Pointlessly, since their sexual selves had already established an understanding.

"Look," Kyle said, softening his tone, "I don't know what you think he's done, but I'm telling you: He's been straight since he got out. No bullshit. He's kept his head down. You know what the first thing he said to me was when I picked him up?"

"What?"

"'I'm never going back. Next time I go to hell it'll be because I'm dead.' Those were his exact words."

"That's what the other hundred thousand said."

"What?"

"California parolees returned to prison after getting out. That's the number, give or take."

"I think you should let me buy you a drink," Kyle said.

Valerie handed Kyle her card. Ropy forearm muscles when he reached to take it from her. His fingertips brushed hers, not accidentally.

"Just call if he shows up," she said.

"Only if he shows up?"

"Just let us know if he gets in touch."

In the car, Valerie called Laura Flynn and gave her the number for Dwight Jenner's cell phone. "All the activity on this number. Incoming and outgoing, locations, the works. Meantime get an APB out. We'll talk to the mother and Jimenez. Call Reno and get them to interview the sister."

"Doesn't sound like you think it's worth it," Laura said.

"If he killed Adam Grant," Valerie said, "he's flown a lot further than that."

# 11

By the end of the afternoon, Dwight Jenner was officially unaccounted for. The sister hadn't seen him since before he went inside. The mother hadn't seen him since he'd got out. Whatever bond Jenner shared with his half brother, it didn't extend to the rest of his family. Salvador Jimenez, former cellmate now bodyguarding the oiled and glittered talent at a Tenderloin lap dance club, had got drunk with him a couple of weeks back and recalled enough to confirm Dwight was getting, in his words, "royally laid," but beyond that the details had dissolved in booze. He did, however, remember the beloved's name. Sophia. Jimenez had grinned, revealing a gold upper incisor with a diamond stud. "Way Dwight said that name: So, Fee, *Ahh*. Like when you taste something good and go *uh-uh-nnnn*." He'd found his own analogy sinisterly hilarious. They were waiting now for access to Jenner's bank records to check the most recent transactions. Kyle Cornell was under surveillance, but so far had done nothing more exciting than take out his trash and drive over to Flamingo Bar on Twenty-first and Castro to start his shift. In other news, the standard homicide toxicology report noted minute traces of zolpidem in Adam Grant's system. Negligible, Ricky Santayana had told Valerie. Half the city's on Ambien. He took a sleeping pill. Zero impact on cause of death. Sorry.

"I don't like any of this," Will said, when he and Valerie were back at their desk.

"Neither do I," Valerie answered. "But there's no arguing with the treasure trove at the scene. It proves he was there. It proves physical contact."

"Still doesn't sing to me."

"What are you—a yogi? Maybe it wouldn't sing to me if he hadn't disappeared."

"Look on the bright side," Will said. "If he doesn't show up, you'll get to interview your new boyfriend again."

"Oh, please."

"It's okay. I won't tell Nick he needs to up his game."

"You're obsessed. I barely noticed that young man's caramel muscles and elegant cheekbones."

Will shook his head, in the manner of a despairing therapist.

"Well," Valerie added, "no more than you noticed Officer Lopez's cute little tits. Correction: 'Maria's' cute little tits."

"Just because *you* don't bother with the names of your fellow officers, doesn't mean the rest of us—"

"Hey," Laura Flynn said, looking up from her desk. "I hate to interrupt vital sexual aesthetics with, you know, *police* work, but here's something you might be interested in." She got up and came to their desk, handed Valerie a transcript of calls to and from Dwight Jenner's cell phone. One incoming number had been circled in red, repeatedly.

"Whose?" Valerie asked.

"Adam Grant's," Laura said. "One of them, anyway. He had two registered. More than a dozen exchanges in the last two months."

Valerie drove out to California Pacific. She was in what she was beginning to recognize as her new state: alert contentment—fractured by perverse agitation. The contentment was a terrible fortune: She had Nick. She had love.

She had the Work. There were random moments—Will making her laugh; starting the Taurus's engine on a sunny morning; closing a case; discussing the night's dreams with Nick over coffee in bed—when she couldn't believe how lucky she was, when the wealth of her life suffused her with delicious guilt. But there was another guilt, not delicious. She was restless. And the conviction that she didn't deserve any of her gifts endured. The dumb flare of lust for Kyle Cornell, for example. On the one hand, it was nothing. Love didn't kill your ability to desire others, it just restrained you from acting on it. Her problem wasn't that she had sexual temptation beyond her husband. It was that the sexual temptation was an apparatus for the *bigger* temptation: to Fuck Everything Up. To the truly perverse, happiness was suspicious, an elaborate joke in which *un*happiness, sooner or later, would turn out to be the punch line. Her wiser self knew this was idiotic, mere juvenile existential paranoia, which insisted it made no sense to *dare* to be happy. But identifying paranoia didn't cure it. Her younger, *un*wise self still tossed and turned and occasionally lashed out with the message that she was, deep down, rotten, and that the best thing she could do for the good people in her life was to leave them the fuck alone. Or, by some giant act of sacrilege, hurt them so badly that they'd leave *her* the fuck alone.

She knew why this was happening. She knew why this was happening *now*. Because as of four months ago she and Nick had dispensed with contraception. Along with quitting smoking, she was more or less off the booze. She'd rejoined the Department's long-neglected physical training classes. She had begun to get her body's house in order.

To be ready for a baby.

After which, her life would never be the same again.

That, both her wise and unwise selves agreed, was the real temptation: to avoid the transformation motherhood was guaranteed to bring. The voice that told her she was rotten was the most elaborate ruse of all. She didn't hate herself. She liked herself—and *that* self, once there was a child to care for, would have to go.

She found a spot in the hospital parking lot, grabbed Jenner's file from the passenger seat, and headed inside. Catching—naturally—the word "Maternity" on one of the signposts.

Officer Riordan was sitting outside Rachel Grant's room, texting.

"Detective," she said, pocketing the phone and getting to her feet.

"Hey," Valerie said. "Sorry you pulled the babysitting gig."

Riordan smiled. "Are you kidding? I forgot what it's like to be able to, you know, sit down and *think* for five minutes. Like a regular person."

"Who've we got in there?"

"Just the daughter and her aunt. Mr. Grant's sister . . ." She checked the list on her clipboard. "Hester Fallon. Elspeth's been staying with her. Mind if I ask what the latest is?"

Valerie flipped open Jenner's file to reveal his mug shot and copies of the more recent picture, cropped to exclude his handsome half brother. "AWOL suspect," she said. "DNA, prints, the works. APB's out. Here, take one. Hand it off to your relief. I think Mrs. Grant was collateral damage, but you never know."

"Got it."

"I'll be sending Elspeth and her aunt out in a few minutes. You want to take them to get coffee or a soda or whatever, that's fine."

"Will do."

Valerie went into the room. Rachel Grant looked slightly better. Her bed was angled up to an almost sitting position. Her short coppery hair had been combed back. The first shock wave had passed but her face was still the traumatized version of itself. The threadbare sanity was there, even in the tan forearms and elegant hands, the fingernails of which Elspeth Grant was in the process of painting olive green. To give themselves something normal to do, Valerie knew.

Elspeth, on the other hand, looked worse. The puppet eyes were red around the rims, younger without the ghost of makeup. Her lips were chapped, making a pale smear of her mouth. She was still struggling with disbelief. For a while the nail-painting might have hypnotized her. Now, with Valerie's appearance, reality was back. When she glanced at her, Elspeth's face looked as if she were expecting the news that someone *else* was dead. Why not—since the world, in taking her father away, had obviously gone mad?

Hester Fallon looked so much like Adam Grant that Valerie felt resurgent shame warming her skin. As if, by virtue of resemblance, she had been in the room with them on the night of failed sex four years ago. The effect was claustrophobic, incestuous. Valerie had the urge to open the window.

None of them recognized Dwight Jenner from the picture.

"Who is he?" Rachel asked, when Hester and Elspeth had left the room.

"Someone your husband put in jail more than six years ago. We found his prints on the murder weapons, on the French window, the balcony rail. You won't remember, but the hospital swabbed your fingernails when you were admitted. DNA confirms another match. You said you tried to get him off Adam. In terms of physical evidence, it's conclusive. All we have to do now is find him."

"What?"

"He's disappeared, but it's only a matter of time. His picture's out with law enforcement nationally. We'll get TV coverage as well. Everything we know about Dwight Jenner tells us he doesn't have what it takes for invisibility."

Valerie was watching Rachel, who couldn't stop staring at the picture. Here he was, the man who had butchered her husband and left her for dead. Just a man, who brushed his teeth and drank beer and watched TV and emptied his bowels. Ordinary in every way—except for his ability to commit murder. Valerie had seen it before, the victim's fear and disgust and hatred and grief—and, like it or not, fascination, when confronted with the mundane fact that a person had done this to them. Not lightning or fire or a heart attack. A person, who might have chosen not to.

"This might be difficult for you to hear, but phone records show Dwight Jenner was in contact with Adam over the last two months."

"What?"

"They spoke several times. Usually not for more than a couple of minutes, but there was definitely communication. You're sure Adam didn't mention this to you? Anything about an inmate getting out?"

"No, nothing. But he wouldn't. He knew how much I worried about the enemies his job made him. I told him . . . I *told* him . . ."

Rachel shook her head, swallowed. Refused to cry. Valerie let her ride it out.

"Another difficult question, I'm afraid," she said. "Is it possible that Adam was in some kind of trouble? Financial? Legal?" she hesitated. "Personal?"

Rachel didn't look at Valerie. Just let the implications settle.

"Why in God's name would you think that?" she said quietly.

"I don't think it," Valerie said. "I'm just trying to find a basis for their communication. Of course it's possible Jenner called with threats—threats that escalated, obviously. But it's unusual. Especially since any direct threat would only lead to increased vigilance."

"You mean if you're going to murder someone why give them advance warning?"

"Yes."

"A man comes into our home and does this—leaves all this . . . his fucking fingerprints and DNA, and you're asking about fucking telephone calls?"

Valerie was surprised by the shift of gear, but she remained calm. "I'm sorry, Mrs. Grant, I know this is difficult. But as I said to you before, we ask the questions so we can build the strongest possible case. In *this* case, the evidence we have is the best we ever get, short of catching someone in the act. But I don't want any surprises when this goes to trial. I don't want the slightest possibility that a mysterious relationship, even a few phone calls, between the perpetrator and your husband, could shift a jury away from a conviction for first-degree murder."

Rachel closed her eyes. Breathed through her nose. Subsided. Opened her eyes again, though she still wouldn't look at Valerie.

"I don't know," she said, defeated. "I don't know anything."

*I don't know anything.* No, Valerie thought, you don't. It came to her again that her position was untenable. She imagined Adam Grant getting home from their abortive night worried she'd left her scent on him. Pictured him scrubbing himself in the shower. Washing away the incriminating evidence.

She'd been wrong to take the case. Yet the more clearly she understood that, the more she knew she couldn't, now, leave it alone. It had a dark gravity. As did all the richly wrong decisions in her life.

"I need your permission to take a look through Adam's stuff," she said.

"What stuff?"

"Computer, emails, correspondence, bank records."

Rachel shook her head—in disbelief. "Jesus Christ," she said.

"If he was in touch with Dwight Jenner it might give us a clue to his whereabouts."

"Are you serious?"

"I'm serious about getting Jenner. I'm sorry, Mrs. Grant, but we have to look at every possibility. We'll be doing the same at his office."

Rachel shook her head again, exhaled: resignation. "Do whatever you want," she said. "I don't care."

Valerie got up and went to the door.

"Detective?" Rachel said.

"Yes?"

For the first time in the interview Rachel Grant looked at her with focus. "Whatever you have to do, do it," she said. "But leave my daughter out of it. She's thirteen years old."

"Of course," Valerie said. "How's she doing?"

"How do you think she's doing?"

"Yeah, dumb question," Valerie said. "You know we have officers on watch with her at your sister-in-law's, right?"

"Yes." A pause. "I just need to get home with her."

"You'll both have protection until we bring Jenner in. How long before you get out of here?"

"They're saying another three days. I'm not staying here for another three days. I'm fine. I need to be with Elspeth."

"She seems a bright girl."

"Do you have children?"

"No."

Saying it laid another veil of guilt on Valerie. *I don't think I'd make a very good mother.*

"I was nothing before I had Elspeth," Rachel Grant said. "I was a waste. If anything happened to her . . ." The composure went again. "If she'd been there that night . . . I keep thinking . . . If she'd been there . . ."

"Don't torment yourself," Valerie said. "She wasn't there, and she's safe."

Rachel Grant recovered. Smiled. Empty calm. "It's disgusting, isn't it?" she said. "My husband's dead and I can still feel thankful . . . *thankful* for something."

"It's not disgusting," Valerie said. "It's natural."

"Natural things are disgusting," Rachel said.

Valerie didn't answer.

Rachel looked away, out of the window. "Ignore me," she said. "It doesn't matter."

# 12

## *August 7, 2017*

Will Fraser's scrutiny of Dwight Jenner's bank records proved fruitful. In among the regular transactions were (a) two cash deposits of three thousand dollars and two thousand dollars within the last two months and (b) six card payments to budget hotels at various locations within the Bay Area for the same period, the most recent less than two weeks ago. Every one of them had date-correlative CCTV footage which showed him checking in (and out, after one night), apparently alone. Since then the account activity had returned to normal—except that there had been *no* activity since July 30.

"Wherever he is," Will said to Valerie on the phone, "he's not leaving a plastic trail."

Valerie was seated in one of five ivory leather chairs in the lobby of Willard & Gould, Attorneys at Law. The space had a headachy green marble floor and soft overhead halogens. It smelled of cold corporate cleanliness. Fleetingly, it made her feel utterly exhausted by the whole concept of the Law, so much of which was in the dirty and dexterous hands of money. "Well, five grand in cash won't last forever," she said. "He doesn't have a passport, so he can't have left the country. Laura check the hospitals?"

"Nada. Needless to say, he didn't show up for his meeting with Difalco. Or for Lady Liberty at the car wash, either. Anything on your end?"

"I'm talking to his colleagues. Nothing flags so far. *His* bank's not being quite so prompt. I'll wrap up here then head over to the Grants'. No sign of So Fee *Ahh*?"

"I'm starting on the hotels' footage right now. Looking forward to meeting her. She sounds like my kind of gal."

Valerie hung up. *Natural things are disgusting.* She couldn't get the phrase out of her head.

"Detective?"

She looked up. A dark-haired woman in spectacles and a cream pantsuit had just exited the elevator. She was made up with precise understatement, nails French manicured, clothes pressed, shoulder-length bob full of controlled glossy life. She had the sort of poise that made Valerie straighten her spine.

"Fiona Perry," she said, extending her hand, which arrived with a waft of perfume. "I wish you were here for a different reason. Everyone here is just devastated. We'll go up and use Adam's office."

Adam Grant was—had been, rather—a senior partner, and his office reflected his position. A giant walnut desk stood on a large Persian carpet intricately patterned in pale blue and gold. The rear wall was glass. Two abstract canvases—shades of deep blue with gashes of silver leaf—hung on each of the flanking walls. The desk photograph was a close-up of Rachel and Elspeth, lying in a field of wildflowers. The room's odor was of crisp technology and polished wood.

The first few minutes of the interview covered what Valerie needed by way of access to Adam Grant's work calendar and correspondence, for which—predictably—Fiona Perry informed her she would need a warrant.

"You'll get one hundred percent cooperation," Fiona said. "But obviously protocols for a law firm require every 'i' dotted and every 't' crossed."

"We'll have it tomorrow. But in the meantime, I want to ask you about Adam personally. You've been his secretary for the last three years, right?"

Fiona looked out of the window and didn't answer. A slight slackening of her posture, as if a thin layer of professional propriety had fallen away. When she looked back at Valerie it was with a new candor.

"You're going to ask me if I noticed anything in his demeanor suggestive that all might not be well," she said.

"Yes," Valerie said.

"You don't buy the home intrusion narrative?'"

"I buy it, but not as the whole story. Adam was in contact with Jenner for weeks before his murder. He say anything to you about that?"

"Christ," Fiona said. "No. Nothing."

"But you felt something was wrong?'"

Fiona looked away again. Valerie wondered if Adam Grant had fucked her. She wasn't particularly good-looking ("handsome" if you were being generous), but that didn't prove anything. Only the sexual realist in Valerie wondered why, if Grant hadn't cheated on his wife with her, Valerie, he would bother cheating on his wife with Fiona Perry. She wasn't proud of the thought, but there it was.

"Adam seemed unhappy to me for a long time," Fiona said.

"Yes?"

"Agitated. I doubt anyone else here would have noticed. But I saw him every day, just the two of us. Professionally he never missed a beat. But there were quiet moments . . . I don't know. He snapped at me a few times, I guess, totally out of character. Some evenings he stayed late, there was a bottle of scotch on the desk. Between you and me that's not groundbreaking news here, but I came in some mornings and it was obvious he'd been here all night, bottle empty. He didn't seem right."

"When did this start?"

"More than a year ago, I'd say."

"You ever ask him what was wrong?"

"Once. He told me to mind my own—quote—'fucking business.' Came in the next day with flowers and profuse apologies. Said he couldn't believe how he'd spoken to me. But I didn't pry after that. It's just that there were times when his mind was so obviously elsewhere."

"You think someone had something on him?"

"As in blackmail?"

"As in blackmail."

Fiona shook her head, not in denial, just in ignorance. "It's hard to imagine," she said. "But then we're in the business of imagining the things that are hard to imagine."

"Was he having an affair?"

"Not with me, if that's what you're really asking."

"I wasn't. But it's noted."

A crackle on the ether here. Fiona Perry didn't like being an object of sexual speculation. And thereby sexual evaluation. It entailed, whether the two women liked it or not, an admission of mutual comparison. For a moment it was as if Valerie's "handsome, if you were being generous" had been spoken aloud. Both of them knew where they stood. Fiona with resignation, Valerie with both annoyance that any of that mattered and in spite of the annoyance a flicker of pleasure because she knew she had what Fiona did not. The uneven distribution of beauty was a grand injustice. But since the injustice was here to stay, better to be its beneficiary than its victim.

"I'll come back tomorrow with the warrant," Valerie said. "Meantime, if you can keep everyone out of Adam Grant's stuff, I'd appreciate it."

"I'll do what I can, but his caseload's already been picked up by Dan Kruger."

"I'm seeing him next. Just make sure the call logs and email correspondence stay intact."


Will Fraser was having a pleasant afternoon, working his way through the CCTV footage from the hotels Dwight Jenner had checked into for his assumed liaisons with Sophia, if Jimenez's memory of the name was to be trusted. Sophia. *Cherchez la femme!* Very occasionally actual police work paid homage to its fictional tropes. Not that that was the only pleasure. It was, Will admitted to himself, enjoyable just to watch people going about their business.

The simple satisfaction of voyeurism, enhanced both by the subjects' obliviousness and by the police knowledge that the vast majority of them had something to hide. Walk up to any random stranger, look them in the eye, and say, with absolute conviction: *I know about it.* Invariably there would be a secret "it" to which they would believe you were referring. It might not be criminal but it would certainly be shameful. Will supposed he thought of himself as one of the exceptions, but only because at some point years ago he'd ambled past shame and into the understanding that even his shameful things were wearily natural. Thanks to the job, yes, but thanks, too, to Marion, his wife, who had no time for being embarrassed by either his or her own imperfections. He had, for example, wanted to have sex with her the day of her father's funeral. What kind of a lousy bastard are you? he'd wondered. What the fuck is *wrong* with you? He'd lain next to her that night trying to think of anything—*anything*—to dispel the aching hard-on that threatened to incriminate him if he turned to face her. It wasn't even that he'd been indifferent to her father. He'd been fond of the old geezer. Nor was he numb to Marion's palpable grief. Be that as it may, there'd been nothing he wanted more right then than to fuck his wife, preferably as filthily as possible. He'd hated himself for it, but there it was. They'd lain for a while in thudding silence. Then Marion had said: I know you want to fuck me. Will had felt the pointless denials massing—then falling away. He was transparent to her. It's no big deal, Marion had said. It's what death does. Makes you crave life. It doesn't mean you're the spawn of Satan. Don't bother making a thing of it for yourself. He'd waited in stunned speechlessness. Then she'd said: Don't get excited, either. I'm not *going* to fuck you. I'm not up to it right now. I just don't want you making a goddamned psychodrama out of it and lying there staring at the ceiling as if you've betrayed the Son of Man with a kiss.

Will had loved her more then than at practically any other moment in their life together. If he hadn't known it before, he knew it then: that there was no other woman for him.

He took a sip of his cold coffee, yawned, gave himself a mental shake. On-screen he was watching a family checking in at the Civic Center Holiday Inn. Mother, father, one boy of about six, crying, uglily, and a toddler in a stroller. The father, a fat guy in a red-and-white bandana, Nirvana T-shirt, and ridiculous leather pants, was having a problem with his credit card. The clerk looked bored rather than uncomfortable. The mother, in an orange bikini top and sawn-off denims, yanked the squawking kid violently by his elbow and said something that made it clear she was out of patience—which just made the kid cry more.

A woman with voluminous blond hair and sunglasses so big they gave her the look of a fly walked past them and crossed to the elevators. Green chiffon dress and trim long legs in killer heels. Snakeskin purse. No jewelry. Beautiful. Not the kind of woman to be checking in anywhere that cost eighty-eight dollars per night. Not the kind of woman you'd forget.

Will hadn't forgotten her.

He stopped the video.

Rewound.

Replayed.

Froze it.

Opened a second window on the desktop.

Ramada at the airport, three weeks earlier. He'd been logging the time codes for Dwight Jenner's check-ins. He fast-forwarded to 12:27 P.M., watched Jenner exchange a few upbeat pleasantries with the girl behind the desk. No luggage beyond a backpack that looked more or less empty, as in all the previous check-ins. Will watched until he walked out of the shot. Then went methodically through the desk footage that followed.

At 1:19 P.M. he found what he was looking for.

Sophia was there again. Ivory silk dress this time. Same purse, same boudoir heels, same bluebottle shades. Straight past reception and across to the elevator doors.

Hello, lady.

There were, he knew, other steps to take. There was the business of *con-*

*firmation*. But her and Dwight being at the same hotel twice was enough to tell him what he needed to know.

No wonder Jenner looked upbeat, Will thought. If that was who he was spending his afternoons balling in a rented bed, it was a miracle he wasn't walking on air.

# 13

Valerie was in Adam Grant's study when Nick put his head around the door. The room was full of warm sunlight.

"Hey, Skirt," he said.

"What are you doing here?"

"Er . . . my job? We're taking Grant's computers, as requested by you."

"I thought you just sat in the basement like a spider and waited for your minions to bring you the gizmos."

"I do. But sometimes I get lonely."

He kissed her. Valerie had a little traffic jam of images: sucking Adam Grant's flaccid cock; Elspeth painting her mother's nails; Kyle Cornell's dark arms; herself living alone in the desert in an adobe hut, bare feet in the dust and a bottle of tequila and bleaching sunlight. Her inner life was roiling these days. So what? So nothing. *The natural things are*—

"For God's sake."

They separated, guiltily, and turned to see Nick's colleague, Nathan, in the study doorway.

"You guys carry on," Nathan said. "Don't mind me. I'm just the removal guy. Once I've cleared the desk there you can spread out."

He hefted the first of the three unplugged hard drives Valerie had earmarked, along with two laptops. "By the way," Nathan said, "there's an old dude here asking about the Grants."

Valerie went into the hall to find a tall, white-haired guy in his late seventies in a blue plaid shirt and khaki pants, standing just inside the front doorway with a look on his face somewhere between apology and bemusement.

"Can I help you?" she said.

"Hello, yes . . . I was wondering how Rachel's doing? I'm her neighbor. Vincent Lyle."

Valerie rapid-scrolled. Lyle. Senior. Insomnia. Saw the perp in the backyard.

"Hello, Mr. Lyle." She extended her hand. "Detective Hart. I'm leading the investigation. Rachel's stable, recovering well. She should be home in a few days."

"Oh, that's good to hear," Vincent said. "What about poor Elspeth? Who's taking care of her?"

"She's fine. She's with family." Leave it vague. His concern was genuine, but there was the predictable fascination as well.

"And the man who did this?" he asked. "I suppose you're not allowed to say. I saw the photograph on the news."

"He's still at large," Valerie said. "But we'll get him. I understand you saw the suspect in your backyard on the night of the incident?"

"I did. It was . . . as with all such moments, simultaneously prosaic and surreal."

"Do you know the Grants well?"

"Not terribly. Rachel more than Adam. We have reading in common. And insomnia. We wave to each other in the small hours, like a pair of sentinels. She's been very sweet about books, seeking my opinion and so on. All redundant, since she knows by her own lights what's good and what's trash. My son's machinations are behind it."

"I'm sorry?"

"I believe Lucas recruited her to the cause: reengaging the moribund literary brain."

Nick and Nathan went past, carrying the last of the tech hardware out to the van. Vincent Lyle observed, with obvious curiosity.

"But you didn't know Mr. Grant well?" Valerie asked him.

"Not really. He kept himself to himself. Struck me as a bit abstracted, in fact, on the few occasions I met him."

"Abstracted?"

"Mind elsewhere. But then I know from Rachel he was a workaholic. To be honest, I hadn't seen him much of late."

"Was Mrs. Grant worried about him?"

Lyle thought about it for a moment. Not, Valerie decided, because he had anything useful to contribute, but because he didn't want their conversation to end. The literary brain might be moribund but it was a rare mind the murder-next-door couldn't hook. Over his shoulder she saw Nick give her a quick nod farewell then get into the van and pull away.

"She never said anything like that to me," Vincent Lyle said. "Why do you ask?"

"I ask everything. It's my job."

He thought about it again. Reached the same conclusion. "No. She never said anything like that to me."

"Well, as I said, Mrs. Grant should be home in a few days. Now if you'll excuse me . . ."

"Of course, of course. I'm taking up your time."

Valerie watched him walk away down the drive. She remembered he was a widower. Not long back she and Nick had had a conversation about getting old. The challenge was to find *good* things about it. They'd only come up with two. The first was that they'd care even less than they did now what anyone thought of them. The second was they wouldn't be expected to do anything on New Year's Eve except stay home and get drunk and watch dumb TV. It occurred to her now that they'd both only imagined growing old together. All these assumptions that did nothing but tempt the gods to prove them false.

She closed the front door (the Halligan's damage had been repaired with a steel plate and new lock) and put her back to it. She had, at last, what she wanted: the opportunity to move alone and undisturbed through Adam Grant's house.

# 14

This was a pleasure that went beyond the job. In fact the job was (à la Rebecca Beitner's) a rationalization of a condition that preceded it, namely, the desire to snoop around other people's lives. Valerie had always been that way. Even as a child she loved poking around her family's and friends' rooms when they weren't there, not with malice or strategy, but out of a fascination with the otherness of others, their things—and the narratives she could dream up to explain them. In her early teens she'd dated a guy who had a fetish for getting into buildings when they were unoccupied. Together they broke into (or concealed themselves in until after hours) their school, the bus depot, the local swimming pool, a couple of cinemas, and three or four private residences. They did no damage, took nothing. Just went through various drawers and wardrobes and cupboards, barely exchanging a word. Neither of them knew quite why, but it was irresistible. Incredibly, they never got caught.

Now there *was* no getting caught. Snooping was what she was paid for. Being Police was a backstage pass to the world behind the world, the people behind the people, the lives behind the lives. The dirty thrill of it had never diminished. Finding what was hidden. The dark secret. The awful treasure. That was the force that drove her. Justice was an incidental by-product.

She left the hallway and went upstairs to Adam and Rachel's bedroom.

The scene hadn't been formally released but all the work was done. She was excited to be alone. She cut the tape and opened the door. She didn't know what she was looking for. The truth was that if she hadn't had the failed one-night stand with Adam Grant she probably wouldn't even be here. Dwight Jenner had killed him. Therefore her job was to catch Dwight Jenner—end of story. There were unanswered questions, yes—but there were always unanswered questions. Adam Grant talked on the phone a dozen times to the man who eventually murdered him. Snapped at his secretary and seemed unhappy. Occasionally got shit-faced and didn't go home. Didn't get chummy with Professor Insomnia next door. So what?

Jenner got five grand in cash from someone and maybe it was Adam Grant. Jenner was punching above his weight with hot, blond Sophia. Jenner's half brother was probably lying. Again, so what? It didn't alter the central fact: Dwight Jenner killed Adam Grant and advertised his culpability by dropping off the grid. Motive might be more obscure than simple revenge, but means and opportunity were beyond doubt. Therefore, aside from corralling the tech hardware there really was no good reason for her to be here.

It didn't matter. She was used to the job's rogue gravities and long past accountability to her rational self.

She spent a few minutes examining the master bedroom's wall of black-and-white photographs, all of which—initialed "A.G."—she assumed had been taken by Adam Grant. (Very vaguely she remembered him mentioning photography somewhere in the middle of their doomed evening, when the booze was already softening the boundaries and swirling the conversation.) To Valerie's eye they were what would once have been regarded as good pictures (in the days before apps gave us the power to make any old shit look like an album cover) albeit with predictable subject matter: desert landscapes, city architecture, a stack of old tires, a burned-out car. A series of high-contrast shots of a derelict ranch surrounded by scrub and saguaro, shadows very black, sand very white. Several portraits of people unknown to Valerie, but many of Rachel and Elspeth, either solo or together. In one shot Rachel was standing looking out the window of a rustic kitchen, wearing nothing but a man's white shirt with sunlight coming through to expose her silhouette. In another Elspeth had been surprised reading a book. You could imagine her father saying, "Hey"—and the girl looking up, not expecting the camera, the puppet eyes inquiring. A second later she would probably have said: "Jesus, Dad, stop *doing* that," but just at that moment she was caught perfectly, without attitude or performance, artless, herself. Valerie imagined her secretly rather loving the photograph.

The guest room directly across the landing had, along with luxury white linen, high ceiling, and blood-and-gold abstract canvas above the bed, two walls of books and a square bay window with a box seat, which, having sat in it, Valerie found gave a view over the alleyway (and bamboo) into the Lyles' sprawling backyard. There was the conservatory, Vincent Lyle's retreat in the small hours. Presumably it was from here that Rachel waved to him when they shared the insomniacs' graveyard shift. We have reading in common. Valerie couldn't remember the last time she'd begun a book, let alone finished one. Being Police shunted so many things into the hard shoulder. You told yourself you'd get around to them. You never did.

Like having a kid.

One of the things that annoyed her was that sex with Nick now was definitively shackled to reproduction. It had to be vaginal, penetrative—every time. A serviceable hand job was sperm-squandering sacrilege. When he went inside her these days she had an image of the school diagram of the female reproductive organs in cross-section. (Which unfortunately had always looked to her like a drawing of a sheep's head.) Hardly a turn-on. Couples complained having kids killed their sex lives. It was worse than that. *Trying to get pregnant* killed your sex life.

Maybe you just don't want a child?

Maybe I just don't.

She was enjoying herself, like a stray dog among the trash cans. The license to snoop, of course—the house was so grand and established, so rich with the Grants' detail that the sense of privileged intrusion went through her like a fabulous drug—but also because it was a family home which, courtesy of the randomly ugly world (the world she knew, the world she dealt with, the world she depended on) would never be the same again. The Grants had had it all. And now look: ruin. They might never recover. Elspeth's face, the shock. Rachel's face, worse, the knowledge that she would have to go on. The fewer people you loved the less you had to lose.

Yes. Quite.

She went aimlessly through the generous, sunlit rooms. Aimlessly, but with casual clairvoyance fueled and prepped. There was an art to it. To knowing when not knowing didn't matter, when the absence of knowing was necessary, in fact, to leave room for the spookier intuitive forces—in which she both believed and did not believe. This was the deal with getting older, apparently. Every year gifted you a new paradox or koan. Like (again!) her desire for and dread of motherhood. *Do you have children?* Even in her ravaged state Rachel Grant had asked the question in the way all mothers did, with a smug flourish of gender credentials and a complacent challenge to yours. Do you have children? Once, drunk at a dinner party, Valerie had answered a particularly annoying woman: No, I'm afraid my cunt hasn't gone on to the Higher Calling. It's still wasting its time fucking for pleasure.

She went into Elspeth's room. The girl's interrupted life was here. She and it had been in tremendous cahoots, the goth jewelry, the tweets, the likes, the clothes, the music. Now the life knew that when she came back it wouldn't recognize her. Valerie sat on the bed. *I was nothing before I had Elspeth,* Rachel Grant had said. Valerie could feel that in here, too, the mother's love like an invisible organic architecture underpinning every hair tie and fad and sulk—now faced with the task of making the unbearable bearable. *If anything happened to her,* Rachel Grant had said. *If she'd been there that night . . . I keep thinking . . . If she'd been there . . .* Yes. Exactly. If she'd been there she'd be dead. Maybe raped, maybe mutilated, maybe you made to watch. Then what would all that love be except proof that love couldn't save her? If you'd really understood you could always lose her like that, would you have had her in the first place?

Prosecution rests.

Valerie went downstairs. Through the living room window she saw the maples' shadows were longer on the lawn. But still she lingered. She went through all the drawers in Adam Grant's desk. Innocuous. For a while she sat on one of the two vast, L-shaped couches in the living room just listening to the birdsong and absorbing the domestically serviced ether of the Grants' formerly comfortable life.

Then, in the basement, she found the darkroom.

The basement itself had been turned into a fully equipped home gym. Whitewashed walls, blue exercise mats, concrete floor. When she tried the steel door between the bench press and the rowing machine she expected a broom closet or boiler room. But it opened into a darkroom, and she realized with a little adrenal "oops" that the let-in light might just have ruined Adam Grant's final photographic work. Thinking it was probably redundant now, she found the safelight switch, closed the door behind her, and turned it on. Soft brown-red illumination that seemed to pixelate the air and within moments made her feel uncomfortably hot.

The place was tidy. The chemistry trays might have been lined up by a robot. The wastepaper basket looked virgin. Enlarger brand-new, leather swivel chair factory fresh. It looked like a darkroom set up for someone as a gift—then never used.

Of course the clairvoyance twitched. She dismissed it. Pavlovian. The lone photographer in his windowless room of brothel light was the villain in too many movies. The mere word "darkroom" suggested secrecy, deviance, subversion, deceit. In any case Adam Grant was the victim, not the perp. An honest voice in Valerie reported that she wasn't searching for the reason he was murdered. She was searching for some clue—however remote—to why in God's name he hadn't fucked her when he'd had the chance. She wasn't surprised at herself. She'd grown used to the lawlessness of her motives, which had long since drifted free of their ethical anchors. She was monstrous in many ways. Of course she was. But so was everyone else, more or less. Being Police was learning to find room for everything—even yourself.

Regardless, she was here, so she might as well take a look. Two steel cabinets with ten shallow drawers stood to either side of the door. She began going through them from top to bottom, starting with the one on her right. Print paper stock, mostly, organized according to grade, finish, and size, but also large black ring binders containing hundreds, actually thousands, of plastic-sleeved proof sheets, transparencies, and prints, labeled, as far as she could tell, chronologically and going all the way back to what she guessed were Adam Grant's college years. A vast variety of images, some of them so heavily abstracted that their original object was hard to guess, plus more of the strictly figurative type displayed on the bedroom wall. The bottom two drawers had a lock, but the lock was open. The drawers were empty.

The cabinet on her left contained more contact sheets, ring binders, grease pencils, loupes, mattes, scissors . . . Nothing unexpected. Mild orneriness kept her checking all the way to the bottom two drawers.

Which, unlike the neighboring pair, were locked.

Not *much* from the clairvoyance. A wry smile, perhaps. Still, there was no *not* getting them open, now.

Naturally none of the keys on Rachel's bunch fit the lock. Valerie went back upstairs. Adam Grant's keys were in an ovoid lapis lazuli bowl on his desk. Aside from house and Audi there were four others on the fob. Two Yale, one brass skeleton, and one tiny stainless-steel key that looked about right for the cabinet. She went back to the basement.

It didn't fit.

She smiled. Now it was a little game with the clairvoyance. She had lockpicks in the car. For a moment she considered just forcing the drawer. Decided that wasn't in the spirit of the game. Up she went again, her thighs asking if she was aware this was the fourth time they'd done this trick in practically as many minutes.

The heat outside surprised her after the house's air-conditioning. The afternoon had swollen. Hot asphalt and the sun-struck Taurus like a big black jewel. The neighborhood was silent, as if the green lawns had absorbed all the sound.

She took the kit and went back inside.

It didn't take long. The first of the two drawers was empty but for a scatter of paper clips and a lump of Blu Tack.

The second contained two packs of unused manila envelopes, neatly stacked. Nothing else. She was disappointed, but not surprised. She riffled the stack nearest to her.

Stopped.

The clairvoyance bristled, then settled in her like a curled-up cat.

One of the envelopes wasn't empty. Its weight had messed up her riffle. She slid it out. From the feel of it, two or three prints inside. She went back to the lockpick kit and selected a thin file. Slit the envelope and pulled out the prints.

In the red safelight, the colors were annihilated. But the representational content was clear. The first photograph was a rear view of a blond woman in nothing but black stockings and high heels bending over a desk. She was looking back at the camera with her pale hair half covering her face. The one eye that was visible was heavily mascara'd and, Valerie suspected, false-lashed. Glossy lips in a half smile, half pout.

In the second she was leaning against a kitchen sink, head thrown back, blouse open, left hand caressing her breasts, right hand shoved inside her panties.

The final image was of her naked on a bed, gagged and blindfolded, hands tied above her head.

Valerie took them out of the darkroom into the full light of the basement for a better look. They were all black and white, the first (desk) and third (bed) looked artificially lit, taken with the same high contrast. The kitchen shot was softer, the light apparently natural. None of them, unsurprisingly, was initialed.

A cop gear shifted. She looked again at the first photograph. Even in black and white the lapis lazuli bowl in which she'd found Adam Grant's keys was unmistakable. She climbed the basement stairs a fifth time anyway. Thighs and calves burning, she stood in the office doorway and held up the print of the blonde bent over the desk.

This desk.

She went to the kitchen. Checked the print. All that natural light came from a window on the blonde's left. To the right of her bare shoulder a red Smeg fridge with a scatter of magnets and Post-its.

This window. This fridge.

Valerie was standing at the foot of the Grants' king-size (and still bloodstained) bed when her phone rang. Will Fraser calling.

"Hey."

"I found Sophia," Will said.

Valerie held the bedroom photograph up in front of her. The naked woman, black cloth blindfold, black cloth gag. Wrists fastened with curtain cord to the head of the bed.

This bed.

"Yeah," she said. "I think maybe I did, too."

# 15

## *August 1, 2017*

The night was too short and the hard work of digging had left her awash with endorphins. Of course the thing to do, once she'd finished, was get the fuck out of there. Yet she found herself in the driver's seat with the door open, easing her boots off and pushing her bare feet into the icy sand. Bliss entered her soles and traveled up through her calves, and for a strange, indeterminate time she sat there with her eyes closed and her knees apart, receiving the earth's cold benediction. She hadn't known murder would be like this. She'd imagined suffocating disgust at best. At worst a continuous raging fever of guilt. At any rate not this curious sensitivity, as if her innocence had been renewed at the cellular level. The desert understood. The masculine silence kept her company without judgment. The constellations absorbed her crime as the ocean would a tear. It was awful, how clean she felt.

But not all her wits left her. Dawn was coming. Whatever allowance this had been, it was over. She tossed the suede boots onto the passenger seat, accepting as she did it that it was a risk, grains of sand, some egghead with a microscope pinning down the exact square of earth, uniquely identifiable thanks to some geological quirk she didn't know about—but she couldn't care. It was enough that she was moving. She put the shovel back in the trunk. Took a last survey of the burial site. Began to tell herself it was completely undetectable—then dissolved a second time into indifference. She really *couldn't* care. This new innocence courtesy of guilt was, she understood, dangerous. It would get her caught. Tried. Convicted. Sentenced to death. Well, que será, será. She was very tired.

She expected disaster all the way back, sirens, a helicopter, the quivering searchlight, the moment of terrible stardom. But it didn't come. The desert lightened and she felt as if the night were a friend she'd lost. Tears welled and fell. She was, she admitted, probably losing her mind.

The house was empty when she got home. As determined. The endorphins had subsided. Now there was the purged feeling, as after a childhood afternoon of wild play and compressed dramas. She remote-opened the garage door and eased the Volvo inside. Got out and went around to the trunk, but for a moment couldn't open it. She leaned the heels of her hands on it, waiting for the next reserve of energy to kick in—the last reserve for this night, she knew. If she didn't get done now what she needed to get done there was no telling how long it would be before she'd have it in her again.

A few minutes passed. Her mouth hung open, a little spittle fell and pooled on the gleaming trunk. Spit was a thing sex had appropriated. Larry had spat on her, many times, after the first time, after he'd established he could fuck her. That first time he'd done everything as if with his mind elsewhere, as if he wasn't seeing her. Even then, young as she was, she'd thought he was trying not to see himself doing what he was doing so that afterward he could pretend he hadn't done it. He'd kept his eyes closed. *If a tree falls in the forest* . . . But later, once he'd got past all that, it was as if he couldn't see her clearly and vividly enough. As if he couldn't find enough things to do and watch himself doing. The first time he spat on her it had seemed involuntary, or at least unpremeditated. It surprised both of them. Then it became something he did every time, sometimes holding her head still so he could be accurate, get it into her eyes or nose or mouth. It was only later she understood spitting was something sex had appropriated. Lots of guys paid to spit on her, or paid her to spit on them. There was nothing, her working years taught her, that sex couldn't appropriate. By the time she was rescued she was saturated with pornography. Sexual omniscience like a dirty overcoat sewn to her skin. At nineteen.

What's your name, honey?

Sophia.

You're just about the cutest blond thing I've ever seen.

She straightened. The garage smelled of turpentine and new steel. She opened the trunk. She wanted to do it quickly. Not just because she was worried the last energy reserve would run dry too soon, but because she didn't want to spend time handling what she'd brought back from the desert.

In spite of which she couldn't stop herself pausing with the plastic bag in her hands, feeling its weight, tracing the padded outlines of its contents. Your curiosity was indefatigable, it turned out. As was your sense of comedy. The absurdity of objects divorced from their natural contexts. Why medical students played pranks with cadavers, presumably. *And if I laugh at any mortal thing / 'Tis that I may not weep.* Byron. Another bit of educational currency. It was only ever fragments. She'd missed the window in childhood for the structural groundwork, the big building blocks of learning that would have allowed proper cohesion later on. Instead she had a whirling miscellany, party pieces, novelties, tidbits.

Well, it didn't matter now.

There were two freezers, one upright in the kitchen, for daily use, small items, and one in the utility room, chest-style, for big joints of meat, some of which, she knew, had probably been in there long past even deep-freeze safe limits.

It took her half an hour to empty it, place the plastic bag in the bottom, then refill.

And that really was the last of the energy gone. Burning the scrubs, the clothes, the props, it would have to wait until tomorrow.

In the shower, simple soap and water sloughed the last vestiges of her violence and she emerged as if prosaically reborn. The soft white towel she wrapped around herself might have been woven by angels. She had thirty-six hours yet of solitary freedom. She was very hungry. She went back down through the clean spaces of the house to the gleaming kitchen. Made herself a cup of black coffee and devoured random food from the fridge: a roast chicken leg; a peach yogurt; a slice of leftover quiche. She ate in blank animal need, standing at the window watching birds flitting to and from the feeders on the sunlit lawn.

Naked, she lay on her bed, limbs spread as if for tanning, though in fact it was the house's cool conditioned air that moved over her like a beneficent spirit. She felt a great tenderness toward herself, a sympathetic exhaustion that tingled from her eyelids to her fingernails. The closed curtains showed pearly blue dawn light. Sleep was very near.

The first part of her giant labor was over—but she knew the worst was still to come.

# 16

## *August 7, 2017*

"So they were both screwing Sophia," Will Fraser said.

"Not necessarily at the same time," Valerie answered.

"I wasn't picturing a three-way."

"Not *seeing* her at the same time, fuckhead."

They were at their shared desk at the station, comparing stills of Will's gathered CCTV with the photographs Valerie had found in the Grants' basement. All but conclusively the same woman, though her face was maddeningly obscured in the photos and behind the giant shades in the CCTV.

"Well, maybe if Jenner hadn't done our guy there'd be mileage in that," Will said. "As it stands it's a no-brainer."

"I can't believe Jenner's that dumb."

"Are we looking at the same woman? I don't go for white girls, but I'd be dumb for this one. And why're you so convinced Jenner's smarter than that? Because his handsome half brother reads Norman Mailer?"

Valerie took a sip of her cappuccino. Here it was again: In among the legitimate reasoning was the irritating fact that Adam Grant had been, it turned out, capable of cheating on his wife. Just not with Valerie. Was there no end to the durability of her ego?

"Okay, look at it another way," she said. "What's a blonde hot enough to turn you into a cretin doing with a roach like Jenner? You're sleeping with a lawyer, chances are you're not sleeping with a recently released ex-con."

"Hooker?" Will asked.

"Not the type you could afford on Gold Star Valet wages."

"Unless you got five grand in cash from God knows where. That'd buy you a session or two."

"Check the escort agencies. Assuming you can handle that without falling in love or picking up an STD."

"What are you going to do?"

Valerie straightened, put her hands in the small of her back and stretched. Heard her vertebrae tick. She'd missed her hour in the gym two days running. If she didn't get in there soon there was a very good chance she'd find herself smoking a cigarette. Followed by twenty more. And a bottle of vodka.

"Well, since I'm not in a hurry to tell Rachel Grant her husband was screwing around," she said, "I'm going to the gym."

Twenty-four hours, she thought, finding her rhythm on the cross-trainer. She'd give Rachel Grant twenty-four hours of ignorance. Then, like it or not, she was going to have to deal with it. However unlikely, it was possible Rachel knew what her husband was up to. It was further possible that she knew with *whom* he was up to it. And Sophia was now, in the professional parlance, *material*.

She shifted from cross-trainer to treadmill, treadmill to bike. It was, she had to admit, good to be back in shape. Over the months her body's tensions had eased. Her circulation had been surprised into forgotten efficiency. Not long ago Nick had woken to find her standing, bent from the waist with her palms flat against the bedroom floor, something she'd been unable to do since childhood. Look at me, she'd said to him. I'm *nimble*. Do you have any idea how much work you'd have to put in to become nimble, like me? For a few moments he'd lain there, frowning through the dregs of sleep. Then he'd said: I'm handsome. I don't have to be nimble. Come back to bed.

Valerie pounded through the last two minutes on the delirious edge of exhaustion, trying and failing to ignore the gym's video screens, all of which showed music videos, all equally alien and annoying. Occasionally she was reminded of how far she'd traveled from such things. Adolescence had been filled with songs and TV shows and celebrities. Now she didn't know who anyone was. Work had stripped her of so much everyone else took for granted. When, as now, she caught glimpses of it, it was like looking back to a prehistoric age. By rapid degrees, and with a sort of frank implacability, Being Police simply obliterated everything else. People who weren't Police seemed like children or fantasists to people who were, diverted by toys and dreams, utterly oblivious to a reality which, unless they were very lucky, would sooner or later take a swipe at them, fracture their innocence, or smash their world to pieces. At which point, like Rachel Grant, they would need Police.

Calories burned: 210. Plus 170 on the treadmill and 200 on the cross-trainer. 580. Plenty. In the last three months she'd dropped almost twenty pounds. She was quietly ashamed of her self-satisfaction. Not quite the body she'd had at twenty-one, but there was no denying the look and feel of rejuvenation. Enjoy it while you can, she thought, enjoy it until it all goes to shit courtesy of *Getting Pregnant*.

She showered, dressed, drank a bottle of vending machine Evian (look at this, her alcoholic ghost scoffed—water!) then went to see Nick in Computer Forensics.

"I don't know how you guys stand this," she said. Nick and Nathan were at their desks. The white room always felt over-air-conditioned to Valerie.

"Each other's company?" Nathan said.

"Working in a windowless fridge," Valerie said.

"We have the warmth of our vocation," Nathan answered. "You two got a date up against the wall—or should I stick around?"

"Well, there's nothing groovy here," Nick said, leaning back in his chair. Valerie joined him to face the desktop screen. "Bank transactions all look regular. There are cash withdrawals, few hundred bucks here and there, but that's walking-around money to a lawyer. Jenner's cash could have come from Adam Grant, but there's nothing here that proves it."

"What about escort agencies? Credit card transactions show anything like that?"

"I wasn't looking for it. I'll check again. Was he doing that?"

"Maybe. Hidden photos of a blonde who looks the part. Same woman Jenner was apparently seeing. I don't expect the name 'Sophia' will crop up, but keep an eye out for it."

"Okay," Nick said. "I'll get on it. Gimme a couple of hours."

On her way out, Valerie ran into Laura Flynn. She was holding a sheaf of papers in her left hand, and a single sheet in her right.

"So we know from Jenner's phone records that Adam Grant called him," Laura said. "But I pulled Grant's phone records anyway. He had two phones registered." She shook the sheaf in her left hand. "These are the calls logged for one of the phones over the last two months. Regular shit, plenty of calls." She handed Valerie the single sheet. "That's the record for the other phone. Two months. Total fourteen calls, all to one number."

"Jenner's."

"It doesn't really help, since it tells us what we already know."

"Different shade, though, someone using a dedicated phone."

"Lawyer paranoia?"

"Probably."

"And that should be a title for an album, I think."

Valerie was back at her apartment and done for the day when Will called. Neither Adam Grant's photos nor the CCTV footage had produced a solid candidate from the Bay Area agencies, although Will hadn't finished his sweep.

"I've got a bunch more places to see tomorrow. Christ, does anyone in this city do anything else apart from pay for sex?"

"You want to trade with Nick and go through the bank records?"

"You don't want Nick keeping this sort of company, trust me. It's lucky I love my wife. Do you know what CIMNC stands for?"

"What?"

"'Come in mouth no condom.' You need money for the escorts and money for a learning course to decipher the fucking lingo. Anyway, if Sophia's a pro it looks like she's freelance."

"All right. Check the rest tomorrow."

"It's a tough job but someone's got to do it."

Valerie hung up. Once, at a house party she and her sister Cassie had gone to in their late teens, a guy had offered her three hundred dollars to blow him. He was older, a freshman back for the first vacation since leaving home. He was drunk, but serious and quite polite. He'd taken the money from his wallet there and then and said, with what appeared to be complete sincerity: Listen. I'm not a pervert or dangerous, but you are unbelievably beautiful and I cannot think of anything I'd rather do. I realize I'm not much to look at, but would you consider it? No one, I swear, will ever have to know. It's just that if I get run over by a truck later I'd like to die happy. She'd had a mix of feelings in response. There was a superficial sense of having been insulted and offended. Also some amusement and even, given the lonely earnestness of his manner, a little embarrassed pity. But the bedrock was her childhood Catholicism and a deeper sense of something like personal pride. She'd known immediately that not only was she not going to do this, now, but that it was something she would never do. It simply wasn't in her. On the other hand, the mere fact of him having put it into words forced her to visualize it—and to understand that if you were a woman in this particular world such transactions were always available. She'd understood not only that she couldn't do it, but that other girls (with whatever damage it entailed) could. Of course she'd known, intellectually, that prostitution existed, but up until that moment the reality of what it was had never fully hit her. At the time, conscious that this story would get told, eventually (if not by him then by her), she'd laughed and said, Not if you had three million and you were the last guy on earth. But secretly it had saddened her, and revealed at a stroke the countless women who, for whatever reason, could accommodate the idea that they had a price. Later, she'd told Cassie about it. Cassie was two years older, wrapped in the armor of artificial cynicism late adolescence demanded. She's snorted and said: Welcome to the world, kiddo. As far as men are concerned, every woman's cunt can be burgled or bought. Get used to it.

Nick got home with Indian takeout around nine. The summer evening was a soft deepening blue in the apartment windows. Valerie had just opened a cold bottle of sauvignon blanc. There was an unspoken understanding between her and Nick that she would restrict herself to two glasses. After the years of commitment to vodka's rough sex this was a mere peck on the cheek. That said, the new restraint and regular workouts—the *health*—had lowered her tolerance. If she swallowed the first glass in a couple of gulps and then sipped the second, she could get some sort of buzz. The trouble was it was the sort of buzz that demanded the rest of the buzz. Nick wasn't stupid: He made sure he drank the remainder of the bottle himself. Valerie had considered not drinking at all. She'd considered it—and rejected it, with a mortified inner shudder.

"No escort agencies," Nick said, unpacking the food. "I went three years back. Zippo. He might have paid an individual girl in cash, but the agencies are PayPal or plastic these days. No reference to Sophia, either."

"Yeah," Valerie said, as her salivary glands discharged at the scent of jalfrezi. "She's not recognized by any of the outfits Will checked, either. *He* had a fun day, at least."

"You going to tell the wife?"

"Have to. And I'm going to have to trawl Sophia through Grant's circle. Someone might ID her. Thank fuck we've got the CCTV stills. At least she's got her clothes on in those."

"Does Rachel Grant work?"

"No. Why?"

Nick helped himself to tarka dhal and tore off a strip of naan. "The photos," he said. "Taken at the Grants' house. Seems reckless, don't you think? Bringing your mistress into the family home? I mean Grant's got the means to bang her anywhere he likes. Why run the risk of your wife coming home early from her coffee morning or watercolor class or whatever?"

"Could have been a one-off," Valerie said. "Maybe Rachel was on vacation. Maybe he liked fucking his mistress in the marital bed."

They both fell silent. When Valerie had cheated on Nick four years ago that was exactly what *she*'d done. Not out of recklessness. Out of calculation. Because she'd wanted to get caught. She'd been so committed to her own worthlessness, love had felt like a grand injustice. So she'd done everything she could to subtract it from her life.

All of which passed between her and Nick now, telepathically. They glanced at each other, acknowledged the scar tissue, conceded it was worn more or less smooth.

"I'd rather wait till she's out of the hospital at least," Valerie said. "But unless we get word on Jenner soon I'm not going to have a choice."

# 17

## *August 8, 2017*

As it turned out, the gods or the random universe gifted Rachel Grant a stay of execution. The following afternoon Valerie got an APB response call from motorcycle patrol officer Niall Fox up in Hamilton City. Apparently, he'd seen Dwight Jenner less than two weeks ago at a rest stop gas station on I-5, just south of Orland.

"You sure it was him?" Valerie asked.

"Pretty sure," Fox told her. "I'd stopped in at the minimart for coffee. He was the customer behind me in line. I got the vibe."

"The vibe?"

Fox laughed. "The little shift in his, you know, force field when he registered a cop. Ma'am, you know what I mean. We see it every day."

Valerie did know. All but the slickest guilty had a sixth sense, alert to police presence. And if you were good police, the sensitivity was mutual. Equipped with thermal imaging goggles you'd be able to see their body temperatures rise.

"I hear you," she said. "Was he alone?"

"He was alone when I saw him," Fox said. "I got my coffee and went back out to the bike. Watched him come out. Didn't see what he bought."

"Vehicle?"

"Unknown. There's a parking lot there but the view's obscured. There were maybe half a dozen vehicles at the gas pumps, but he didn't get into any of those. To be honest with you, I was going to check him out, but I got a ten-forty-six southbound."

"You got a date for me?" Valerie asked.

"July thirty-first. I checked with Dispatch. The ten-forty-six came through just after nine forty P.M. And yeah, the minimart has CCTV."

"Someone looking at it?"

"Ma'am, I wish I could tell you they were, but we're a pretty small shop up here. I'm up to my neck and we've got a grand total of two detectives—"

"No sweat. Give me the number."

"I've been trying it, but phone-answering isn't their strong point."

After fifteen minutes of listening to hold music courtesy of On-the-Go roadside convenience, Valerie gave up and headed for her car, knowing it was probably a waste of time. Jenner had killed Adam Grant in the early hours of August 5, four whole days after this alleged sighting. Even if Fox's ID was sound—where did that get her? Nowhere. The good stuff, if there was any, lay *in* those four days.

Still, it was better than nothing. Motion was better than rest. Going somewhere was better than admitting you had nowhere to go. Between his last day at Gold Star Valet and the night of Adam Grant's murder, Dwight Jenner's movements were wholly unaccounted for. This would, Valerie told herself, put at least *one* fucking pin in the map.

Boredom on the road kept her trying the minimart's number. She'd done a hundred miles before a clerk picked up and transferred her, after what seemed a ludicrous delay and a lot of background yelling, to the manager, who listened, understood, but insisted, in only very slightly accented English, that he would have to see her badge before releasing the material.

"It's fine," Valerie said. "I'll be there in thirty minutes."

Pamu Ranasinghe was a weary, ironical Sri Lankan immigrant in his midfifties with a moonish face and hefty mustache. Dark eyes of amused skepticism and a small gap between his front teeth. Having spelled his name for Valerie's notes he added, "Yes, I'm the Asian socioeconomic cliché made famous by *The Simpsons*."

It took Valerie a moment to make sense of this. Then she did—and making sense of it left her not quite knowing what to say. "It's been a long time since I saw that show," she said, with an involuntary tone of apology, though she didn't know what she was apologizing for, except, vaguely, the racial stereotyping inherent in American popular culture. Ranasinghe studied her, with his head on one side. This was a man, she thought, resigned to being undervalued and misunderstood. It had bred in him a remote, inert superiority. She liked him.

"So, if you could let me take a—"

"Yes, I know what you need to see. You gave me the date and time. Come this way."

Valerie followed him to the back of the store and through a stockroom to his very small office, a scrupulously tidy place with one barred window of frosted glass.

"It's set up ready for you," Ranasinghe said. "Just hit Play. Since I assumed you'd like a copy on disc," he tapped a CD case on the desk with his fingernail, "I've made one for you."

Smart, disappointed, and bored, Valerie revised. There was a copy of *The New York Times* and the latest edition of *The Lancet* next to the disc. It made her imagine a professional life before the U.S., before whatever upheaval had driven him here. She groped, mentally, for anything she knew about Sri Lanka. Got the word "Tamil," along with a vague notion of civil war. Tsunami? How long ago was that? The world gobbled its news too fast. You couldn't hold on to anything. Like millions of others she harbored the thought that one day—when she had time—she would get a grip on global current events. Her wiser self knew it would never happen. There was only one kind of current event she gave a shit about: whatever homicide had most recently landed on her desk.

"Thank you very much," she said. "That's very helpful." It sounded patronizing.

Ranasinghe smiled, manifestly in a way that said he'd found it patronizing too, though the gap in his teeth gave him a look of impish delight. "There is no end to my talents," he said. "Would you like a cup of coffee?"

Cappuccino in the making, Valerie examined the footage. There was no doubt it was Jenner. Beyond that it had nothing to offer, except that even through the pixels she could see Fox was right about the vibe. Jenner entered the store with a take-no-shit buoyancy—then checked it when he saw the uniform. For a moment it looked as if he was considering turning on his heel and getting the fuck out of there. But he didn't. He loosened his shoulders and took his place in line, hands in the pockets of his khaki combat jacket. After the officer paid for his coffee and exited (with a backward glance) Jenner bought a pack of Marlboros, then left.

Ranasinghe brought her cappuccino. "On the house," he said, setting it down next to her.

"Thanks."

"Officer Fox is a regular here. Hospitality by extension." Then, seeing her look, he added: "Sorry. I was being petulant. You're welcome."

"Do you have external CCTV?"

The smile reappeared. "You want a vehicle," he said. "I'm afraid you won't find anything. But once again, with my remarkable prescience . . ." He reached past her, selected another video file from the desktop, hit Play. "It's a single wide-angle," he said. "You can see here, your suspect exits. He crosses the forecourt, and . . . Ah. You see?"

It was as Fox had said: The bulk of the parking lot was obscured by a combination of gas pumps and a few small trees on its border. The camera was positioned to optimize the view of vehicles taking gas. Obviously. For drive-aways without payment.

"And you've never seen this guy before?" Valerie asked.

"No. And I've checked with my team, barring one who's on vacation. No one recalls seeing him before."

"What about . . ." Valerie took out her phone and pulled up the best still of Sophia. "This lady?"

Ranasinghe studied the image. "No," he said. "Not to my recollection. But obviously, given a fallible memory and the vast number of customers, that doesn't prove anything. Besides, I'm not always on the shop floor. You can, of course, check with my staff, but frankly since they spend most of their time here in what appears to be a catatonic state, I wouldn't hold your breath."

She didn't hold her breath, but she checked anyway. No joy. She was almost back in the city when Will called to say he'd had a fruitless day of it with the remaining escort agencies. No one recognized Sophia.

"If she's a hooker," he said, "she's not on anyone's books in the Bay Area. Now what, Sherlock?"

Valerie pulled out to pass a station wagon driven by a young black girl singing along to something with complete oblivious conviction. The sun was low and molten on the horizon.

"We'll pull the traffic cam footage for the rest stop entrance and exit. Couple of hours either side of Jenner's sighting. He didn't *walk* there."

"Fun viewing."

"And I think we should try the brother again."

"Half brother."

"Half brother. He's not telling us everything."

"Maybe you should offer him sex?"

"You've spent too long in the world of prostitution. You at the station?"

"Will be in about fifteen. Meet you at Cornell's?"

"Don't bother. I can handle it."

"I was *kidding* about offering him sex, you realize?"

It wasn't entirely self-serving. Valerie did think Kyle Cornell was holding something back. Mainly though, she hoped an interview with him would take long enough to justify postponing the *other* interview until tomorrow. The one in which she'd have to break the news to Rachel Grant that her late, murdered husband had been, prior to his brutal departure from this mortal coil, screwing another woman.

# 18

Ed Perez was on surveillance outside Kyle Cornell's building when Valerie arrived, just after 9 P.M.

"Nada," he told her. "Trip to the grocery store this afternoon. Watered his window plants and took out the trash. Girlfriend turned up a couple of hours ago. Guess it's his day off."

"What time's your relief?"

"Ray's on at eleven." Ed smiled. "Tell me you've got nothing better to do."

"Go ahead," Valerie said. "I'll take it for a couple of hours."

"Every time I begin to doubt the existence of God," Ed said, "he presents me with another small miracle."

"Forget God. I want a dozen of Sondra's empanadas by Friday."

"It's my recipe. She's not even Mexican."

"And some of that mango jalapeño salsa, too."

An unfortunate parting exchange, she realized, as Ed pulled away. She was starving. Another consequence of low alcohol consumption: The need to *eat actual food regularly* had reasserted itself. Now she was stuck with hunger for at least two hours. She should have left Ed in place, gone in and talked to Kyle, then called it a night. But en route she'd changed her mind about a second interview. Partly (she told herself) because she wasn't convinced mere questioning would get her whatever it was he was hiding, but mainly (she *admitted* to herself) because she didn't relish a repeat of the sexual frisson between them. Picking up surveillance at least took care of the duty hours for tonight, providing a rationalization, however feeble, for leaving the bad-news delivery to Rachel Grant until tomorrow.

So much for surface logic. Beneath it, she knew, was raw instinct's directive to watch and wait. Kyle's alleged indifference to his brother's whereabouts—to his brother's predicament as a murder suspect—didn't square with the relationship the two of them apparently shared. By Kyle's own testimony, they'd always been close. You didn't give your ex-con half brother a room in your apartment then do nothing more than cross your fingers and hope for his good behavior. The I'm-not-my-brother's-keeper nonchalance was smoke for the cops. Even if Kyle genuinely didn't know where Jenner was, it wasn't credible that he didn't care.

Just before 10:45 P.M. Kyle came out of the building. With The Girlfriend, a lithe, pretty white girl in her very early twenties, with long straight dark hair, center parted. Skinny jeans and a tan suede jacket big enough on her that Valerie decided it actually belonged to Kyle. She carried herself haughtily, shoulders back, chin up. Valerie caught a glimpse of a broad silver bracelet with a chunky turquoise stone on her left wrist. She tossed her hair over her shoulders, once. She was proud of the hair, its glossy fall, practically down to her ass. She was altogether proud of herself, in fact. Valerie assumed controlled rebellion against affluent, conservative parents. An interrupted college degree and a flirtation with the wrong side of the tracks. Daddy, in particular, would be grinding his teeth over the half-black boyfriend. Mommy would be saying things like *Let her get through this, don't rise to it, the more you disapprove the farther away you'll drive her . . . .*

Ridiculous, Valerie thought, as she turned on the Taurus's ignition to follow Kyle's Ford. You can't know any of that. Still, the movie ran on in her head. Did Kyle Cornell know he was just an instrumental feature of a predictable white family psychodrama? Maybe he did. Maybe he didn't care, as long as the sex was crazy enough. She had an image of the two of them fucking, Kyle on his back, the girl astride him, hair tossed back (naturally, he'd like that) cat eyes fierily focused, ostensibly on him, really on how appalled her mother and father would be, watching their precious little princess . . .

For Christ's sake. Enough. If you want to think about fucking him, have the decency not to use a fantasy proxy. There's no harm in thinking. It's not what you think that counts. It's what you do.

And no, she told herself, you're not going to do *that*.

She called Rayner Mendelsund and told him she'd picked up the surveillance shift. Then (a *little* guiltily) she called Nick to tell him not to wait up.

"Fine," he said. "But wake me if you want biology."

Valerie hadn't kept her feelings about baby-making sex to herself. "Biology" had become the euphemism. "Wow," she said. "You're making me wet."

"Yeah, we're so hot together. How do we stand it?"

The Ford stopped outside a corniced white four-story apartment block on Twenty-fifth and Sanchez. Noe Valley: She'd been right about the affluence, at any rate. The girl got out and went with regal pertness and jouncing hair up the whitewashed stoop. Waved back at the car from the door, then went in. A moment later, the Ford pulled away.

Valerie followed.

North on Castro. Northeast on Market. Right on Fourth Street. East on the 80. He was taking the Bay Bridge.

There was, of course, no explanation for how mere taillights could testify to a driver's nefarious intent, but that didn't stop her reading them that way. Valerie was well aware of the long list of legitimate reasons Kyle Cornell might have for leaving the city at this hour, and similarly aware that she'd dismissed all of them. She'd lived too long with the occult intuitions of Being Police to question them now.

At Emeryville he picked up the 580 and stayed east on it until it joined Highway 99, where he turned south. She checked her fuel gauge. Less than half a tank. The insistent physics of the non-police world. How far was he going?

Ten miles north of Fresno he took a left toward Fraint. The moon was out, full and cream-yellow. In a minute, she thought, he's going to pull over, get out, walk up to me, and ask me why I'm following him. She let the tail lengthen, very sincerely hoping all her previously ordered surveillance hadn't given itself away.

Smaller roads. Lanes. Millerton Lake to the north, Table Mountain to the east. Scrub gave way to woodland, big conifers that leaned toward each other above her as if trying to embrace. A narrow avenue of sky showed between them. She shouldn't be doing this by herself.

She slowed. The bends made keeping her distance—

Fuck.

He'd stopped.

She hit the brakes and killed the lights.

The Ford was parked fifty yards ahead, half up on a bank at the edge of the trees. Lights off. It looked like the vehicular equivalent of a dog cocking its leg to pee.

She squinted. The driver's seat was empty.

The thing to do, obviously, was call it in. Precious seconds. Maybe a minute, two minutes. Plenty of time for her to lose him—and he already had a head start, in the fucking *woods*.

She grabbed a flashlight from the glove compartment and got out. It was close to midnight.

# 19

Left or right? She was at the parked Ford, flashlight off, eyes still adjusting to the moon's illumination. The night reprioritized her senses. *Listen.* She was about to go right—when she heard, unmistakably, the clank of metal. Across the lane. Left.

In the dark she caught her jacket on what turned out to be a barbed-wire fence. Beyond it the trees thinned into a rough meadow. She could see him now. He had a flashlight of his own. Its white ellipse shivered on the grass. He was maybe fifty feet away, moving directly across the field. She turned to her right and followed the fence, grateful for her standard wardrobe choice: jeans, leather bomber jacket, and the Van Gorkom hikers that were halfway between a shoe and a boot: tough, pliable, and in their own humble way capable of convincing her there was no physical gearshift she couldn't handle. Unless you were either a moron or inveterately vain, the job soon swept the aesthetic niceties aside. "Lady clothes" as she called them—skirts, dresses, heels—were for leisure time only. Nick had no complaints. As he had put it: The great thing about you dressing like a guy 90 percent of the time is that it makes the 10 percent when you dress like a woman worth the wait. It's pornography.

The clank of metal, she discovered after twenty paces, was a small five-bar gate with a chained padlock. Someone's land. A farm? She grabbed the chain to muffle it, got a foot up, slithered down the other side, and set off after Kyle. She left her light off. The bobbing flicker of his was easy to follow. The field was maybe seventy meters across but its length disappeared into darkness. The air was warm and still. Smell of the pines and dry grass—then rust: an abandoned water trough she skirted just as she saw Kyle go over a second gate and into another belt of trees.

These, too, gave onto a field, more baked dust than grass, crumbly under-foot. He stopped, checked his bearings, looked to his left. She crouched down, tracking his look: barely visible fifty meters away, a fenced yard of pale asphalt and a couple of low-lying outbuildings lit by a weak security lamp, presumably barns or sheds. He went the other way. Valerie followed. She was sweating. Underarms, forehead. All he had to do was turn around and he'd see her. She reached under her jacket, popped the shoulder holster, and took out her Glock. She didn't believe he was armed, but belief was a long and potentially lethal way from certainty. He didn't turn.

She lost sight of him when he entered the woods bordering the bottom edge of the field, but it was obvious where he'd gone: A tiny, derelict trailer missing both wheels stood on cinder blocks in a small clearing. A scatter of litter around it: beer cans and plastic bags, a busted and weather-rotted armchair, half its stuffing coming out like ectoplasm. The door was open but there was no light from inside.

She stopped. Watch and wait. Police version of the Hippocratic oath: In the first instance, do no harm. She got her back against a tree, crouched down, trained the Glock on the doorway.

Silence.

A minute passed. Two.

Nothing.

She waited. Her left leg started to cramp. She was thirsty.

After maybe five minutes of soundless stasis, she lost patience. She eased herself upright. Felt the blood flow back into her leg. Took a moment to plot her route avoiding the garbage, then—

She heard him a split second before he hit her, side on, with his full body-weight. He must have been barely three paces to her left, behind a neighboring tree. She got a sudden whiff of him: denim, cigarette smoke, light sweat, and something synthetically fruity, as if he'd washed his hair with a strawberry shampoo—then the wind went out of her as his shoulder struck her just below her ribs and she felt the dark ground swing up and smack the side of her head.

He was half on top of her, their legs tangled, his left hand buried in her hair, his right grappling for the gun. Adrenaline went through her in a rapture, scalp to toenails. The sound of his breath and hers was abrasively intimate after the silence. His fingers fought for a grip on her sleeve. She didn't have long. The speed of events had an expanding mass of their own. In seconds it would eclipse her options.

But the recent physical training classes had refreshed her Academy circuitry, unlocked the drilled routines and maneuvers, the angles, trajectories, leverages, shifts. The impulse, in this position—the untrained impulse—was to push against your attacker. The reflex was *resistance*. Which was precisely what the Academy taught you to override. Kyle was behind her, almost (her lawless imagination let it in without fuss) in the lovers' spoons position, and what he wanted was to force her onto her belly. All his energy right now was devoted to rolling her over. The math and physics were simple. She feigned for a moment, pushed against him—then as soon as he pushed back, she went with it. One horrifying instant when she was, actually, facedown in the dirt with him on her back—then it was done. He was a victim of his own momentum. Their roll left him on *his* back with her on top of him. She lifted her head then smashed it backward into his face. He cried out as she wrenched her gun hand from his grip, scrabbled off him, and got to her knees. She made sure he could see *very clearly* the Glock held two-handed and steady, trained on him.

"Jesus," he spat. "*You?* What the fuck?"

"Over on your front, hands behind your head."

"What the fuck are you doing?"

"On your front, hands behind your head. Do it."

"I didn't know it was you!"

"Otherwise you'd have invited me in for a beer? Move."

"I think you broke my goddamned *nose*."

But, struggling, he assumed the position. Best she could do without cuffs, which, of course, she hadn't brought. She moved forward, held the nozzle to the back of his skull, frisked him. No firearm, no weapons.

"You can't do this," he said.

"And yet here I am, doing it." She stepped back a couple of paces. Shot a glance at the trailer doorway. Empty. No sounds of movement within.

"Jenner?" she called. "Dwight Jenner? SFPD. Come out with your hands where I can see them."

"He's not in there," Kyle said. "He's not here, for Christ's sake."

"Get up," she said. "Keep your hands behind your head. Move slowly toward the trailer. When you get there, get back on the ground just as you are now."

"He's not *here*."

"Don't make this a labor. It's undignified."

He laughed, once, half into the dirt. "You're something," he said. "Jesus."

But again, in awkward increments, he complied.

The trailer, a quick look showed her, was empty. Relics of furniture, a camping stove, more garbage. A ragged hole in the floor the size of a soccer ball, long grass growing through as if with shy curiosity. Smells of kerosene, cat piss, mold.

"Look, this is ridiculous," Kyle said. "I'm not armed. I'm not resisting. And more to the fucking point, I'm not doing anything illegal."

"Assault, I think you'll find, is illegal," Valerie said. "And assaulting a police officer is, you know, illegal deluxe."

"I told you: I didn't know it was you. Can we just calm down here? Because I'm starting to think you're getting more than just professional satisfaction out of this. I know you like me, but how about we go out for dinner first, like normal people?"

"Are you early or late?" Valerie asked.

"What?"

"For the rendezvous with Dwight."

"There's no rendezvous."

"Look, we can go through all the boring crap of commandeering your phone and finding out when you talked to him, or you can just tell me now. You tell me now and I'll think about not charging you with obstruction."

Kyle didn't answer.

"Or as an accessory after the fact, for that matter," Valerie added. "I'm pretty sure your girlfriend wouldn't be thrilled."

Kyle laughed again. There was genuine warmth in it, as if Valerie had admitted a collusion. As if the girlfriend was the object of their shared superior awareness.

"You've been watching me," he said. "Nice."

"Not me, personally. Come on. Let's not waste each other's time."

"We still talking about Dwight?"

"You can hit on me later. For now, tell me where your brother is."

For a moment Kyle just lay there with his eyes closed. The trees around the clearing were a quiet collective, observing. Valerie had a brief intimation of how small this event was in the earth's history. Countless tiny dramas. Billions of lives like scraps of paper being sucked into a furnace. It made your own urgency absurd. Which was why she shut all such thoughts down. They got in the way of the Work.

"Can I get up?" Kyle said. "If I lie here much longer I might doze off."

Valerie stepped around in front of him, kept the Glock trained. "You can sit up," she said. "But for God's sake don't try anything gymnastic, will you?"

Kyle got into a sitting position. Knees bent, elbows resting on them, wrists loose. He had the gift of looking wholly at ease in his body. A black-guy thing, Valerie thought, that languid assurance. (A racist thought, she supposed. All right, not *all* black guys. But certainly *very few* white guys.) He looked up at her, then away. Smiled. Some inner capitulation.

"I haven't seen Dwight," he said. "I haven't seen him or spoken to him, like I said, for more than a week. His phone's off, or dead. This place . . ." He shook his head. "It's my aunt's. My mom's sister. Used to be an alpaca farm, believe it or not. We used to come here when we were kids. Me and Dwight."

He lowered his head for a moment. Exhaled. Valerie could sense his mix of anger, resignation, fear. This shift into candor softened her, slightly.

"It's nothing," he said. "Me being here. Just a long shot. We used to say we'd come here, you know, if things . . . If some shit went down. If ever we needed a place to hole up." He shook his head. "I didn't really think he'd be here. There's no sign of him, nothing."

Valerie observed him for a moment in silence. Decided he wasn't lying. Decided nonetheless that she was going to have to request a watch on this place, too. More manpower. More resources the department didn't have.

"The truth is I don't know whether I'm worried about him or sick to fucking death of him," Kyle said. "Way I feel right now, if I knew where he was, I'd probably tell you."

Valerie doubted that. Still, the gun pointed at him felt a tad redundant. She lowered it. No reaction from Kyle. Her flush of adrenaline was subsiding, leaving its characteristic afterglow, a heightened sensitivity to her body, its simple miracle of breathing in, breathing out.

Kyle looked at her again. "You'll think I'm naïve," he said. "But I just don't believe he could've done something this crazy. He was getting his act together. He really was."

"People surprise us," Valerie said, surprising herself, her tone of sympathy. It wasn't good that there was such ease and directness between them. It wasn't good that they understood each other. Kyle looked at her—as if he'd had precisely the same thought. He ought, she thought, to have smiled or winked, with deliberate sexual mischief. She could have dealt with that. But he didn't. He just looked. It was appalling, the silent, palpable attraction. It made *her* look away. And though he said nothing, she knew he was reading her. She even sensed him letting it go, deciding this wasn't the moment. There won't be a moment, hotshot. It's nice, but there won't be a moment. I'm a little cracked, a little perverse, but I'm not completely fucking insane.

"And you really don't know anything about this woman he's seeing?"

Kyle shook his head. "Name's Sophia. Former pole dancer. That's all I know. Way Dwight told it, she's a class act. Gave him instructions, where to meet. *Hotels.* At first I thought he was making it up. He's susceptible to his own fantasies. It didn't sound feasible."

He handled certain words with precarious satisfaction in having acquired them. *Susceptible. Feasible.* Precarious because he didn't yet trust his entitlement to them. Valerie imagined the hours of community college. The determination that would have required. With what must have been an extraordinary act of will, he'd marshaled his rogue energies, forced them to submit to education like wild horses to a harness. If he hadn't, there was no telling where such energies would have taken him. He'd saved himself just in time. Unlike his half brother.

"You're not going to call me if he gets in touch," she said. Not a question.

"Neither would you, in my shoes."

Would she? If it were her sister? If it were Nick? Did love trump the law? She felt the admission that it did coming off her like heat. Another illicit understanding between them. Nothing to do but consign it to the collection of ignorable truths. Know it was possible and hope it never happened. Moral consistency was a doomed enterprise.

"Time to go," she said. "Walk ahead of me."

He waited a moment, then got with that same provoking lazy grace to his feet. Now he did smile—and there was the sexual mischief. "Yes, ma'am," he said.

# 20

## *August 10, 2017*

Against her doctor's advice, Rachel Grant had discharged herself from the hospital and was back at home under police protection (Officer Riordan on babysitting duty again) and attended by a private nurse, a dyspeptic Filipina with a small face and very large eyes, so small and well proportioned a woman that she looked like a specially designed miniature.

"I don't like hospitals," Rachel told Valerie. "Besides, I need to be with Elspeth."

A hospital bed had been set up in the TV room, though Rachel wasn't in it. She was reclined instead on the couch, wearing a white bathrobe over a pink T-shirt. Gray fur slipper boots. Her face looked as if she'd scrubbed it too hard. Or as if it had reached the phase where no more tears would come. The short coppery hair was greasy. The olive-green nail varnish was still on, an incongruous touch of goth glamor in the atmosphere of dreary convalescence.

"The nurse changes the dressings and keeps the pain meds flowing. I don't need anything more than that."

"How's Elspeth doing?" Valerie asked.

Rachel closed her eyes for a moment. Opened them. "She's in a night-mare," she said. "She's awake in the middle of a nightmare."

Valerie groped mentally for something encouraging. Rachel Grant got there first.

"She's strong," she said. "She's got strength like stubbornness. She amazes me. I thank God for it. I thank God for *her*."

Valerie nodded, feeling sick. Along with her purse she had a manila envelope on her lap. Containing the photographs of Sophia. She'd bought Rachel Grant another day of innocence yesterday by checking the CCTV images with Adam Grant's friends and colleagues—none of whom could ID the subject, nor knew that Adam had a relationship with anyone named Sophia. Now there was only Rachel left to ask. Obviously the best thing was to get it over with. But the celluloid evidence of Adam Grant's secret life had refreshed the fact that she, Valerie, had been (however drunkenly and without consummation) a player in it. Again, the sense of her own bankruptcy needled her. She'd done the wrong thing in taking the case. The sort of wrong thing that expanded, fractally, around you, until as far as you could see in any direction there it was, *wrongness,* an inescapable matrix of your own making.

"Have you found him?" Rachel said.

"No. I'm sorry. Not yet. But we will."

Rachel looked as if she believed her. The belief wouldn't last forever. Right now it was fueled by grief and the need for vengeance. Soon, Valerie knew, it would turn to frustration, then anger, then cynicism, then a sort of nullity, an acceptance that this was not, after all, a world in which the good were rewarded and the wicked punished.

"Mrs. Grant," she said, "this is going to be difficult. I'm sorry. I have something I need to ask you."

"What?"

Valerie took out the photographs. Selected the best single shot from Will's CCTV stills and handed it to Rachel. "Do you know this woman?"

Rachel's force field shifted. There was no physical sign, but Valerie felt it. Fear, she thought. She already knows what I'm going to ask her.

Rachel studied the image. "No. I don't know her. Who is she?" Her eyes were already on the other photographs, still held in Valerie's lap.

"We don't have her surname," Valerie said. "But we think her first name is Sophia. It's almost certain that she was involved with Dwight Jenner. As far as we can tell, they met regularly, at various hotels in the Bay Area."

A lesser woman than Rachel Grant might have allowed herself the reflex response: *So? So what? What's that got to do with . . . ?* But Rachel Grant wasn't that sort of woman. The inner calculations were being worked through. Her hand holding the print, Valerie now saw, was trembling. Her face was stark, the green eyes wildly alive.

Valerie chose what she regarded as the least explicit of the Adam Grant shots: Sophia sitting on the kitchen worktop, head back, body lit prettily by the window-filtered sun. She handed it to Rachel. "This is the same woman," she said.

Then said nothing more. Instead watched Rachel Grant recognizing the kitchen, the fridge, the Post-its.

Silence. Valerie's face was warm.

"You recognize the—"

"Yes."

More silence. The nurse put her head around the door, big eyes inquiring.

"I'll take the pills later, Tala," Rachel Grant said. The nurse tutted and withdrew.

"I'm sorry," Valerie repeated. (How many times was she going to say "sorry" to this woman, knowing that no amount of apologies would ever, if she knew the whole truth, be enough?) "The fact is I found this picture in Adam's darkroom. In one of only two drawers that were locked."

Rachel Grant stared at the image. Her effort not to succumb—either to rage or tears—was all but audible. The big window behind her showed a cruelly perfect afternoon. Blue sky and a flawless green lawn. A laburnum tree's yellow blossom brilliant in the sun. Beauty carried on, regardless of human misery.

"How can you know it's the same woman?" Rachel said, not looking at Valerie. "You can't see her face." She spoke quietly. A terrible forced calm. Valerie looked down at the next of the Adam Grant photographs. Sophia, blindfolded, tied to the bed. Rachel's bed.

"Oh," Rachel said. "You have other photographs."

"I'm afraid so," Valerie said. "Clearly the same woman, and clearly taken here in your home. I'm really—"

"Show me," Rachel said.

"Mrs. Grant, it's not going to—"

"Show me the rest of the pictures."

Valerie understood. Rachel Grant had received her first hit of horror through the murder of her husband—and horror was masochistically addictive. Now she wanted more, all of it. Now she wanted to know exactly how much shit the world was made of, and exactly how stupid she'd been to believe otherwise. There was satisfaction in it, experiencing your nude self, stripped of its delusions. If not for her daughter, Valerie thought, Rachel Grant was the sort of person for whom a brush with monstrosity would be more than enough to turn her into a monster herself.

She handed her the rest of the photographs. Observed first the shock then the quivering disgust as Rachel went through them. And beneath both shock and disgust yet another stratum of sadness, when she'd thought there could be no more. The death of your husband. Then the *lie* of your husband, so that even the grief couldn't be clean. Valerie felt another "I'm sorry" burgeoning. Suppressed it. Pointless. And craven.

Rachel passed the photographs back to her. Elsewhere in the house the nurse opened and closed a cupboard door.

Then Rachel smiled. This, too, was one of horror's demands, that you saw the possibility of laughing along with it. "I was going to say you still can't really tell if it's the same woman," she said. "But where does that get me? *One* of these women was in my house. Being photographed by my husband. Being *fucked* by my husband, presumably, since that's what you're not saying." Then she added, vaguely: "All these things we don't say."

"I wouldn't have brought this to you," Valerie said. "But there's good reason to suppose this individual was one of the last to see Dwight Jenner before he went off the grid. She could be crucial to finding him."

Rachel lay back on the couch and looked at Valerie, still with a slight smile. The saying was *Don't shoot the messenger.* One of the dumbest sayings, Valerie knew. The messenger always got shot. And police were always the messengers.

"How do you do it?" Rachel asked her.

"Do what?"

"This. Every day. Bring people ugliness and betrayal and death. It must do something to you."

Well, here was the messenger, getting shot.

At the last moment before Valerie replied, she changed what she was going to say. She'd been going to offer something professionally platitudinous. *It's part of the job, Mrs. Grant. The worst part. Believe me, if there were any other way . . .* But Rachel Grant was looking at her from the calm eye of her hurricane as if she really, in her new state of raw curiosity where anything was permissible, wanted to know.

"It probably has done something to me," Valerie said. "I'm not sure what. Pushed me past surprise, I suppose. Burned out some human circuits. But without being that way we don't catch the people we need to catch."

For a moment the two of them looked at each other. Rachel's face was a fusion of exhaustion and energy, fascination and despair. Again, Valerie thought how easy it would be for this woman to surrender, to break down into madness, perhaps even death. If not for the daughter. *I thank God for her.* Maybe, Valerie thought. But loving a child was a vicious blessing: It took certain options off the table, no matter how much you were suffering. If you loved your child then you had to survive. You had to survive anything. For them. That was love's price.

"Yes," Rachel said. "I suppose it has to be that way."

For a crazy moment Valerie thought Rachel Grant had read her mind. Then realized the response was to what she'd *said*. Burned out some human circuits, etc.

"I hope you're right," Rachel added. "I hope that being the way you are means you get him. Whatever Adam . . ." She didn't finish. Just shook her head, looked away. Then said, still with her face averted: "Unless I'm supposed to care less now that you tell me he was fucking another woman. Is that what's supposed to happen? Am I supposed to think it served him right?"

Rhetorical. And in any case irrelevant to Valerie's purposes. But it didn't stop her wondering. *Did* it make a difference? Did betrayal register at all in the din of loss? Maybe not now—but Rachel Grant would have the rest of her life for the emotional math to settle. Time's subtle recalibration.

She got to her feet. There was nothing left here.

"I'll call you as soon as we have anything," she said.

Rachel didn't answer.

"Oh, actually, one last minor thing." She didn't even know why she'd remembered it. Desperation?

Rachel exhaled. Rose above her contempt. Looked Valerie in the eye.

"Did Adam take a sleeping pill that night?"

At first Rachel's look was just one of disbelief that the questions were still coming, that there really was no end to it.

But she rose above that, too. Shook her head, looked away. Didn't care. "I don't know," she said. "It's possible. Sometimes he took one of my Ambien if he was wired and had an early start."

The nurse, Tala, appeared in the kitchen doorway when Valerie was on her way through the hall.

"Are you finished?" she asked, with distinct peremptoriness.

"Yes," Valerie said.

"Good. We're late with the meds."

Tala went back into the kitchen. A sound made Valerie turn and look up. Elspeth was sitting halfway up the glass stairs, hunched with her arms wrapped around her shins, watching her. The girl looked exhausted. The big eyes were bright. One pale knee showed through a (designer) tear in the dark blue jeans. Her white T-shirt had a small brown smear on the left shoulder. An elf in the process of transforming into something much darker.

"Hello, Elspeth," Valerie said. Mainly because the girl's stare was discomfiting. She couldn't, Valerie decided, have overheard the conversation with Rachel Grant. "You doing okay?"

Elspeth didn't answer. Valerie couldn't look away.

Suddenly Elspeth wrenched herself to her feet, turned and, with a strange, low mewling sound, ran up the stairs and disappeared.

# 21

## *August 1, 2017*

The alarm clock on her phone went off, as set, at 11:00 A.M. She woke in the bedroom's pale light with her body aching. Had it not been for what she'd done the night before, she would have thought she was coming down with the flu. But she had done what she had done. Look no further for explanation. This was how it would be now: She was in new territory. There would be surprises. Existence itself would be one long surprise for the rest of her life.

Besides, the flu—any illness, debilitation, weakness—was prohibited. She had work to do.

Still, for a few sweet, illicit moments, she lay where she was. The white muslin drapes were an oblong of mother-of-pearl light. The bedroom was sparsely populated by expensive things, each occupying its space with a distinct, assured personality. Life had brought her so much of what she'd wanted. But only after doing sufficient damage to prevent her ever enjoying it. Her sense of her own worth was one of the things Larry had needed to destroy. He had known she was better than him. Which had been unacceptable to him. *Not such a princess after all, huh*, he'd said to her, after coming on her face, though even as he said it she knew it hadn't been enough for him, that he was still raging. In some part of herself she'd understood the drab truth that nothing he did to her would ever be enough for him. His hatred was an infinite disease no finite object could satisfy, though he was compelled to keep trying, to keep repeating the failed cure.

Enough.

She got up, washed her face and brushed her teeth, dressed. She wanted coffee but dismissed the desire as more procrastination. In the kitchen she opened the cupboard under the sink and tore open a new pack of heavy-duty rubber washing-up gloves. (Redundant items, if anyone had bothered to check, given the state-of-the-art dishwasher, but the kitchen and its equipment were under her sole jurisdiction.) Wearing them, she took last night's clothes and the scrubs from the Volvo, stuffed them into a plastic garbage bag, and carried it into the sprawling green backyard.

It was already warm outdoors. A high blue sky with low-lying quills of cloud. The roses were soft knots of color. Red. Yellow. Peach. The jasmine needed trimming. Here it was again: People made sonnets or gas chambers. The planet carried on cashing out its flora and fauna regardless.

The chiminea was in the shed. In fact there were three chimineas (if that was the correct plural), since affluence insisted that one of any given thing was rarely enough. She wanted the biggest of the three, which, her rehearsals had established, she could just about shift by herself. She'd bought kindling and wood a week ago. Firelighters. A can of lighter fluid just in case.

She dragged it outside to what she decided was a safe distance from the shed, set it on its wrought-iron stand, loaded it with fuel, and got a small fire started. Then she went back inside the shed, selected the large garden shears, and began work on cutting up the clothes, the scrubs, the props.

It turned out to be a calming ritual. She went through it four times, feeding in only enough material as wouldn't choke the flames. The discomfort was that her need to watch the evidence being consumed kept drawing her closer to the open grate. She had to keep backing away, face hot.

Eventually, satisfied that everything had been reduced to ash, she tipped the residue into the storm drain at the back of the yard, bleached the grate for good measure, then went inside to shower.

# 22

## *August 12, 2017*

There were two different kinds of murder, Valerie knew, one engaging, the other dull. The engaging murder was one in which you had to figure out who'd done it. (Fiction didn't mass-produce "whodunnits" for nothing. They engaged police for the same reason they engaged audiences, the perennial appeal of solving the central mystery of *responsibility*.) The dull murder, on the other hand, was one in which you already knew who'd done it—but you couldn't *find* the fucker. And unfortunately, with every day that passed, it was becoming increasingly obvious that the murder of Adam Grant fell into this second category. The question was migraine-inducingly simple: Where is Dwight Jenner? The answer was migraine-inducingly simple, too: Somewhere in North America. In the twenty-first century, allegedly an age of public passivity in the face of ubiquitous national surveillance, surely it was only a matter of time before your culprit popped up on film? The U.S. had an estimated thirty million CCTV cameras in use, recording four *billion* hours of footage every week. How hard could it be to find someone?

*Quite hard,* Valerie imagined herself saying, through gritted teeth. *Especially if he knows you're looking for him.*

The traffic cam footage was a washout. Both blind. The entrance camera (as I said, she repeated, mentally, *quite hard*) simply wasn't working. It had been out for days. The camera covering the exit road *was* working—and had allowed the gods to cook up a subtler frustration. Highway maintenance crews were at work just beyond the slip road. Along with the cones and diggers and the high-vis jackets of the beavering crew were half a dozen mounted LED balloon lights, two of which bounced their illumination directly off the windshields of exiting vehicles, nicely obscuring their drivers. Ed was running the number plates through DMV (Valerie hadn't *entirely* ruled out the possibility that Kyle Cornell's Ford would show up) but so far nothing had flagged.

Her desk phone rang. It was coming up on 9:30 A.M.

"Hey," Nick said. "Want a straw to clutch at?"

"I'll take a blade of grass. I'll take a *hair*."

"Where'd you go to check out the bike cop's Jenner sighting?"

"Orland rest stop."

Nick paused. "Orland . . . Hold on a second . . ." She could hear him hitting keys. "Okay. That's maybe forty miles from what I'm looking at."

"Which is?"

"Scanned deeds to the Grants' country place. They've got a house just outside Campbellville. You put that with Jenner and Adam Grant's phone calls . . ."

"They met."

"Maybe. Unless you know some other reason Jenner would've been in the neighborhood."

"Christ, maybe it was a three-way with Sophia after all."

"What?"

"Nothing. I'm kidding—I think. Wait. You got Adam's work calendar? Check what he had for July thirty-first."

It took Nick a few moments, during which Valerie shuffled the facts. Met for what? To negotiate screwing rights? And if Jenner was going to kill him, why not do it there? Why the fuck would he—

"Oh," Nick said. "Not very cooperative. According to his calendar, Grant was in Los Angeles. Four-day law symposium at UCLA. Keynote speaker on the opening day, in fact."

"Fuck. Okay. I'll check."

Which she did, and got the obstructive confirmation that Adam Grant did in fact speak to at least two hundred people—a mix of professionals and final-year law students—on the afternoon of July 31, commencing at 2 P.M. He stuck around at the drinks reception, then according to his colleague from Willard & Gould (a fellow speaker, who had taken the early-morning flight down with him) retired to the hotel around 5 P.M. They got together for dinner at nine and went for drinks afterward. There was simply no way Adam Grant could have met with Dwight Jenner on the night of the 31st. Credit card transactions proved he stayed in L.A. for the symposium's duration. He didn't fly home to San Francisco until the night of August 3.

Two steps forward, three steps back.

Still, Jenner had been forty miles from the Grants' country house with no good reason for being there. Or no known reason, at least. Valerie called Kyle Cornell.

"Can't get me out of your mind," he said. "I know how it is. Don't feel bad about it."

Valerie pictured the smile with which this was being delivered.

"Dwight have any business up north?" she asked. "Any buddies? Job interviews? Additional lady friends? Think Orland, Hamilton City, Campbellville. Anything that would take him upstate on the 5."

"You've got a beautiful phone voice. You know that?"

"Please don't fuck around. Yes or no?"

In the pause that followed, she had a little pang of regret (and guilt) that she'd used the word "fuck."

"No," Kyle said. "Nothing I know of. Why?"

"Forget it," Valerie said, and hung up before she said anything else she'd regret.

She drove to Pacific Heights, mentally grinding the options. Maybe it *had* been Jenner's plan to kill Adam Grant at the Campbellville place, assuming he had somehow (via Sophia?) found out about it. Maybe he was casing it. Maybe he just got tired of waiting for Adam to show up there.

She had other, more elaborate theories. Suppose the intention *wasn't* murder? Adam Grant had money. By Dwight Jenner's standards, plenty of money. Put blackmail aside for a moment. How about kidnapping? Could Jenner (and Sophia) have planned to snatch Elspeth—or Rachel? Sophia starts fucking Adam as leverage against him going to the cops when the ransom demand comes in. Keep it out of the press, keep your career, keep your life—just pay up with no shenanigans. Maybe Adam wasn't supposed to be home that night? Maybe Elspeth wasn't supposed to be at a friend's for a sleepover? Jenner gets in, realizes Sophia's intel's for shit, panics, ends up with a homicide on his hands. Valerie pictured him going over the Grants' bedroom balcony in a flurry of adrenaline, thinking *fuck . . . fuck . . . fuck . . .* Dropping the knife. In the dark. Can't find it. More panic. Murder. Back to San Q—or the Chair. Get out. Get the fuck out of here *now*.

Maybe, maybe, maybe. They were all maybes. And none of them explained Jenner's not bothering with gloves. Kidnapping wasn't murder, but that was no reason to leave your prints all over the scene.

"You can't see her," Tala told Valerie, when Officer Riordan had let her into the Grants' front hall. "She's sleeping."

"I'm afraid I have to," Valerie said.

"As it is she's moving around too much. It's ridiculous."

"Is she under sedation?"

"No. She is *sleeping*."

Emphasized as if to get through to a moron. Valerie was mildly amused. The nurse was so small and neat and had such compressed annoyance. Presumably she wasn't happy. Presumably Rachel Grant was not proving to be a biddable patient.

"Well, as I said, I'm afraid I have to see her," she repeated. Then she smiled and bent a little closer toward the nurse's face. "If she is *sleeping* I will *wake her up*."

For a moment Tala simply stood there, hands in her uniform pockets, tiny nostrils flaring.

"Fine," she said, turning her back on Valerie and walking away. "Do what you want. It's on your conscience."

Rachel and Elspeth were asleep together on the couch, the girl with her head in her mother's lap. Valerie watched them. Even asleep, Rachel's face wore its recent trauma like a thin veil. Elspeth looked worse—and on closer inspection was, if REM was an indicator, dreaming. Her lips moved, though they didn't part, as if a nightmare had them sealed with duct tape.

*I was nothing before I had Elspeth.* At the time, Valerie hadn't paid much attention to that, but on reflection it seemed extreme. Rachel Grant didn't strike her as the type for metaphorical excesses. Still, the woman had been in shock. And in any case these were superfluous preoccupations, derived, Valerie admitted to herself, from the perpetual subsonic noise of her own potential motherhood. Nick hadn't asked her what time she was likely to be home (for which she would have read: Are we going to have biology?) but he knew her menstrual cycle. Right now she was in the golden zone. She didn't know which irritated her (irrationally) more, the fact that he was tracking her like the goddamned fertility police or that he was doing such a good job of not mentioning it. She was being, she knew, completely unreasonable. *That* was what irritated her (rationally) the most.

Elspeth screamed.

Two small whimpers—then a full, piercing, wide-eyed horror-movie scream.

She sat up, shaking, crying, hands over her face.

"Honey, it's okay, it's *okay*," Rachel said, having been wrenched awake herself. "Baby . . . ? Did you have a—" She saw Valerie in the doorway. Stopped. Frowned. Her face went tight with fury. Valerie held up her hands in silent apology. Backed out of the room. Elspeth hadn't seen her.

Serves me right for being such a bitch to the nurse, Valerie thought. Shit.

It was almost twenty minutes before Rachel came out of the living room, alone. The TV had been switched on. *Shrek*. Comfort. Elspeth was being allowed to be a little kid again, to return to a time before anything ugly had happened to her. Since the murder of her father, Valerie guessed, Elspeth was being allowed *anything*.

"What the hell?" Rachel Grant whispered.

"I'm so sorry, Mrs. Grant. I just arrived."

"What is it? You found him?"

"No. But we have something. Jenner was spotted not far from your place in Campbellville on the night of the thirty-first. It's possible he was watching the house. I'd like to go up there and take a look around."

Rachel Grant stared at her as if the information had frozen her into incomprehension. She opened her mouth to speak—then shook her head, and waved Valerie toward the kitchen.

"What do you mean?" she said, once they'd switched rooms. "How would he know about the house there?" She was standing against the island worktop, arms wrapped around her middle.

"Well, he knew about this place," Valerie said. "And as I said before, Adam's phone records show he spoke with Jenner several times. Obviously, we still don't know what they talked about."

"This woman," she said. "That's what you think they talked about."

Not a question.

"We really can't know," Valerie answered. The kitchen was benign with sunlight. As it had been (she imagined Rachel Grant thinking) when Adam had photographed Sophia. On the worktop barely ten feet away. Her ass had rested there. Maybe they'd fucked right here, where Rachel Grant was standing. Valerie wondered if Rachel was already thinking of selling the house, getting out, starting over. A forced rebirth. She saw it in survivors, the realization that the life they'd thought established was gone, the future of vague plans and approximate certainties reduced to a blank canvas.

"In any case," Valerie said, "I need to check it out. Do I have your permission?"

Rachel smiled. The same masochist's smile Valerie had seen before. "It goes on, doesn't it?" she said. "Even when there's nothing left, it goes on."

Valerie didn't want to answer, since she had nothing but the truth to offer. But there was a bitter strength to this woman that demanded your honesty.

"Yes," she said. "Unfortunately, it does."

Rachel stared at her. Then said: "I can't do this anymore."

For a moment Valerie thought this was just an admission of exhaustion. Rhetorical, if so, since she knew Rachel would find the strength to keep going—for her daughter's sake.

But she'd misread it.

"I knew about her," Rachel said. "I knew about Sophia."

And here we are, Valerie thought, in the short silence that followed, that point in an investigation when the camera angle shifts and you see a whole different side to the object you thought you knew.

She waited. Assimilated. Put the next question in its simplest form.

"Why didn't you tell me?"

Rachel shook her head. Mild self-disbelief. Then self-acceptance. "Because I'm pathetic," she said. "Because I don't want Elspeth to know. Because I thought it was dead and buried. Because it still matters to me that people don't think of him as worse than he was. Take your pick. The real reason is I'm such a fucking narcissistic egomaniac I'm still angry with myself that I forgave him and took him back. I doubt you'll believe that, though it's the truth. You can love someone so much it makes you ashamed of yourself. I didn't tell you because it was an indictment that I wasn't enough for him, and a double indictment that that wasn't enough for me to kick him out. Astonishing, isn't it?"

Again, Valerie assimilated. Astonishing? No, it wasn't. Nick had taken *her* back when she'd done exactly the same thing.

"I understand," she said.

"Sure you do."

No point pressing that. Just get the facts. Valerie took out her notebook and pen. Carefully. Anything *not* done carefully might pitch Rachel away from saying anything more. "Tell me," she said. "Let's start with her surname."

Rachel stared at the gleaming floor, arms still wrapped around herself. "I don't know it," she said. "I didn't ask." Pause. "She was a whore."

Not figuratively, Valerie decided, but best to make sure. "A prostitute?"

"A *dancer*. Some strip club in L.A. Where the girls weren't restricted to dancing, obviously."

"Do you know the name of the club?"

"No."

"When did it happen?"

"Two years ago. He was down there for a *funeral*. I'm sure you can imagine the narrative. Death. Sex. A heightened sense of mortality so you suddenly need to grab life. It would've been better for me if I didn't understand. But that's the curse of a generous imagination. I *did* understand."

"Whose funeral?"

"An old college friend. Massive aneurism, totally unpredicted." She glanced up and saw Valerie's pen poised, waiting for the name. "Noah . . ." She searched, mentally. "Levine. I think the surname's Levine."

"You don't recall the exact date, do you?"

"Summer. Early June."

"Well, we can get the exact date. Did he go to the club alone?"

"He said he did."

More CCTV joys. Some strip clubs had them, some didn't. And how many strip clubs were there in L.A.? "Sophia" most likely a working name. Finding the real one would require a tax-legit establishment. And that was assuming she'd given them her real name to start with. Another needle in another haystack.

"But it wasn't a one-off, clearly," Valerie said.

"No. It wasn't."

"How did it continue? I'm sorry, I know this is—"

"I only had his word for it, but he said another four or five times. According to him, she moved up here not long after they met."

"Still dancing?"

"Who knows? There was a limit to the details I wanted. I wasn't inter-ested in her biography. Just in what she did that I didn't."

*And what was that?* Valerie didn't ask, since she knew. The photograph of Sophia tied, gagged, blindfolded. The old dreary story: sexual territory a marriage left unmapped. There was a sadness emanating from Rachel now, beyond the grief. Releasing this information had lowered her, with a strange, inevitable gentleness, to a new level of ordinariness. The ordinariness of im-perfection. *Don't speak ill of the dead,* we were in the habit of saying. But the dead had always been real people, and real people's imperfections couldn't be erased, even by death. The world was everything the world contained. Reality had no patience with the need for delicacy.

"How did you find out?" Valerie asked.

"He told me. It's not as if I caught them in the act. Maybe if I had I wouldn't have forgiven him. He knew me well enough to know that."

"How long ago?"

Very wearying to Rachel, Valerie could see, to dredge through the facts, the dates, the logistics. There was a dull horror to it, that these seismic events in the heart were anchored to particular times, places, mundane de-tails. Her husband zipping up his fly, afterward. The dismal plainness of small atrocities.

"He told me in the fall. October, I guess." A pause. "I didn't know he ever brought her here. He swore he didn't."

So *that* part of the shock when she'd seen the pictures was real. She hadn't known the sacrilege had gone so far, into her home, into her bed.

"Maybe he lied," Rachel said. "Maybe he didn't end it when he said he did. Maybe I don't even get that consolation. Maybe I don't get anything."

Maybe you don't, Valerie thought.

"Did you ever see her? In person?"

Rachel paused. Nowhere to go now but back to the truth. "Yes," she said. "It was before he told me. A total coincidence, as it happens. I was pulling up outside his office and I saw him talking to someone in a car parked half a block down. A glimpse. Nothing, really. Just the blond hair and too much makeup. I suppose if I'd been blond he'd have gone after a redhead."

Or a brunette, Valerie thought. Like me. Maybe he sensed I didn't want to be tied up and blindfolded and gagged. Her own guilt bristled anew. How could it not? It could have been her. It *had* been her, up to a point. And here was the evidence of what that would have done to his wife. The questioning now felt bankrupt. The words were unclean in her mouth.

"By the time I parked she'd gone and he was back in the building," Rachel continued. "I asked him about her, of course, teased him in that idiotic way, when you make light of something because you can't let it be anything. He said it was a client. That was all."

"You weren't suspicious?"

"Not really. Things were good between us. I had the great reservoir of false confidence." She smiled again. "And then later you find out, see the dots join with comical obviousness. It's like your own stupidity's been with you the whole time, walking right next to you, but you've only just turned and noticed it. You think your life's immune to cliché. Turns out it isn't."

"You don't happen to recall the car she was in, do you?"

"No. Black, I think."

"Sedan? RV? Compact?"

Rachel fought through tiredness for the memory. "Sedan, I guess. I don't know."

Valerie was on the verge of asking if Adam had taken his mistress to the Campbellville house—but she abandoned it. It wouldn't make any difference. And in any case Adam might have lied.

"Is there anyone else who might have known about the affair? A close friend of Adam's? A work colleague?"

Rachel shrugged. "He told me no one knew about it," she said. "But then he told me he never brought her here and that was a lie. His friends *were* his work colleagues. Maybe he told Dan."

"Dan Kruger?"

Rachel nodded.

"Is there anything else you can tell me about this woman that might help us find her?"

"Not that I can think of."

Valerie closed the notebook and put it away.

"I suppose this is all going to come out in court," Rachel said. "If there's ever a trial. If you ever get Jenner and . . ." She left it unfinished, defeated, Valerie thought, by the sheer sordidness: If you ever get Jenner and it turns out he and my husband were fucking the same woman.

"It might not be necessary," Valerie said, desperate to give her something. "As I said before, the physical evidence is overwhelming. We just have to find him. That's the only reason Sophia's material. It's possible she knows where he is. There's no reason to think beyond that."

Bullshit, of course, and Rachel's face said she knew it.

"It's for Elspeth's sake. For myself I'm past caring. As you can probably tell."

Quite, Valerie thought. Rachel looked as if, for herself, she didn't care if she lived or died.

"I'll do everything I can," Valerie said. "I promise you it'll be kept out unless it's crucial to securing a conviction, which at this stage I don't think it will be. In the meantime, I still need to take a look at the Campbellville house."

Rachel eased herself away from the island with a wince. "Come with me," she said. "I'll give you the keys."

# 23

The Grants' country house was a couple of miles east of the small town of Campbellville, a roomy, two-story place set in an acre of evergreen woodland. White-graveled driveway at the front, a wildflower garden with a few dwarf apple trees at the back. At the rear of the garden a grand sycamore with a rope swing, the pleasures of which Elspeth had probably long since traded for inane hours on her cell phone or iPad.

Inside, the house was a smaller and more homely cousin to the one in the city. Appliances and furnishings still displayed West Coast professional wealth (as did the mere ownership of a second home, obviously), but without the urban residence's visible straining for minimalist chic. It looked, in other words, comfortable. Original stripped-oak floors and a kitchen in which you could actually imagine someone cooking. The common denominator was *books*. The smallest of the downstairs rooms (with a view into the backyard) was walled in them, an eclectic selection ranging from classics to popular science, with a lot of what Valerie assumed (she had to assume, since she didn't read anything these days) was serious or "literary" fiction in between. Rachel's domain, she figured, recalling Vincent Lyle and the insomniacs' reading club he and Rachel shared, waving to each other in the small hours.

In gloves and shoe guards Valerie spent three hours going through the place, top to bottom. It satisfied her insatiable snooper's appetite—but she found nothing. No locked drawers, no hidden photographs, no diaries (although there was a desktop computer that would have to be trawled), no evidence that Dwight Jenner, or Sophia, for that matter, had ever been in the place. She hadn't expected any other result. There was, naturally, an alarm system (Rachel had given her the entry code) linked to the security company, but it was unsupported by CCTV. If Jenner had been inside he'd either had the code or been let in. The only way to know for sure would be to get a team up here and dust for prints. Should have done that in the first place. But there would have been a wait, and she was impatient. Impatient and (let's be honest, Valerie) overinvested in her own occult intuitions, her ability to pick up what patrol officer Niall Fox would have called the Vibe.

Well, she thought, closing the front door behind her, so much for that.

She checked the time. 6:18 P.M. Traffic on I-5 would be moving like molasses. Fuck it. There was an acre around the place and more than an hour of daylight. Might as well take a stroll.

In the rest stop footage, Jenner had bought a pack of Marlboros, so Valerie kept her eyes trained on the ground for a telltale butt. Movie-inherited optimism. She found none. Tire tracks in the drive she told herself would only turn out to belong to the Grants' vehicles. Away to the right a rough, narrow trail led into the trees. She followed it.

Daylight didn't count for much in here. The dry smell of the evergreens was pleasant, like an old wardrobe. Again she thought of Elspeth. This place would've been an enchantment to her a few years back, bottle-green light, fairies in the ferns, adventures beckoning. Valerie's own childhood had been imaginatively rich, courtesy of mild Catholicism and her grandfather's penchant for cooking up outlandish and religiously incorrect mythologies. The Pope, he'd told her, was visited by the Holy Spirit, who told him what rules to make for the Church. To Valerie the Holy Spirit was the white dove of traditional iconography. According to her grandfather there was a secret dumbwaiter in the Pope's bedroom in the Vatican, a narrow shaft that reached all the way up to heaven. Sometimes His Holiness woke to the sound of beating wings. A message from the Dove! It had all made perfect sense to her. Unfortunately it had also made perfect sense to her that, as further according to her grandfather, a deformed goblin lived in their hot water tank, and that the occasional noises emanating from there were sounds of him *trying desperately to get out and come for her.* She had no clue what this creature could have against her, but it didn't stop her living in fear of its eventual escape and her own mysteriously deserved destruction.

She smiled, remembering. She'd been awed and terrified by her grandfather's revelations, but always went back for more. Grown-ups were compelled to frighten children, she theorized now (as the trees thinned ahead of her), a narrative inoculation to lay the psychological groundwork for the realities of adulthood, in which the world would sooner or later turn out to be a frightening place. Get used to fear now, kiddo, because there's plenty to be afraid of coming your way.

Would she do that if she had a child of her own?

She stepped out of the undergrowth into fresher air—and found herself on the shore of a small lake. The path, apparently, circled it. Maybe fifteen minutes to walk around. Annoyed that her mind had wandered (back to children again, parenthood, for Christ's sake give me a break), she set off with renewed dedication to scouring the ground, a rationalization she was well aware was growing more risible by the second.

More than fifteen minutes, it turned out. The lake's circumference was deceptive. Nonetheless she found herself back where she'd started with nothing to show for her walk.

The sun was lowering toward the tree line on the opposite bank, but a shaft of late light fell on the turf and shingle around her. She lifted her chin and closed her eyes, enjoying the warmth. Then she turned to head back to the house.

Something glinting in the short grass caught her eye.

Without any expectation (she'd resigned herself to the fruitlessness of this sojourn) she stepped over to see what it was.

At the last instant, excitement having *almost* eclipsed the protocols, she remembered to pull on fresh gloves.

Then she bent and picked it up, carefully.

It was a man's wristwatch.

# 24

Skeleton crew at the station by the time she got back, around 10:30 P.M. Laura Flynn and Rayner Mendelsund were at their desks, both with a look of resigned night-shift misery. Everyone hated it, the quiet, the coffee, the fluorescents' reflection in the black windows, the thought of all the other San Franciscans out there, drinking, watching TV, *relaxing.* Or worse, committing some crime that would, with the ring of a phone, come their sleep-deprived way.

"If you're going to keep these hours," Laura said quietly, "what's the point of me being here?" She was eating McDonald's fries and chicken nuggets.

"I have dedication," Valerie said.

"You have a sadistic desire to make the rest of us look bad."

"Someone has to."

"What've you got?"

"The rewards of detection. You should try it sometime. Now shut up and get on with your nuggets. I'm in the zone."

It had been too much to hope. The rest stop footage of Dwight Jenner buying his Marlboros showed his right hand only. If he was wearing a wristwatch it was on the left, unseen. She looked again at the actual watch in its sealed bag. A distinctive design. The face was composed of two concentric circles, an outer white one containing the numerals and a pale coppery one inside it. Hour, minute, and second hands were metallic red. It looked, in fact, like something from the fifties. The strap was pale tan leather and appeared new. It had barely been marked by its time on the ground—with the exception of one small, faded brown droplet splash. *Blood* was where her mind had gone, immediately, though unless they were extremely lucky that wouldn't be DNA-friendly. Practically the first forensic fact you learned was that DNA identification relied on nucleic cells, which ruled out three of blood's four major components: red blood cells, platelets, and plasma. The fourth component, *white* blood cells, did contain nuclei, but since there was only one white to every six hundred red, you needed a lot more than a drop to score.

There was, however, a legitimate alternative.

She took a photo of the watch with her phone camera, dropped the watch itself at Forensics, then drove out to see Kyle Cornell.

Well, yes, a legitimate alternative.

*He* wasn't going to see it that way.

Did *she*?

No. It was the work. The necessary work. And afterward she'd go straight home and make biology with the man she loved. Thinking only about the man she loved while she was doing it.

*The lady doth protest too much, methinks.* Her high school Shakespeare was for shit—except for those quotes that reflected badly on her ability to remember them.

The great thing about cigarettes, she thought, as the city's storefronts and digital hoardings went by, was that when you reached a tricky mental juncture you could distract yourself by lighting one. Small wonder she'd been on two packs a day.

Flamingo was an aggressively hip cocktail bar on the corner of Haight and Belvedere, and either coincidentally or via sexual radar Kyle looked up and saw her as she walked in. His face said annoyance and excitement. It also said he wouldn't appreciate her flashing her badge under his manager's eye. So she took a vacant seat at the bar and waited. She'd give him, she decided, five minutes. Meantime his shift-mate, a beautiful young Japanese girl with a bleached-blond skinhead, tattooed forearms, and eyes the color of espresso, came over to take her order. Fuck the white wine allowance, Valerie thought. She ordered a Moscow mule.

Halfway through it (oops, *slower,* Valerie) Kyle got a gap between customers and approached her.

"Seriously?" he said.

"Don't get excited. Something I want you to take a look at."

"That's how it starts."

She took out her phone and selected the picture of the watch. Enlarged it so the face was clear.

"This Dwight's?"

Kyle leaned closer. He was wearing a plain white T-shirt and faded Levi's. No jewelry. Good call, Valerie thought. Jewelry—even a ring—on a guy this good-looking would be overkill. Forget the accoutrements. Just give the eyelashes and the smile and the easy muscles room to do their thing.

"Looks like it," he said. "Where'd you get it?"

"Doesn't matter. You're certain it's his?"

Kyle straightened. He hadn't had to do more than glance at the image. "No," he said. "I'm not certain. I'm sure he's not the only person in the world with this particular make of watch. But if it's not his, he's got one exactly like it. Used to be his dad's, or so he told me. And his *grand*father's before that. Lund and Blockley."

"Sorry?"

"The make. Lund and Blockley. It's written right there in the middle. Don't you have a magnifying glass? I thought all detectives had those."

Valerie drag-enlarged and scrutinized the image, embarrassed that she hadn't noted the make. But there it was, in microfine italics just below the hands' axis. *Lund & Blockley.*

"Dwight got it valued," Kyle said. "Eight hundred bucks, guy said. Always amazed me he never sold it. Again: Where'd you find it?"

"Again: Doesn't matter. But I can tell you it wasn't on Dwight's wrist."

Valerie looked at him: Let's be honest with each other. Can we?

"What is it?" Kyle said. (Okay. Honesty.)

"I think something might have happened to Dwight."

"Something like what?"

"Something like nothing good. There's a stain on the watch strap might be blood."

"His."

"Kyle!" the Japanese girl called. "Two mojitos and an old-fashioned. You can flirt later."

Kyle's response was to close his eyes for a moment, then open them. He'd had a lot of practice, Valerie thought, in not losing his temper.

"Give me a minute," he said. "Would you?"

And here was the mutual ease again. The vodka had gone straight to her thighs. She'd drunk the rest of it while they were talking. Fuck. Don't order another one.

"Sure," she said.

It was ten minutes. She spent them (a) not ordering another drink and (b) calculating exactly how much to tell Kyle Cornell.

"Look," he said, when he'd squared a break and they'd moved to a vacant table, "are you going to be straight with me?"

"I'll give you everything I can."

"So, no, then."

She leaned forward in her seat toward him. Their hands were only inches apart on the table. A blue floor lamp's light shone on his left side.

"The guy who put Dwight away was murdered eight days ago," she said. "Dwight, I'm sorry to tell you, is the prime suspect." *I'll give you everything I can.* Which didn't—yet—include the fact that Dwight wasn't a prime suspect but a known perpetrator.

"He wouldn't kill anyone," Kyle said. "It's not in him. Obviously you'll say what do I know. Fine. Just remember I said it."

"I'll remember," Valerie said. "Meantime we know that the victim and Dwight had a woman in common."

"Sophia."

"Sophia. Dwight's been AWOL since August first. Now his watch turns up at the victim's country house with blood on it that may or may not be his. Whoever this woman is, it doesn't look to me like she's doing your brother any favors."

"Apart from the obvious ones."

"And maybe those aren't favors."

"You think she's a hooker?"

Valerie pulled up the picture of Sophia in black lingerie, bent over Adam Grant's desk. "This look like Dwight's regular speed?"

Kyle looked. Raised his eyebrows. Gave a nod of no-brainer male approval. Then looked back at Valerie. "I guess not," he said. "But like I said, he told me she was a pole dancer. Those girls aren't known for being plain and fat."

Valerie returned her phone to her pocket. She could have chosen one of the CCTV stills, where Sophia wasn't half-naked and sticking her ass out. But of course that wouldn't have kept *sex* humming quietly between them. Really drank that mule too fast.

"I take it you don't recognize her?" she said.

"Unfortunately, no, I don't."

"And that's really all you've got for me? She's a dancer?"

Kyle leaned back in his chair. Appraised Valerie. The look now said: I'd still rather have you. Followed by one of resigned capitulation.

"A *former* dancer," he said. "Way Dwight told it, she looked like she had money, or had got money from somewhere. The clothes, the way she carried herself. Smart, too, according to him, but then relative to Dwight most people were. He thought *I* was a genius." A smile.

"Stop fishing," she said. "We both know you're in no doubt of your abilities."

"Yeah, but what kind of half-black guy would I be without a chip on my shoulder?"

Please, Valerie thought, can we stop *getting along*? She looked down at the tabletop to conceal her own smile. When she looked back up at him his face said he knew it was working. The charm.

"How did Dwight meet her? He must have told you that."

"In a bar. I don't know which one. Genuinely. Not this one, at any rate."

"She picked him up?"

"And gave him the night of his life."

"That doesn't seem odd to you?"

A broader smile this time. "You mean what's a woman like that want with a lowlife like my brother?"

Valerie opened her hands. Saw Kyle note the wedding ring. Yes, let's not forget that.

"There's no accounting for taste," Kyle said. "Sure, it's hard to picture her and Dwight shopping for curtains together, but clearly that wasn't what she had in mind. You're a cop. You know this city's full of crazy people. Some of those crazy people are women. I doubt Dwight was worried what the agenda might have been. I doubt he was concerned with the psychology."

"Let's note that you didn't tell me any of this before," she said.

"Hey, I was still getting to know you. Intimacy breeds honesty."

"So there's more to tell?"

"Unfortunately for me, no. That really is everything I know. Now you've got no incentive to come see me." Pause. Smile. "No police incentive, I mean."

Okay, she thought, time to go. Before I discover I am, in fact, completely fucking insane. She got to her feet.

"You really think something's happened to him?" Kyle asked.

Valerie shrugged. "He's not in any of the Bay Area hospitals, I can tell you that."

She turned to go.

"Hey," Kyle said.

She looked back.

"I get off in two hours."

Well, I asked for that.

"I don't," she said. "But thanks for your help."

# 25

## *August 13, 2017*

Dan Kruger's office was no smaller than Adam Grant's but testified to an even greater commitment to minimalism. The wall of books was screened by opaque glass, matched by the glass of the big desk. Bare cherry parquet with a demonic sheen. The two large canvases appeared, at first glance, blank—until you shifted your angle and saw that they were in fact shades of the very palest creams and grays. No family photographs. The room's only concession to color was the client seating, three chairs of tubular steel and dark green leather. Kruger's chair was *white* leather, so clean it made Valerie wonder if he ever actually sat in it.

He wasn't sitting in it now. He was leaning against the edge of the desk with his hands in his pockets. A dark blue suit, white shirt, green tie exactly the shade (by design?) of the client chairs. Either way his wardrobe somehow set off the whiteness of his close-cropped hair. Valerie couldn't tell if it was premature gray or a self-inflicted bleach job. He was altogether a striking physical specimen, tall, muscular, with light blue eyes that managed, weirdly, to be both calm and fierce. The big windows behind him showed San Francisco sunlit, occasional details—cornices, skylights—picked out as if with tenderness.

"I'd hate to think you were wasting my time almost as much as I'd hate to think I was wasting yours," he said. "You already showed me the photographs. I don't know the woman."

"Yes," Valerie said. "But that's not what I asked you. I asked you if Adam told you he was seeing her. Seeing anyone other than his wife, in fact."

Kruger took his hands out of his pockets and rested the heels of them on the edge of the desk. He'd come straight from the gym. Smelled freshly showered and cologned. A little aura of wholesomely spent male energy. "Nope," he said.

Valerie looked at him. Really?

"Scout's honor," he said. Then smiled. "You sure this is a smart line of inquiry?"

"What?"

"Adam's alleged infidelity?"

Her body heat went up—but she did her best to look puzzled. "I don't follow you," she said.

Kruger held the smile, then eased himself away from the desk and walked around it, lowered himself into his chair. Valerie was thinking that for the right kind of guilty client this was exactly the sort of guy they'd find reassuring: strong, merciless, in it purely, *purely* for the money. He gave the impression of mild amusement at his own professional acumen, as if he knew he could win your case with less than half the weapons in his arsenal.

"Adam wasn't the only lawyer in Carlton's that night," he said.

Shit.

Her stupidity hit her. The slap she knew she deserved. *Serves you right.* How many times hadn't she said that to herself? Put it on her headstone. The perfect epitaph.

Still, she said nothing. Just continued with what she hoped was a look of bafflement.

Dan Kruger laughed, gently, dismissively, a laugh that said he had bigger fish to fry—unless he discovered frying this *little* fish might come in particularly handy. "It's a funny thing," he said. "As these things always are, if you've got the right sense of humor. I saw you and Adam tête-à-tête at the bar. I was going to come over and ask him if he knew he was fraternizing with the SFPD, but I got a call, and when I looked again you guys had gone."

There was more to it, his complacency said. Valerie kept her mouth shut, but in spite of her efforts it was clear he could see her discomfort.

"Of course that would have been the end of it," Kruger said. "Except I had an early flight the following morning. Cab took me right past your building. Guess who I saw staggering out just after five A.M.?"

Four years ago. Lawyers, like cops, required a perversely talented memory. Kruger was a man who never mislaid his wallet, never forgot an appointment, never missed an opportunity to file away a snapshot detail that might, one distant day, be put to his service. Valerie found herself at a perfect impasse. Saying nothing was as incriminating as saying something, saying anything. The simultaneous need for and absence of a response filled her, stalled her, mapped her body at what felt like the cellular level. A detached part of her marveled at how rarely this happened: *speechlessness*.

Kruger let the moment stretch, relaxed into it, savored it. Then made a slight movement with his hand, a bored colossus shooing away a fly. "Don't sweat, Detective," he said. "I outgrew sadism years ago. For the record—for your peace of mind—Adam's story when I quizzed him about it was that nothing happened. You went to dinner, drank late, shared a cab, he walked you up to your apartment, he left."

And *still* Valerie found herself without words. What she wanted now was to turn and walk out of the room. That would be an admission of something. But so was standing here like a moronic mute.

"Anything you want to add?" Kruger asked.

Suddenly, boredom released her. Mental math had, in fact, been going on. There was no way of knowing whether that *had* been Adam Grant's story. And if it hadn't been, there was no way of knowing what Dan Kruger planned to do with whatever story he'd really been told. She shrugged, gave him a little indifference of her own, and quite deliberately used his own version of the earlier negative: "Nope," she said.

"Good. Glad to hear it."

She turned to go, but he got to his feet and came toward her, hand out-stretched. They hadn't shaken hands when she'd arrived. She took it—back on guard. His grip was stronger than she liked. The moment when he should have let go came and went.

"Let's be clear about this," he said. "I know you've got a job to do. I also know you're one of the good ones, one of the best. Your record speaks for itself. But Adam was a good friend and a good man."

Pause. He still had her hand in his.

"I want you to get Jenner. But I don't want Adam's memory dragged through the shit. You're a smart enough professional to avoid that. Rachel and Elspeth have suffered enough. Do we understand each other?"

Valerie tightened her own grip. Now that the words were available it felt good to say them. "*Let's* be clear," she said, with a smile. "I'm going to pursue any line of investigation I believe will lead to the resolution of this case and the conviction of Adam Grant's murderer. Whatever the consequences. To anyone. That's my job, and that's what I'm going to do. So, yes, I have a strong feeling that we understand each other."

For a moment they stood in silence, eyes locked. Then Kruger released her hand. She turned, walked to the door, exited without a backward glance.

# 26

## *August 2, 2017*

Fuck. *Fuck.*

This is what it's going to be like, she thought, interrupted halfway through applying the day's lipstick by the realization that she'd forgotten the sigil. This is what it's going to be like: hours of blithe complacency—then the drenching shock of your own incompetence. She was an idiot. She deserved everything that was coming to her.

She wanted to take the makeup *off*, now, since putting it on had been so wildly precipitate. Instead she completed her bottom lip, tore out of the bathroom, and raced downstairs.

Her purse was still on the Volvo's backseat. Of course it was. It had been sitting there, innocently guilty, all night and half the day. She opened it, scrabbled through the contents, found the folded piece of paper with the hand-drawn copy of the symbol she'd made. No time for fun and games with the chiminea now—but setting light to it indoors was out of the question. The odor of burning would linger, especially in a house like this, where mere empty space smelled as if it had been piped in from some dimension utterly unsullied by life.

She hurried back to the shed, found the matches, then went over to the storm drain. Matches. Sulfur. There'd once been a brand called "Lucifer," she thought.

She'd read it somewhere, or seen it in an old movie. Murder threw up these charming synchronicities. With the whimsy of the real Lucifer, in fact.

The single sheet of paper burned quickly, though she had to keep shifting her fingers to avoid the flame. When all but a few blank scraps remained, she fed them into the storm drain's grid and stood for a few moments in the warm afternoon air, forcing herself to go over her actions again. What other oversights or fuckups littered her criminal wake? Maybe she'd left the gun in a ladies' room? Maybe she'd neglected to flush the bleach or dump the tools in the lake? Maybe she'd neglected to *bury* him? If you were an idiot—as, manifestly, she was—anything was possible.

Eventually, after perhaps five minutes of wild speculation, she gave up and went back to the house. Either she'd made no other mistakes or she'd lost the ability to identify them. Regardless, the philosophical calm had returned. *Quod scripsi, scripsi*, as Pontius Pilate had said. There was no undoing it now.

She went to the kitchen freezer and took out a steak for tomorrow night's dinner.

The right freezer, she told herself, with a mad Shakespearean image of what going to the wrong one would cost her. The right freezer, the right kind of meat.

# 27

## *August 30, 2017*

It can't be postponed any longer, Valerie thought. Just get on with it.

Nonetheless, she didn't move. It was morning on her day off and she was still in bed. Nick had left for a racquetball game with Will, and for the time being it was simply too good to have the bed—the whole apartment—to herself. Not enough time alone these days.

Really? She imagined not living with Nick. She remembered what not living with Nick had been like. What *she* had been like. The word "feral" offered itself. Not just the booze and wretched one-night stands, the chain-smoking, the more or less perpetual exhaustion and compulsive self-distraction, but the domestic reality of living in a pigsty. When Nick moved in, things came with him: calm, order, pleasure, civilization. Someone coming over for dinner no longer required forty-eight hours' labor to make the place fit for human occupancy. It was as if after years of flailing in a dark ocean she'd washed up on a sunlit beach. On the island of Happily Married.

And? *And?*

She got out of bed and stood naked in front of the mirror. A lull in the traffic had brought an unnatural urban silence. The curtains were open a few inches and through the gap a single shaft of sun lit a swirl of motes her movements had disturbed. The quiet and warmth and stillness combined to form a subtle intelligence, an invitation to the truth of herself. She looked at her reflection in the mirror. Conceded with manageable vanity that the new trim suppleness was a gift that refused to stop giving. Imagined Kyle Cornell describing her. Brunette, five eight, nice tits, all the requisite knowledge . . .

She moved closer to the mirror, examined her face. Her dark eyes were honest. Childhood innocence overwritten by the world's reliable violence. The childhood was still there, its astonishment a stubborn irrelevance. All her earlier selves were still there, in fact—the curious girl, the stealthy teenager, the burgeoning woman—and the moment her wild energies found their focus and she knew she was Police. Look hard enough, she thought, and you could see a person's whole life in the eyes. Windows to the soul, obviously. Her own said she'd had love, urgency, horror, self-loathing, and the humor or luck to outgrow it. They said she wanted the real world, no matter how ugly. They said she trusted her judgment. Just.

Further postponement beckoned. She could make breakfast. She could go *out* for breakfast. She could drive to the mall and buy something indulgent. She could—oh, the crazy, beautiful freedom!—go see a movie.

But the subtle intelligence was shifting its weight. Not an invitation, now: an insistence.

As if to emphasize the point, a truck broke the silence, roared, rattled, and downshifted with a gasp of hydraulics at the junction.

Okay, okay. *Fine.*

She went to the living room and took the Rite Aid packet from her purse. She'd fudged the dates with Nick. Partly because after years on the pill her period wasn't a stickler for punctuality, but mainly because she wanted to give herself as much time to think about it by herself before it became something they'd have to think about together.

All well and good, but biology was running this particular show. Even by her own elastic standards she was minimum three days late.

In the bathroom she speed-read the instructions. Redundantly, since she knew exactly what they involved.

*One-Step hCG Urine Pregnancy Tests are used for qualitative (visual) determination of hCG (human chorionic gonadotropin) in urine specimens for early detection of pregnancy.*

*Immerse the strip into the urine with the arrow end pointing toward the urine. Do not immerse past the "max" line. Take the strip out after 3 seconds and lay the strip flat on a clean, dry, non-absorbent surface (e.g., mouth of the urine container).*

*Wait for colored bands to appear. Depending on the concentration of hCG in the test specimen, positive results may be observed in as short as 40 seconds. However, to confirm negative results, the complete reaction time (5 minutes) is required. Do not read results after 10 minutes.*

She sat on the floor with her back against the side of the bathtub and set the stopwatch on her phone. Decided not to actually stare at either the phone or the test strip. Instead she looked out the open bathroom door, through the living room, and out the window. On a balcony of the building opposite, a guy with a short gray beard and no shirt was reading something on a sheet of paper and scratching his belly. On the next balcony someone had tied helium party balloons to the rail: red, pink, white. The day was so still they barely moved. Above the building the sky was deep blue. Two jet contrails crossed each other, miles apart, one curved, the other straight, the leftovers of vague, giant geometry. Her eyes came back to her own apartment. Her leather jacket on the back of a chair. A white bowl of clementines. Last night's empty green bottle. Her shoes still where she'd kicked them off next to the couch. All the details were suddenly vivid. The way they must be, she thought, in your last moments just before a firing squad.

The problem was she'd outgrown the cop clichés. She'd had the cases that had damaged her. She'd done the monstrosity. She'd done the booze. She'd done the sex addiction. She'd done the rejection of love. She'd done the obsession, the monomania, the *Work*. Time had passed and she'd found herself awkwardly larger than all of it. Merely not killing herself had allowed her to forgive herself her trespasses. Astonishingly, even to forgive some of the trespasses against her. Love had come back, with a calm admission of its finiteness, its wonderful inadequacy. Now she was a creature of durable approximations. It had left her wondering what else she might become. It had left her a curious, large, quiet space, into which, with a sort of thrilling lunatic sacrilege, the word "motherhood" had insinuated itself.

When her phone *rang* it startled her so badly that she dropped it. And the test strip.

Carrie Wheeler Calling, the screen said. For a moment she had no idea who Carrie Wheeler was. Then remembered: Victim Support. The woman who had brought Elspeth to the hospital.

She let the call go to voice mail. The screen reverted to the stopwatch. One minute thirty-eight seconds.

She turned the strip over.

Then stayed where she was, naked on the floor, with her eyes closed.

She didn't pick up the voice mail until after she'd showered and dressed, as if for work, despite the official day off. The Adam Grant file she'd been looking at last night was still open on the desk. Among other things it contained a results sheet from Forensics based on analysis of the wristwatch. Obviously, Kyle's recognizing it as his half brother's heirloom was enough for her, but for the record, prints and skin cell touch DNA had confirmed it. Also for the record, the droplet stain was blood, though *whose* blood was still unknown. Aside from that, they'd had zero movement on the case for going on two weeks. Still no sign of either Jenner or Sophia.

Carrie Wheeler's message was a request to call her ASAP.

"What's up?" Valerie asked her.

"Hi," Carrie said. "I'm sorry, they told me you're off today, but I thought you'd want to know right away."

"Yes?" No matter the circumstances, Valerie thought, important news inflated the bearer. The short pause was the counselor's reflex concession to dramatic effect.

"I'm back at California Pacific," Carrie Wheeler said. "Elspeth Grant tried to kill herself last night."

# 28

"Class two hemorrhage," Dr. Jacob Loomis told Valerie. "Maybe twenty percent blood loss. No biggie. She's young and healthy. She'll be fine." He was a tall guy with designer glasses and a haircut intended to look as if he'd just tumbled out of a hot girl's bed. Carried himself very much in the manner of a man who had his mind brightly elsewhere. On the lifestyle his profession afforded him rather than on the profession itself, Valerie decided. She didn't like him.

"Fine?" she said, not quite without judgment.

Loomis smiled. "Physically, yes," he said. "You'll have to talk to the shrink as far as the rest of her well-being goes. She a smart kid?"

"As far as I know, yes. Why?"

Loomis shrugged. He was about to toss out a tidbit from his casually acquired omniscience. "Probably not a serious attempt," he said—then left it at that.

Valerie counted to five, mentally. "Because?"

Loomis smiled again, delighted to have the door to his condescension opened. "Smart suicides don't cut their wrists," he said. "Two minutes on the internet will tell you it's a lousy method. Slow and painful. Serious contenders go femoral or carotid."

Valerie had seen this sort of chipper arrogance in surgeons before. To the right kind of assholes, saving lives on a daily basis simply made them bigger, happier assholes.

"Good to know," she said, turning away. "I'll bear it in mind when someone's smugness finally pushes me over the edge."

There was no answer to her knock, so she opened the door, gently. Elspeth was in bed in a hospital gown, sleeping, hooked up to an IV. Both arms outside the covers, wrists bandaged. Rachel Grant was in the chair next to her, also apparently asleep. She stirred, opened her eyes, saw Valerie.

"Hey," Valerie whispered. "How's she doing?"

Rachel Grant just stared at her. Then put her head in her hands. When she raised it again she drew her palms down her face, as if to wipe away something clinging there.

"What happened?" Valerie said.

It took Rachel a moment. Her voice, when it came, sounded as if it hadn't been used in years.

"I found her," she said. "Why would she do this? Why would she . . ." Rachel shook her head. Struggled. Recovered. "She's been sleeping downstairs with me," she said. "We've been watching movies. It's all she wants to do. There's all this time . . . She can't stand it."

To Valerie neither mother nor daughter looked like they'd slept much. Their new shared exhaustion had stripped their features, returned them to the essential animality formerly soft-lensed by an untroubled middle-class life.

"Last night I did sleep," Rachel said. "But I woke up and she wasn't there. She . . . I found her in her room."

She paused and looked down. Swallowed. "When I think of her, when I think of her lying there, *bleeding* . . . All that time. If I hadn't got up, if I hadn't woken up and gone upstairs . . ."

"But you did," Valerie said. "And the doctor says she's going to be—"

"That's all it is," Rachel interrupted. "It's just whether you happen to do something. If I hadn't . . . She's just a *child*. Is that all it is? Whether you happen to wake up?"

"I know," Valerie said. "But you *did* wake up. She's okay. And she's going to get whatever help she needs. Both of you."

"It's my fault. I've been useless. If I didn't have her . . . If I didn't have her there'd be nothing. Just . . . There would be absolutely *nothing.*"

Valerie tried to imagine Rachel Grant recovering from a second loss, this loss. She couldn't. There *would* be absolutely nothing.

"She never . . ." Valerie hesitated. "She never did anything like this before?"

"Of course not. Why in God's name would she?"

"No, of course. I understand."

"I keep seeing her . . ." Rachel locked her jaws for a moment. Rode out the horror. "It was a box cutter. She went to the utility room. I keep seeing her, going there by herself . . . How could she do that? How could I not know?"

Valerie kept silent.

"It's my fault," Rachel repeated. "I sat there and told you how strong she was. I'm a fucking monster."

"Don't blame your—"

"She was strong because she could see how weak *I* was. God, I'm disgusting. It should be me lying in that bed, not her."

"Mrs. Grant, I'm not a shrink, but I've seen enough to know that a lot of survivors end up feeling guilty about the simple fact that they have survived."

"She's not going to go that way. I'm not going to let her go that way."

Rachel's voice had risen. Elspeth stirred. Opened her eyes.

"Mom?"

"I'm here, honey." Rachel took Elspeth's hand, carefully. The girl focused. Saw Valerie. Looked sick at the sight.

"I'll leave you two in peace," Valerie said.

She glanced back from the open doorway. Rachel had moved to the edge of the bed and was embracing her daughter. Elspeth looked at Valerie over her mother's shoulder. The big puppet eyes were unblinking—but there was plenty going on behind them. A pitch of tension so extreme it manifested itself as perfect calm. For the first time it occurred to Valerie that maybe Elspeth knew about her father's affair.

*Leave my daughter out of it,* Rachel Grant had said.

So far that hadn't been a problem.

Maybe it was time for it to become one.

# 29

## *September 5, 2017*

Be careful what you wish for, Valerie thought. Or half wish for. Or dread. *I was nothing before I had Elspeth*. Perhaps hers was the opposite condition: *I'm too much already. There's no room for anyone else*. Except now there was someone else. Literal room for someone else had already been found. Inside her.

She'd done two things. The first was to check the time limits on legal abortion in California. Eight weeks for medicated, twelve weeks for a D&C, and twenty-two weeks in Los Angeles County for an E&C, should she be dumb enough to leave it that long. She'd done this in a state of dreamlike cognitive dissonance. She'd told herself such information was irrelevant, since she wasn't going to get an abortion. She'd told herself that even to check was a betrayal of Nick. She'd told herself she wasn't going to check. And here *I am, not checking*, she'd thought, as she looked up the information.

The second thing she'd done was a deed by omission: She hadn't told Nick she was pregnant. He was well aware of the calendar, but he hadn't asked. He'd read her silence at her period due date as negative, and read the particular *brand* of silence, accompanied by what Valerie thought must surely be a perceptible shift in her aura, as her desire not to *be* asked. She knew what he was thinking: Ease back. Don't make it a big deal. Take the pressure off her. Hell, take the pressure off *both* of you. Perhaps another couple of months would go by before he might quite reasonably float the idea that they should get themselves checked out, to see if they were, well, you know, capable of conceiving.

Every day since the positive test result she'd woken up certain that would be the day she broke the news. She went over the imagined exchange endlessly.

*Guess what?*

*What?*

*I'm pregnant.*

Pause. A moment for the glitter from the quiet explosion to burst, flicker, fall around them, settle.

Then Nick's face, smiling. Warmth. Happiness. Relief. Love.

And no fear.

Which was, of course, why she hadn't told him. It wasn't just that the thought of herself as a mother—the new vast arena in which she could fuck things up—terrified her. It was that her miscarriage of five years ago had re-attached itself to her like a sad and silent ghost. It was with her in the morning and with her during the day and with her when she lay down to sleep. She told herself she was being ridiculous. In gentler moods she told herself she was being understandably cautious. Most of the time she didn't tell herself anything, just carried on existing in an awful condition of heightened tension and draining uncertainty. And now a week had gone by and Nick still didn't know.

Work wasn't helping. Her requests to interview Elspeth had been rebuffed three times by Rachel Grant. Not well enough yet. Stay away. Valerie had legal options, but she wasn't, quite, at the stage of exercising them. Mainly because there was no hard evidence that Elspeth knew anything, but partly because she, Valerie, was loath to risk an interrogation that might push a manifestly unhinged minor into a second (and God forbid) successful suicide attempt.

It would have been easier if she'd had any other leads—but there were none. Jenner was still missing. The pictures of Sophia had been circulated among the Bay Area strip clubs, but as with the escort agencies the list of possible candidates—based on blond hair, a trim body, and an obscured face—was laughably long and wholly inconclusive. There were four Sophias, all of whom claimed never to have heard of Adam Grant, and none of whom had been working in L.A. when he'd been there for his friend's funeral. The LAPD was (cursorily, Valerie knew) going through the same routine on their turf, but given the time lapse, forty-plus establishments, personnel turnover in the clubs, and the department's own prior commitments, she wasn't holding her breath. It was a mild, seductive torment to her, that somewhere out there Sophia was going about her business, putting on her makeup, shopping for groceries, watching TV, dressing and undressing (perhaps for men, perhaps for money) with so much Valerie needed to know locked up in her beautiful blond head. Sophia—*The Life of Sophia*—was a drama series in Valerie's head, with no amount of episodes sufficient to explain the central mystery of the plot. Even sleep didn't protect her: The other night she'd dreamed she was talking to her in a supermarket parking lot. The wind was blowing and Sophia was struggling to keep her bright blond hair out of her face. In the dream, Valerie had asked her all the pertinent questions—and Sophia, laughing with what seemed a genuine ignorance, had told her she had no clue what she was talking about. There had been a strange sisterly goodwill between them.

"I'm going home," Will said. "You?"

It was dusk. Outside the office windows an evening of deepening blue, accompanied by the city's simmer of preparation for the night's crimes and misdemeanors.

"Yeah, in a minute," Valerie said.

Will put on his jacket and pocketed his phone. "This gig's no fun now I'm not interviewing escorts," he said.

"Work Vice for a month, see if you like it."

"It's not that they were hot. It's that they were *nice*. You know, *charming*. Especially the Eastern Europeans. They really seemed to like their work."

"Imagine sucking Ed's cock," she said. "Imagine *rimming* Ed."

"Jesus."

"Still think they like their work?"

"There's no talking to you. You're a pathological ruiner. I'm going home."

In sheer dull desperation, Valerie was going through the entire case file on Adam Grant, rereading every statement and fine-combing every financial document culled from the computer hardware. Currently she was halfway through the DMV output for license plates the exit traffic cams had registered leaving On-the-Go at the Orland rest stop. Ed Perez had already done this, but Valerie was at the stage where she'd decided to trust no one's scrutiny but her own. Jenner was not the registered owner of any vehicle, nor had he hired one—at least not with his own credit card. Kyle Cornell's Ford wasn't on the footage, nor, according to Ed's report, were any of Dwight's known family or acquaintances. But the fact remained Jenner had been there, and he couldn't have been there except courtesy of a vehicle, even if he'd hitchhiked—and Christ, surely in these paranoid times no one did that anymore?

Licenses, registrations, and photographs (invariably terrible) of drivers. Valerie was so bored she found herself trying to imagine the characters and lives behind the names and images. Drake Lennon was thirty-two last birthday. African American. Plump face, disastrous cornrows. Valerie imagined him cooking up doomed business ideas, entrepreneurial zeal turning to annoyance, then a sense of deep betrayal. Jessica Reynolds, forty-five. Ash blond with green eyeshadow. Good-time girl who'd made too many bad decisions. Never quite had what it took to get out of waitressing. Sadness creeping in. Rick Chesney. Thirty-eight. Boyish dark hair, blue-eyed and gaunt, with a little artistic righteousness burning away. Independent filmmaker, with nothing actually made—

Holy fuck.

She stopped. Read the next name again. Looked at the photo ID. Are you kidding me?

She took the printout sheet over to Ed's desk. Had to wait a moment while he got off the phone.

"*Qué?*" he said.

"No gold star for you this month, Eduardo."

"What? Why?"

She handed him the sheet. There were a dozen licenses per page. "Look again," she said. Then observed while Ed scanned the page. It still took him two attempts.

"Oh," he said. "Fuck me. Fuck *me*."

"Not after this performance," Valerie said. She checked her watch. 8:03 P.M. Still early enough to go and see Rachel Grant.

# 30

"I told you, you can't see her," Rachel Grant said. She had come downstairs after Tala had gone up to tell her Valerie was here. "I thought I made myself clear. Don't you think she's got enough to deal with?"

As before, they were in the kitchen. Tala, Valerie assumed, was keeping an eye on Elspeth. Suicide watch.

"I'm not here to speak to Elspeth," Valerie said. "I need to ask you something."

"For God's sake, what?"

"Traffic cameras at the Orland rest stop record your vehicle leaving there on the night of July thirty-first. Were you there?"

Again, the question baffled Rachel. Not its content, but the bare fact that she was being asked.

"What?" she repeated.

"The same place we know Dwight Jenner was spotted. The same night. Within minutes. It was when Adam was in Los Angeles for the symposium."

Rachel's face said she was working it out. "Was he *following* me?"

"So you were there?"

"Jesus Christ. Jesus *Christ*."

In what Valerie saw had become a reflex action, Rachel wrapped her arms around her middle. All the questions livened the wound Jenner had left there.

"I was . . . I stopped there on the way up to the house."

"The Campbellville place?"

"I can't believe he . . ." She shook her head. Valerie had seen the look on the faces of countless victims, the one of dawning realization: You went about your business without a clue that close by a criminal was going about his. A criminal for whom you *were* the business.

"I'm sorry to tell you this, but we're pretty sure Jenner was watching the house."

Rachel just stared at her.

"It's possible he followed the car thinking it was Adam."

"My God."

"We found his wristwatch by the lake."

Rachel raised her hand to cover her mouth for a moment. The sickness of discovering you were the hapless object of someone's surveillance. The feeling of invisible assault.

"You're sure you didn't see him? At the rest stop? In the store?"

Rachel shook her head. "I didn't go in. I just . . . I only stopped for a minute. I realized I'd left my phone in a bag in the trunk. I just got out to get it."

"Was Elspeth with you?"

"No, she was at camp. The summer camp." She looked like she might throw up. "I was there by myself."

Yes, you were, Valerie thought. Crossing the windows. Walking in the grounds. Getting undressed. Sleeping. And now you know he probably watched it all. Amazing, isn't it?

"I take it you and Adam didn't always go to the Campbellville house together?"

"Mostly we went together. Or sometimes, if he wasn't free, Elspeth and I would go up for the weekend. Take one of her friends."

"Adam ever go there by himself?"

"Yes, but not often." Rachel met Valerie's eye. "Often enough for what you're thinking."

Sophia. That *had* been what Valerie had been thinking. Why not? Clearly Adam Grant had fucked his mistress in the family home, but obviously the place in the country would have served him better.

Rachel looked at the floor. "It's quite something, you know," she said. "I don't have what it takes."

"What do you mean?"

"It should be nothing, shouldn't it? I mean, compared to the fact that he was murdered—compared to the fact that he's *gone*—it should be nothing that he was making a fool of me with some dumb cunt."

Valerie started at the word. It went off between them like a gunshot. She was Police: It took a lot more than a sexual obscenity to ruffle her. But it was utterly at odds with the image of Rachel Grant she'd built through the interviews. For a moment she thought Rachel was going to catch herself, cup her hand over her mouth a second time as if she'd fallen victim to an otherwise suppressed Tourette's. But she didn't. She simply carried on staring at the spotless kitchen floor.

"I realize this is a stupid question," Valerie said, "but have you talked to Elspeth?"

Rachel looked up at her. Another look Valerie had seen innumerable times before. It meant: What is wrong with you? Why are you making this suffering worse? Why can't you just *stop*?

"I'm sorry," she said. "But—"

"You mean have I asked her why she tried to kill herself?" Rachel interrupted. "What do you think? That I might *not* have asked? Just put it down to an adolescent mood swing and bought her a new Xbox?"

Valerie didn't answer. Sometimes allowing someone's anger to hang in the air diffused it.

Rachel sighed. Relaxed her shoulders.

"She said she didn't know why she did it. She said she just got sad. She said she just couldn't stand it." Rachel smiled bitterly. "Isn't that why anyone does it? Because they can't stand it anymore?"

"Yes," Valerie said. "I suppose it is."

"I deserved it. I wasn't there for her. Lesson learned. I don't need to be told twice. Everything will be different now."

"Are you getting everything you need? Is she—"

"I'm not a fan of shrinks," Rachel snapped. Then mastered herself again. "But yes, she's seeing a counselor." She softened. "I'm sorry," she said. "I know you're just doing your job."

And a lousy version of it at that, Valerie.

Unless of course she admitted the wilder hypotheses with which she'd been flirting. When she'd told Rachel Grant about the initial sighting of Jenner at the rest stop, Rachel hadn't mentioned that she'd stopped there herself. Understandable, perhaps. Valerie hadn't given her the date (July 31), and in any case Rachel might simply have not remembered pulling in just to get something from the trunk, especially given the state she was in during the interview. On the other hand, if Jenner was following the Grants' car, why would he take the risk of losing it by waltzing into On-the-Go for cigarettes? So maybe he already knew where the car was going. No reason to suppose July 31 was the first time he'd been there. There remained the fact of his phone calls from Adam Grant. All of them, according to the records, less than two minutes in duration. Some of them barely thirty seconds. Rendezvous instructions?

Go a little wilder. Could it be *Rachel* the two men had in common, rather than (or as well as) Sophia? Maybe Jenner had had enough of sharing? He goes to the Grants' bent on removing his rival (his nemesis, in fact) but Rachel leaps to her husband's defense and ends up almost dead herself.

More than a little wild, dear Valerie. Certainly she could see Adam Grant with Sophia—but Rachel with Dwight Jenner? Hardly.

Very well. Forget Rachel fucking Jenner. How about good old-fashioned money? Valerie had assumed life insurance for Adam Grant, and the assumption had been correct. Given his profession and assets, enough to take care of Rachel and Elspeth for the rest of their days. Could Rachel have recruited Jenner to kill her husband for a cut of the payout? Since she'd admitted knowledge of Adam's affair with Sophia she had double the motive.

That would make sense—except, again, Rachel had ended up a victim. If Jenner was getting a share of the money, he needed Rachel alive to give it to him. Dead, she was useless.

Rubbish. Bogus. Bad police. You worked with the evidence in front of you. This crap was to kid yourself you were thinking outside the box. Only cops on TV thought outside the box and solved the case. The fact was the box was just a depressing dentist's waiting room. In that environment even *People* magazine felt like worthwhile reading.

Will called her with the results from the CSI sweep at the Grants' country place: small amount of blood near where the wristwatch was found, matching the blood on the wristwatch. Scarring on the turf caused by oxygen bleach. Cashmere fibers, DNA clean. No signs of a struggle. If something had happened to Dwight Jenner by the lake, there was no telling what it was or whether it was fatal.

"Suppose it doesn't happen," Valerie said to Nick, later. He was in the bath. She was sitting on the floor next to the tub. He was drinking his second glass of white. She was still sipping her first, half of which (oh for God's *sake*) was sparkling water she'd added in the kitchen. They had a lot of their tender conversations in the bathroom. The white wood paneling and one circular wall light always gave Valerie the feeling of being in a snug ship's cabin.

"You know, as you get older," Nick said, "you're developing a weakness for *non sequiturs*."

"Suppose I *never* get pregnant."

"Suppose you don't. So what?"

"It raises the question, doesn't it? Of whether we'll be enough. Of whether *just us* will be enough. For each other."

"That hadn't occurred to me."

"Really?"

"Really. This is another of your problems, things occurring to you, pointlessly."

"How can it be pointless?"

"Because it's not something you can know ahead of it happening."

"So you admit it's a possibility."

"Yes, it's a possibility. Unless of course you *already* know I won't be enough for you. In which case it's not a possibility, it's a certainty. Let me finish my bath and I'll move out. Move back in if and when you give birth."

"You know that's not what I mean."

Nick didn't answer. Valerie was past wondering at herself. She felt bleak and thrilled. She put her hand on her belly. The wrong place, she assumed, at this stage, but symbolically irresistible. Because there was no end to her madness, she imagined getting run over and killed in the next few days. Nick never knowing she'd been carrying his child. It was an appalling secret, but holding on to it gave her a perverse feeling of power. The loving part was that she knew how happy it would make him. She had this precious gold coin and wanted to choose exactly the right moment to spend it. The unloving part was that she still had the freedom to toss the same precious gold coin down the nearest drain—and none but herself any the wiser.

"Look," Nick said. "You're right. If we don't have a kid it might turn out we're not enough. If that happens, it happens. Jesus, it might turn out we're screwed even if we *do* have a kid. *That* happens all the goddamned time." He stood up. Stepped slightly awkwardly out of the tub next to her. Took a towel and began drying himself. The levity (and whose fault is that, Valerie?) had gone. "For what it's worth I think you'll always be enough for me," Nick said. "So I guess you're really only worried I won't be enough for you. Well, I'll take my chances, kid or no kid. I don't want a kid because I'm scared we won't survive without one. I want a kid because I think having it with you would be fun. Although at the moment every time I say the word 'kid' I go off the idea a little bit more."

He walked out of the bathroom.

"Look on the bright side," he called back. "If we don't have one at least we can stop drinking sauvignon fucking blanc and get back on the good stuff."

Well done, Valerie. Really. First class. Any amateur can deliver good, life-affirming news to a loved one. But to hold on to it, to let it turn to secret toxic shit—that takes a consummate professional.

*I'm disgusting,* Rachel Grant had said. *I'm a fucking monster.*

Yeah, Valerie thought, getting to her feet and sinking the remains of her feeble drink in one gulp, you and me both, sister.

# 31

## *September 6, 2017*

She'd been at her desk the entire morning when Will called her.

"It's your day off, William," she said.

"That's why you're going to Exquisite. Spelled 'X-q-u-i-s-i-t-e.' Got a message from one of the dancers there, says she talked to Sophia three months ago."

"Finally, Jesus. What's the story?"

"Gina Johnstone, aka Gigi. The club's at 301 Columbus, southeast of Little Italy. I'm texting you her number but I'm guessing she sleeps late. The message was she's not a hundred percent sure from the photos, but it's got to be worth a follow-up."

Valerie tried Gina Johnstone's number and got voice mail. She called X-quisite. "Gigi" was due in at 3:30 P.M. for the club's opening at 4:00 P.M.

It wasn't the first time the job had taken Valerie into the world of Adult Entertainment, and X-quisite yielded precisely the vibe she recalled from previous forays: the smells of dry ice and booze and upholstery, the ether of boredom and desire. Underneath it all a residue of sadness. A neon-lined bar with a silver counter ran the length of one wall, currently being prepped by two pretty girls in Lycra bras and hot pants. Dancer podiums either side of the main stage, maybe twenty tables. A lot of velour and leatherette. Smaller rooms off, for the private dances. Mundane thrills. A labored effort to cover ordinariness with glamor. A stripper she'd interviewed on a different case years ago had said to her: In this business you've either got to really love men or really hate them. Anything in between and you'll go off your goddamned head. It had stuck with Valerie, the lonely self-evidence of that insight.

Gigi hadn't arrived, but was expected momentarily. The manager, Francis, looked as if he'd designed himself to defy the industry stereotype. Early thirties, boyishly handsome, and cleanly healthy in a khaki linen suit and crisp white shirt. Kind green eyes and a warm smile. He had a paperback copy of *Wuthering Heights* in his hand when he approached her. On top of these absurdities he was British, with an accent so charming she almost laughed. She asked him about CCTV.

"Well, yes, we do have it, but not in the ladies' dressing rooms, and if I'm being perfectly honest it doesn't *quite* cover the whole club. If we can get a date from you, obviously, we might be able to pull the requisite footage. It depends on whether Gigi can recall . . ."

"You don't remember Sophia yourself?"

"No, I'm afraid not. I might not have been here. Or at any rate, not on the floor."

Valerie didn't know what to make of him. He seemed a sheer impossibility.

"You guys completely legit?" she asked.

"Completely. We're owned by Magisteria, the international chain of which you've no doubt heard. They insist on full compliance with California state law, fiscal transparency, *rigid* enforcement of health and safety regulations. You name it, we don't hide it. Ah—here's Gigi."

Valerie turned to see a petite girl in her early twenties approaching. A dark Cleopatra bob and heavily made-up eyes. Not yet—the ripped jeans and cropped Aerosmith T-shirt said—dressed for work. Francis did the introductions and left them to it. Valerie and Gigi took seats at the nearest table.

"Quite a character," Valerie said.

Gigi rolled her eyes. "I thought it was totally an act, at first," she said. "But he's really like that. The stuff the guy knows is insane. Speaks *Japanese*, for Christ's sake. I've been here a year and I still have absolutely no clue what his deal is. He told me he's writing a book. *Sex and the Soul of America*. It's probably true. Either way, the dude knows how to run a club."

Valerie pulled prints of all the Sophia images from her purse. Gigi nodded. "Like I said when I saw them, I can't swear to it. I mean apart from the stage it's not exactly bright in here. But the hair looks right, the mouth. She had terrific hands, really beautiful. And she did say her name was Sophia."

"What did you talk about?"

"She was asking about working conditions in the club. You know, customer scum-rating, what the management's like, are the girls easy to get along with. Said she was looking to pick up maybe six months' work before heading back to L.A."

"She was from Los Angeles?"

"That's what she said."

"Did she come in alone?"

"As far as I know."

"She mention any guys? Boyfriend?"

"Breakup. Apparently she'd been seeing some guy but it had gone sour. Some *loaded* guy, I figured, given the wardrobe."

"Did she tell you his name?"

"No, not that I remember."

"Not Adam? Or Dwight?"

"I really don't think she said his name. We spoke for like, ten, fifteen minutes tops. I'd finished my shift and I was pooped. Just wanted to get home and crash."

"How did she seem to you?"

"What do you mean?"

"Nervous? Scared? Confident? Experienced?"

Gigi thought about it. "Tired," she said. "I mean, don't get me wrong, she was in terrific shape, but she was definitely the wrong side of thirty. Couple more years, she's a niche market. She looked like she knew that. But not nervous. Definitely not scared. To be honest I thought she had an ace up her sleeve."

"How so?"

Another pause, while Gigi wrestled with articulation. "She had a sort of smiling calm," she said. "Does that make sense? Like she knew something the world didn't. Like maybe she had something good coming. I mean, this is just me guessing, you know? This is just . . ." She shrugged. "It was just the vibe I got."

"What about where she was staying in San Francisco? Did she say?"

Gigi tilted her head and looked away, searching the mental files. "Might have been Nob Hill," she said. "I *think* she said Nob Hill. Which would fit with the loaded guy, I guess."

"Exactly when did she come in?"

"Yeah, I knew you were going to ask me that. I'm hopeless with dates. It was back in early summer. Maybe three months? I don't know. I honestly don't. It could have been June or even like, the end of May?"

Valerie made the notes.

"This is something I think about," Gigi said. "You know on all the TV shows when someone's on trial for something and they say, like, where were you on the night of so-and-so between six and nine P.M.? Jeez. I don't know where I was *yesterday*. I should start keeping a diary. I used to, when I was a kid."

Valerie nodded. "Anything else you can tell me?"

"I don't think so. But can I ask you something?"

"What?"

"What'd she do? I mean, you're Homicide. She kill someone?"

Valerie got to her feet. "It's just a line of inquiry," she said, for about the thousandth time in her life.

"You like being a cop?"

"Sometimes." Lie. All the time. *All* the time. Mainly because I don't know how to be anything else. She looked down at the girl in front of her. She seemed a child. Valerie began to wonder what the story was, what had led her here, whether there was hope for anything better. Who her mother was.

Stop. No point.

"Do me a favor," she said, handing Gigi her card. "If she comes in again, try to get her surname, her number. And call me—okay?"

"Okay. Oh, hey, there's one thing. It probably doesn't matter."

"Yes?"

"She didn't sound L.A. Her accent, I mean. Sounded East Coast to me."

"New York?"

Gigi shrugged. "I don't know. But definitely East."

"All right, thanks."

Gigi smiled up at her. For no reason she could explain, Valerie felt afraid for her, suddenly. There was still brightness here. The soul hadn't quite lost its expectation of happiness. Borrowed time.

"You get any trouble from anyone here, you let me know," she said, surprised at herself.

"Trouble?"

Valerie felt ridiculous, ambushed by sentiment. "Just . . . You have my card."

"I can take care of myself," Gigi said with a grin. It was piercing to Valerie, the buoyancy, the optimism. She nodded, turned, and hurried away, practically tripping over her own feet. You are losing your mind, Valerie.

"But thanks!" Gigi called, laughing.

Francis was hovering at the exit.

"Any joy?" he asked.

"You have the pictures. If Sophia comes in again, you know where to contact me. In the meantime we're going to need to see the CCTV footage for May and June. Call my office when you've pulled it and someone will arrange for its collection or transfer."

"Will do," Francis said. "I'll have to clear it with the head office, naturally."

"Naturally," Valerie said. "And if it takes longer than forty-eight hours I'll be back with a warrant."

# 32

## *September 7, 2017*

When the left rear tire on his 1989 VW camper blew in the desert just after 4:00 P.M., it felt to Pete Jardine like the first time he'd stopped since leaving New York five days before.

Five days? Six? Time had ceased to be a measurable line. Instead a series of snapshots that bloomed and faded. Silver mountains under a blue sky. A burned-out Texaco. A lake on which he'd watched a solitary cormorant preening itself, savagely. He had continued to function. He had eaten, gone to the bathroom, slept. But like a quiet automaton, a melancholy robot that had been given all the (insufficient) programming it was ever going to get. Somewhere back there on the road, he'd turned forty. When he thought of the digits, four and zero, they seemed the definitive notation of precisely where and what he was right now: an ordinarily betrayed American man, stranded in the middle of nowhere.

He got out of the VW, followed immediately by the dog, Pablo, a rangy mongrel the color of burned toast. He and Vicky had got him from the ASPCA shelter on Ninety-second Street six years ago, when love had been the central certainty and the world a bright arena designed solely for their own adventures. Pete hadn't decided to bring him when he left New York.

Pablo had just followed him out of the apartment and got into the van and Pete hadn't had the capacity to turf him out. Hadn't thought about it, even. In those moments, everything had happened in a dreamy, inevitable flow.

The desert afternoon simmered. Pete stretched, looked up at the blue-white sky. Sun-heat fitted the back of his head like a skullcap. He set Pablo's bowl down and half filled it with water from the plastic bottle. He didn't know if he was in Nevada or California. He'd kept off the interstates. Lonely blacktop and small towns he'd never heard of. He'd begun with the clear thought of driving to the Pacific. Don't think about anything until you get to the Pacific. Everything could be postponed until he stood with his bare feet in the cooling surf. But now that he was within reach of it he didn't feel ready. Maybe he would head north for a while, if only for the milder weather. The Pacific went all the way up to Canada, after all.

He went to look at the tire. It was a write-off. The thought of changing it gave him some pleasure. It would provide him with meaningful action for the first time since New York. Manual labor. There was honor in it. He opened the trunk and took out the jack and lug wrench. Pablo, tongue lolling like a little pink scroll, went mooching off into the scrub.

Vicky's face from that last afternoon. It had happened in the way these things happen, courtesy of simple cause and effect. He had come home from work just after midday with the beginning of a migraine. It was a Friday. Vicky was supposed to be having lunch with her friend Nadine. As soon as Pete entered the apartment he knew it wasn't empty. There was a reflex flurry of panic when he thought: Someone's broken in—but his body had barely tensed (he'd felt his scalp tighten at the thought of a burglar, a man he'd have to confront, fight) when he heard Vicky in the bedroom. And in that moment he had known not only what was happening but that everything for quite a long time had been leading him to it.

The desert around him was bone-pale. The lug wrench was already hot in his sweating hands. Fix this and pull off at the next town. Drink an ice-cold beer. Eat a refrigerated ham sandwich. The last few days had returned him to simple needs and impulses. It was a quiet, blissful madness to have left his life behind him—but he knew it couldn't last. It made him sad to think of going back. Doubly sad, given the smallness of what had happened. Next to the world's genocides and famines it was nothing. At the time he had thought it was unbearable. But the word "unbearable" made a liar of you if you didn't kill yourself. And he hadn't. Wasn't going to. The death of another middle-class marriage was nothing—yet his reaction to it had felt like the most natural thing he'd ever done. As natural, in fact, as getting married in the first place.

He and Vicky had met at a party six years ago. Vicky had arty energy and ambition and petite bitchy blond good looks, but not enough talent for any of it to come to anything. There were unfinished novels. Acting classes. Poetry slams. A year singing in a band that never played anything but bars. Whereas Pete had graduated NYU film school in '98 knowing that he didn't have what it took to be a filmmaker, and had instead gone to work in his uncle's interior design company, where, as of four years ago, he'd become a partner. Vicky didn't mind the money, but after a while she dropped the pretense of having a creative career of her own. Then it was just the dangerous energy and petite bitchy blond good looks. As a couple they understood what they had: Pete was the steady force keeping Vicky—just—from going off the rails. It was a joke between them, that he was reliable, romantic, conservative. It was what she loved in him, his tender sanity.

Somewhere along the line, Pete had understood that she had decided to love his tender sanity because she feared how much she would hate him for it if she didn't. He loved her, on the other hand, without inversion or compromise. The only fracture was his suspicion that he wasn't enough for her. In spite of her artistic failures she was hungrier than him, riskier, more imaginative and more violently alive. Worse, it became apparent to him after the first flush of mutual adoration that he wasn't entirely floating her boat in the sack. There was a yearning impatience in her when they had sex, as if she were confined to a space too small for her. She often, post-coitally, picked a fight with him. (A lousy reversal of make-up sex, in fact.) Without asking, he knew she'd had better lovers before him. He wasn't rough with her, for one thing. They'd worked their way through a little bondage and spanking at her insistence, but it was clear his heart wasn't in it. Again, it had been made into an affectionate joke, what a *gentle* guy he was. But the yearning impatience in her remained, sometimes became outright anger. The last couple of years, their evenings had featured stretches of uneasy silence, intolerable if not for Netflix. They saw more of their friends, separately. Sunday mornings, which had formerly been filled with lazy potential—brunch, cocktails, the *Times*, sex—became the week's dreaded low point.

And yet there was still love. There was still, from time to time, sex. They didn't have the arguments. It was worse: They didn't *bother* having the arguments. They were like a couple standing on a damp lawn at night watching, sadly, as their house burned to the ground.

Which was why, when he pushed open their bedroom door that afternoon five or six or ten days ago to find Vicky facing him, naked on all fours, getting pounded in the ass by a muscular guy with Celtic tattoos on his forearms and his hands wrapped in her short blond hair, Pete's overwhelming feeling was one of sad recognition, as if he was seeing the obvious punch line to a bad, long-winded joke. There was even (he thought now, unscrewing the last lug nut) a feeling of wretched relief.

He hadn't said a word. Vicky had looked up at him with cat eyes full of ecstasy and heartbreak. The guy fucking her had *his* eyes scrunched shut, as if performing a feat of tremendous concentration. Absurdly, he didn't see Pete the whole time. Pablo walked out of the study and joined Pete in the hallway. Pete watched for a moment, felt his entire life deflate, then turned and walked out of the apartment. Pablo followed him. Pete had got into the VW, started the engine, and begun driving. The Pacific was a blue promise on his mind's horizon. He would get there and wade in up to his shins. Until he'd done that, he couldn't imagine doing anything else.

All four lug nuts were off. He eased the wheel from the threaded bolts. Somewhere in the scrub the dog was barking. It sounded quite a way off. Pete straightened. "Pablo!" he called. "Pablo?"

More barking.

"Pablo! Here, boy. Pablo, come on."

Silence. Then more barking. It sounded, incredibly, like there was more than one dog. Someone *camping* out here? Pablo wasn't the friendliest canine when it came to other dogs. Pete sighed. The heat and the work with the wheel had brought out a sweat. He squinted in the direction the dog had gone.

"Pablo?"

Nothing. Low stunted dry bushes obscured his view. The air in the distance rippled. He locked the van. Deal with the spare when you've found the dog. Urban reflex made him check his phone. No reception. He took the lug wrench with him, though he didn't quite know why.

In the heat it felt like a long time before he heard the dogs again. He looked back toward the road. The white roof of the VW was visible, but it was farther than he'd imagined.

"Pablo?"

Growls and the sound of scuffling, off to his left. Maybe fifty meters. Then snarls—and a yelp of pain.

"Pablo!"

Pete started to run.

The dog was bent low, hackles up, facing off two coyotes over a dark patch of dug-up earth. There was blood on his muzzle. More blood on his flank.

Pete didn't think. For a moment absolutely everything left him except fear of the coyotes and fear for his dog.

Blank, surrendered wholly to an instinct he didn't know he possessed, he screamed and charged the coyotes, flailing with the wrench.

The animals turned tail and fled.

Pablo got, trembling, to his feet and limped to his owner,

"Jesus, Pab . . . Hold on, let me take a look. Easy. Easy, boy."

The wound in the flank wasn't deep, but the left foreleg was gashed to the bone. Pete stuffed the lug wrench into the back of his jeans and picked the dog up. Pablo was oven hot, panting.

Quick with the spare wheel. Vet. Shots. Fuck. Rabies?

Pete was trembling himself. Adrenaline in this heat. His arms felt weak and light. He was drenched in sweat. The afternoon silence was a kind of noise.

He glanced down into the earth the animals had dug.

Even with the adrenaline flowing he wasn't prepared for what he saw.

# PART
# TWO

# 33

## *1991–2003*

Long before she became Sophia, desired by men and envied by women, she was Abigail. Her middle name, which everyone preferred. Even her mother.

The sad thing was that Abigail loved her mother, in spite of everything. If Joanna Lake had been bad all the time it would have been easier: Abigail could have hated her, simply. But Joanna wasn't bad all the time. Sometimes she was wonderful. Or at least had wonderful impulses.

"Let's go somewhere," she said to Abigail one afternoon. It was a raw Philadelphia day, the wind hurling itself around in the rain. Joanna was in bed under the comforter, shivering. A loose windowpane rattled in the room next door. Abigail was supposed to be at school, but Joanna had been sick when she got home late in the night. Abigail had found her asleep on the bathroom floor with her hair in a sour splatter of puke and her makeup in ugly streaks on her face. She'd been fully dressed in the clothes she'd gone out in, skinny jeans and the short green leather jacket over a gray roll-neck sweater, silver hoop earrings, and the dozen clinking bangles Abigail loved. Even passed out, Joanna's magical glitteriness had still been plain to see, but spoiled and dirty. It had made Abigail think of the Christmas tree she'd seen that time stuffed into a garbage can, still with its tinsel crushed and clinging.

"Where?" Abigail asked. She was gathering up clothes from the bedroom floor. It had been her plan to get quarters from Joanna for the laundromat down the block, where the owner, Mr. Lee, knew her and usually gave her a Coke or a donut for free. She'd been wearing her current clothes, including the torn red parka that was too small for her, for three days. Besides, the laundromat was filled with dreamy heat. The house, on the other hand, was freezing since the gas had been cut off. You could see your breath.

"Anywhere," Joanna said. "The world's our oyster."

"I want to go to school."

Joanna sighed. "For Christ's sake," she said.

"Okay, let's go somewhere. I just—"

"No, no, I wouldn't dream of it. Why would you want to go somewhere with me when you could be doing fucking algebra or whatever?"

"I didn't mean it. Let's go somewhere. I really want to."

Joanna stared at Abigail as if she hated her for being her only friend. In these moments of wonderful impulses the girl knew everything could go wrong. She had to be careful.

So she kept still and said nothing. Her mother's eyes were fierce and pleading. Then they filled with tears and Joanna rolled over onto her back.

Abigail put the clothes down on the floor. She wanted to get into bed and wrap her arms around Joanna. No matter how many times she saw her mother cry, she never got used to it. It was as if her chest cracked down the middle and a hurrying emptiness filled her.

Instead she went to the kitchen, stood on the stool to reach the counter, poured a cup of coffee from the pot (lots of cream and sugar), and took it back to the bedroom.

"Mommy?"

Joanna was staring at the ceiling's brownish stain from where the roof had leaked last winter. The stain was roughly the shape of an elephant. Abigail imagined it trapped there, separated from its normal elephant world. She felt sorry for it.

"I made you some coffee."

No reply. Abigail set the cup down on the nightstand and went to find her mother's purse. It was still in the bathroom. Purple fake leather. With its zipper open it was like a soft face with only a mouth. She hunted through the makeup and loose change until she found a crumpled pack of Winstons and a yellow plastic lighter. There were three bent cigarettes left. She took the pack and the lighter to her mother.

"Here's your cigarettes," she said.

The last time she'd done this, a couple of days ago, Joanna had held her and kissed her and said, Oh, honey, you're my angel, do you know that? You're my guardian angel. For Abigail it had been as if the icy house filled suddenly with warm sunlight. But then the phone had rung and her mother had put on her makeup in a hurry and gone out and not come back until the following day. When she went out that way, with urgency and a kind of sheen to her face, it was as if Abigail had stopped being a person and had instead become just an ordinary thing, like a cushion or a shoe or an old TV magazine. It was as if her mother didn't even know she was there.

"Mommy?"

Joanna hadn't moved. She was still staring at the elephant.

"Get me my purse, would you?"

This was for the other things, Abigail knew. The medicines. She'd brought the coffee and the cigarettes but she'd left the medicines in the purse. She didn't know why she didn't trust them. They definitely made her mother better, sometimes happy and full of a sort of bright craziness—but there was something about the whole business Abigail didn't like. It was as if the medicines knew something about her mother that she, Abigail, did not.

Nonetheless, she went and got the purse.

"Go look out the front window and tell me if the car's still there," Joanna said.

Abigail knew her mother didn't like to take the medicines in front of her. She also knew the car was still there. This was just to get her out of the room. But she went anyway.

"I've thought where we can go," Joanna said, as she pulled the battered Ford out of the driveway.

"Where?"

"You'll see. It's a surprise."

The medicine had done its thing. Joanna had put on fresh makeup and perfume, and when she drove it was as if everything about driving was a delight to her.

"Where?"

"You'll see. You'll like it."

"Have we got any money?"

"Some."

Abigail didn't ask what she wanted to ask. But her mother had the magic now.

"Enough for a hot dog and soda, probably," Joanna said.

They went to the recently opened New Jersey State Aquarium across the Delaware River. It was an ugly concrete building with a white dome on top, and inside was a strange smell and a lot of echoey noise bouncing around like at the indoor swimming pool.

Abigail was nervous when they had to pay. Sometimes her mother would hunt through her purse and find she didn't have enough. But this time it was okay. Abigail decided she wouldn't say anything about a hot dog or a soda unless her mother asked.

"Do they have sharks here?"

"I guess so. I guess they have everything. Turtles, dolphins, jellyfish, hell, maybe they've got a whale."

"A whale?" Abigail had school facts about whales. *Beneath the skin lies a layer of fat called blubber. Whales can be up to 110 feet long and weigh up to 150 tons.* The thought of one of them being in a glass tank in a building made her feel queasy.

"Well, maybe not a whale," Joanna said. "What do you want to see first?"

"Sharks."

"But what if you fall *in?*"

"I won't fall in."

"But what if I *push* you in?"

"I'll pull you in with me!"

"You will, will you? We'll see about that, missy."

Her mother was glimmery with the magic. When she smiled it filled Abigail with excitement. But always in the excitement was the thought of the medicine and the fear of when it stopped working. She tried not to think about it.


There were no sharks. There wasn't anything apart from fish, and most of them were gray or brown. All of them were ugly, with bottom jaws longer than their top ones. They looked as if they were in a bad mood, though they just kept gliding back and forth in the tanks, doing nothing.

For a while the magic lasted, though Abigail could see her mother was only pretending to find the fish interesting. Abigail wasn't interested either. Common carp. American shad. White sucker. Brown bullhead. They all looked pretty much the same. Only the catfish were different, with their whiskers that made them look like Chinese wizards. Her mother got tired of reading the names. "*You* read them," she said (as the magic wobbled). "You're the one reads everything." Then she seemed to catch the wobble and steady it. "Look at this dude," she said, pointing to a largemouth bass. He's like: 'I hate this goddamned place. I get out of here, I'm going to Florida.'"

That became the game: Abigail would point to a fish and her mother would do an impersonation of what it was saying to itself. She did different voices. It was funny.

———

They were leaving the aquarium when Joanna remembered the hot dog and soda.

"It's okay, Mommy, I'm not hungry."

"Don't be such a drama queen. You can have a hot dog or a soda. Which do you want?" Her voice had changed. The words "which do you want?" made Abigail's throat tighten with a feeling of selfishness. It was like she was doing something mean to her mother.

"Come on, which? I don't have all day."

Abigail's mouth was dry. The thought of eating a hot dog made her feel sick. But she wanted to go to the bathroom (she didn't want to say that, because the restrooms might be miles away) and if she drank a Coke that would be worse.

"Hot dog, please," she said.

She had only taken two bites by the time they got back into the Ford. Her mother was moving briskly now, as if the trip to the aquarium had made her late for something. The day had darkened and the wind rocked the car.

Joanna turned the ignition.

Nothing happened.


Joanna sat back in the seat and closed her eyes, breathing hard through her nose. Abigail kept trying to think of something to say. She was afraid of saying anything, but her mother's silence and closed eyes and hard breathing were unbearable. It had started to rain.

"Could we . . ."

"Could we what?"

"Could we take the bus?"

Joanna opened her eyes. She laughed. "The bus?" she said. "Oh sure. Or what about a taxi?"

Abigail knew she'd said the wrong thing.

"Shall we take a taxi?" Joanna said.

Abigail shook her head. No.

"No," Joanna said, smiling. Her forehead was shiny with sweat, though the car was so cold. "No, maybe we won't take a taxi. You know why?"

Abigail didn't answer.

"Because we just spent the last of the fucking money on your fucking hot dog. Which you're not even fucking eating."

Abigail said nothing. Hot tears hurried out of her eyes. The empty space in the car, the whole empty space of the day and the rain and the darkness pressed around her. Weirdly, in the middle of everything, it made her picture a whale in a huge tank of dirty water, not moving.

Her mother went through her purse, throwing every item one by one onto the floor. She found a quarter and a dime.

"Stay here," she said, and got out of the car.

"Where are you going?"

Joanna just slammed the door and walked away.

The only thing Abigail could think to do was finish the hot dog. If she ate the hot dog at least her mother wouldn't hate her for not eating it. It was almost impossible. Each bite made a bigger, drier ball in her mouth, and each time she forced it down her throat got tighter and more tears came.

She couldn't see out the windshield for the rain, which was heavier now, so she rolled down the window. Her mother was standing at an unsheltered pay phone across the parking lot, talking fast into the receiver, getting drenched.


Zeke came and picked them up in his car. Abigail didn't like him. He had a magic of his own, soft and musical, and when he talked it was like a lullaby— but the sort that made Abigail think that if she fell asleep she'd never wake up again. His skin was smooth and brown and he had strange marks tattooed on each of his knuckles. His car smelled different than theirs, a sour cigarette odor something like herbs and molasses. He blinked slowly, his long eyelashes meeting and parting with a kind of sly tenderness.

They were still a ways from home when Abigail began to feel she couldn't hold her pee any longer. The whole ride back to Philadelphia she'd been in agony. She was terrified of asking to stop and terrified of wetting herself in Zeke's car.

Meanwhile Zeke and her mother said things she didn't understand.

"*Quid pro quo*. That's Latin. Know what it means?"

"I can guess."

"You got a fat tab already, girl."

"You know I'm good for it."

Zeke laughed.

They pulled up in front of the house. Neither Zeke nor Joanna made a move to get out.

"Mommy? Can I have the keys? I need the bathroom."

"You got heat?" Zeke said to Joanna.

"No."

"Jesus."

"Mommy? Please can I have the keys?"

Zeke looked up and down the street.

"There's heat in *here*."

"Yeah. Sure, what the hell."

"Momm-eeee!" Abigail wailed. Her legs were crossed so tightly her thighs ached.

"Give the kid the keys, for Christ's sake. She's gonna piss herself."

Abigail got out. Uncrossing her legs made her feel dizzy and wide open, as if she were on stilts. She went to her mother's side window. Joanna hunted in her purse. Seconds. She couldn't hold it. She couldn't. Not one second more. The window rolled down.

"Go in and stay upstairs," Joanna said.

Abigail snatched the keys and ran. There was a wooden side porch and a door that led into the back hall and the downstairs toilet. She would make it. She would.

But in her hurry she tripped on the top porch step. Without time to get her hands from between her legs she went thud-rasp flat on her face on the boards—and the pain and shock made her let go of holding her bladder—and she wet herself.

The first moments were pure joy. Hot pee spread through her jeans and she didn't care about anything. She felt her face smiling, even.

Then the warm wetness began to cool and the joy went and she tasted blood in her mouth. Two splinters of pain shot up the length of her nose. She didn't stop peeing. Just lay there and let it come.

She got to her feet. Her face was hot in the cold air, nose and mouth throbbing. She looked back to the car to check if her mother had seen what happened. But Joanna was talking to Zeke.

After a moment Zeke put his hand on the top of Joanna's head and guided it down toward his lap until it disappeared from Abigail's view.


Despite her ravaged education, Abigail learned and understood things quickly. Their house in Harrowgate had belonged to Joanna's mother, who had left it to Joanna. They'd been losing it ever since they moved in, and one day when Abigail was eleven they lost it for good. Nothing was said about it. Money and possessions traveled in one direction only: away from them. One minute they were in the house, the next they were in a bare apartment in which the sole fragment of beauty was the blue flame in the immersion heater.

Abigail accepted the changes, adapted, found whatever new minimal footholds were available, assumed it would all change again. She was a skinny girl with her mother's blond hair and green eyes and a fierce privacy that put people off her. She had a big, erratic intelligence. When she realized Joanna was a drug user and a prostitute and by most people's standards at least half-crazy, she realized, too, she could feel sorry for her own younger self, the four- or six- or eight-year-old Abigail who'd had to cope, without knowledge. She realized this, but turned away from it, as if it were a dead thing.

She missed too much school and, despite her intelligence, never racked up the hours vital to putting the various things she learned together. Her life was one of forced practicality, in which all actions derived from a single goal: keeping Joanna alive. Which meant food, the laundromat, cleaning up vomit, lying to people, stealing. She had to keep her mother alive because her mother was all she had.

Joanna, meanwhile, came in and out of reason, manageability, presence. There were periods in which she willed herself into competence. Even, occasionally, jobs: washing hair in a salon; waitressing; cleaning. For a while she helped Mr. Lee in the laundromat. None of it lasted.

Still, her beauty held, precariously. The blond hair and green eyes emerged from the wreckages more or less intact, renewable. Her glamor was a fortune resistant to all but the most reckless spending. And even by the time Abigail turned fourteen the spending wasn't, quite, reckless.

Then, in the winter of 1999, everything changed.

"Honey, you got something to eat tonight?"

They were in the bathroom, Joanna drying herself, Abigail in the tub. The latest was that Joanna was dancing at a club called Jezebel's in Frankford. An attempt to shed Zeke, whose protection skills weren't what they had been. Abigail knew her mother couldn't possibly just be dancing, though Joanna sometimes came home bearing traces of glitter and smelling thrillingly of dry ice.

"Ariel's bringing pizza," Abigail said.

"Girls' night in, huh?" Joanna said.

This friend, Ariel, wasn't quite mythical, but Abigail had exaggerated their relationship, which only very occasionally involved hanging out for a couple of hours after school.

"Well, at least you can watch a movie this time," Joanna said.

The television was out of hock as of yesterday. Courtesy of Jezebel's they had light, heat, hot water.

Joanna got dressed, plainly by her standards, in a pink puffer jacket from thrift, jeans, and shit-kickers. Her dancing gear was at Jezebel's. Abigail leaned against the radiator, looking out of the window. The black streets were gashed with frozen slush. Tiny snowflakes swirled in the dark.

"Don't stay up too late," Joanna said from the doorway.

Abigail spent the evening in what she supposed other people would think was a strange way. It had become her habit to eavesdrop on the building's inhabitants. Best, of course, were the overheard conversations. Often very ordinary, but occasionally something valuable.

You knew I didn't want to.

No, I didn't.

You knew I didn't want to and you went ahead anyway.

You're talking crazy.

You like it better that way, if you know I don't want to.

For God's sake.

This was the other world, with sex running through it like a dark river. She'd been masturbating regularly for some years now. Initially it had been nothing more than instinctive physical self-comfort. Later it was attended by images from magazines and the Adult section of the video store—and eventually by the inevitable shock of knowing, really knowing, that this was her mother's life, too. Abigail didn't know what to do with the feeling of empty sickness and compelling excitement. The guilt just seemed to heighten her pleasure. It was as if she'd come into a dirty inheritance, a wretched legacy that had been waiting for her since birth.

After working her way up all four floors (nothing particularly good tonight) Abigail went out onto the building's roof through a security door that should have been locked but never was.

This, too, was something she liked to do, stand up there under the sky and know that below her all the overheard lives were going on, and to imagine herself and her mother, one day soon, getting far away from the city, to a time and place where everything she knew now would be a distant memory.

————

She was asleep on the couch in the small hours when she heard the apartment door open and her mother, breathing heavily, slam it behind her. It was still night. The snow had stopped.

"Mom?"

Joanna stumbled in the dark to the bathroom and turned on the light, then the shower.

Abigail went to look. Her mother was sobbing, pulling off her clothes. With the exception of the puffer jacket, not the clothes she'd gone out in. These were clothes Abigail had never seen: a short dress of green spangles and a pair of white knee boots. One of the white boots had a splash of red down its side. More red on Joanna's thigh. Abigail knew it was blood.

"Mom, what happened? Are you hurt?"

Joanna didn't say anything. The tiny bathroom was filling up with steam.

"Mom where is it? Where are you hurt?"

Joanna yanked the dress over her head. She wasn't wearing any bra or panties. She was shaking.

"I'm not hurt," she said. "Oh God, Abby. Oh God." She covered her face with her trembling hands. The unstained boot was still on. "Shit," Joanna whispered, behind her hands. "Shit, shit, shit."

"Please tell me what's wrong," Abigail said.

Joanna uncovered her face. Her green eyes were alive and desperate, her skin moist. She put a hand on Abigail's shoulder for balance as she lifted her leg to unzip and pull off the boot. "I'm so stupid," she said. "I'm so fucking stupid. Let me . . . I need to get in."

She pulled back the curtain and stepped into the tub for the shower. But a moment later she whipped the curtain open again, stepped out, and pushed past Abigail. She dropped to her knees and threw up in the toilet.

Abigail, as she had many times before, held her mother's head. It was a strange thing, she supposed, to know the weight of your mother's head like that, the way it felt with heat in the bone and the brain inside and vomit coming out of the mouth.

———————

The next day Joanna didn't leave the house. Nor did she tell Abigail what had happened. All she would say was that there had been an accident and someone had got hurt.

At the club?

No. Afterward. At a friend's place.

What friend?

Just a friend. Jesus Christ. Stop interrogating me.

Joanna was horribly alert. She couldn't sit still. She called Zeke twenty times, but he didn't answer.


On the morning of the following day, Abigail woke to find her mother gone. All her clothes were still there. Only her purse and the jacket were missing.

Abigail walked up and down in the apartment. She spent an hour at the window, looking out into the wet streets, where slivers of frozen slush remained, dirtied by the traffic.

It had been dark for an hour when Joanna came back. Her hair was damp and Abigail could smell the cold on her skin. Joanna went straight to the bedroom and took the battered Nike tote bag from the wardrobe.

"Pack your clothes," she said to Abigail.

"Where are we going?"

"Never mind. Just do it."

"Mom, I don't—"

"For Christ's sake just do as I tell you!" Joanna screamed.

There was a knock at the door. Joanna froze. Grabbed Abigail and put her finger to her lips.

More knocking. Louder this time. Then a man's voice:

"Police, open up."

Joanna stared at Abigail, not seeing her.

"Joanna, for God's sake we know you're in there. We just watched you come in. Don't make us break it down."

Joanna exhaled, heavily, as if she'd been holding her breath for a long time. She straightened up, smiled at Abigail, sadly, then went to open the door.

It was just one guy, with his badge held out. He wasn't in uniform. He was slightly shorter than Joanna, with broad shoulders and narrow black eyes. He looked like a Native American who'd cut off his long hair and forced himself into regular clothes. His face was slightly pockmarked on the left side. He had beautiful hands and a big wristwatch like the ones divers wore. Abigail wondered why he'd said "we."

"Detective Garner, Homicide," he said. "Need to ask you some questions."

"About what?" Joanna said.

"About Tuesday night."

Pause.

"Joanna, we know you were there. We can talk here or we can talk at the station. Up to you."

Joanna let him in. The detective saw Abigail standing in the bedroom doorway. He smiled at her, showing perfectly straight white teeth. The smile changed his whole face.

"Playing hooky?" he said.

"She's sick," Joanna said, closing the front door. "Honey, go in the bedroom while I talk to the detective."

In the bedroom Abigail sat on the unmade bed staring at the worn gray carpet, listening to the murmur of their voices. She couldn't hear what they were saying, but it was mainly her mother talking. Until the last few minutes, when the detective spoke, very quietly, for what seemed a long time.

The apartment door opened and closed. Abigail heard the detective walk down the hall. It sounded as if he were trailing his fingernails against the wall. She listened until she was sure he was going down the stairs. Then she went in to see her mother.

Joanna was sitting on the couch holding her knees, gently.

"I'm in big fucking trouble," she said.

"What is it?"

Joanna just shook her head. Closed her eyes. Opened them. She looked as if she was going to cry.

"Is he going to send you to jail?" Abigail asked. She had a clear image of her mother stepping into a barred cell, the door closing slowly behind her. A clang of mctal.

"No," Joanna said. "He's going to help us."

There was initially a strange period when Detective Lawrence Garner, "Larry," was simply Joanna's boyfriend. For a while he showed up at the apartment two or three times a week. On more than one occasion he took Joanna and Abigail out for dinner.

"I don't like him," Abigail told her mother, when they'd come home from one of these uncomfortable evenings at a Korean restaurant.

"Why?" Joanna asked. "What's wrong with him?"

"*You* don't like him."

Joanna laughed. There was a brittle brightness to her around Larry, around the subject of Larry. To Abigail it was as if her mother was terrified of something and had convinced herself that as long as she didn't look at it then it couldn't really be there.

"What a thing to say," Joanna said. "Of course I like him."

"You hate him. It's like he stinks and you're holding your nose."

Joanna laughed again. It wasn't even her real laugh. "You're crazy," she said.

"He hates you, too."

"What?"

"He hates both of us. You know he does."

Joanna's smile faltered. Since Larry, she had a new version of the magic, the same unreliable glitteriness, but with panic right underneath it.

"Don't be silly," she said. "He's looking out for us." Then she forced herself back into brightness. "I wish you'd let me cut your hair," she said. "You look like a goddamned gypsy."

One night not long afterward, Abigail woke in the small hours and heard her mother and Larry laughing in the living room. There was an odd atmosphere, as if the apartment were alive and had whispered something to her while she'd slept. She went to the bedroom door and opened it, carefully.

Larry was sprawled on the couch, still wearing his shoulder holster, though his red shirt was half unbuttoned, showing plump chest muscles so smooth and hard they looked plastic, like a G.I. Joe's. He had a glass of scotch in his hand, ice cubes tinkling. Joanna was down on her knees, cutting lines of coke on the coffee table, her skirt bunched up around her waist. She tucked her hair behind her ear and looked up at him. Larry opened his mouth and curled his tongue up like a happy lizard.

School (Abigail was there more now that her mother had Larry on the scene) was an escape and an imprisonment. Escape because in spite of everything her mind went into some of the stuff. She was good at biology, math, geography. (Later she would theorize that she liked these subjects because each of them in its own way took her far away from the regular world: to the invisible molecular level; to the clean realm of numbers; to countries and people thousands of miles away.) More than anything, though, she loved literature. *The Adventures of Huckleberry Finn. The Old Man and the Sea. To Kill a Mockingbird. The Pearl.* She read *The Heart Is a Lonely Hunter* five times. Before she'd begun reading seriously, she'd assumed half her thoughts and feelings were uniquely insane. But it turned out other people had such thoughts and feelings, too. In spite of this—or perhaps because of it—she kept her mouth shut in her English class and scored lousily on her papers. For her it was private and inarticulable. While she was reading them, the books and their characters were living, fluid things. Talking and writing about them in class killed them.

So much for escape. School was an imprisonment because she had no friends and most of the teachers seemed afraid of her. They treated her as if she were a bomb that might go off if they got too close.

Ariel had abandoned her. The two of them had been to a party where Abigail had hit a guy in the head with a big glass ashtray because she'd overheard him call her mother a whore.

One strange thing happened. It was her last day of junior high. She was coming down the steps that led out into the parking lot when the strap of her shoulder bag, which had been rotting for months, snapped. The bag dropped and spat out some of its contents. Abigail got down on her haunches to retrieve them. When she stood up she saw Daniel Coulter leaning on his motorbike, watching her. Daniel was two years older. His kid sister was in the year below her. Abigail remembered Daniel in the way she remembered all the older boys who had gone on to senior high, as remote figures utterly unconnected to her. Daniel beckoned to her. As if it were a movie, Abigail found herself checking over her shoulder that there wasn't someone else he was beckoning to. There wasn't. Daniel grinned and repeated the gesture. She went over to him. She knew it was going to be something unpleasant, since he was cool—had *been* cool even two years ago—but she couldn't stop herself.

"Anyone fucking you yet?" he asked her.

This struck her as such an outlandish question that she thought she must have misheard.

"What?" she said.

Daniel laughed. He had a glamorous face, with blue eyes and shoulder-length dark hair. A silver hoop earring.

"I said," he repeated, smiling, "is anyone fucking you yet?"

She wanted to walk away. Her face was hot, her legs strands of chiffon. But he stared at her, full of brightness. She was confined to a terrible privacy with him.

"No," she said.

Daniel shook his head, smiling. He glanced down at the ground, then back up at her. "Someone *should* be," he said.

Abigail was speechless. She couldn't stop staring at him.

"Listen," he said. "I'm doing you a favor. Get your shit together. Put on some goddamned makeup. Stop dressing like a fucking tramp. Shave your pussy and come see me when you're ready. Now exit."

Abigail walked away. Not because she'd been told to but because her impulse to walk away finally got the better of her.

Was it a joke? No one had ever said anything like that to her before. She didn't consider herself pretty. It was a joke. Some ruse to shame her in public. Daniel would wait until she was naked, then open the door for everyone to look and laugh. This was what she told herself.

But that night when Joanna was out with Larry, Abigail took a shower and blow-dried her long hair and put on some of her mother's makeup. Eyeshadow, liner, mascara, bloodred nail polish and lipstick. When she'd finished she stood naked in front of the full-length mirror on the back of the bathroom door.

She was slightly astonished. She was slim, and her breasts were small and firm. She had Joanna's features and coloring, the rich blond hair and green eyes, but she'd always taken her own invisibility for granted. In her mind, Joanna's beauty was something unrelated to her, an impenetrable phenomenon like lightning or an earthquake. Now, with the cosmetics, Abigail felt a thrilling share in it. She went to the bedroom and put on a pair of Joanna's high heels. They were black suede, with open toes and a strap across the ankle like something a slave girl would wear. She returned to the bathroom. More astonishment. She'd never worn high heels in her life. It alarmed her that the image in the mirror was her. A different her. She looked like Joanna.

In the days that followed, she repeated this ritual often, when she was alone. Outwardly nothing changed. She never wore makeup in public. She continued to dress the way she always had, featureless jeans and tops, sneakers that looked exhausted. But she had, whether she liked it or not, a new secret to share with herself.

One evening, after performing the transformation ritual, she masturbated in front of the mirror. The resulting climax was a delicious explosion of shame. It frightened her. It frightened her because even telling herself (in the immediate profane afterglow) that she wasn't going to do this again, she knew beyond any doubt that she certainly was going to do it again.

Which she did, the very next time she had the place to herself. It became a cloudy, wonderful addiction. For a while, each time she did it, it felt as if she were daring God to punish her. She imagined the sins like a heap of stolen coins, a dirty fortune getting bigger and bigger. But after a while she stopped thinking in that way. The heap of coins was sprawling, but she just didn't bother about it.

That summer they moved into Larry's first-floor apartment in Manayunk. To Abigail it seemed huge, but there was too much dark wooden furniture. The couch and armchairs were deep green vinyl. Larry had a black electronic recliner only he was allowed to sit in. She had her own room, with nothing in it but a bed, a badly put-together wardrobe, and two empty filing cabinets with rust around the edges. There were office blinds instead of curtains over a small window that looked out onto Grape Street.

Abigail spent as much time as she could out of the apartment. When she wasn't reading she wandered the city and fantasized about leaving. She went to the Schuylkill River, since the water gave her the sense of a route into distant openness. The leaving fantasies had a treacherous duality. They began with her and her mother on a bus, pulling away from the city with a feeling of millions of tiny threads tearing. There would be hot coffee and icy sandwiches, dusty sunlight and the bus's wheezing gears, signs saying West. Freeways and eventually prairies; soft, giant sunsets. Intercut with this footage, flashes of Larry coming home, seeing they'd gone, raging, gradually realizing his helplessness. But the fantasies that began this way always morphed into a version in which, by the end of the journey, Joanna had disappeared and Abigail got down from the bus in a strange city alone. When she imagined this, the feeling was of waking from a dream, as if her mother had never been with her on the bus at all and she'd made the entire trip by herself.

———

One evening she came home from the river and heard her mother and Larry talking in the kitchen. They hadn't heard her come in.

"This is going to be something fucked up," Joanna said. "Otherwise why the big money?"

"It's not going to be anything fucked up," Larry said. "I told you: This is a solid guy. I *know* this guy." His voice sounded different. Softer. Full of gentle reasonableness. "Plus, he's not dumb. He knows *me*."

"I really don't feel like it, baby. Really."

There was a pause. Abigail stood perfectly still.

"Look," Larry said. "Just go to dinner. He wants to take you to dinner. If you get the wrong vibe, just get up and walk out of there, no sweat. Absolutely no sweat."

"I just . . . Why do you want me to do this?"

"I don't want you to do anything you don't want to do, Christ, you know that. But I'm in a cash-flow jam right now. I'm in a tight spot and this would really help me out. It'll help *us* out. This guy is *loaded*."

Another pause. Then the sound of a chair moving slightly and the creak of Larry's leather jacket. Abigail heard her mother sigh. Abigail could picture Larry with his hands resting on her mother's hips. He had a habit of doing that, then sliding his right hand up and gently squeezing the back of her neck in a soft massaging movement that always made Joanna close her eyes and let her whole body go loose.

"The kid's gonna need new stuff when school starts next month," he said. "You said yourself you're sick of her walking around looking like a goddamned homeless person. I mean I'm doing what I can here, but . . . You know?"

"I thought you said you were working on a deal?"

"I am, but it takes time. And money. I got two more mouths to feed, after all. Say you'll do it."

"Jesus," Joanna said. Then sighed again. "Dinner first. And if anything feels wrong—"

"You don't like it, you walk. I'll be close by, I promise."

Abigail tiptoed back to the front door. Opened it and closed it, loudly, as if she'd just come in.

She hadn't realized how glad she'd been that her mother had stopped fucking men for money. The relief had been eclipsed by her loathing of Larry, whom her mother was fucking not for money but because she was afraid of him—which was worse. But when Abigail saw Joanna getting ready to go out one evening a few days later and understood that the date of the arranged dinner had arrived, all the desolation of her childhood came back, and with it, this time, a fresh ache for her mother and, weirdly, a disgust with herself.

"Don't do it," she said.

Joanna was getting ready in front of the mirror. She was wearing a white halter-neck dress and her hair was pinned up, with two artful long blond curls dangling down each cheek. "I don't know what you're talking about," she said.

"Don't do it," Abigail repeated. "You don't have to do this anymore."

Silence.

"Mom?"

"Leave me alone, will you, for Christ's sake. You have no idea."

"No idea of what?"

"Of what I do for you."

For a moment this silenced Abigail. She was standing behind Joanna, who was struggling with the clasp of her silver neck chain.

"I don't know why you didn't just have an abortion," Abigail said. "Think of all the shitty stuff you wouldn't have to do for me."

The room tightened. She'd never said anything like that before. The words coming out of her mouth surprised her.

What surprised her more was that Joanna hit her. A hard blow with the back of her hand as she spun on her heel away from the mirror. The still unfastened silver neck chain went flying across the room. They found themselves facing each other. It had been years since Joanna had hit her. And when she'd done it in the past it hadn't been like this. Smacks on the bottom or the legs, humiliating rather than painful, no more than an offshoot of Joanna's general craziness.

In shock, Abigail stood there, her hand to the side of her face where the blow had struck. Joanna grabbed her by the shoulders and shook her.

"You don't know *anything*," she hissed. "He can put me in fucking jail. Don't you understand?" Tears sprang from her eyes. "He can send me to prison, Abby." Speaking the name "Abby" fractured her. She pulled Abigail tight against her and wrapped her arms around her. "I'm sorry, baby. Oh, God, I'm so sorry."

Abigail held her. Her face was still stinging, as if a hot leaf rested on her cheek. All the feelings jammed: rage; fear; hurt; sadness; disgust. She and her mother hadn't held each other like this in a long time. Abigail had forgotten the warmth, the shape, the smell of her hair. For a couple of seconds even the jammed feelings fell away and she felt only a deep physical peace.

"Hey?" Larry called, coming in the front door and slamming it behind him. "You ready, babe?"


When they'd gone, Abigail paced the apartment. *He can send me to prison.* The phrase repeated itself, gave shape to an understanding that had been vague. Not even vague. Just denied. All those hours she'd spent trawling the city, fantasizing, reading, escaping—doing nothing about what she knew except pretending not to know it. She was disgusted with herself.

All right, she was disgusted with herself—but no more pretending. She had to think what to do.

It was a muggy night and the apartment's air-conditioning was feeble. She would take a quick cold shower and go out. Cold water to wake herself, then the city's spaces to think in.

The bathroom had changed its nature since becoming the arena for her illicit transformations and the pleasure she'd discovered in herself. The dirty fortune of sins was beyond measure now. She knew God was still counting the coins even if she wasn't. This was how God worked. His patience was a kind of cunning, to see how far you'd go. It didn't sadden Him, as her early teachers had said. It satisfied Him, proved He'd been right about you all along. The scale of her deviance frightened her, suddenly, added to by the dizzying feeling of having somehow cheated her mother. *You have no idea of what I do for you.* Was that true? Could everything her mother did . . . ? The thought was vast and terrifying, a weight which, if she accepted it, would suffocate her.

She showered, quickly, in icy water.

She didn't hear Larry come in. One minute she was alone in her room taking clothes from the wardrobe, the next he was in the open doorway. She was wrapped in a pale blue bath towel. Her hair dripped on her bare shoulders. When she turned and saw him, some inner gear shifted in her and she knew. She supposed, now, that she'd known *this* all along, too.

"Get out," she said.

Larry opened his arms and rested his hands, one on either side of the door frame. His leather jacket spread like the wings of a bat.

"That's not going to happen," he said, quietly, with a smile.

All the things she could say rose in her—then dissolved, uselessly.

Larry stepped into the room and closed the door behind him. His smell came in with him: cigarette smoke and aftershave, leather, alcohol on his breath. He used a hair wax that had an odor of concentrated coconut.

"Princess, you and I need to come to an understanding," he said.

Abigail was trembling. The water dripping on her bare shoulders was a torment. Larry leaned back against the closed door. "Let me ask you something," he said. "How do you feel about your mother going to prison and you going into CPS?"

She didn't know what CPS was, but she knew if it was anything good it wouldn't be an option.

"That won't happen," she said. It was nothing. Just a reflex refusal. She had no argument.

"Well, the great thing is," Larry said, "that's *exactly* what'll happen. Do you know your mother's an accessory to murder?"

Abigail's insides lurched at the word "murder." It was a dark presence in the room with them, suddenly.

"I don't believe you," she said.

"I think you do. My guy was there. And will testify. Your mom made some bad friends at Jezebel's. I'm pretty sure you know *that*."

"My mom wouldn't kill anyone. You're lying."

"I didn't say she killed anyone," Larry said. "I said she was an accessory. Do you know what that word means?"

Abigail didn't answer.

"Sure you do. You're a smart kid. Smart and pretty. The problem is," he continued, moving toward her, "you've got no modesty. You're *smug*."

He was right in front of her now. "You need to come down a couple of notches," he said.

"You touch me and I'll—"

Larry grabbed the towel where it was tightened around her chest. His fingers against her flesh were hard and cold. Abigail flung up her hand to try to hit him, but he blocked it and pushed her back onto the bed. In a moment he was sitting astride her, kneeling on her arms. She thrashed under him. His jeans smelled freshly washed. He put his hand around her throat and tightened it. Enough to let her know he could go on tightening it, if he liked. In the middle of her horror, she realized that he had literally never laid a finger on her before.

"Lie still," he said. "I haven't finished talking to you yet. Lie still and I'll let go."

Abigail stopped struggling. Larry eased his grip on her throat. But he left his hand there. Her solitary pleasures in the bathroom massed in her body like a disease she hadn't known she was carrying. She had the clear thought that this was her fault. For enjoying looking like Joanna.

"You say a word to your mother, she goes to jail. You run away, she goes to jail. In fact, princess, there's only one way now Mommy doesn't go to jail, and that's if you start pulling your weight around here and being a little more appreciative of just what I'm doing for you."

"I'll tell," Abigail said.

"Didn't you hear me? If you tell your—"

"I'll tell your boss."

Larry looked at her incredulously. Then he laughed, as if she'd genuinely amused him. "Go ahead," he said. "You think he's going to believe you? Or your mother? Her lifestyle, it's a miracle she isn't *already* in the fucking slammer. And just so we're clear: You tell *anyone*, including my boss, and your mother goes to jail, even if he does believe you. Even"—he laughed again—"if he sends me to jail."

Abigail felt the room pressing around her, in addition to his weight on her. A long time seemed to pass in silence, but for the sounds of their breathing. She turned her head from him and stared at the ceiling. The need to find something to say was a stone in her chest.

"I'll kill you," she said, at last.

Larry slid down slightly, releasing her arms from under his knees. She tried to leave her body. For the briefest moment it seemed she had succeeded. She had a view of herself as if from above, with him crouched over her like a giant beetle.

Then he put his fingers back under the towel and yanked it open. His face warmed, visibly, as the air touched her exposed flesh.

"Yeah," he said. "I'm sure you'll try."

He began undoing his belt. "Meantime I'm going to take charge of your education. Think of it . . ." He laughed as the buckle tinkled and his cock sprang out. ". . . as homeschooling."

Abigail had only ever had one recurring nightmare. There were several versions, but the central element was always the same: She had killed someone. Sometimes by accident, sometimes on purpose. The lead-up in the dream didn't really matter. What mattered was that the victim hadn't deserved it. She would wake from this nightmare and for the first few seconds not know it was a dream. In those first few seconds it was as if the blood was still warm and wet on her hands. She would lie there in silent horror, knowing that she had done something—the *worst* thing—and it could never, ever be undone. The stain on her soul was indelible. She was damned.

Then, as the moments passed and she realized it was a dream, that she *hadn't* killed anyone, the relief was such joy it brought tears to her eyes. She would lie there filled with extraordinary tender happiness, repeating to herself that it was *just a dream . . . It was just a dream . . .* The feeling was so good it was almost worth the horror she had to pass through to get it.

After the first time with Larry she had only the horror. It wasn't a dream. The relief couldn't come. The stain was indelible. She had done something that could never, ever be undone.

Except she hadn't done it.

It had been done to her.

From then on her life reduced to a single imperative: Stay out of his way. There was no end to the contortions she produced to keep herself out of the apartment. For a while Larry seemed to accept that it was a game between them. Seemed to relish it, even, as if the rarity of getting her alone increased his pleasure when he did. But soon enough the novelty of cat-and-mouse wore off for him.

He showed up at her school, leaning against the side of his car, grinning.

"Fuck off."

"Get in the car, princess. You know how this goes."

She did know. No matter how many times she went over it in her head, the logic didn't change. She couldn't tell and she couldn't leave. The only option was to get herself and her mother away. *Far* away. And Joanna wouldn't risk it.

"Jesus, why *not*?" Abigail asked her, when the nightmare had been going on for six months.

"I've told you," Joanna said. "You don't know what he's like. He'll find us."

"Mom, this is a big country. We could go . . . I don't know. We could go anywhere."

"He's a *cop*, for God's sake. You don't think a cop could find us?"

"Not in *Alaska*. Or Mexico. What's to stop us going to—"

"Oh, yeah, sure, I didn't think of that. We don't have any money. Or did I miss you winning the goddamned lottery?"

The just-this-one-time trick had, of course, become Joanna's regular obligation. Larry handled the money, of which neither Joanna nor Abigail saw a cent, short of minimal disbursements to keep them alive. The only concession (to Joanna) was that Larry kept the drugs coming.

"If I get money, will you go?"

"Oh, *God*," Joanna moaned. "Just leave it, will you? I don't understand why this is such a fucking crucifixion for you. I mean for Christ's sake. What do you want? What do you *want* from me?"

Abigail adopted a new strategy with Larry—of complete deadness when he raped her. Struggling had in any case proved useless. Instead she learned pages of biology or geography by rote, and forced herself to repeat them, mentally, word for word, while he did what he did. The new frozen passivity gave her something, though she couldn't say precisely what. He didn't like it.

"Fuck is wrong with you?" he said, the third time he found her inert in his hands.

She didn't answer. He hadn't yet hit her in any way that would leave marks.

"Hey," he said, shaking her. "You think this is going to make a difference?"

Abigail stared at the ceiling. "'Plants and various other groups of photosynthetic eukaryotes collectively known as "algae" have unique organelles known as chloroplasts,'" she said.

"What the fuck are you talking about?"

"'Chloroplasts are thought to be descended from cyanobacteria that formed endosymbiotic relationships with ancient plant and algal ancestors.'"

For a few moments he didn't respond. Then she felt him understanding that she hadn't lost her mind but was doing this for herself. He laughed.

"I get it," he said. "That's a neat trick, princess. Let's see if you can keep it up." He grabbed her by the hair and yanked it, tugging her shoulder so that she was twisted over onto her belly. She felt him spreading her legs with his knees.

"I've been saving this for a special occasion," he said. "And I'm damned if this isn't it. Ready? Here we go . . ."

One afternoon at school she had cramps so bad she could barely walk. She didn't tell anyone. Just got up and left. All the way home pain came and went. There were moments when she stood still, eyes closed, teeth gritted, riding it out.

When she made it home, Larry's car was outside the apartment. She sat down on a nearby stoop, wrapped her arms around her shins, leaned her head on her knees. Watched and waited. The pain embraced and released her like a demon that couldn't make up its mind. All she wanted was to get in, take some of her mother's painkillers, and sit in a hot bath.

After more than an hour, Larry came out carrying a crumpled-up plastic bag. He got in the car and took off. Abigail pulled herself to her feet and hobbled across the street. In the sunlight after the stoop's shadow she felt herself shivering. She hadn't realized she was cold.

"Mom?" she called. No answer. But when she pushed the bathroom door she discovered Joanna fully dressed, slumped on the floor as if she were taking a nap. Abigail shook her.

As soon as her mother's eyes opened, Abigail knew this was a different drug.

"Oh . . . Hey, sweetie," Joanna said, smiling. Her speech was soft-edged, struggling back through a veil of bliss.

"Mom, what . . . ?"

Joanna's eyes closed again, though the smile remained.

"Mom!" Abigail bellowed, shaking her again. "What did you take? Jesus Christ, get up. Get *up*."

"No need," Joanna whispered. "I'm fine. I'm resting."

Abigail scanned the bathroom for needles. Checked the trash. Nothing. Except of course what could have been in Larry's plastic bag. She got Joanna up and onto the couch—then doubled up at a fresh assault from the cramps. She sank to her knees, rested her head on the couch, breathing carefully. Joanna put her hand in her hair and made a slight massaging movement with her fingers.

"It's so nice you're here," Joanna whispered. "We don't do this often enough. I love you so much . . ."

Abigail stayed where she was. There seemed no absurdity in it. For a while the hopelessness itself was a kind of obliterating peace.

Eventually, when she could stand again, she got up, took some Advil, then curled up next to Joanna on the couch.


There was no reasoning she disallowed. One night on the bridge over the Schuylkill, with a full moon silvering the slow-moving water, she found herself considering calling his bluff. She would either leave or go to the authorities. Not the cops, obviously, but to CPS, which she now knew stood for Child Protective Services. Suppose the bluff failed and he got her mother convicted? Okay, Joanna would go to prison. Abigail found herself trying to make room for that in herself: the girl who got her mother locked up. Maybe it was the one thing that would fix Joanna? The other drug was the only drug, lately. Abigail could actually see that people would understand. Some people would applaud. It wasn't, if you took the feeling of betrayal away, the wrong thing to do. Intellectually she knew it was possibly the right thing to do. The problem was she couldn't take the feeling of betrayal away. It was an impossible subtraction. No amount of intellectual honesty could shift the belief that Joanna simply wouldn't survive in prison. And in any case, prison for how long? It could be years. How long would she, Abigail, last in a place like that? Days? Weeks? Definitely not years.

She couldn't do it. She went over it so many times it was worn smooth in her mind—but always the same end point: She couldn't do it.

Which left killing Larry.

Another mental object worn smooth. She didn't doubt she could do that—only that she could get away with it. The months had gone by and she hadn't done it. Not least because Larry knew she was capable of it and exercised an uncanny vigilance. He was scrupulous with his gun, for a start. When he wasn't wearing it he kept it in a home safe in his closet. Nights he was home and sleeping with Joanna, he locked the bedroom door. Even wasted, apparently, he kept half an eye open. I wouldn't try that, sweetheart, he'd said once, when Abigail had crept in from the kitchen carrying a knife. He and Joanna were on the couch, Joanna passed out with her head in his lap. Abigail had assumed, from his closed eyes and slack mouth, that he was in the same state. Not so. Gonna have to do better than that, he'd said, then winked at her.

The breeze lifted her hair. She looked down at the water, and for the first time (this was a shock to her, that it was the first time) thought of killing herself.

It was an exciting prospect. She was a month from turning sixteen. She let the idea in, enjoyed it, imagined soft darkness covering her like an angel, a whispered shshsh . . . then the peace of nothingness.

But she couldn't hold it. Rage got in the way. She would be gone but Larry would still be alive, and her mother's situation would only get worse. It was impossible.


She got back to the apartment late, to find Joanna in a state. She was half-dressed, and had applied all her makeup except lipstick. It made her mouth look cruel. The place was a mess, drawers open, cupboards turned out.

"I can't find my purse," Joanna said. She was shaking.

"You're strung out," Abigail said.

"How can I not find my purse? Jesus Christ, it was right there on the couch."

"Sit down," Abigail said. "I'll look for it."

Joanna ignored her, carried on rummaging frantically. She had on a black T-shirt and a denim jacket. Panties and unmatching ankle socks. There was a plum-colored bruise on her left thigh.

"Where is he?" Abigail asked.

"He had to go to Jersey. Fuck. *Fuck.*" She stopped and looked at Abigail, glassily. Her face was moist. "Did you take it?" she asked.

"What?"

*"You took my purse."*

"Mom, for God's sake—"

"You took my fucking purse."

Joanna went to Abigail's room. Abigail followed her. Joanna was on the floor, looking under the bed.

"Mom, stop for a second, will you?"

"Why do you do this? Why do you do this to me?" Joanna got to her feet and pulled back the comforter. Nothing. She stood there, trembling, mouth open.

Abigail went to the kitchen and unhooked her mother's purse from where it was hanging by its strap on the edge of the door.

"Here," she said, tossing it on the bed.

Joanna snatched it up, hunted, found a twenty-dollar bill. Her face thrilled.

"You know about it, don't you?" Abigail said.

It was the strangest thing. She hadn't thought she was going to say that. The words were out before she could stop them. *You know about it.*

There was only a split-second fracture in Joanna's eyes—but in that split second the world shifted for Abigail. It wasn't, she understood, that Joanna did know. It was that even if she knew, it might not be enough to make a difference.

Something between them, the invisible umbilicus that had always been there in spite of everything, snapped, silently. For the first time in her life, Abigail realized she was absolutely alone.

She thought of her mother being dead. And realized without horror or even surprise that it would open the door to something, a dark space in which, because she would care about nothing, anything would become possible. She tried, immediately, to unthink the thought—but it was too late. She felt old, suddenly.

"What?" Joanna said. The split-second fracture was gone. Now she was back in the flow of urgency, clutching the purse and the twenty, moving toward the door.

Abigail felt the thought forming and knew there was nothing she could do to stop it.

*I hate you.*

It was pure and clean. The stale air she'd been breathing her whole life was replaced, suddenly, by a cold, fresh alternative. She felt empty and light-headed.

"Nothing," she said, as her mother pushed past her.

———

Abigail woke to the sound of the phone ringing. Either from exhaustion or from the aftershock of the truth, she'd slept long and without dreams. The light and the sounds of Grape Street said the day had been up and running for hours. Her body was sweetly rested and alert. She got up.

As she entered the living room, the answering machine picked up the call. It was Larry.

"Joanna, for Christ's sake where are you? I'm still in Jersey, but I'll be back around four. I got a big job for you tonight, so get your shit together."

He hung up.

Joanna's bedroom door was half-open. Abigail could see her mother's bare leg outside the covers.

She went to the kitchen and drank a glass of water. Then refilled the glass and took it to Joanna's room.

Her mother's face was turned away from her, the thick blond hair half covering it. She was still wearing last night's T-shirt and denim jacket.

"Mom?"

Joanna didn't stir. Abigail sat down on the edge of the bed and set the glass of water on the nightstand. Outside in the street below, someone went past on a skateboard.

"Mom, wake up."

She put her hand on her mother's knee to give her a shake.

And the moment she touched the flesh she knew Joanna was dead.

It wasn't just the coldness of the skin. It was that the sound of her own breathing caught up with her, suddenly, the loud absence of any other breathing.

The room had known. The whole apartment had known, while she'd been sleeping, with the day growing bright and warm outside.

She moved Joanna's hair off her face. There was a small brownish stain next to her open mouth. Abigail pulled the comforter back. An empty syringe and a length of thin rubber tubing on the mattress. These objects were witnesses, too, bright and distinct with what they'd seen.

Abigail sat very still, knowing nothing except that last night she'd thought about her mother being dead and now here was her mother, dead.

*I hate you.*

In the street outside, the rear door of a delivery truck opened up with a soft roar. Abigail imagined the driver climbing in the back with his clipboard, looking for the right package. And the person the package was for coming to the door, signing for it, taking it inside, opening it. Maybe it was something they'd mail-ordered, or maybe it was a nice surprise.

She thought of her mother saying: I love you so much.

For a long time she drifted into this, knowing nothing.

But eventually she came back. She heard the delivery van start up and drive away and somewhere else a police siren whooped, once, as if asking a question.

She imagined herself returning to this room, to her mother, to everything that was real. But somehow in the meantime there was this unreal time to be got through. She thought of calling an ambulance, imagined herself answering questions, watching while the medics loaded Joanna onto a gurney and wheeled her out the door. Things would follow from that, the authorities, something would be done with her. Vaguely, she accepted that at some point these things would happen—and yet she couldn't accept that they would happen right now. Picking up the phone was not in her power. Every atom of her failed at the thought.

She looked at the clock. 3:22 P.M.

*I'll be home around four.*

If she went away and came back later this might turn out not to be real at all. She knew this was impossible and that she had to give it a chance to be possible.


It was a Friday and the city was winding down, people leaving their offices early. She could feel the mood of tired celebration even in the thickening traffic. She walked without knowing where she was going, though it was a gentle necessity to keep moving. Some instinct said that if she walked long enough she would eventually arrive at the next thing to do. She hadn't eaten since yesterday morning, and now her hunger was like a friend keeping her company. Her face throbbed in the warm air.

She found herself outside their old house in Harrowgate. A pretty black woman in a sundress of tiny red and white flowers was watering some potted plants on the side porch. All the woodwork had been repainted in a pale blue that made her think of a rare bird's egg. She thought how strange houses were, that people came and lived in them and had all their conversations and meals and dreams—and then moved out to go somewhere else and some other people moved in. Houses were helpless things, being invaded and abandoned. They must have a kind of wisdom, she thought, though they could do nothing with it.

Zeke was outside his apartment building, tinkering under the hood of his car. Abigail would have thought she'd forgotten where he lived, yet when she saw him it felt inevitable. He looked exactly as she remembered, still with the maroon suede jacket and white shirt and black Levi's. His face had the same smooth calm, like a wood carving. For a moment he didn't see her. She stood on the sidewalk watching him doing whatever he was doing to the engine.

Then he looked up and noticed her. He didn't recognize her immediately— then he did, and smiled.

"Holy moly," he said. "Look at you, all grown up."

Abigail didn't answer. Something was happening.

"Your momma still sleeping with the enemy?" he said.

She was thinking of herself masturbating in the bathroom, wearing her mother's makeup and shoes. Larry had said to her, once: *You won't ever wash clean, princess.* Don't waste the soap and water.

"Hey," Zeke said, straightening up. "You spaced out, kiddo?" With a kind of reflex, he looked up and down the block. Then back at her.

"I need some money," Abigail said.

Zeke laughed. "Who doesn't?" he said. "You got a direct approach, I'll give you that."

"Can you loan me fifty dollars?"

"Can I loan you . . . ?" He laughed again. "Holy shit, girl."

"I'll pay you back."

Zeke just stood there, smiling and shaking his head, as if his disbelief were a delight to him.

"I'll pay you back," Abigail repeated. "I swear."

Zeke put his hands on his hips. "You are sensational," he said. "How old are you now?"

"Eighteen," Abigail lied. She didn't know why she lied, only that she had to.

Zeke, still smiling, turned back to the engine, made a final adjustment, then unlatched the hood, lowered it, let it drop.

"I'll tell you something," he said. "I believe you. Even as a kid you were a serious little soul. If I loaned you fifty bucks I'm pretty certain you'd pay me back." He leaned against the car, took out a cigarette, and lit it. The daylight had gone while they'd been talking. Abigail was seeing Larry standing over the bed. Her mother just as she'd left her. Somehow, with the lighting of Zeke's cigarette, she knew she wouldn't go back to the apartment. The chance she'd given it to be a dream was over. The street and the world beyond it gathered its reality, hard and clear and beyond any argument.

"Trouble is," Zeke said, blowing out smoke through his nostrils, "I won't be here to collect. I'm leaving."

"Where are you going?"

"Sin City."

She didn't understand. He grinned.

"Las Vegas, sweet pea. Entertainment capital of the world." He put his hands together as if in prayer. "Where a fool and his money are easily parted, forever and ever amen."

In Manayunk, Larry would be doing things. Whatever things it would take to make none of it cling to him. She could sense the mass of his lies like a rapidly growing organism only a couple of miles away. You won't ever wash clean, princess. The girl who'd killed her mother by hating her.

That wasn't true.

But its truth was in her anyway. It gave her what she'd been waiting for.

"Take me with you," she said.

Prostitution was something to her, a kind of homecoming. She hadn't known she was looking for a life to give shape to her rejection of life, but when she began it was like slipping into a set of dirty clothes that had been waiting for her to come and claim them. It helped her perfect the art of never quite seeing herself. Her consciousness remained otherwise occupied, though she couldn't have said what occupied it, except superficially: a movie; a great vanilla shake; banter with the croupiers; looking good in a new dress; room service on a client's tab. She gave herself a working name: Sophia. People didn't expect a blonde to be called Sophia, for some reason. It added a curiously valuable frisson.

For nine months she worked the Strip, the casinos, for Zeke, who, after the first time, didn't touch her. He fucked her once, experimentally, to see what being her mother's daughter had made of her. Didn't like the result. She knew he was a little afraid of her.

Eventually she shed him. Got a fake ID and started working for an agency. She was good. Most tricks, she knew within a minute what she was looking at. Men either hated women or worshiped them and hated themselves for it. Either way, hatred was the currency. She had a numb curiosity about it. A man might start as a worshiper—*oh, baby, you're so sweet, you're a fucking angel, how can you be such an angel?*—but she generally knew ahead of time if he was one for whom the worship would segue into hatred—*that's right, move your ass, bitch, show me what a filthy little cunt you are.* She wasn't infallible: More than once she misjudged a trick and ended up taking a beating, one of which left her with a concussion and a lost molar, another in which she narrowly escaped a knife—but she forced her instincts to improve by giving them no alternative. If she got the wrong vibe, she walked. Very soon she had all of them, *men*, calibrated. Some vaguely functioning analytical part of her said she ought to relish the genuine masochists, but she found them frustrating. There was one guy, for example, who paid her five hundred to whip him until he was bleeding, then piss in his wounds while he jerked himself off. Her curiosity, initially engaged, was derailed by the absurdity of him having to get in the bathtub because he was worried about the hotel room carpet. These slapstick accents took her back to herself. Comedy towed the larger world and life's generosity back in—and it was the larger world and life's generosity that she didn't want.

She got to the end of a good year. Almost subconsciously for months she'd been creating order for herself based on a very simple logic: The better she was at what she did, the more in demand she would be, and the more in demand she was, the more she could charge. The more she could charge, the more money she had, and the more money she had, the more she could control her life. If anyone had asked her, she would never have admitted to a need to control her life. In fact she would have said the opposite, that she lived to see where life would take her. Yet by the time she turned eighteen (twenty-two as far as the agency was concerned), she had a rental apartment in North Cheyenne, a tiny battered Honda, regular health checks, and a list of clients for whom no one but "Sophia" would do. She moved through her time as if it were a bridge collapsing behind her with every step she took. She lived as if there were nothing to look back at.

But in the spring of her second improving year, something in her changed. It was as if life had lulled her into accepting it could get better, seduced her into a dream of expectation, a fantasy of hope. It was as if life had been on the verge of making a fool of her—and she'd spotted the ruse just in time.

She started doing coke. She'd always drunk, and occasionally shared a joint with some of the other girls, but hitherto she'd stayed out of Class A. Couldn't afford the compromised judgment. Risk assessment depended on clarity. Then one night, when a client had chopped a half-dozen lines and invited her to join him, she did. No premeditation—just a reflex kicking in. The drug gave her a sense of hurrying with delight toward something that would change her forever, like rushing through driving snow, happy and magically impervious to the cold.

Naturally it ate into her money—and her professional competence. The good second year eroded into blurred decisions and bleak comedowns. She lost first the apartment, then the car. Moved into a rented one-room. There was a satisfying soft flow to it, like a receding tide she'd been waiting for.

As with Joanna, her looks endured. She was a lithe, striking creature. A current of glamor crackled in the green eyes and fabulous blond hair. One customer said to her: You've got the most exquisitely formed hands and feet of any woman I've ever seen.

But her arms ached, putting on her makeup. She got a urinary infection. In the clinic waiting room the fluorescents' buzz was deafening. When she vomited there was no one to hold her head, as she had her mother's. And all the while the Vegas neons and bleached afternoon skies offered her a bright, flat endorsement, as if they were happy she'd come back into her correct alignment, her proper mode.

She went with sleepy deliberation further away from herself. When she wasn't working, she wandered the malls or drank tequila in the casinos, where there were neither windows nor clocks and time dissolved in the coin-gobbling slots and the subdued jabber of the tables. Any noise was preferable to silence.

Joanna's ghost wasn't with her, but as the weeks and months passed, Abigail had a sense of her mother somewhere not far off, as if each of them inhabited different rooms in the same big civic building.

"Hey, angel, buy you a drink?"

She'd sensed the approach from her left. She was at a joyless bar of black and red vinyl, walls plastered with music posters, on the north side of the Luxor. Her dealer had called ten minutes ago, postponing till midnight. Four hours. Time bristled and fizzed ahead of her. Her rule was agency work only. She turned.

Dark hair, blue eyes, tall, well dressed. Coyote-handsome, comfortable in his own charm.

"No thanks."

"Come on, that glass is just melting ice."

"I'm waiting for someone."

The word "waiting" hurt, stretched the four hours to a vanishing point, an empty desert road. She realized her need was visible, tried to gather and tighten her atoms.

"No problem," he said. "I'll leave you to it. But thanks for bringing a splash of beauty to an otherwise lousy day."

He moved back to his stool at the end of the bar. Ordered a screwdriver and salted peanuts. Turned his face up to the wall-mounted TV and began to watch the soccer game with a pleasant smile of benevolent superiority.

On her way out a few minutes later, he said: "If you've been let down, I can offer you more than a drink. No pressure. Just saying."

His name was Karl, and his Audi was in the Luxor's lot. As soon as she got in, he gave her a hit from a little silver tin and snort spoon. "It's not altruism," he said. "It's just more fun with company."

All the way from the bar she'd kept up an inner mantra: It's okay, it's cool, you're all right . . . but after the coke's first glittering lift it faltered, and she relaxed into the Audi's dark embrace, the pixels of her spirit vivified.

His house in The Lakes was a sub–Frank Lloyd Wright structure of flat roofs and white walls, cut, it seemed, into the side of a slight hill. Inside, glass and steel and big, lonely looking furniture. Native American art. Copper pans hanging from the kitchen's suspended rails. Granite patio and kidney-shaped pool out back, a garden of cactus and dark cypress trees.

He put on music, saying: "Don't ask me what any of this shit is. My nephew just sends it to me. He's cool, so I play it."

Champagne and more coke. He said: "So do you want a simple barter system, or do you want to pay me for the coke when I give you the cash?"

It halted her for a moment, though she was in the middle of laughing at something, at nothing.

He studied her, straight-faced, earnest—then burst out laughing himself.

"You should see your face," he said. "Jesus, I'm *kidding*. You've been spending too much time with assholes, obviously. Marching powder's on the house, angel. Wait here."

When he returned, he handed her five crisp hundreds. "Okay?" he said.

"Okay."

She felt good, better than she had in a long time. Something dragged at her, a killjoy spirit, but she shrugged it off.

While he took a shower, she swam naked in the pool. The water was soft and cool under the warm desert night. She floated on her back and looked up at the stars.

Afterward he made her lie in the sun lounger and gave her a long, slow foot massage with scented oil. It wasn't news to her. Worship was just another thing. She ought, she knew, to be adopting the tone and demeanor of a haughty and spoiled princess (it was what he was angling for) but the coke got in the way. They talked. He used to be in the music business, now didn't do anything much, didn't need to. Restlessness, he said, was a problem.

In the spotless bedroom she lay facedown on crisp white sheets that smelled freshly laundered. The massage and the talk continued, as he eased his fingers around her shoulder blades, up and down either side of her spine. It was impossible for her to let go completely. Caution was a small, permanently glowing red light, like the standby indicator on a TV, but she was as relaxed as she had ever been with a client. His kisses had returned repeatedly to her feet and anus. It was a slight weariness to her that in all likelihood she would soon have to inhabit some version of the dominatrix role, say the things, express the controlled contempt with conviction—crucially without laughing, despite the coke's continual good-natured prompting.

"Feel like a princess?" he asked.

"Yes."

"Good."

He grabbed her by her hair and yanked her head back so hard it almost snapped her neck.

———

At some point she passed out.

Flashes came in the darkness. She smelled the night. Then the Audi's pine air freshener and cold leather.

She vomited. Went back into darkness.

Hit the ground and tasted dust on her tongue.

Joanna's voice said: Well, you wanted me dead, didn't you?

When she woke it was to the smell of antiseptic. A white ceiling and the hum of technology. Hospital.

She turned her head.

A guy she'd never seen before sat with his chin on his chest in the chair next to her bed. His dark hair was tousled and there was faint stubble on what looked as if it would at all other times be a meticulously clean-shaven chin. Boyish and slim. Twenty-five or thereabouts. Long eyelashes. White shirt and black pants. City shoes.

She opened her mouth and tried to speak, but only air came out. She cleared her throat—and immediately her body fired up in a protest of pain.

He opened his eyes.

"You're awake," he said. "Hold on, I'll get someone."

He got to his feet and went out. His black jacket hung on the back of the chair. She was in a room by herself. Windowless. There was a drip attached to her left wrist and a weight on her chest which she discovered was her right arm, in a sling and plaster.

When he returned a few moments later it was with a doctor, a tall, freckled woman with a froth of dark curly hair pulled back in a ponytail.

"I'm Dr. Manion," the woman said, taking hold of Abigail's wrist and checking her pulse. "You're at the Valley Hospital Medical Center. Can you tell me your name?"

Abigail swallowed—and winced. Her throat ached.

"Wait a second," Dr. Manion said. She took a cup with a straw from the table by the bed and gently raised Abigail's head. "Here. Drink some water."

Abigail drank. It was one of the sweetest physical sensations she'd ever experienced. Can you tell me your name? The familiar anxiety massed. She'd spent so long avoiding or scamming officialdom it was as if she'd been asked for an incriminating secret. Sophia? Abigail? Abigail wasn't even her first name. It was her middle name (after her grandmother) but it was what Joanna had always called her. It seemed extraordinary, suddenly. Her given first name was like a ghost that walked ahead of her, ignored except for the occasional form-filling or school report. The name on her fake ID was Samantha Holmes, but her ID was in her purse and she doubted she'd made it out of the house with that. She had a memory of Karl buttoning her bloodstained shirt and jamming her shoes onto her feet. Through the pain it had felt like a brutal version of her infancy, being dressed for kindergarten hurriedly by her grandmother.

"Samantha Holmes," she said. She needed to sound alert, capable, well enough to get out of here. She had no medical insurance. As the doctor dropped her wrist, Abigail thought of the hundreds—probably thousands—of dollars she must have already racked up. The meter was running even now, just by her lying in this bed. She had to get out.

"I'm fine," she said. "I need to get home."

"Please don't worry about anything," the guy said, as if he'd read her mind. "It's taken care of."

"You're not fine," Dr. Manion said, albeit with a slight impatience, the suggestion that there were other (legitimate) people she should be attending, people far less fine than Abigail. "You have three broken ribs and a broken ulna. It's a miracle your spleen isn't ruptured. Do you want to tell me what happened?"

"Car hit me," she said.

Dr. Manion looked at her, shook her head. Too tired to bother exposing the fiction. She'd seen it all before.

"For future reference," she said, "large amounts of cocaine and alcohol get your liver to produce cocaethylene, with which the body has a very good chance of killing itself. Something you might want to consider."

"I need to get home," Abigail repeated.

"That's against my advice," Dr. Manion said. "But we can't keep you here if you want out."

An odd little atmosphere of unsaid things between the three of them. Then the doctor turned on her heel and left.

Abigail was flailing, mentally, trying to reconstruct. She was surprised to be alive. But at the cost, it seemed, of this subtraction of time.

The guy was standing next to her bed. There was a quiet intensity to him. He looked as if he didn't know what to do with his hands.

"Who are you?" she said.


His name was Adam Grant, and it was a curious relationship.

It wasn't going to *be* a relationship, as far as Abigail was concerned.

"I don't understand," she said. He was driving her home from the hospital. She was fuzzy with codeine and disproportionately confused by the fact of her arm in its sling. She had never broken a bone before. Amidst the churning thoughts it was a delicate novelty, an intimate signature of the violence she'd suffered and a terrible, distinct affirmation of her mortality. Adam had tried to talk her into remaining in the hospital, but she had stood there, with her legs' gravity all wrong, saying no, repeatedly. The only thing she wanted was to get out from under the scrutiny of authority, even an authority with her own well-being as its goal. Dr. Manion had made her sign a notice of voluntary discharge against medical advice and told her to ice the ribs regularly. Beyond that it was obvious she regarded Abigail (Sophia, Samantha) as time wasted, a lost cause.

"What's to understand?" he said. "I saw you lying on the side of the road. I stopped. I called an ambulance. It's nothing. It's ordinary."

She couldn't work him out. He seemed happy about something entirely private. She didn't know if it was her intuition or just come-down paranoia.

The sunlit city went by outside the car windows and refused cheerfully to settle into her comprehension. It was as if she'd lost not hours but days, months. She had no apparatus to bring to what he'd done, except that she assumed he found her desirable.

"Is it a walk-up?" he said, when they pulled up outside her dismal apartment building.

"I can manage."

"Don't be crazy," he said. "Let me help you."

She was light-headed, partly from having to shallow-breathe around her ribs. There was no-nonsense pain there if she dropped her guard. The thought of climbing even the four steps of the front stoop made her feel sick. Genuinely nauseated. She opened the passenger door and swung her legs out, but for a moment she could only sit like that, wondering if she was going to vomit on the sidewalk.

He came around the car and squatted down on his haunches in front of her.

"I wish you'd stayed in the hospital," he said. "You're really not well."

The word "hospital" brought back the reality of cost and money. He had paid. He must have paid. It was an awful betrayal to her, as if the ground beneath her feet was no longer solid.

Suddenly, out of this image, she realized that her keys were in the purse that hadn't made it out of Karl's house. She couldn't get into her apartment.

Something extraordinary happened. She found herself in tears.

"What is it? What's the matter?"

She couldn't get a word out. Her apartment was a tiny, bleak, functional thing and at that moment it was all she wanted. To lie down on the bed and hold her ribs and close her eyes. And yet there was a great space behind this simple need that terrified her with a kind of demand. It was as if the world had, without warning, decided to want something from her after all.

The time they spent waiting in the car for the building manager was very difficult for her. Something had caught up with her. She didn't know what, only that she was afraid. Meanwhile he was giantly normal, as if this were the sort of thing that happened every day. She was aware of him not asking her what had really happened, beyond a token inquiry about whether she got a look at the car that had hit her. He seemed utterly unruffled by the obviousness of her lie. He was clerking for a judge in San Francisco, he said, had come to Vegas for a college friend's wedding, was staying on for a week.

In the middle of it she heard herself say: "What do you want?"

"What do you mean?"

Anger kept offering itself to her, impotent in the face of her fear. "Jesus Christ," she said. "What do you want?"

He waited a long time before answering. Whatever aftershave or deodorant he'd been wearing the day before had thinned. Now he smelled of tired skin, hospital coffee on his breath. Aside from his black jacket draped over her shoulders, she was in the stained skirt and blouse of the night before. One of the nurses had discreetly given her a pair of disposable underpants. Her own, like her purse, hadn't made it out of Karl's house. She had an image of Karl sitting naked on the bed, with the bloody underwear hanging from his fingertips. There was a swelling on her left cheekbone where he'd hit her.

"Nothing," Adam said. "Just to make sure you're okay."

"I'm fine," she said. "I can wait on the stoop."

It wasn't the first time she'd said that. But still, here she was. It was frightening to her, that she hadn't been able to get out of the car.


He came to see her every day. She couldn't, obviously, work. Without the codeine she would have been in real trouble. Four days passed without cocaine. It wasn't good, but she was practically broke. He took her to restaurants but she had no appetite. She picked at salads, melon, ice cream. She told him she was a telemarketer. Which was the cover job, a few hours a week, the paltry legitimacy. She knew he knew she was lying. It infuriated her, but always, underneath and far bigger than the anger, was fear.

His family, far back, had made its money in eastern steel. Seven generations later it had become microelectronics. The Grants had followed their money west, had been in California since his grandfather's time. The whole thing was a story to her, as remote from her experience as Snow White or Aladdin. She wondered why he worked, since he didn't have to. He had gone to Berkeley. Law. He was, she thought, sad when he talked about it.

The week passed and he didn't leave.

Very gradually, her strength came back.

One night they had dinner at his hotel and she stayed with him. All her instincts had told her to get rid of him, but she was at the mercy of some other force that made her a stranger to herself. They lay in bed together side by side, holding hands. He hadn't, yet, even kissed her. To her it was like a TV show that didn't make sense but which she couldn't stop watching. She had no intimation of her mother, though she reached for it, mentally. Her past was a shoreline she'd lost sight of. There was just open dark water in every direction. In a spirit of sheer blind experiment, she turned toward him in the bed. He hesitated, then kissed her.

"Be careful," he said, meaning her injuries. The soreness from Karl's abuse had abated, but her tender parts were firmly closed on themselves in determined, self-healing sleep. It occurred to her that she had never had sex with anyone except when she'd been forced or had forced herself, for money. For her that was all sex was. The thought that it could be anything else filled her with hopelessness.

In the small hours she woke to see him standing by the window, looking out through a gap in the curtains at the city's neons.

"What is it?" she said quietly.

It startled him. He came back to bed, didn't touch her. They lay for a while in silence. A gentle panic was in her limbs, as if they were only now coming back to her from their trauma, shocked at their own survival.

"You know what I do, don't you?" she said. The words were out before she'd really known what she was going to say.

"Yeah," he said. "I know."

"And?"

He lay in silence for a few moments, not blinking. To her it seemed as if some long calculation on which his brain had been working was coming to its conclusion.

"And it seems to me you don't want to do it anymore," he said.

# PART
# THREE

# 34

## *September 15, 2017*

"We can stop looking for Dwight Jenner," Will said to Valerie, entering the office with the coroner's report. "DNA confirms it. It's him."

News of the discovered body had come through five days ago from Reno, where it had been sent because none of the three towns—Mina, Luning, and Gabbs—closest to where it had been found had the facilities to deal with it. (Mina, for example, had a population of a whopping 155 souls.) Valerie had plugged Dwight Jenner into NCIS two weeks back, since notwithstanding the APB he was still a missing person, and Reno (God bless their belea-guered diligence) had made the match. Valerie had interviewed Pete Jardine, the poor bastard who'd found the remains, heard the story of the dog, the coyotes—and, redundantly, the sad tale of Pete Jardine's broken marriage and subsequent existential road trip. Finding the body, Valerie thought, had probably done him good. Put his own losses into perspective.

"You're going to want to see the pictures," Will added, dropping the file onto Valerie's desk. "It's wonderful shit."

"Good or bad?" Valerie asked.

"Probably bad," Will said. "I'm going to Ashan's. What do you want?"

"Two chicken tikka samosas. And one of those fancy lemonades."

"Christ, for breakfast?"

She couldn't lay off Indian food. *You may notice cravings for particular foods, or aversion to others, as well as to certain odors.* She'd started skipping Nick's breakfasts at home so she could eat what she really wanted. And she still hadn't told him. She knew she wouldn't get through faking another period. That, in her perverse or outright insane system, was the date she'd set for breaking the news. She'd bought herself just under two weeks. Her conscience wouldn't stand any more than that.

"Don't be so conventional," she said to Will, trying not to look guilty. "Where's your spirit of anarchy?"

"Anarchy's for teenagers. I'm having an egg on a roll with ham and cheese."

She looked down at the file. "This going to gross me out?"

"Not with your constitution. Talk to Rayner and Sadie."

"Why?"

"You'll see."

She didn't, at first, see—but there was plenty to occupy her. Chiefly that the body was missing its hands and feet. They had been amputated (not professionally, according to the coroner) and the amputation sites ravaged by oxygen bleach, royally fucking up the chances of finding lasting DNA from the perp. Cause of death three gunshot wounds: head, abdomen, chest. Toxicology clean. No other signs of physical trauma except for several carefully inscribed linear flesh wounds on the chest, probably (the symmetry implied) a symbol of some kind. Between them, forensic entomology and climatology put time of death at four to six weeks prior to discovery on September 6, and their reports were riddled with caveats courtesy of the desert's geo-bio-peculiarities. There was no conclusive evidence for a primary scene elsewhere, though the entomologist's studies suggested it wasn't, quite, where the body was discovered. Valerie didn't require conclusive evidence to draw her own conclusion: oxygen bleach to cauterize the stumps and wipe out DNA, traces of oxygen bleach found by the lake at the Grants' house in

Campbellville. Dwight Jenner had his hands and feet cut off up there by the water before being driven out to the desert and buried. By whom, for God's sake?

Great. Trade one murder case for another. The upside was she could put Adam Grant (as it were) to bed. How would Rachel take it? Probably the outcome her head wanted: her husband's killer—dead. But her heart wouldn't be satisfied. Her heart would have wanted something more protracted and personal. To see him arrested, mangled through the machinery of Justice, visibly shackled to what he'd done—and *then* ended. Victims' families had the right to be present at executions. Rachel Grant, Valerie thought, was the type who would want to see it all, to savor the desolate pleasure of an eye for an eye. Not only would Rachel have been able to handle it, she would feel short-changed without it. Valerie, of course, would do her best to soften the blow. The moratorium on state executions, thanks to a judicial review and the subsequent legal battle that had been going on for more than ten years, meant that Dwight Jenner wouldn't have been put to death any time soon, probably not for decades and possibly not before he died of natural causes. Would Rachel want that? Death row wasn't, to allow hilarious understatement, any kind of fun, but it was still *life*. You could still eat, talk, read, have a conversation, jerk off, dream. None of which, thanks to Dwight Jenner, was available to Adam Grant. Surely, Valerie would say, it was better to have Jenner gone, regardless of how he'd been done away with? She could picture Rachel's face on the receiving end of this, the fierce green eyes unable to hide her sense of betrayal. Her ideal was probably to have tortured Dwight Jenner to death herself.

So much for the upside.

The downside was that Valerie was going to have to visit Kyle Cornell and tell him that his half brother was dead. *Murdered*.

Sophia was still unaccounted for. They'd located her on X-quisite's CCTV on May 30. A poor shot of her at the entrance booth (still wearing the goddamned shades, though the place was dark enough already) and later at a corner table chatting with Gigi. All you could see was the back of the spectacular blond head. Since then no report that she'd returned or contacted the club for a job. Valerie was pessimistically convinced, courtesy of *The Life of Sophia's* latest episodes, that she'd gone back to L.A., which, unless and until she showed up again on the pole-dancing circuit (assuming the LAPD was giving it *any* attention, which they probably were not) reduced their chances of finding her practically to zero. It hardly seemed credible that the damage done to Dwight Jenner's body was the work of a part-time dancer, but Sophia was still most likely one of the last people to see him alive.

"This mean anything to you?" she asked Sadie Hurst, having walked over to her desk with the photos of Dwight's corpse. Sadie's partner, Rayner Mendelsund, was out on a lead.

"What is it?"

"The Reno body. Well, not Reno. The desert body. Will said you should take a look."

Sadie was the sort of early-thirties woman you might unthinkingly describe as a girl. Milky blond hair and a sharp, blue-eyed face Will had concluded was "weaselly attractive." She had a quiet alertness and self-containment. Valerie was openly envious of her dress sense. Sadie had the knack of using the same staple gear as Valerie—jeans, sweaters, T-shirts, a leather jacket—and somehow making it look both effortlessly hip and as if she couldn't care less.

"Oh," she said, arriving at the photograph of the carefully made knife wounds on Dwight Jenner's chest. "Seriously? Fuck."

"What is it?"

For a moment Sadie sat back in her chair studying the photograph. Then she leaned forward again and placed it on the desk for Valerie to see. "These marks," she said, indicating the wounds. "They're a sigil for Lucifer."

"A what?"

"A sigil. A symbol."

"Lucifer as in the Devil?"

Sadie shrugged. "Depends which lunatic you consult. According to the less obviously mad, Lucifer's an entirely different angel to Satan, a good one, in fact—but that doesn't really matter. What matters here is that you're looking at work I've seen before." She took a pen and tore off a sheet from her yellow legal pad. Reproduced the symbol as if she knew it by heart.

"Three murders seven years ago. Me and Rayner worked the first two. Made an arrest. Suspect went to trial. Halfway through, with this dude still in custody, a third murder, same symbol—which had never been made public. Our guy walked and the Feds took over. As far as I know they never got anyone."

"Could this be your guy?"

"Not unless he's working from the afterlife. He died of pancreatic cancer four years back. So either the MO got out and you've got a copycat, or it's the original perp still rocking in the free world. Who's the victim?"

"Dwight Jenner. The guy who killed Adam Grant. Did the other victims have their hands and feet amputated?"

"No. And they were all female."

"So not quite the MO. How busy are you?"

Sadie smiled. Made a gesture miming tied hands.

"Do you want in?"

"Obviously."

"Well, it might not come to that. If the Bureau's happy it's their guy, fuck it, they can have it. It's on Nevada turf anyway. Jenner killed Adam Grant, and Jenner's history, so technically I'm done."

"You don't look done."

"My looks are deceptive."

Valerie got halfway to her desk before she stopped, turned, and went back to Sadie.

"What was your guy's name? The one who walked."

"Webb . . ." Sadie narrowed her eyes, searching her memory. "Grayson Webb."

"And the trial?"

"Would've been winter of 2000—no, actually it was after New Year's. Early 2001."

Valerie made a note on the same sheet on which Sadie had drawn the symbol. Folded it in half and headed back to her desk.

"I told you you didn't look done," Sadie said.


There were, of course, coincidences. This wasn't one of them. Valerie called the DA's office. The information she got gave her a satisfying flush of confirmed intuition. The state prosecutor on the Grayson Webb trial was Logan Myers, now retired. He had been assisted by Sylvana Bianchi, still in office, and one Adam Douglas Grant, now deceased.

The satisfying flush morphed into a constellation of unjoined dots. Dwight Jenner murders Adam Grant. Okay. Then Dwight Jenner is murdered by someone with a previously established MO (more or less): the symbol or "sigil" (Valerie enjoyed the acquisition of a new word) for "Lucifer." Said MO is central to the trial on which Adam Grant worked. Leaving aside the copycat option (info did leak, but somehow she doubted it in this case), that left the conclusion that the original "Lucifer" was up to his old tricks—with a difference: Dwight Jenner was male, and the MO had now grown to incorporate the amputations. Plus two luminous facts: (1) Jenner was connected to Grant, and (2) Grant was connected to the failed prosecution of the original murders. The notion that there was *no* connection between the two murders was, to put it mildly, a stretch.

Valerie called Vic McLuhan at the Bureau's local office over on Golden Gate Avenue and gave him the story. An hour later he called her back.

"Case is still open," he told her. "But he's been cold since the third victim in early 2001. Well, cold, as in, we haven't found any bodies that fit either the MO or the physical evidence gathered from the first three. Which means either he stopped until now, assuming this latest is him, or he's got better at it and we just haven't found the other victims' remains—or the MO got out and someone's aping his style."

"Could it have got out?"

"Any boat can leak, Val."

"But the timeline's atypical, right? I mean assuming he's just started up again, why the long gap? The pattern should be acceleration."

"We can't assume he *has* just started up. He could have killed plenty in the last sixteen years."

"You're not exactly blowing the Bureau's trumpet here," Valerie said.

Vic laughed. "You know how many unsolved murders we've got that are linked by DNA?"

"No."

"Neither do I, exactly, but it's close to two thousand. And that's based on a sample check ignoring cases where we don't have the luxury of DNA. It's a floor figure, not a ceiling."

"But your guy wants the bodies found, surely? Otherwise why leave the Lucifer signature? You don't write anything unless you want it to be read."

"Yeah, maybe. But you should talk to Profiling. They've got a lot better at not blowing their own trumpet, too. And if you're right about wanting the bodies found, why bury your guy in the middle of nowhere? I take it, obviously, that there's no perp DNA on offer?"

"Not according to Reno."

"That doesn't count for much. We're going to have to send our people over. Either way it doesn't seem it's your problem."

"Well, yeah, but the victim's my doer for the Adam Grant murder. Can you keep me in the loop?"

"Fair enough. We'll see what we'll see."

Valerie hung up and considered her options.

1. Go and tell Rachel Grant that her husband's killer is dead.
2. Go and tell Kyle Cornell that his half brother is dead.
3. Don't tell anyone anyone is dead and go get a massage instead.

Sometimes she gave herself alternatives like this just as a reminder that she was, existentially speaking and contrary to all habits of behavior, *free*. One of these days, she thought, she'd surprise herself. She'd shock the world.

But not today.

She drove over to the Grants' house in Pacific Heights and, having rung the doorbell, prepared herself for the pugnacious nurse. But the door was opened by Hester Fallon, Adam Grant's sister, who was talking on her cell phone as she opened it. She beckoned Valerie into the hall. She looked very tired. She was still in the new world of her brother's death, draining herself to cope with it. The first fatigue was trauma. The second was the persistence of the mundane in spite of trauma. A stubborn, demanding contradiction. It had been six weeks.

"Listen, hon, I have to hang up. Someone's here. Aha . . . Okay . . . I'll let Rachel know. See you soon. Bye." She hung up the call. "Detective?" she said.

"Hi, I was hoping to talk to Rachel."

"She's not here," Hester said. "She took Elspeth out on the boat this morning."

"There's a boat?"

Hester smiled sadly. "Adam was nuts for the water. Ever since we were kids. He bought it when he moved over to Willard and Gould. It's not a *big* boat."

A slight note of apology. As if Hester didn't want anyone thinking her late brother was bothered about *status*. "He'd have been out on it every day, given the choice," she added. She was still, Valerie saw, getting used to talking about Adam Grant in the past tense. She had a pleasant, high-cheekboned face. Almond eyes. Like her brother.

"Is Rachel well enough? The nurse . . . ?"

"The nurse is gone. Rachel decided she didn't need her anymore. I don't know that she should have done that, though I have to confess we were all glad to see the back of her."

"I'm not surprised," Valerie said. "But should Rachel be driving a boat?"

"No, she should *not*. They told her she'd be okay to drive a car by now. They didn't say anything about a goddamned boat. Still, you can't tell her anything. She goes her own way. They should be back at . . ." Hester looked at her watch. "Six. It's just past four now. You're welcome to wait if you like, but I've got a couple more interviews to do."

"Interviews?"

"Housekeeper," Hester said. "I got sick of telling Rachel she can't handle this place by herself, especially given . . . I mean everyone's been trying to pitch in, but she's resisting. In the end I just called the agency. And landed myself the job of weeding out the undesirables. By the end of today I'm going to have three candidates. If she doesn't like any of those I'm giving up. The fact is they should never have got rid of Isabella in the first place."

"Isabella was the former housekeeper?"

"She was a marvel. But Adam didn't get along with her."

"No? How come?"

"Oh, I don't know. I never got to the bottom of it. Some people just rubbed him the wrong way—"

Hester stopped, snapped out of dreaminess, looked at Valerie as if recognizing her for the first time, as if, during the preceding banalities, she had forgotten who Valerie was, why she was here, what had happened. Now it looked as if someone had, via an invisible choke chain, yanked her back to reality.

"What's happened?" Hester asked. "Did you find him?"

"I really need to speak with Rachel first."

"Tell me. For God's sake just please tell me."

Valerie considered. Hester would find out soon enough, and in any case she had a right to know. Fuck it.

"Confidentially," Valerie said. "Understood?"

"Yes. What?"

"The body of a man we believe to be Dwight Jenner has been found."

Pause.

"He's *dead*?"

"Yes."

Hester opened her mouth—then closed it without saying anything. Valerie gave her a moment. Let the information settle.

"Good," Hester said, looking away. "I'm glad he's dead."

She wasn't made of the same psychic stuff as her sister-in-law.

"How did he—"

"Really, I'm sorry. I can't tell you anything more yet. Not until I've spoken with Rachel. The boat . . . Is it a city mooring?"

Having emerged, briefly, from her dream of exhaustion, Hester appeared to have slipped back into it.

"What?" she asked vaguely.

"I'd like to speak to Rachel as soon as possible. Where's the boat kept?"

It took a few moments. Hester knew it was at Pier 39, but had to consult her phone for the details. Mooring E11.

"But they might be on their way back by now," she said, as Valerie headed toward the door.

"It's okay, I'm going to call her. One other thing: Do you have contact details for Isabella? The housekeeper?"

"Isabella . . . ? No, I don't know. It was months ago. Why?"

Yes, Valerie thought. Why? Because Adam Grant's secret life remained unexposed? Because there was no limit to her indiscriminate curiosity? Because it bothered her that there might still be someone who could identify Sophia? Maybe Isabella walked in on Adam photographing his lover, bent over his desk, blindfolded and tied to the bed, bare-assed on the kitchen worktop. *Adam didn't get along with her.* Probably not, if she'd been an eyewitness to his infidelity.

"Nothing important," she said. "We just need all the details of everyone whose name comes up in an investigation, no matter how peripheral. Bureaucracy. You know how these things are."

Hester nodded, though it was obvious her head and heart were elsewhere. Back with the vividly refreshed fact of her brother's death.

"I don't have a number," she said. "I don't even know her surname. But I guess you can call the agency. Hold on a second." She consulted her phone a second time. Gave Valerie the number. Bay Domestic. Market and Dolores.

"Great," Valerie said. "I'll do that."

# 35

Rachel Grant wasn't answering her phone. It was past 5 P.M. by the time Valerie arrived at the marina to discover the boat was still out. But the late afternoon was blue-skied, warm and soft, with a salt breeze coming off the bay, so she bought herself a bottled water and sat down on a bench to wait.

She'd been sitting only five minutes when her phone rang. She didn't recognize the number.

"Valerie Hart."

"Hey, Detective. It's Dan Kruger."

Instant irritation.

"Yes?" she said.

"How's the investigation going?"

She didn't answer straightaway. For no reason other than that she could imagine exactly the sort of conversation Kruger had in mind: bullshit cat-and-mouse, a reiteration of the original threat.

"Incomplete," she said.

"Did you find Sophia?"

"Not yet."

"But you're still looking?"

"Yes."

Pause. She could feel him winding up to something elaborately under-stated.

"Perhaps I didn't make myself clear," he said. "When we spoke a few—"

"Dan," she interrupted, with facetious gentleness. "Do you have any-thing you'd like to add to your earlier remarks? Anything new, I mean? As opposed to some slicker version of the original attempt at intimidation? Be-cause if you don't, I really feel like I can save us both some time."

"Really? And how is that?"

"Well," she said, "it goes like this: Fuck off."

She hung up. Reckless, yes, but irresistible. Every now and then the world of men used to the luxurious exercise of power concentrated itself into a single intolerable individual. When that happened, something essential in her reacted. Let Kruger do what he had to do. She'd deal with it. And if it got her kicked off the case, fine. She'd have her dignity. To say nothing of the pleasure she had at this moment, the image of him staring at his phone in disbelief.

Why, in any case, was Kruger making such a fuss? She hadn't, until now, mistrusted the idea that he wanted to keep Adam's name out of the dirt. But maybe there was more to it? Did *he* know Sophia? Was he involved with her? It seemed ludicrous. Every time this woman's name came up in the investigation it added to the list of guys she might have been fucking. She was either sexually voracious or possessed of some strategy that depended on calculated promiscuity. If she (and Jenner) had been blackmailing Adam Grant, could that somehow have compromised Kruger? Valerie let her mind wander into grander theories: that Sophia specialized in high-profilers, that she'd uncovered malpractice or corruption at Willard & Gould, that there was more at stake than a lawyer's reputation. Was there some fuckup—or cover-up—in the original prosecution of the Lucifer murders?

Reluctantly, she conceded that she was going to have to start looking—carefully—into Dan Kruger. Without him knowing. Great.

Twenty minutes later Rachel appeared, pulling into the dock at the helm of a nifty cabin cruiser, a forty-footer in gleaming white with a pale green trim. Not, as Hester had said, a *big* boat, but big enough, Valerie estimated, to have set Adam Grant back upwards of $300,000. Rachel was wearing a red baseball cap and aviator shades. Elspeth sat in the stern in a white T-shirt and yellow life vest, staring back out at the water. The breeze lifted a single lock of her long dark hair, dropped it again. She looked as if she were gazing into an alternative dimension only she could see.

Valerie watched them tie up, gather up their backpacks, disembark. They didn't exchange a word. She went to the end of the gangway. Rachel saw her, started slightly. Took off her sunglasses as she approached.

"What is it?" she asked Valerie. Then quickly to Elspeth: "Go wait in the car, honey." She went into her purse and brought out the car keys. "Here. Go on."

Elspeth didn't move. She was staring at Valerie. The dark puppet eyes and full lips had a terrible look of blocked life. It occurred to Valerie that she'd never once heard the girl speak.

"Elspeth," Rachel said. "Wait in the car, please."

Elspeth still didn't move. For an awkward moment the three of them stood there, Rachel holding out the keys, Elspeth apparently oblivious to everything except Valerie.

"Actually," Rachel said, going back into her purse and pulling out a twenty-dollar bill, "here. Go get yourself something from the stand. Wait for me on the bench." There was a hot dog and ice cream concession over to their left. "Come on, sweetheart, the detective is waiting to speak to me."

Elspeth turned to her mother, slowly, as if the movement were tearing her from an invisible membrane. She took the twenty and moved away like a sleepwalker. Valerie watched Rachel watching her. Every atom of the woman was charged with anxiety. Elspeth ignored the concession. Instead drifted to one of the benches with her hands hanging loose by her sides, the money clutched. She didn't sit down. Seagulls walked back and forth in front of her on the decking as if in compressed collective outrage at her intrusion.

"What's happened?" Rachel said, turning back to Valerie.

"We found Dwight Jenner."

Rachel didn't answer. The only indication that the news had gone in was that her fingers tightened their grip on her purse.

"You found him?"

"Dead. His body was discovered in Nevada nine days ago. We got confirmation of his identity this morning."

Rachel looked away, out over the glittering water. The disappointment Valerie had imagined wasn't immediately apparent. For a few moments neither of them spoke. Then Rachel said: "I don't understand. How can he . . ." She shook her head, eyes closed. Here, perhaps, *was* the disappointment. It had taken time to filter through.

"He was murdered," Valerie said. "And I'm afraid it looks connected to Adam's death."

"What? How?"

"Back in 2001, Adam worked a prosecution case against a murder suspect, Grayson Webb. Both murders of which Webb was accused carried a distinctive MO—I mean, a distinctive signature, marks left on the victims' bodies. But while Webb was in custody, a third victim, also with the distinctive marks, was found, more or less establishing Webb's innocence. The charges were dismissed, and four years ago Grayson Webb died of cancer." Valerie took the folded sheet of paper from her pocket and opened it. She showed the "Lucifer" sigil to Rachel. "This is the mark found on all three bodies," she said. "The same mark we found on the body of Dwight Jenner."

Rachel stared at the "Lucifer" sigil. Struggling with incomprehension.

"Does it mean anything to you?" Valerie asked her.

"No. Nothing. What is it?"

"It doesn't matter. But it's too much of a coincidence that it's shown up again on the body of Adam's killer. Adam ever discuss the case with you?"

"I don't . . . Adam didn't talk about his work. I don't know what any of this is."

Rachel glanced over to make sure Elspeth was still there. She was. She didn't appear to have moved an inch. Valerie resisted the urge to ask how the kid was doing. And further resisted asking to speak to her.

"Did you find anything out about the woman?" Rachel asked. Her tone changed for this, for Sophia, for her husband's lover. "Is she involved in this, too?"

"We don't have anything on her," Valerie said. "The fact is, we don't know who she is."

"It's not enough," Rachel said. The familiar bitter smile. "It's not enough that he's dead. I wanted . . . I wanted . . ."

"I know," Valerie said. Then amended: "I can imagine." Redundant to trot out the line about Jenner dead being better than Jenner lingering indefinitely on death row. Reasonable, yes, but Rachel wasn't interested in reason.

"And now that's it, I suppose," Rachel said sadly. "Line drawn under. Case closed. Someone's life—gone." She turned her head away again to look out into the bay. "You must be pleased." Delivered with a mix of sarcasm and disinterested understanding.

"I wish we'd gotten to Jenner before someone else did," Valerie said. She left other things unsaid. That they still didn't know why Jenner killed Adam. That Sophia remained a mystery. That there was no explanation for Adam's phone calls to his killer. That the unanswered questions still vastly outnumbered the answered ones. That as far as Valerie was concerned the murder of Adam Grant was just one bloody corner of a much bigger—and bloodier—picture.

"It was my fault," Elspeth said.

Both women started. Rachel spun around. They hadn't heard the girl approach. She stood there still holding the twenty-dollar bill. Still, apparently, seeing the other dimension.

"Elspeth, for God's *sake,*" Rachel said. "I told you to wait." She put her arm around her daughter, shook her slightly. "Jesus *Christ.*" Rachel turned to Valerie. "I need to get her home," she said. "This is— We can't. It's enough. It's *enough.*"

Without another word she turned and hurried Elspeth away.

Valerie watched them go, Rachel clutching Elspeth as if afraid the girl might bolt.

*It's my fault.*

You don't look done, Sadie had said earlier that day. At the time, with the Lucifer killing fresh to the equation, Valerie had admitted to herself a wretched burgeoning interest in the serial case it reopened.

But she'd been wrong.

Never mind the serial case.

She wasn't done with this one yet.

# 36

"The truth is I've been worried about that girl for a while now," Dina Klein told Valerie. "And not just about her. Julia's impressionable. I mean, don't get me wrong: Elspeth's super-smart. She's a sweetheart. But then all this craziness started and I was worried some of it would rub off."

From the marina, Valerie had driven over to see the Kleins in Presidio Heights, where Elspeth had been for a sleepover with her friend Julia on the night of Adam Grant's murder. The grand house on Cherry Street couldn't have been further from the Grants' in style—classic 1930s Mediterranean Revival—but it wouldn't be much lower down the price chain. The sitting room into which she'd been shown (by a cheerful young Eastern European maid) had a dark walnut floor, double-height ceiling, plenty of paintings, and a curved teal suede couch that could have seated eight. But for all that, the feel of the place was comfortably lived-in.

Dina Klein was early forties, tall and tan, with no-nonsense breasts and hips around which all the weight that could conceivably be gym'd and dieted away had been. Wildly highlighted light brown hair pinned up haphazardly, a face that said intelligence, humor, and an ironic approach to life. She'd lost the weight, Valerie thought, but with an eye roll and a shrug, knowing it would probably come back, and if it did she might not bother to lose it again. She and her husband, Marty, had started one of the world's first wedding websites in the mid-nineties (when, incredibly, such things barely existed) and had sold it less than ten years ago for a sum that catapulted them into the good life. They'd both since been headhunted by Google, where Marty was now, according to Dina, doing blue-sky research just for fun. She, on the other hand, had used the financial security to give something back, and now worked pro bono on web content for various nonprofits.

Marty wasn't home. Julia was upstairs in her room. It was her Valerie really wanted to interview, but she needed the mother on board first. She hadn't mentioned Elspeth's suicide attempt, and from Dina's tone it was obvious she hadn't heard about it.

"Could you be a little more specific?" she asked Dina.

"I'm assuming you've had all this from Rachel?"

"Yes," Valerie lied. "But I'd like a perspective from outside the family. With all due respect, most mothers think their children are wonderful."

"Elspeth *is* wonderful," Dina said, eyes livening. "Or at least she was. Of course I talked to Rachel about it at the time, but she said she was dealing with it."

"You said there was a shoplifting incident?"

Dina made a no-big-deal face, nodding. "Yeah. Stupid, of course. Kids go through the can-I-get-away-with-it phase. I probably shouldn't be saying this to an officer of the law, but I did it myself when I was her age. You know, CDs or glitter pens or candy. Dumb stuff just to prove you've got the balls. I hope I'm on the right side of the statute of limitations?"

"I used to break into public buildings," Valerie said. "So your secret's safe with me."

Dina smiled. "The difference was we didn't want to get caught. We really didn't. I mean stores back then, not all of them had cameras and whatnot. It was a calculated risk. But these days? Elspeth's bright enough to know you pretty much *can't* get away with it, not in a goddamned *mall*. Three times she got caught with high-end gear. Just tried to walk through the door. She knows all that stuff's tagged, so the conclusion's obvious."

"She wanted to get caught."

"Which means it's not about getting new stuff—of which she's not short in any case. It's about something else."

"You don't want to get caught unless you want to be seen to be guilty."

"It wasn't just that, either. She stopped eating. Well, no, she ate, but according to Julia she started making herself throw up."

"Did Rachel know?"

"I told her. She said she was getting Elspeth help."

*I'm not a fan of shrinks.* Valerie wondered what sort of help Rachel had commissioned.

"What happened with the thefts? Were the police involved?"

"Yeah, but I'm pretty sure Adam pulled some strings. Rachel implied as much. Nothing happened to Elspeth, as far as I know."

The maid brought in coffee on a tray.

"Oh, thanks, Kristina. Detective? How do you take it?"

They waited for the maid to exit.

"I know what you're thinking," Dina said, having taken a sip. "Shoplifting and an eating disorder—it's Teen Girl 101."

"Well, it's not unusual."

"Half of Julia's friends are so messed up she's starting to feel neurosis-poor. Like she's missing out on some essential rite of passage. And this obsession with social media—Christ. As it is she goes on as if her life depends on likes and thumb ratings. *Followers.*"

"But she's okay. You're not worried?"

Dina laughed. Confidence in her own motherhood. The knowledge that the groundwork had been done. "No, I'm not worried. She's okay. We make too much fun of her for her to take herself that seriously. Deep down she knows what's what. But she does think Elspeth's dangerously cool. I think there might even be a little crush there. Which is why I was worried, really. Not in case she's *gay,* you understand. I don't care about *that.* I just don't want puppy love landing her in Juvenile."

A disarming ease to this woman, Valerie thought. She'd been hard enough on herself in her youth to afford wry self-gentleness now. The moral life was established, had yielded happiness without smugness. She had no need for concealment. Meanwhile here *I* am, Valerie conceded. Secretly pregnant and investigating the murder of someone I secretly almost fucked. And while we're at it, secretly flirting with the late perp's half brother. Fabulous.

"There's something else," Dina said. "And I only know a little. It must've been seven or eight months ago. Rumor started that Elspeth had been sleeping with boys. *Boys,* plural—and older boys at that. Julia says it's completely false, vicious gossip started by this little posse at Drew who've got it in for Elspeth for whatever reason. But I know Rachel got involved. There were meetings with the principal and the other girls' parents. It seems to have died down, but I'm sure I don't know the whole story. Rachel made light of it when I brought it up."

"You're close to Rachel?" she asked.

Dina made a noncommittal face. "I wouldn't say *close,*" she answered. "Rachel's very private. We can make each other laugh, but there's a definite boundary there. She's one of the few people I know who doesn't talk about herself. *At all.* It's embarrassing. She comes over for coffee and by the time she's gone I feel like a raging narcissist."

"And Adam? Did you know him well?"

"Hardly at all. Neither did Marty."

"But they were okay together, Rachel and Adam?"

"There was nothing to make me think otherwise, but that's not saying much. And given Elspeth's recent shenanigans you've got to wonder— Oh, hey, sweetie."

Valerie turned to see a young girl—Julia, obviously—observing them. Barefoot in cut-off denim shorts and a white vest top, tawny hair in a plait. She had her mother's gray-blue eyes and leonine features. Her mother's look, too, of lively curiosity, albeit overlaid right now with what Valerie was coming to think of as standard teenage suspicion.

"Come and say hello," Dina said. "This is Detective Hart, who's investigating what happened to Elspeth's father. I think she might want to talk to you."

"To me?"

"Yes, come on."

Julia entered (putting on a face of exaggerated incredulity Valerie knew was for her benefit) and took a seat next to her mother on the couch.

Valerie was mentally drafting how she might ask to speak to the girl alone, but Dina anticipated her. "I'll leave you ladies to it," she said. "I've got some calls to make." Then to her daughter: "Jules, no nonsense, okay? Answer straight."

For the most part, as far as Valerie could tell, Julia Klein did answer straight. At least insofar as she confirmed what Dina had said about Elspeth's shoplifting and eating disorder. But there was clearly, as Dina had suggested, a wall of adoration that wouldn't be breached easily. When Valerie asked her about the rumored promiscuity, Julia was less forthcoming.

"That was just some mean girls trying to spread dirt," she said. "Pathetic."

"What exactly were they saying about Elspeth?"

"It was stupid," she said, looking away. "Just stuff so idiotic no one believed them anyway."

"No one?"

"No one worth bothering about."

"Did they say Elspeth was having sex with boys? Several boys?"

Julia pulled her knees up to her chest and sank back into the couch. "Yeah," she said. "I guess."

"Do you know which boys?"

"What's the point? It wasn't true. It was a *lie*."

"I know that," Valerie said. Then, after a pause: "You know everything in this room is just between us, right? No one apart from your mother will know about this conversation."

"Okay . . . ?" Julia said, intoning it as a question to imply: Why should that make any difference? I've got nothing to hide.

"So who were the boys they were saying Elspeth was involved with?"

"I don't know."

"Honestly?"

"Honestly. I mean I know one of the names, but I don't know him, personally. He doesn't go to Drew. Why d'you need to know, anyway?"

"It's nothing, really," Valerie said. "Just background. But to tell you the truth I think Elspeth's still very unhappy—not just because of what happened to her father. I imagined you'd be the best person to talk to about it. I wonder if she's over it, lie or no lie. You don't need to tell me anything you don't want to. It's fine." She would get the names from the principal, if she had to.

Julia looked out of the window.

"Listen, Julia," Valerie said. "I'm going to level with you. And I hope the confidentiality can go both ways here?"

Julia looked back at her. Uncomfortable, yes, but excited, too, to be involved. And a little flattered to be adultly leveled with. She nodded.

"I think Elspeth blames herself for something. I don't know what. Whatever it is, it's making her extremely miserable, and if we don't get to the bottom of it it's going to make her worse. I think in some bizarre way she even feels responsible for her father's death. That's how confused she's feeling right now. I know you care about her. And I hope you can trust me. If there's anything you think I should know, it would be a good idea to tell me."

Julia looked worried. "If I knew anything I *would* tell you," she said. "But I don't. Honestly I *don't*. She's barely talked to me since her dad died. I know she's miserable but she doesn't want to see me. I've tried."

Genuine, all of this, Valerie saw. There was no concealment. Only the pain of having lost the beloved. Dina Klein was justified in her confidence: She'd raised a good kid.

"I'm sorry," Valerie said. "That must be lousy for you. But she's been through a terrible time. If I were you I'd keep trying, gently. She'll come around."

She got to her feet. "Anyway, thanks for being straight with me. I appreciate it." She headed toward the door. "I should just say good-bye to your mom . . ."

"The name of one of the guys is Tanner Riley," Julia said. "I don't know the others."

## 37

It was too late in the day, Valerie decided, to track down Tanner Riley. And since she'd neglected to get the former housekeeper Isabella's surname from Rachel Grant, that stone, too, would have to wait another day for its turning. Besides, she was tired and famished. She'd eaten nothing since the samosas that morning. Suddenly, having slid into the Taurus's driver seat, she felt faint. The car was chilly after the day's warmth. There were the remains of a sunset, a few blood-orange flakes of cloud dissolving up into the dark blue, where the first stars were out. She looked at her watch: 7:38 P.M. She'd been on the go for thirteen hours. Not unusual for her—in fact below her daily average—but right now it was an entitlement to go home.

She put the key in the ignition just as a text from Nick came through:

*S&L ETA 8:30. Can you pick up cilantro?*

For a moment she sat without a clue. Then remembered—and wilted. "S&L" were Serena and Lou, Nick's sister and her husband. The dinner had been arranged two weeks ago. Nick had reminded her this morning. And of course she had forgotten.

Fuck.

She didn't much mind her in-laws (though Serena let it be known in the subtlest ways that she hadn't yet *quite* forgiven Valerie for breaking Nick's heart first time around, while Lou was one of those people drawn to provocative abstract questions despite a near complete inability to think in abstract terms) but at the moment the thought of a sit-down dinner at home with company made Valerie want to curl up in a blanket on the backseat of the Taurus.

Too bad she hadn't declared her condition, she thought, starting the engine. She imagined the chirpy text: *Have to cancel. The Pregnant Woman is NOT WELL. So sorry!* Pregnancy could get you out of all kinds of shit. Yet here she was squandering hers on secrecy.

*Because we still haven't made up our mind, have we?*

Hadn't she? Was it credible that she was still genuinely considering—plain speaking, Valerie—*getting rid of it*? Somewhere back there had been a figurative thought of tossing a precious gold coin down the nearest drain. That word, "*drain.*" Not so figurative after all. A drain was what she'd imagined the remains of her miscarriage swirling down, though of course she realized afterward that it would have been incinerated. Pre–twenty weeks, clinical waste. Or biomedical waste. Whatever they called it. At any rate, *waste*. In the absence of a need for lab testing, that was what happened, unless you had the wits to say otherwise. She'd had neither the wits nor the desire.

And now?

She sat with the engine running, unable, yet, to put the car in Drive and move off. She was, she knew, resisting thinking of her condition as anything other than "it." Loss had only one lesson to teach—namely, that anything could be lost—and she had learned it. The more you cared, the worse the loss. She knew what accepting it as anything more than "it" would mean, what it would sign her up for, how madly it would raise the stakes. She told herself she wasn't thinking about it. Superficially she wasn't. Superficially her consciousness was elsewhere. Superficially she'd settled on running down the clock until it was too late to do anything but go ahead and Have It. But beneath the surface—beneath *thinking*—she was engaged with virtually nothing else. Look at the investigation, for God's sake. These mothers and daughters. What did it matter whether Elspeth felt responsible for her father's death? Or that Rachel claimed she would be nothing without her daughter? So what if Elspeth had been slutting around because she felt guilty about something? What did it matter whether Dina Klein had raised a good girl, or whether Julia trusted her mother? Rhetorical: *None of these things mattered to the investigation*. But here she was, Valerie Hart, Homicide, preoccupied by them, contorting them into lines of inquiry, warping them into leads. She'd done the *relevant* investigative work, yes, but on autopilot. It was all this nonsense of mothers and daughters that was really running her motor.

She hadn't told Nick she was pregnant for the simple reason that that would be the end of thinking of it as "it." Once Nick was in on the deal, "it" would be "he" or "she," or some other cutesy designation of personhood, and the only way out then would be via breaking his heart, *again*.

Was she capable of that?

Sadly, she knew she was capable of anything, if the circumstances were right. It was one of the differences between her and Nick. He had lines drawn to keep his idea of himself intact. (It was a good idea, worth keeping intact.) She, unfortunately, did not have lines. She did not have an idea of herself, except as something that might, depending on the variables, become something completely different. She had started out—as a child, a girl, a young woman—with a quiver full of absolutes, Rights and Wrongs and Onlys and Nevers, but time had done its thing and now the quiver was empty. Being Police had given her infinite protean potential.

Oddly, she imagined Rachel Grant feeling the same—except in Rachel's case there was only one variable: Elspeth. The fact of Elspeth, Valerie thought, could allow Rachel Grant to become absolutely anything.

Her phone pinged a second time:

*And white wine vinegar.*

She sighed, allowed herself a mental *fucking hell,* put the car in Drive, and pulled away.

The dinner did not go well. Valerie and Nick's "trying for a baby" was supposed to be just between them, but Valerie got the impression Nick had blabbed to his sister. There was a little triumphal glint in Serena's eye, a sly satisfaction that Valerie had, at long last, capitulated to biology. Serena's narrative of her own motherhood was one of ditzily making it up as she went along, flailing from one screwup to the next and somehow getting away with it. As with all such narratives, it was a failed attempt to disguise her real estimation of herself, which was that she was probably the best mother history had yet produced. Valerie simmered through the evening. Sobriety ought to have restrained her. In fact it made things worse. There was nothing to dull her perception. Every nuance of Serena's self-congratulation landed on her like a spark. Eventually, without premeditation, she found herself at the end of her tolerance. A liberating moment. Like realizing you were flat broke.

"It's amazing, isn't it," she said to Serena, "how all these mistakes you make turn out not to be mistakes at all."

Bad timing. Nick and Lou had been chuckling about something, but it petered out just as Valerie said this. That the remark had center stage made its intent unequivocal.

"What?" Serena said.

As soon as she'd said it Valerie knew she shouldn't have. Not because it wasn't true, but because it wasn't the problem. The problem was that Serena's and Lou's life screamed domestic introversion; bright, middle-brow complacency; curtailed imagination; clan narcissism; and an indifference to anything that didn't affirm it. Their life smelled small and cozy and dumb and smug—and Valerie was terrified hers and Nick's might, via parenthood, end up just the same.

There was a moment of pure social horror. Fortunately, Lou was sufficiently drunk not to pick it up, and before Valerie could either try to climb out or dig herself deeper, he said: "Oh, yeah, Serena gives out like she doesn't know what she's doing—until you suggest doing it a different way. Then it's like . . . It's like she's Stephen Hawking."

"Stephen Hawking?" Nick said, happy to grab this thread since he could see how pissed his sister was, not to mention his wife.

"Like the Stephen Hawking of whatever the fuck it is. Cooking tomatoes."

"There's conflict over tomatoes?"

"She wants the *skins* off. Tomatoes don't need their skins off. The skins are where all the nourishment is, for Christ's sake."

"We're letting it go then, are we?" Serena said, to everyone. She'd had a few drinks, too, and was ready to go either way.

"Tomatoes reduce your risk of testicular cancer," Lou said to Nick, having missed the import of his wife's remark. "In Italy they found that guys who ate raw tomatoes every day were sixty percent less likely to develop cancer."

"With the skins or without?" Nick asked.

"What do they do for you if you don't have testicles?" Valerie asked.

"Perhaps I dreamed it," Serena said.

"They keep your boobs healthy, too," Lou said.

And so they let it go, approximately, though very shortly afterward Serena said it was time to head home.

"Do you want to tell me what the fuck is wrong with you?" Nick asked Valerie, when the guests had left.

"Nothing. What?"

"I'm not just talking about tonight."

"Your sister's smug. Sometimes she needs reminding."

"I repeat: I'm not just talking about tonight."

"Did you tell her?"

"As a matter of fact no, I didn't. But you're the sort of person who, if she stops drinking, people notice."

"Wow."

"Don't make this into a fight. Just tell me what's going on."

"Nothing."

"Incredible. You're actually going with that. Okay. Before abandoning this altogether I'll just point out that you've been acting fucking weird for days. Weeks, in fact. I don't know what it is and apparently you've decided I don't need to know. Fine. But, shocking though this might be, I am, actually, here. You know, experiencing the effects of your actions."

"Stop talking like a prick."

"Then tell me what's going on."

"Nothing's going on. It's just work. I'm sorry."

"Only that you've been rumbled. And it's not work."

She didn't contradict him. Didn't say anything. Just closed herself off.

"Okay," Nick said, starting to clear the dining table. "Forget it. Although there's only a certain number of times saying 'okay, forget it' works."

There was no limit to the perverse universe's appetite. Perhaps it was the repetition of the word "forget." Perhaps her guilt for taking a shot at Serena sang out in her psyche to other guilts lurking there. Either way Valerie remembered, suddenly, that she hadn't yet told Kyle Cornell his half brother was dead.

She checked the time. Thanks to the abortive dinner, it was only just past 11:30 P.M. Early enough for a man of Kyle's hours. He was probably at the bar. Obviously there was no reason she had to break the news to him now. It would keep until tomorrow. *Doubly* obviously the thing to do was get into bed with Nick and very quietly and sanely and tenderly tell him she was sorry for being such a pain in the ass, but she was pregnant and scared that she wasn't going to be up to the job. What? Yes, you heard right. I'm pregnant. Are you happy about it?

She was very clear that this was the thing to do.

But the universe *would* have its perversions.

"What the fuck?" Nick said, emerging from the kitchen to see her putting her jacket on.

"I know," she said. "Sorry. I have to. I just remembered something. It won't wait."

He didn't say anything. Just stood there, watching her put her boots on. She knew she was doing the wrong thing. She could feel herself doing it. It was fascinating.

"I'll be an hour, tops," she said.

She got all the way to the door before Nick spoke.

"Take your fucking time," he said.

# 38

And is there some reason you couldn't just call him on the phone?

Well, yes, actually. You don't break the news of a next-of-kin death over the phone.

But there's more to it than that.

The fascination gave her a gentle momentum, and it was a relief to be out of the apartment. Without calling ahead, she drove to Flamingo. Kyle wasn't working. The beautiful black-eyed Japanese girl gave her an ambiguous smile along with this information. Possibly: *I know you're hot for him.* Possibly: *I don't blame you.* Possibly: *But you'd be better off with me, hon.*

The momentum continued. Valerie was happy to get back into the Taurus. There was comfort in driving, which let her lose herself in it, gave her an immunity to thinking.

But too soon she was at his apartment—and had already pressed the buzzer before the dream state dissolved and left her confronted, suddenly, by reality. It occurred to her that she hadn't thought what she was going to say. It further occurred to her that the princessy girlfriend might be here with him. She hoped for that, now. It would shut down the potentialities. A little coldness came up from the stone stoop. It made her catch up with herself, completely. She felt hot-faced, foolish. Sad, too, that she was still so susceptible to her least reliable self.

"Yeah?"

"It's Detective Hart. I need to speak with you."

Short pause. Valerie pictured him lifting the princess off himself, bending, pulling on his pants.

But in less time than that would have taken the entry buzzer sounded. She pushed the heavy door and went into the lobby. Kyle was standing in his apartment doorway, fully dressed. Shit-kickers, black jeans, white T-shirt, Levi's jacket. The jacket—along with some vibe of wide-awakeness or still-lingering scent of the streets—suggested he'd only just got in. Alone.

"Hey," he said quietly. No smile this time. It wrong-footed her. She'd been readying herself to cut him off before he got started flirting. No need, apparently.

"It's not good news," she said.

"Come in," he said, turning back into the apartment.

She went in after him and closed the door behind her. Neither of them sat down. As always, the search for a good way of delivering the worst news turned up nothing. As always, there were only the facts. The one fact, rather.

"Dwight's dead," she said. "I'm sorry."

He stared at her in blankness, not seeing her. It was as if his soul had left him. But after a moment it came back and his consciousness flowed again.

"What happened?" he said.

She exhaled, a breath she hadn't known she'd been holding. "Five days ago a body was found buried in the desert in Nevada. We only got DNA identity confirmation today. It's Dwight. I'm sorry."

Not a politeness this time. She was sorry, for the man in front of her, who looked now as if he'd undertaken his half brother's rehabilitation knowing all along it would end like this.

"Murdered," Kyle said. Trying out the word. Understanding he'd have to get used to it.

"Yes," Valerie said.

Silence formed between them. When their eyes met, Valerie knew they wouldn't lie to each other now.

"You don't seem surprised," she said.

Kyle leaned against the back of the couch, loosened slightly. Looked up at her and smiled sadly. "I had a dream last night," he said. "Dwight down on his hands and knees with gasoline coming out of his mouth. Obviously I don't believe in these things."

"Some dreams have a kind of authority," she said.

Another silence. They kept looking at each other—then away.

Kyle straightened, went to the kitchen, came back with a half-full bottle of Lagavulin, two glasses, set them down on the dining table.

"I can't," Valerie said.

He poured anyway. Swallowed his in one gulp, refilled, then brought hers over to her. They were both still standing. There seemed no alternative. Sitting would have felt wrong.

"Tell me what you know," Kyle said.

Valerie told him. All of it. Everything from the incontrovertible evidence that nailed Dwight for Adam Grant's murder to the Lucifer sigil carved on his chest.

Kyle listened, drank, refilled once more, but with a look of knowing it would be the last, that drink didn't have enough to offer him.

"There's something else," Valerie said. "Dwight's hands and feet were amputated."

Kyle looked up at her as if this were the first piece of information that didn't make sense.

"We don't know why," she said. "It doesn't fit the original Lucifer MO, but that's neither here nor there. It's disgusting for you, I know. I'm sorry you have to hear it."

"You mean they're *missing*? You didn't . . ."

"They weren't with the body."

"Jesus fucking Christ."

Kyle stood with his head bowed, staring at the floor. This, the mutilation of his brother's body, was a source of fury, Valerie saw, more, even, than the murder. The murder conformed to the doomed view Kyle had of Dwight's life. The murder was, at the amoral level, unsurprising. But this additional violence was a gratuitous desecration.

It took him a few moments to subside.

"This serial killer shit. Lucifer. You don't buy it?"

"I don't know. Adam Grant worked for the prosecution on the trial that went nowhere. Can't be just a coincidence."

"And Sophia? You find her yet?"

"No. But she's the key. APB's been out for weeks. I have a feeling she's gone back to L.A."

"You say she was screwing Grant. Dwight was killed at Grant's country place. She's more than the key. She's the suspect."

"She's a strong contender."

"The right woman could lead Dwight like a bull with a ring through its nose."

In spite of everything there was no missing the subtext: *Unlike me.* Valerie thought of the princess girlfriend. Kyle looked up as if she'd thought it out loud. The mutual visibility was pure and terrible. He smiled, with soft bitterness, shook his head.

"She doesn't lead me anywhere," he said.

And here they were, without innocence.

The detached part of Valerie looked on like a third person, noting, calmly, that life had an endless supply of these moments, in which certain of your little micro-thoughts and actions culminated in a conclusion to which you never knew you were being led. Or to which you never admitted you were *letting* yourself be led. The missing admission was your own blind cunning: You did always know, deep down. It depressed her that this was still the way she was, that there were still decisions she couldn't make except when the two alternatives were put right in front of her like a pair of salivating dogs. What was the flirtation with Kyle Cornell if not an attempt to push herself into either keeping the life she had or wrecking it?

She didn't know, as he straightened and moved toward her, that she *was* choosing to keep her life. She only knew that this wasn't, after all, the moment she was choosing to wreck it.

He was facing her, close enough so that she could feel his body heat. She opened her mouth to stop it going any further—but he got there before her.

"This isn't that movie," he said quietly.

She waited. But his silence insisted it was her job, not his.

"No," she said. "It isn't. I know."

The heat coming off him wasn't just grief. It wasn't just desire, either. It was, she saw, anger. Justified.

"You really are a piece of work," he said.

Valerie kept very still. She deserved this. Here was his half brother's death, reduced by her to a factor in the math of desire.

"You need to think about something," he said.

She saw him beyond this moment, alone in the apartment with nothing to do but let the realization that Dwight was dead do its work of emptying him. She hoped the girlfriend would come over. Let him lose himself through his body, the humble solace of flesh and blood, if he could be kind enough to himself to accept it. She doubted he would. It was just as likely this would be the thing to make him dump her. Somewhere back in his life he'd acquired the belief that strength came through the self's searing. Comfort was cheating. Comfort was for the weak.

"What do I need to think about?" she said. She didn't know specifically how he was going to put it, but she knew what he was going to mean.

"Whether there's a limit to your narcissism," he said.

Deserved that, too. She didn't say anything. He was too smart not to take an apology as condescension. And who could blame him? Even as she thought this she thought, too, that he was using this as part of the self-searing, refusing himself something he wanted, rising above it. Afterward, when the grief and anger had lessened, he might wish he'd fucked her, even if only to have *spent* the anger.

And so, Kyle, no, I don't really need to think about it. I already know there's no limit to my narcissism. Maybe having a kid will cure it.

They were still looking at each other, face-to-face. Instead of the apology, Valerie looked away. Hoped it would give him something, a feeling of superiority. He was entitled to it.

She turned and went to the door.

"I'll arrange for Dwight's body to be brought back to the morgue here," she said. "Shouldn't be more than forty-eight hours."

She opened the door.

"Hey," he said.

"Yes?"

"You better get whoever did this."

She nodded, still not looking at him.

"Because if you don't, I will."

# 39

## *August 2, 2017*

Problems. The skin. The gloves. The prints. The time. They were like precious jewels of horror, these problems. No matter how often she turned them over in her mind they never lost their luster. Like the memories of Larry.

She was in the kitchen. The big white house was quiet. It knew what was coming. It raised no resistance. She was its mistress. It was afraid of her now that she'd shown it what she could do.

No such thing as the perfect murder. She'd absorbed this maxim, culturally, she supposed. It didn't stop people from committing murder. Why should it? Murder might be imperfect by definition but that didn't mean it wasn't necessary. She had an image of herself saying this, calmly, to students in lecture theater. *Intro to the Philosophy of Homicide. Week 1: On Doing What You Have To Do.*

The question was, having done what she had to do, would she have the strength to do what else she had to do to get away with it? Not a moral question, a practical one. The biggest unknown was the physical state she'd be in in those moments immediately afterward. When she tried to imagine the pain—the necessary pain—all she got was a red, soft-edged sensation of heat and dizziness. She would be swimming. In blood. She was in no doubt about the murder. She already knew—had proved—what she was capable of. That Rubicon had already been crossed. There was no question of what she could do to someone else. The question was what she would be capable of doing to herself.

She went to the utility room and unpacked the chest freezer, methodically. (All the food would have to be trashed and replaced afterward, obviously, albeit by stealth. The prospect of eating any of it was repellant, even in her new state of dark hilarity.) The large, plastic, airtight freezer box, the biggest Kmart had to offer, was intact, its contents still snugly sealed and duct-taped in the heavy-duty garbage bags.

Shed or greenhouse? She'd been vacillating from the beginning. Her main concern was wildlife. In twelve hours this would be fully defrosted. Animal noses would know. They'd had rats in the shed before, though not for some time. She'd been diligent with the poison in both outbuildings. Coyotes? She'd never actually seen one in the neighborhood, though there were stories in the papers now and then about someone's dog or cat getting mauled. Foxes, too, apparently, had been spotted in the city.

In the end she decided on the greenhouse. It had a concrete floor and base wall beneath the glass, and according to her last inspection showed no sign of critter incursion. Besides, the whole caboodle was going inside an old tin chest she'd picked up at a garage sale, ostensibly to use as a novelty plant holder. It even had a working lock.

The greenhouse warmth was palliative, the smell of ripening tomatoes and the glow of chilies. It had been an astonishment to her that she—she!—had the capacity to grow things she could eat, after her life of food in cardboard and plastic and cans. There had been so many chapters in the world's book her childhood should have opened. And too many it should have left closed. That, she thought, had been the story of her youth: an absence of the simple things and a superabundance of the complex. She'd been empty of innocence and stuffed with guilt. Her stubborn irony pointed out that at least now she had something to be guilty of. Give a dog a bad name.

She fitted the freezer box into the chest, locked it, and set it on a length of tarp. It couldn't, she thought, leak, but in murder there was no such thing as an unnecessary precaution. In murder the capacity for precaution was infinite—and insufficient. She dragged the tarp back under a bench and concealed it with four hefted bags of potting compost. For a few moments she stood there in the green light, letting her muscles relax in the magnified warmth. Nature's indifference was the dependable endorsement, if you needed it.

But time was passing. She went back to the house.

In the kitchen she opened the cupboard under the sink and took a pair of gloves from the box. *Gripstrong Vinyl 4.2 mil Powder-free Gloves, Kitchen and Dining. FDA approved for food handling. Size: Small.* She plucked the knife from the block. It livened in her hand, gave her a silent admission of its blameless potential.

Her legs were weak going up the stairs. The greenhouse's drug had worn off. In the moments since coming back indoors, her body had acquired a faint tremor. Hadn't been like that three days ago. Three days ago she'd been smooth and steady. Three days ago it had been as if invisible forces—in the car, in the woods, in the lake air and the desert darkness—had surrounded her with suave support. Her movements had been seductively choreographed. A trick of the psyche, she supposed, to relieve you of responsibility, to persuade you that it wasn't, when you got right down to it, *you, doing this.*

In the bedroom she opened the French windows and stepped out onto the sunlit balcony. The potted plants were distinct personalities in the static heat. Fuchsia. Golden bamboo. Lavender. Daphne "Eternal Fragrance," which even without a breeze gave her its sugary citrus scent.

Only one of the pots was light enough to lift out of its tray, a little photinia "Red Robin" she'd bought a month ago. By design? Not consciously, she thought now. But of course even a month ago the jewel-problems were established, winking in her head. You'll need somewhere to stash the gloves. Somewhere close to hand, somewhere that even swimming in blood you'll be able to . . .

She brought the photinia pot as close as she could to the bedroom, while still leaving it clear of the French window's opening arc. She scrunched up the vinyl gloves in her left hand, then lay down on the floor on her side and slid herself toward the pot. What she'd thought of originally was preparing a hole in the soil, stuffing the gloves in, and covering them over. But that would leave soil on her hands, under her nails. And her nails, above all, had to be protected. Hence Plan B.

And now the dress rehearsal.

Even unimpeded it wasn't easy. In her prone position she could only just lift the pot with one hand. She put the gloves in the tray, replaced the pot. It had weight enough to press the gloves flat, more or less. They wouldn't see it unless they knew exactly what they were looking for. But the blood. The blood was going to be an issue. *Being careful* was going to be an issue. The only issue, in fact, once she'd done what she had to do. And in that state, how careful could she be? Flailing in the red darkness, precision would suffer. Everything would suffer. Including her. Her most of all.

*No such thing as the perfect murder.* These compromises were the imperfections. They were written into the contract, the small print that could grow large under the right eyes, become the pertinent print, the only print, the damning print.

There was no alternative. *I am in blood stepped in so far that should I wade no more / Returning were as tedious as go o'er.* Another fragment. All the belated education, never knowing it would gather to this redundancy. The power of fictional murder died once actual murder arrived in your life. Of course it did. If Shakespeare had really lived, he'd never have written. Art was a kind of envy of life's wealth. It was absurd that she was capable of these thoughts. But the Absurd was unsurprising.

She removed the gloves and replaced the pot.

Her hands were hot. Sweat nettled her hairline.

She fitted the knife handle into the French window's hinge. Carefully eased the door toward its closed position until the handle was, effectively, clamped. The tip of the blade was a question for her.

Well, yes, that was the question.

There was only so far a dress rehearsal could go.

# 40

## *September 16, 2017*

Tanner Riley, sixteen, worked part-time at his uncle's auto repair shop in North Beach, and was just rolling up the shutters when Valerie arrived the following morning.

The night, mercifully, had passed without further damage. Nick had been in bed when she'd got back; eyes closed, but not, she thought, asleep. She'd undressed quietly and slid in beside him, without touching. There had been an hour of silence in which she could sense him weighing up whether to speak—but he'd kept his mouth shut, and eventually *had* fallen asleep. She'd lain awake herself until just before first light, then risen, dressed, and left before he stirred. But the postponement was over. Tonight, for better or worse, she was going to tell him. Everything. Even that she wasn't sure if she wanted to go ahead. One way or another, life *after* tonight wouldn't be the same.

"Morning," Valerie said to Tanner Riley, flashing the badge. "Got a minute?"

She'd watched him from the car for a while before approaching, a skinny, suntanned kid with blond and brown hair and a flinty blue-eyed face that said yes, this was the auto repair shop, but so obviously a fleeting irrelevance en route to greater things that it was all he could do to keep a straight face while it lasted.

His face went straight, however, confronted with a cop.

"What?"

"Detective Hart, Homicide," she said. "What can you tell me about Elspeth Grant?"

"Who?"

"Elspeth Grant. The thirteen-year-old girl from Drew."

Tanner was so suddenly and comprehensively scared shitless, she knew the direct route would be the most profitable. "Word is you and your buddies had a little encounter with her a while back. I need you to tell me about it."

He blinked, mouth open, stunned. Where the fuck had *this* come from? Jesus! Valerie was tempted to smile herself: All that teen cool—gone in an instant, as if a trapdoor had opened under him and the whole lot had dropped through. The sunny morning was blue and silver around them. For him, she knew, it would be spinning, sickeningly. Normally he wore the auto shop overalls with patient irony. Now they were a hot torment.

"I don't . . . I don't know what the fuck—"

"You don't know what the fuck I'm talking about."

"I *don't* know what the fuck you're—"

"Well, let's start with the fact that she's a minor and I'm a homicide detective. We can talk here or at the station. I'll square it with your uncle when he gets here."

"Jesus Christ. I didn't do anything. She said she was fifteen. I didn't *do* anything!"

She had to work fast. First because she wanted to press him while his fear was still fresh, and second because she wanted to get what she needed before his uncle showed up and started making difficulties. She found his story, once she'd burned through the fumbling denials, depressingly unsurprising. Elspeth had been with a trio of older girls (one of whom, Anita Willox, he knew through his sister) at the mall one Saturday afternoon, when Tanner and a couple of his friends had run into them. There followed an hour of driving around, then they'd all gone to Anita's home in Laurel Heights. Her parents were away for the weekend. Valerie filled in the predictable blanks—a raid on the domestic booze, maybe a joint or two, some version of Truth or Dare. The upshot was that at some point in the afternoon, Elspeth found him alone in one of the bedrooms. According to Tanner, he was half-asleep—and woke up to find her standing there in just her T-shirt and panties.

"I don't care what anyone's told you," Tanner said. His face had thickened as she'd wrung the narrative out of him. It had brought a much younger version of himself to the surface. "Nothing—absolutely *nothing* happened. I told her to get the hell out."

"Why?"

"What?"

"Why'd you tell her to get out? She's a pretty girl. You thought she was fifteen. You telling me you didn't even make out a little? There's no law against that."

Tanner dragged his hair off his forehead. He was sweating. Not, Valerie decided, out of guilt, but out of the realization that you could be deemed guilty even if you were innocent.

"Look, Jesus, I'm telling you the truth. I didn't . . . There was something wrong with her. *Mentally*. She gave me the fucking creeps, okay?"

Valerie believed him. More or less. It might have taken a little more than Elspeth's appearing half-undressed to give him the creeps (perhaps the beginning of making out, when her not-fifteenness might have insinuated itself) but unless she'd completely lost her mojo, Tanner Riley wasn't, substantially, lying.

"All right," she said, putting away her notebook. "If I need to talk to you again I'll know where to find you."


She drove to Bay Domestic and picked up contact details for the Grants' former housekeeper. Isabella Hernandez. Who, it turned out, was neither at home nor answering her cell. Valerie went back to the station.

She was eating a chicken chat and paratha when Nathan came up from Computer Forensics.

"All the Grant hardware," he said. "We're done, as far as I'm concerned. Okay to release it?"

"I didn't know we still had it," Valerie said. The computers from Willard & Gould had been returned, cleared by Deerholt, and she'd assumed he'd done the same for the domestic equipment.

"Yeah, normally they're breaking down the door to get their stuff back. You good to sign the release?"

"Sure. Nick in yet?"

"No, he's over at the Pullman for the CTIN conference today. Didn't he tell you?"

"Oh, actually, yeah, I forgot about that. You not going?"

"I'm going tomorrow. It's three days. Nerd heaven. I'll email you the release."

The paperwork arrived in her in-box ten minutes later. She'd just put pen to paper to sign the printouts when something stopped her.

Or rather, something and nothing.

The nothing was Nathan's remark about hardware owners normally clamoring for the return of their gizmos.

The something was a combination of two facts.

Fact one was that with the exception of tracking down the housekeeper in the fragile hope that she had useful intel on Adam Grant's secret life, Valerie had absolutely nothing practical to do.

Fact two was that she'd never looked through the computer material herself.

So what? There was no reason to suppose Nick and Nathan had missed anything. They knew what they were looking for, and they hadn't found it.

Maybe that was the problem. They'd known what they were looking for. She'd given them specific targets. It invited selective scrutiny. But what about the other way of looking? When you *didn't* know what you were looking for?

You looked peripherally, intuitively, tangentially—all the fancy words for simply opening yourself to whatever might be there.

She was glad Nick was at the conference. The state they were in right now, he'd take her going through material he'd already trawled as an insult. Nathan wouldn't be convinced either, but he wouldn't be offended. He was in on the half joke of Valerie's reputation as an instinct-follower, a left-field merchant, a practitioner of Police Occultism. She was in on it herself, unashamedly. It could only be a half joke, because her results were beyond question. When her colleagues laughed it was openly, the laughter of baffled admiration, since so many of her hunches proved her right.

She went down to Computer Forensics. Nathan was on his way out for lunch.

"You're not going to like me," she said.

"I don't like you already. No one does."

"Can you set me up with the Grant stuff?"

Nathan looked at her. Understood.

"I know, I know," she said.

He closed his eyes.

"Is it boxed up?"

"Naturally. Where's the fun for you if it's not boxed up?"

Twenty minutes later she sat alone in the windowless lab. Four hard drives, no cigarettes, no booze—and no idea what she was looking for.

It was a long, *long* day, and she realized halfway through it that she'd chosen this partly to eat up the hours before the conversation she was going to have with Nick at its end. The realization brought panic—but she squashed it. She'd done all the inner wrangling she was going to do. Granted, there was still a blank space when she tried to imagine what would *follow* from that conversation, but there was stark comfort in knowing that soon everything would be out in the open and at the mercy of their shared forces. At least she'd be free of the burden of secrecy, which—not surprisingly—was now a physical sensation in her belly.

She worked methodically through the files, the emails, the receipts, the photographs, the videos. She kept her mind open, intuitions limber—but she found nothing.

Nathan came back, worked at the other desk in silence, stood over her when he was ready to go, said, "You're wasting your time, Val," then left.

By 10:00 P.M. her eyes were aching. There was only the hard drive from the Campbellville desktop left unexamined, but she doubted she had the energy or the will to start on it. She sat back in her chair and stretched. A text from Nick arrived.

*Going for drinks with the nerds. Don't wait up.*

No endearment. No *x*. Fair enough. She'd earned it. It didn't matter. Trivial hostilities that would evaporate in the face of what she had to tell him.

Still, the idea of going home to an empty apartment and waiting for him didn't appeal. There would be time to kill, and space in it for her confessional resolve to weaken.

She opened up the Campbellville hard drive.

Sick of looking at print, she started with the My Photos file. Not, truthfully, because she expected them to yield anything, but because there was still, whether she liked it or not, a fascination with this family which, for all the time she'd spent considering it, remained strangely opaque.

The photos were what she'd expected. Thirteen years of ordinary life, albeit of the well-heeled variety. Christmases, Thanksgivings, vacation beaches. A lot on the boat. There was a nightmarish mesmerism to looking at so much normality in full knowledge of where it would end up, namely with Adam Grant murdered. All those moments and days, smiles, glances, poses and funny faces, each snapshot testifying to a terrible ignorance of what lay ahead. It was as if Death was an invisible presence in every picture, smiling, waiting patiently for its appointed time, while the subjects went about the bright business of Being Alive, never for an instant suspecting they weren't alone. From which it followed, Valerie knew, that we were all in the same predicament. Which person's photos wouldn't, in retrospect, have the same invisible guest—if they ended up murdered?

One folder was titled "Better Late than Never." Opened, it revealed a dozen or so pictures of Rachel Grant's university graduation—though surely not more than six or seven years ago. Interesting, if irrelevant. Rachel had presumably gone back to school, as what was euphemistically called "a mature student." Valerie wondered what she'd majored in. Maybe literature, given the omnivorous nocturnal reading. Which thought took her back to the neighbor, Vincent Lyle, he and Rachel exchanging a small-hours wave of shared literary insomnia. Again, it niggled: Dwight Jenner spotted on the Lyles' back lawn, kitted out in black gear and ski mask. What the fuck, exactly, was he doing there? Okay, better concealed access to the Grants' from the rear—but why not just get into their yard to start with?

No answer.

Too many no answers.

The next folder was marked "Kruger Party."

Dan Kruger, obviously.

He appeared in the first of the pictures—though it took her a moment to recognize him, since he was bare-chested in leather trousers with his hair wet, holding what appeared to be a live white dove. He was standing with his arm around a guy dressed, as far as she could tell, as Humphrey Bogart. Costume party then. Kruger, she realized, had made use of his natural coloring (and indeed a basic resemblance) to present himself as Rutger Hauer's replicant from *Blade Runner*.

The rest of the pictures—interior and yard of a swanky and clearly very large house—confirmed the theme was movie stars or movie characters. It was only the third time Morticia Addams cropped up in a shot that Valerie recognized her as Fiona Perry. The only people *not* in costume were the hired hospitality crew, glimpsed here and there bearing trays loaded with champagne flutes or canapés. The guests had taken the dressing up seriously, since they could afford to. All the gear looked professional, tailored, rented. Costume parties, Valerie observed, revealed two kinds of person, one who was happy to put glamor aside, and another who used the opportunity to enhance it. The demographic at Kruger's bash fell squarely into the second category. There were no King Kongs, Mickey Mouses, or Big Birds. On the other hand there were two Barbarellas and three Jack Sparrows, though none of the men who fancied themselves Johnny Depp looked remotely convincing, and one of them should really have put himself in a corset first.

It took her a while to spot Adam Grant. He was Indiana Jones, pictured raising his glass to the camera, flanked by Liz Taylor's Cleopatra and Raquel Welch's fur-bikini'd cavegirl from *One Million Years B.C.* The latter looked like she'd spent a year working out for it, and the result was, Valerie was forced to concede, impressive.

There were a lot of photographs, and the quality suggested Kruger had hired a professional photographer. Examining them was—after the dreary hours of scouring the other documents—fun. Count Dracula. Princess Leia. The Joker. Scarlett O'Hara. Valerie's heart warmed to one small guy in his sixties who'd gone, with convincing hilariousness, as Norman Bates's mother from *Psycho*. Not surprisingly, since the photographs appeared to be chronological, the costumes and makeup suffered as the evening wore on and people got drunk.

It occurred to her—with a dumb belatedness that scolded her for losing focus—that Rachel Grant hadn't shown up in any of the images so far. Either that or Valerie had been fooled by a costume. Not invited? Unlikely. Maybe she couldn't go. Maybe she was away with Elspeth. Maybe she was sick. Clearly, since here were the photographs, Adam Grant hadn't kept it a secret. Maybe (this seemed feasible, given the little Valerie had seen of her) this just wasn't Rachel Grant's kind of thing.

She began going through the remaining twenty or so images with renewed concentration.

Then stopped. At a picture near the end of the collection.

The photograph she was looking at showed Adam (Indiana) with his back to the camera. And his hand resting in the small of a blond woman's back. She, too, was facing away from the lens. She was wearing a white halter-neck fifties dress that left her arms and shoulders bare. Marilyn. From *The Seven Year Itch*. The dress of the famous scene where the skirt blows up over the subway grille.

The next picture—Valerie could all but hear the photographer shouting "Hey, you two!" over the noise of the party—changed everything.

In it, "Marilyn" had turned to glance back over her bare shoulder.

The hair wasn't quite accurate. It was a little longer and more voluminous than its screen original's.

And shorter than Sophia's in the three pictures from Adam Grant's darkroom.

But there was no doubt it was her.

What Adam's three hidden pictures had obscured—courtesy of the tilted-back head in the kitchen, the fall of the hair in the study, the gag and blindfold in the bedroom—namely the *face*, was, in this snatched shot, visible.

Even then Valerie's circuits jammed. All she could think was why on earth would Adam Grant take his mistress to a party where surely *some* of the guests would have been expecting his wife? Moreover (sweet satisfaction), it proved Dan Kruger had lied when he said he didn't know her.

Then she looked at the final photograph in the sequence.

In it, Sophia was staring straight into the camera, frowning.

Valerie forced herself to resist what her eyes told her. In the moment of resistance she heard some inner voice—or rather a combination of voices, only one of which might have been her own—saying *How could you not, but why would she, he took it or she did with a timer, you only see what you're expecting to see, that's the trouble, expectation. You see what you're expecting to see. Expectation is blindness. You never saw the face, really. You never, clearly, saw it.*

She enlarged the image.

The resistance melted away.

The woman dressed as Marilyn Monroe, the woman in the photographs from the drawer in Adam Grant's darkroom; the woman bent over the desk; half-naked on the kitchen worktop; bound, blindfolded, and gagged in bed; the woman from the hotels' CCTV, hidden behind a bigger blond wig and giant sunglasses—Sophia—was Rachel Grant.

# 41

## *September 17, 2017*

Valerie didn't go home, didn't sleep.

Laura Flynn came in at 7:30 A.M. and set her regulation giant latte down on her desk. "You been here all night?" she said, seeing Valerie's face.

"Found Sophia."

"No shit. Really?"

"It's Rachel Grant."

"What?"

"There is no Sophia. There's a redhead in a blond wig and shades whose face we've never seen clearly. Rachel Grant."

Laura was halfway out of her jacket. She stopped. Processed. "Rachel *was* fucking Jenner?"

"Apparently."

Laura shed her jacket and joined Valerie. Traffic cam stills were running in sequence on the desktop.

"What're we looking at?" Laura asked.

"Just got this from ALPR. Last point of coverage between Orland and Campbellville."

"Great. But I'm only three sips into this, so, you know . . . er . . . What?"

Valerie didn't answer. Three more stills of vehicles clocked by the camera.

"Or I could just guess," Laura said. "But I wouldn't hold your breath."

"This is July thirty-first, the junction just east of Chico," Valerie said. "Where the 99 meets the 32. Which is what you take for Campbellville, the Grants' country house. We know Jenner was at the Orland rest stop a few miles west of there that night. As was Rachel Grant. Ergo . . ."

Two more stills. A third. Valerie froze it. Zoomed. Enlarged. No reflection on the windshield this time. The faces of the vehicle's occupants were visible.

"Jesus," Laura said.

"That's Rachel. In blonde mode. And that's Dwight Jenner in the passenger seat next to her."

"I can't believe she was screwing him."

"There's more to it than that."

"Yeah?"

"Yeah. I think she killed him. After getting him to kill her husband."

"But she was . . . I mean *she* was—"

"Stabbed, yeah, I know. Not fatally. Either something went wrong or it was part of the arrangement."

Will Fraser arrived just as Valerie was getting off the phone. He knew her well enough to pick up the gearshift.

"Fuck," he said, after she'd brought him up to speed. "For the money?"

"Partly. You've seen the will and the insurance payout. A trust for Elspeth and enough for Rachel to live like a queen for the rest of her life."

"She was *already* living like a queen. Why risk it? A simple divorce would've seen her royally set up. There's Grant family money goes way back, and Adam had a chunk of it."

"*Partly* for the money, I said. There's more to it."

"What?"

"I'm working on it. Meantime, we know Rachel and Dwight were at the Campbellville place on the night of July thirty-first. That was the last time Dwight was seen alive, and it's now pretty obvious he was killed by the lake.

The question is: Was he killed that night? If not, he's still in the frame for Adam Grant's murder. If he was, we're looking at a brand-new suspect."

"When did entomology say he bought it?" Will asked.

"Four to six weeks prior to discovery of the body. Useless, thanks to the two-week gray area. We're getting an ALPR cross-check for Rachel's plates on the Chico cam from July 31 to the estimated date of Jenner's death. If it flags they'll send the relevant footage. Ed and Laura can go through it. We need to know Jenner was alive long enough to have killed Adam. If he was, there's a chance he'll show up on the cam again with Rachel. For now she's officially under investigation for conspiracy to commit murder. Find out everything you can about her. Personal history, vital records, all of it."

"So you get the rock and roll and I get the desktop?"

She got to her feet and grabbed her purse. "Even God needed angels for the grunt work," she said.

Captain Deerholt's office door opened when she was halfway down the corridor.

"Val, in here, please."

Nothing good. As long as you were doing your job, Deerholt left you alone. It was only when you fucked up that he wanted to talk to you. Valerie entered and closed the door behind her. She knew what was coming.

"One question," Deerholt said. "What happened between you and Adam Grant?"

Pause. Kruger. Naturally.

"Nothing," she said.

"Why do you do this?"

"Sir?"

"Put a crack in the foundation of every house you build?"

"I take it Dan Kruger called?"

"Yes, Dan Kruger called."

"Sir, nothing happened. I had dinner with Adam Grant four years ago. We shared a cab home. He dropped me off. He left."

"Nothing else?"

"Nothing else," she said.

A great deal passed in the silence that followed, as they looked at each other. Deerholt knew the way she'd been back then. The booze, the guys. Morally it made no difference to him. Aside from the Work, Valerie knew, *nothing* made a difference to him. It was what they had in common. They were like a father and daughter between whom the love was so obvious they had no need to acknowledge or express it. In everything except the Work they were liberated into complete mutual indifference. But this, unfortunately, *was* the Work.

"For the record," Deerholt said, "Kruger says Adam Grant told it otherwise."

"Then you either believe him or me."

He nodded, unsurprised. His face said she was telling him exactly what he knew she'd tell him. And that what she was telling him might very well be a lie. That didn't matter, either. All that mattered was whether the investigation was compromised.

"Is there any way Kruger can prove anything?"

"No."

Not, strictly, true, but short of Adam Grant having secretly recorded their evening or photographed her half-naked and asleep, true enough.

Another silence. More volumes unspoken.

"You know the consequences," Deerholt said.

"Yes, sir."

He looked down at the papers on his desk. "Fine," he said. Then, when she was at the door, added: "I hope you're right."


Sylvana Bianchi, part of the team at the DA's office who, along with Adam Grant, had prosecuted the doomed Grayson Webb "Lucifer" trial, was on vacation in Bali. Former DA Logan Myers, however, was at his home in Sausalito. He sounded spry enough on the phone, for a man pushing eighty. Yes, he knew about Adam's murder, and yes, he was willing to talk to Valerie—in person only. Even on the phone she could tell he was quietly delighted to be involved, however peripherally, in a case. Beyond his voice she sensed the months and years of deeply pleasant and wholly unsatisfactory retirement. Golf. A boat. The Sunday papers over long breakfasts. Boredom.

Nick called her when she was halfway across the Golden Gate Bridge. She thought twice about picking up.

"Hey," he said. "I'm sorry."

"You're sorry?" She'd assumed she would be the one apologizing.

"Yes, I'm sorry. I was pissed at you."

No mistaking the tone of voice. Guilty. No mistaking it because it was *rare*.

"Yeah," she said. "I don't blame you."

A pause.

"Seriously?" he said. "I wasn't expecting that."

Valerie was baffled. She was also aware that whatever advantage she had at this moment was precarious. Silence was the smart option.

"Nothing happened," he said.

She waited.

"I got wasted, that's all," Nick said. "I passed out and Lomax put me in his room."

"Where are you?"

"I'm still at the Pullman."

*I'm sorry I didn't come home last night.* She almost laughed. Almost.

"Right," was all she said.

A long pause.

"I was expecting to wake up to an angry message," he said.

She flirted, briefly, with lying. She had a sudden glimpse of breaking up with him. A conversation in which staleness expanded between them, became a solid wall. Not without a flicker of excitement, she imagined the peculiar scintillating emptiness of losing him. A return to the old familiar wealth of inviolate selfhood. The challenge was to make yourself enough. No husband, no kid, no love. Just the stark geometry of your own choices and actions and thoughts and dreams. It was clean and cold. With an extraordinary clarity she thought: If we break up I'll take a vacation somewhere with snow and mountains. Scandinavia. A big wooden lodge hotel with schnapps and fire and the muted conversations of strangers. The image made her present reality—of hard city sunlight bouncing off storefronts, people in T-shirts and sunglasses, the secret life growing in her womb—a profound irritant.

"Or maybe a message saying, you know: Are you okay?"

So the guilt was ready to morph into injury. It added to her irritation. And made telling the truth easy.

"I didn't go home either," she said.

A longer pause. His silent calculations. Her disappearance after the dinner with Serena and Lou. Their shared silence in bed when she'd got home.

"Oh," he said.

Here was the perverse fascination again. She could ruin it all, let it all go. It was heady temptation. You let it go and flowed on into the freedom of loss. It was appalling that you could have such power in your hands. Appalling and, of course, if you were a monster, thrilling.

"I was at work all night," she said.

The logic of which was luminous: I *wasn't* wasted. I could have called. But I didn't. You don't call, it's because you're unconscious. I don't call, it's because I'm preoccupied. One more scrap of evidence to add to the case for you caring more than me.

"I have witnesses," she said. Unnecessary. Irresistible.

He didn't say anything.

"Look, I'm in the middle of something right now," she said. "I'll call you later."

Hung up before it could go any further.

In pale green chinos and an ivory flannel shirt, Logan Myers came out to meet her on the white-graveled driveway of his detached Sausalito home. Tall, balding, liver-spotted, with silver-rimmed glasses and a magnificent hawkish nose showing a peck of gray hair in each nostril. Blue eyes visibly nostalgic for the pre-retirement days of putting away the bad guys. Her hand felt small in his when he shook it.

"How's the investigation going?" he asked her.

"Tangled."

"And there's a limit to what you can tell me, though my hunger must be obscenely plain to see."

"I wanted to ask you what the case-file-handling protocols were when you were in office," she said. "These days it's all digital, security encrypted. Were you guys still using paper on the Lucifer case? I mean, did you actually take physical documents home with you to work on after hours?"

"Yes, of course. One had to be extremely careful, obviously. But even in those days the ethical parameters weren't rigidly defined. Even now, unless I've missed something, there's no national consensus. It's amazing, isn't it, that less than twenty years ago we actually trusted human discretion?"

Valerie nodded. It was only confirmation of what she already suspected.

"From which I gather someone has seen something they shouldn't?"

"It's possible. We found a body with the Lucifer mark on it."

"What makes you think it's not the original killer?"

"Victim's male. Different MO."

"Different how?"

Valerie was about to answer—when the picture in her head shifted.

Fuck.

An object of two dimensions suddenly tilting to reveal that it was, in fact, three.

In the moment of revelation she felt a genuine, separate astonishment that she could so grossly have underestimated Rachel Grant.

"Jesus," she whispered. To herself. For a couple of seconds, Logan Myers, the yard, the house, everything—disappeared. Valerie was in the Grants' bedroom. Seeing it. All of it.

"Detective?"

She snapped back.

"You're smiling," Logan Myers said. "Something I said?"

"Sorry," Valerie said. She *was* smiling. "Nothing. Well, yes, actually. It was something you said. But . . ." She waved it away. It was still difficult to keep the shock—the pleasure—down.

"The different MO?" Myers prompted.

Valerie hesitated. Myers laughed. "Don't worry," he said. "I'm well aware that no one is above suspicion. Even"—he drew himself up and flared his nostrils in mock self-importance—"a former district attorney."

"There was some mutilation not common to the previous victims."

"I see. And why spoil a pretty morning with the gory details?"

"I'm sorry."

This time it was Myers who waved it away.

"Adam wasn't married when you worked with him," Valerie said.

"Correct."

"Girlfriends? Any sense of what his personal life was like?"

"Not as racy as mine," Logan Myers said—and as if on cue, a silver-haired woman Valerie assumed was Mrs. Myers appeared in the front doorway. She was dressed, cutely, in Bermudas, a Raiders T-shirt, and red espadrilles. Gardening gloves, a wicker basket over one arm, a pair of pruning shears in hand. She looked a good ten years younger than her husband.

"I'm just telling this nice young lady about the constancy of my love," Logan Myers called to her.

"Don't listen to anything he says," Mrs. Myers said. "He's demented."

"We could use some iced tea out here," Myers said.

"There's a jug in the refrigerator. Assuming you remember where that is."

Mrs. Myers walked off to the colorful beds bordering the lawn. As if mildly hypnotized, Valerie and Logan Myers watched her, until she bent to snip the first shrub. In the midst of her tiredness (the missed night's sleep had draped itself on her like a veil) Valerie was vaguely aware that there was a happy marriage here. Children launched, successfully, into the world. Grandchildren already with their own cell phones and dramas.

"Irony is one of the paltry consolations of age," Myers said. "To answer your question, I honestly don't know. I think he dated a little, but as far as I know nothing serious. The women in the office called him 'the Enigma.' The general opinion was that he was too good to be true. Polite, proper, professional. Naturally the assumption was of a secret and probably deviant life. To me he just seemed superheroically focused on his career. To be completely honest I was surprised when I heard he got married."

"You keep in touch? Ever meet his wife?"

"Nope. Adam and I didn't have that kind of relationship. I was sorry we lost him to the sharks, but we were never really more than work colleagues, and we didn't keep in touch after he went corporate. The loss was professional. He would've made a hell of a chief prosecutor."

The Enigma. Polite, proper, professional. Hadn't she thought something similar that abortive night with Adam Grant? That something sexual was missing?

"Well, I can see you have thoughts of your own," Myers said. "I'm not asking you to share them with me."

"You know how it is."

"It's one of the things I miss. I know *your* work, by the way. I read the papers."

Valerie looked away. Mrs. Myers was down on her haunches, snipping with precise viciousness.

"I'm no good for anything else," Valerie said.

"In it for the long haul?"

It was all she could do not to give in to what was becoming the reflex gesture—of putting her hand on her belly.

"Can't really imagine an alternative," she said. "Hard as I try."


At Willard & Gould, Valerie had to wait almost forty minutes to see Fiona Perry, who was in a meeting. On the upside, the Grants' former housekeeper, Isabella Hernandez, returned her call, and agreed—with audible reluctance—to meet with her later that afternoon.

"Detective?" Fiona Perry said, finding Valerie seated in the corridor outside her office.

Valerie rose. "Got a moment?"

"Sure." Fiona opened the door to her office. "Come in. It's a bit of a mess, I'm afraid."

Valerie followed her in. There were stacks of boxed files and a plastic crate containing Fiona's personal effects.

"You leaving?" Valerie asked.

Fiona was, as per Valerie's last visit, immaculately turned out, this time classically, in a white silk blouse and black pinstripe pencil skirt and heels. Her makeup looked as if it had just been applied. She was sans glasses this time, which made her jaw look heavier. "Not leaving," she said. "Moving. upstairs, at least temporarily. Fortunately for me, Ben Willard's secretary's just taken maternity leave, so I've got three months to make myself indispensable—again. I've been kind of a fifth wheel since Adam . . ."

"But you'll stay on, right?" The phrase "maternity leave" had, along with the Myerses' happy marriage and all the world's other jolly reminders, pricked Valerie.

"Who knows? I thought I was dug in here. Life resents assumption, it turns out. But I'm sure that's not what you're here to discuss."

"Right," Valerie said. "I realize this is going to sound stupid, but how many phones did Adam have? I mean, was there just the one number?"

"Only one that I used," Fiona said. "Although God knows he upgraded his phones often enough. He was a bit of a geek for the latest hardware."

"Do you recognize this number?" Valerie handed her a slip of paper with the number on it from which the caller had contacted Dwight Jenner.

"Can't say I do. Whose is it?"

"Well, it's registered to Adam."

Fiona shook her head. "Must be an old one. In my time Adam's only had one number."

Back at the station Valerie got an update from Laura Flynn.

"No-show on the Volvo from ALPR," she said. "If Rachel went back to Campbellville after the thirty-first, she either took an alternative route or used a different vehicle. It's not conclusive, obviously. For all we know she could've taken a cab. Or a bus. All we know for sure is that the last time she took the Volvo via 32 was on the night of July 31. Which still doesn't prove that was Jenner's last night in the land of the living."

"It doesn't matter," Valerie said. "I know Jenner didn't go back there after the thirty-first."

"You know?"

"Pretty much."

"How can you know?"

Valerie sat down at her desk. Opposite her, Will was just getting off the phone. She had to make a great effort to conceal herself, *what* she knew. Or almost knew. There was still a piece missing. To say nothing of the gap between what she knew and what she could prove. Even *if* she found the missing piece.

"So?" she asked him.

"Humble beginnings. Rachel Abigail Grant, born Rachel Abigail *Lake* at Penn Hospital, Philadelphia, in 1984. Known as 'Abby,' which was her grandmother's name. Mother, Joanna Lake, unmarried, father unknown. Sketchy employment and residence for Joanna, lost a house inherited from her mother and pretty much dropped off the grid. Zero tax records, so whatever she did, she did for cash. Any guesses?"

"Go on."

Will pushed a printout of a school records photograph in front of her. It showed a girl of twelve or thirteen years with long, untidy blond hair and a forced smile. The green eyes and fine mouth. Rachel. Who'd grown up to ditch the long blond hair in favor of short, snazzily chopped red. Except when she needed it back again. Except when she needed to go back to who she'd been.

"Rachel attended school in Philly until she was sixteen—pause for drum roll . . . At which time Joanna dies of a *heroin* overdose. Her body's found in woods off the 23 just east of Bryn Mawr. Investigation—more on this in a minute—eventually gets an ID and alerts CPS, by which time Rachel's long since AWOL and it goes to NCIC. Next and only thing we have is an address for her in Vegas, 2004. Employment says part-time at a tele-sales outfit that died in 2005. Not enough to live on, for sure. So there's money or support coming from elsewhere."

"NCIC never found her?"

"Apparently not."

"For Christ's sake. And Joanna's investigation?"

"Curiouser and curiouser. No doubt about the cause of death, but apparently she'd been keeping police company. Neighbors said she'd been living with homicide detective Lawrence Garner, who disappeared shortly before her body was found. Garner—get this—was found shot dead himself in Jersey less than two weeks later. Murdered by a New York drug dealer named Cole Pruitt. Pruitt's on a life sentence in Trenton. Claims Garner was as dirty as they come."

"Nice."

"Changes Mrs. Grant's profile, don't you think?"

"Adam must have known. *Surely* Adam must've known."

"Maybe. Or maybe he saw what he wanted to see."

"If he found out, it would explain the career shift," Valerie said. "If you're headed for chief prosecutor, do you really want a wife with that backstory? Corporate doesn't give a shit. Corporate'll make a virtue of it if the money comes in."

"All right. Maybe. What'd you get?"

She sat back in her chair and smiled at him.

"I know you're trying, Val, but you still look like the cat who got the cream. *All* the cream."

She didn't answer.

"Come on. Jesus."

She looked at her watch. 4:15 P.M. She was meeting Isabella Hernandez at 7:00 P.M.

"Ask me again in a couple of hours," she said. "In the meantime we're going to need a search warrant for the Grants' properties. Including the boat moored at Pier 39."

# 42

## *August 3, 2017*

It was still dark when the alarm woke Rachel for real. For real because the night had had many brief wakings between dense explosions of dreams. In those false wakings she hadn't known where she was, who she was, even. The room and the darkness could have been anywhere. Each time she'd groped and flailed to gather her history, to get some basic bearings—and each time the dreams had sucked her back under before she could. Of the dreams, all she recalled now was a sense of trying repeatedly to free herself from some suffocating muscular redness, as if she were buried like a maggot in a lump of raw meat.

She was exhausted. An enormous energy was pouring into her to compensate. A finite allowance. Move fast. Hurry while it lasts. Even as she'd lain there—surely only a few seconds?—the darkness outside had lost a layer of its conviction. She should have set the alarm for earlier. She should have done what she had to do in the middle of the night. But she'd been so tired. Just sitting on the couch had drained her. She'd watched television with the sound down and felt all the house's ordinary objects in awe of what she'd become. She was like a supernatural entity who'd somehow torn through into the natural world.

Without turning on the lights she crossed the landing to the reading room, knelt on the window seat, and parted the curtains a couple of inches. Vincent Lyle was, as always at this hour, seated in the pink velour wingback in the conservatory of the big house that backed onto her own. She couldn't make out the book in his hands, but he'd confessed he was struggling through *The Corrections*. She had a copy herself and had promised him she'd start it soon to keep him company. He never retired before first light. His sleeplessness outlasted hers, generally (she usually gave in sometime after 3:30 A.M. and crept to Elspeth's room) though their mutual small-hours acknowledgments had become a nightly routine. He must have wondered, these last couple of nights, what had kept her. Perhaps he thought she'd finally cracked her insomnia. Be there tomorrow, Vincent. You have to be there tomorrow.

In the bathroom she took off her T-shirt and panties and stood naked in front of the full-length mirror. It was required, this moment of nudity, this reduction to her absolute physical self. She had to look at her body, her face, her limbs, see, accept. It's you. You're doing this and it will be all right. *All shall be well and all manner of thing shall be well.*

She put on the fresh scrubs and old sneakers and went downstairs. In the kitchen she took several pairs of the disposable gloves from the cupboard under the sink, pulled one pair on. Five plastic ziplock bags. You only need two—so take five. Plastic for the organic material. Paper for the evidence. And for right now, for between the shed and the house, a Met Foods carrier bag.

The backyard was very still and tender in the twilight. She was tempted, courtesy of adrenal sensuality, to take the sneakers off and feel the cropped grass between her bare toes. These temptations, too, were murder's potential imperfections. You were hopelessly susceptible in your new world where anything was permissible, where there was only one answer to any question of possibility, namely, *Why not?*

She resisted, however. Her rational self labored toward its goal, the single sane navigator when the rest of the crew had gone happily mad.

The same rational self made her look up beyond the bamboo at the yard's edge. At ground level, of course, Vincent wouldn't be able to see her, but there was always the chance one of the Lyles was awake upstairs.

Nothing. The upper rooms were in darkness, blinds drawn.

She went first to the shed.

For a man who, as far as she knew, had never undertaken a single DIY task, Adam had an abundance of tools. Wealth, again, demanded acquisition. In addition to a complete set in the utility room there were many random bits and pieces here, including several hammers of various sizes. Two of them— claw hammers—were almost identical, albeit with different-colored grips. One was slightly larger than the other, but not, she decided, sufficiently to make a difference.

She took them both, checked the bleach and bucket were where she'd left them, then slipped out, closing the shed door behind her. The scent of night jasmine filled her nostrils, a sweet, insinuating headache. She went softly to the greenhouse and turned on the small plug-in lamp she'd set ready on the bench.

Aside from the mild tinnitus of her new lunacy there was a detached curiosity. A *biological* curiosity. Would it smell? Would there be blood, as with (she realized now) the raw meat of her dreams? Her inner voice repeated: Carefully and methodically . . . Carefully and methodically. Imagine every single gesture as part of a sequence you have to commit to memory—so that when the doubts creep in afterward you'll have some certainty to bring to bear against them: No, I was careful. First I did that . . . And then that . . . And so on. Memorize the map that will guide you home to innocence.

No, not innocence. Just guilt invisible to the eyes of the law.

She set the hammers on the floor and heaved the bags of potting compost to one side. Opened the metal box, the Tupperware one inside it. The greenhouse plants were a congregation of shy witnesses.

The first prod with her index finger told her the contents of the duct-taped bags had, as they were compelled to, thawed. Not surprisingly it brought to mind the instructions on frozen meat packaging. *Defrost thoroughly before use. Do not refreeze.*

She removed enough of the tape to get the bags open, then shifted the angle of the box to catch the beam of the lamp.

Right-handed. She'd established that early on. Therefore, she'd placed the right hand on top. The wristwatch—God *damn* it—had been on his left. A family heirloom, he'd said, clearly as proud of the word "heirloom" as he was of the watch. Even now, when there was no point in self-reproach, she cursed herself for not noticing he'd taken it off that night by the lake. Another imperfection. They were murder's lice, these oversights.

Eliminate the physical evidence. Operate as if every single one of your movements sheds glittering cells, a fairy dust of incrimination that will lead the right kind of investigation step by step back to you. She had an image of a CSI team with halogens, magnifiers, chemicals, black lights, their collective will bent on re-creating the picture of her guilt, a painstaking but inevitable restoration. It was hopeless. They would find her out. They had twenty-first-century technology at their disposal. She had nothing but her own amateur violence. For a moment the thought of getting caught gave her a thrill of liberation. If nothing else, getting caught would free her from the burden of worrying about getting caught.

But that would leave Elspeth alone.

Therefore it couldn't be allowed to happen.

*Radial and ulnar arteries. Anterior interosseous. Median nerve.* Elspeth's illustrated book from years ago: *The Human Body: How It Works.* Rachel had memorized some of the basics. A madcap instinct had insisted the Latin would desensitize her to what she had to do when the time came. It hadn't. When the time had come there had just been the ugliness of serrated metal and wet meat, the heat in her face and the ache in her arm. The blood had been a heavy softness in the air, in her breathing. When the time had come her mind had just repeated: *Sawing off his hand . . . Sawing off . . . his . . . hand . . .* She'd done the hands first, fearful she only had fuel in the tank enough for that. Astonishingly, she hadn't thrown up, though the first rasping stroke of saw against bone had brought her close. Since all connections were allowed, she'd found herself thinking of the movie in which the guy trapped by a boulder had to amputate his own arm with a dull blade to free himself. She and Adam had watched it together. Adam had said: Christ, if it wasn't true you'd never believe it, would you? All those ordinary things between them. Movies, dinners, conversations. Her and Elspeth making fun of him trying to choose a woolen hat.

Enough. What had happened had happened. Other women, other wives, would have been surprised, shocked to their cores. She had been surprised only in the upper strata of her being. Her core was immune to shock. Thanks to Larry, the worst had happened to her and made her core a place where the worst was expected, received, absorbed. After that it was just a question of what you did in response to the worst.

And here she was, responding.

She opened one of the ziplock bags and held it ready. Then she picked up Dwight Jenner's amputated right hand and examined it in the light. Comedy, as before, was available. Comedy was durable. She resisted the impulse to wave with it or perform a mock handshake, though there was no denying the impulse was there. Comedy to block the pathos, the understanding that this was really his hand, that had recorded his life's history of touch. Childhood. It had run over warm stone and delved into chilled sand, swished water, clutched hot coins.

But it had touched her, too, greedily delighted, rich with his contempt and blind to her purposes. He'd grabbed her hair, once, in spite of her telling him it was the one thing off-limits. Even when she'd told him, she'd known he'd try it sooner or later. That was men: Whatever you told them you didn't want them to do became the thing they wanted to do above all else. At the time she'd frozen (she'd been on her hands and knees) and said: Let go of my hair right now or I walk and you'll never see me again. He'd said, For Christ's sake—but he'd let go. Not that the wig would've been a deal-breaker for him. She had too much else to offer. But he would have started asking questions, and, as per the male logic, would have started wanting to fuck her without her wearing it. In her natural state. She'd had no control over how much he might tell people about her. She had to be sure his description was inaccurate. When they started looking—as they would, inevitably—they had to be looking for a blonde. For Sophia.

She sealed the hand in the ziplock bag, peeled off the gloves, set them aside, and put on a fresh pair. Put the first bag in a second. Resealed the duct tape, closed the Tupperware box, then the lid of the tin crate. Locked it and stowed it under the bench. She put the amputated hand and the two hammers in the

Met Foods carrier bag (imagined them nestling among packaged tomatoes, a carton of milk, bunched parsley—horror in suburban shopping!) then turned off the lamp.

Quicker across the yard this time. The sky had lost another layer of darkness. Still an hour till dawn, but she'd been too leisurely. There was a terrible tendency to let time drift, to be beguiled by herself, by what she was doing.

In the kitchen she took a clean polishing cloth and plucked the knife from its block.

She went up the stairs.

Prints. Hammers. Knife. Bedroom.

She set the carrier bag down on the landing, took out the slightly larger of the two claw hammers, and went into the reading room. Checked on Vincent. Still there, now holding a steaming red mug. Caffeine, he'd told her, made absolutely no difference one way or the other.

The window seat lifted. Storage space inside, occupied by spare cushions, throws, blankets, and, as of a week ago, half a dozen plain new brown paper bags (you only need two, so you get six), one of which she removed and set down, open, on the floor. She wrapped the larger claw hammer in an Indian-print throw and stowed it at the bottom of the pile. Then she went back out to the landing and changed her gloves.

Move as little as possible. Every gesture sheds the lethal fairy dust. She took the knife and the second hammer, along with the ziplock bag, back into the reading room. Went to work, vigorously, with the polish cloth until she was confident the surface was clean of all previous marks of contact.

The next wasn't easy. (Nor, if she were being honest with herself, was she sure the prints would either take or last. Freezing and defrosting—would that fuck it up? Nothing she'd read indicated it would, but murder was the land of no guarantees.) There wasn't much pliability to work with, and simulating an actual *grip* on either the knife or the second hammer was impossible. There was nothing to do but apply pressure with the fingertips and hope it was enough. The delicate trick was not to handle either the knife or the hammer where she'd placed the prints. Whatever she lost between now and tomorrow night was lost for good. There was only one shot at this.

When she'd finished, she put the hammer in one brown paper bag, the knife in another, rolled the tops of the bags into a loose seal, deposited them in the left corner of the storage space, and covered them with a blanket, arranged to allow only minimal contact between itself and the bags. As little friction as possible. The prints were her sleeping babies, now. On no account must they be disturbed—until it was time for them to wake and go to work.

She lowered the window seat. One brief vision of herself coming back here tomorrow night, lifting it again, unwrapping the hammers, the knife. The feel and weight of them in her hands, her lifeless accomplices. The last few minutes. *I am in blood stepped in so far . . .*

Let it go. No point. It would be what it was.

In the master bedroom she applied the dead fingertips—hard not to overdo it—to the frame and handle of the French windows. Have to keep Adarn away from them. Turn up the air-conditioning? More comedy. Jesus. She stepped out and very quickly (she was, after all, outside) pressed a set to the balcony rail. And if it rains?

It won't rain. It can't.

By the time she was back out in the yard, dawn was a burgeoning excitement, like a crowd outside a concert hall knowing it would soon be let in. She hurried again to the greenhouse.

This last preparation was, she admitted to herself, wildly optimistic. But at least it didn't increase the risk. She took the smallest ziplock bag, a Swiss Army penknife, and a set of tweezers from her pocket. Her original idea, she knew, wasn't going to work. Her fingernails simply weren't strong enough. Instead she used the smallest of the knife's blades and made three tiny incisions in the skin around the edge of the hand's stump.

It took some work, a concentration that taxed her. But eventually, via a combination of blades and tweezers, she had an approximation of what she wanted: three minute, ragged parings of skin. She placed them in the last ziplock bag and put it in her pocket. The Swiss Army knife went in the Tupperware box. Along with all the used gloves—and Dwight Jenner's right hand.

She allowed herself a long, hot, meticulous shower. The heat and water and steam were good. Good in an archetypal or Old Testament way: *And God saw the light, that it was good.* The coconut scent of the hair conditioner gave her pleasure out of all proportion. Deep soft towels and Shalimar body lotion. She went again into a spell of self-beguilement, rubbing it into her skin. Her physical details were renewed and strange with life. The lines in her knuckles, the creases behind her knees. The flesh of the dead vivified the flesh of the living. Her thoughts fluttered. Did morticians enjoy a sensuous advantage? Doctors and nurses? What could handling the dead do but remind you you were fabulously alive?

In the bedroom she painted her fingernails and toenails metallic blue, dressed in her favorite blue jeans, a crisp black T-shirt, and snug white sport socks with slightly padded soles. It was a ridiculous bliss to pull them onto her feet. Brand-new red Nike high tops that made her feel springy and strong. The world beyond what she had to do was filled with the sprawling promise of baked asphalt and brightly lit stores and good coffee and the hiss of the ocean pressed thin at the shingle's edge. She had an image of her and Elspeth in a convertible on Route 1, Elspeth with her bare feet on the dash, her long dark hair wild in the rushing wind.

She ate a bowl of cereal and a peach yogurt and drank a cup of black coffee. The sky now was dark salmon-silver, a few horizontal shreds of thin cloud in silhouette in the lower reaches. An anarchy of birdsong in the backyard when she opened the patio doors and stood for a few minutes, going over everything one last time. Elspeth was due back at Drew at 5 P.M. She had almost eleven hours. Adam's flight didn't land till 8 P.M.

At which point the countdown would really begin.

Daylight. She put the metal tin in a cardboard box with a few paperbacks on top to hide it before stowing it in the Volvo's trunk, alongside the ten-pound weight she'd brought up from the gym. There was always the chance she'd run into one of the marina staff or a boat neighbor. She was moving ahead to the investigation, picturing a tired-eyed but die-hard detective in a crumpled suit.

—*Did you notice what Mrs. Grant was carrying in the box?*

—*Yes, books! She's a great one for reading.*

"Carrying books" the detective would write in his notes. Hardly a sign of homicidal guilt.

She didn't run into anyone. The marina was quiet at that hour, though the city at its back was already going brashly about its business. With the tools and the extra ten pounds the box was heavy. The upper sky was deepening blue, the sun liquid on the green-bronze water, the white hulls blinding. Presumably because the universe couldn't resist occasional symbolism, the last thinning tuft of a morning fog clung along the edge of Alcatraz Island. She'd taken the audio tour of the prison by herself, years ago, when Elspeth had first started kindergarten. Like every other visitor she'd tried to imagine herself as an inmate. Sometimes they put you in solitary and turned out all the lights. One prisoner so confined had passed his time by pulling a button off his shirt, tossing it somewhere in the pitch darkness of the cell, spinning himself around, then getting down on his hands and knees to find it. Find it, toss it again, and so on. The minutes, the hours, the days. Wandering among the rusted cells and bare concrete, Rachel had recalled the night she'd considered sending her mother to prison. She'd wondered whether Joanna might still be alive if she had.

Now the question was hers: How long will you last, incarcerated? Prison was what she saw on TV, the pumped inmates and the bare forearms of overweight guards. Women's prisons, the assumption was you became someone's bitch or made someone yours. At least she had violence and sexual malleability in her favor. In the early Vegas period she'd done couples, occasionally, until she tired of seeing that the men who got the most out of it were the ones whose women were putting up with it, reluctantly. Reluctance was wearily arousing to men. Larry had made that plain from the start.

Larry. So much of what she'd become circled back to Larry. And Joanna. Larry had determined what she hated in men. Joanna had determined the sort of mother she, Rachel, was never going to become.

And here, in these last days, the fruits of that tree had fallen.

True to form, Adam's effectively living on the boat for the last two months hadn't made much of a dent. Marina regulations prohibited residing on board, but Adam found a way around proscriptions. She supposed money had changed hands. In any case, the *Aqua Nova* was clean, tidy, organized. Order went with him. In the early days it had been one of the things she'd liked about him, the absence of mess, clutter, chaos. Living with him had been everything that living with Joanna had not.

She eased the boat out and headed west toward the Golden Gate Bridge. It was colder out on the water, and after only a few minutes she had to put on one of the windbreakers kept ready on board. The bridge itself never failed to astonish her, the extraordinary perverse human will that had pushed through the physics and math, sunk drills and hoisted steel. Such engineering was like a joyful insult to the old idea of God: He could divide land and water as He liked. It didn't stop us altering such arrangements for our own convenience.

The old idea of God. She pictured the benevolent Old Man sitting distraught with his head in his hands, wondering how it had turned out that he wasn't God after all. Just one more frail and redundant aspect of the actual and much larger God, by whom he was contained, and who had offered him to the human imagination as a parent offers a teddy bear to a child, to be a comfort for a few years—then discarded, when all such comforts were shown to be false.

Fresh, open space rushing toward her like the future. Liquid blue sky and her collar's rattle in the wind. There wasn't much traffic on the water. She kept west through the Gulf of the Farallones at a steady eighteen knots, turned slightly northwest to pass the islands themselves.

Fifteen minutes later she stopped the boat. In spite of the sun, cold came up from the deep water, spoke of the onyx darkness down there.

On deck she spread the tarp, put on gloves, opened the cardboard box, and lifted out first the metal one, then the Tupperware. Along with the books, the gym weight, and the duct-taped bags were a steel mallet and chisel. Corpses, notoriously, filled with gas. The sea all too often gave up its secrets. She didn't imagine mere amputated hands and feet would float up to betray her, but she was taking no chances. She removed the books, weight, and tools, transferred the bags from the Tupperware box directly into the metal one, and gouged a few holes in them with the chisel. She put the weight in, closed the lid, and punched several large holes in that as well. Let the water get in. Little fish, crabs, scavengers. The Tupperware and tarp she would discard on the way home, since even if it was found it would prove nothing—and so much the better if it was found on dry land.

There was a moment, standing with the now locked and vandalized metal box balanced on the handrail, where all her risk gathered and pressed upon her. Once this went overboard it was beyond her recall. She was tempted to retrace her actions again—there had to be something she'd missed—but sheer mental fatigue got the better of her. She let it go.

For a second or two she thought the weight wasn't enough. It canted, seemed to bob a couple of times . . .

But it went. The water crept in through the holes as if in eager investigation, as if she'd given the ocean a gift—then it was gone.

She held on to the handrail, feeling empty. Then she gathered up the mallet and chisel and hurled them as far from the boat as she could.


"So?" Rachel said to Elspeth when she picked her up at Drew later that afternoon. "How was it?"

"Please don't make me go there ever again," Elspeth said. They had both just got in the Volvo.

"It smells weird in here," Elspeth said.

"I had it valeted."

"It smells like bleach."

"Roll the window down. I'll turn the AC off. Was it really that bad?"

Elspeth shrugged. She hadn't wanted to go to the summer camp, in spite of it being the countryside equivalent of the Waldorf.

"It was okay," she said quietly. This was her daughter, now, Rachel knew, everything accepted with submissive resignation.

"Lana and Jeanette sounded nice."

"They were okay," Elspeth said.

"Mica must've been a drag. Now that she's had her braces out she must be swaggering around like Beyoncé."

Humor. Weak, admittedly, but come on, baby. Don't go under. Don't let it be the only thing. Not long now. After tomorrow we'll be free.

"Did you . . . ?" Elspeth said.

Mild telepathy, always, between them.

"Yes. Tomorrow night he's coming to the house to sign the papers. After that we're gone."

There were no papers. Papers weren't part of the plan. She hoped the telepathy didn't go that far.

"You're going to Julia's for a sleepover."

Elspeth looked at her in disbelief. Dark eyes filling with injustice.

"I don't want you in the house while we have to deal with it. I don't want you anywhere near him."

Elspeth subsided, kept her mouth shut. *He. Him.* The pronouns were contaminated for her now. Of course they were.

# 43

Valerie was in the Taurus, en route to the Mission to see Isabella Hernandez, when her phone rang. It was Dina Klein.

"We've had a bit of drama here," Dina said.

"Yes?"

"Last night Julia was very upset. I'm afraid she thinks she's in trouble. She wasn't, apparently, entirely honest with you."

"Oh?" Valerie spotted a gap, pulled over outside a Ben and Jerry's. It was a golden late afternoon. The car's interior was comfortingly sunlit.

"Yes," Dina said. "Look, it's probably nothing . . ."

"Go ahead?"

"It was what you said about Elspeth feeling somehow responsible for her father's death."

There was, of course, satisfaction. *Seeing the full picture.* But beneath the picture was a sprawling space, drearily and expansively occupied by her inability to prove the picture was genuine. For Valerie, closing a case was a mix of pleasure and emptiness. Pleasure because she'd penetrated the mystery, seen what there was to see, how it had happened, who had done it and why. Emptiness because all any case revealed was that there was really no such thing as a mystery. The reasons, the motives, the hows and whys—they were all drawn from the same small human pool: greed; anger; envy; lust; vengeance. Every murder sprang from ordinary sources.

Every marriage, too, she thought, now, with a feeling of melancholy.

"It was months back, according to Julia," Dina said. "The girls were talking and Julia was bitching about her dad. Marty had nixed her going to some mini-festival without adult supervision—anyway it was minor, it was nothing. But in the middle of Julia's nonsense, Elspeth blurted something out. She said she wished her father were dead."

"I see," Valerie said.

"Obviously kids say this sort of thing, but Julia . . . You know? It wasn't said in the usual way."

"I hear you."

"I realize it's irrelevant," Dina continued. "To the investigation, I mean. I'm just worried Rachel doesn't know how bad it is for her daughter. If Elspeth *does* feel responsible, then someone professional needs to be addressing it."

"You're right," Valerie said. "But I'm pretty sure Rachel has a very good idea of how serious it is. My understanding is Elspeth's seeing a counselor. But let's keep that between ourselves, okay?"

"Got it," Dina said. "I just wanted to make sure she's getting some help."

"No problem."

"Are you . . . ? Are you making any progress? I know it's none of my business."

It would have been some relief to be able to tell Dina Klein the truth: Progress? Well, yeah, I pretty much know the whole story, which, by the way, your latest bulletin has just solidified. Problem is I can't prove any of it.

"We're still working," was all she said. "Can't really tell you any more than that."

"I get it. Of course. Well, good luck . . ."

"Thanks for calling."

They hung up.

———

Isabella Hernandez was a small, quick woman in her early sixties with a tight-skinned face and deep eye sockets, short curly hair dyed several shades of copper and gold. She lived in a two-bedroom ground-floor apartment on York Street with her youngest daughter, Felicia, and her grandson, Gabriel. Isabella's husband had died of a heart attack three years ago, and the bereavement had coincided with the collapse of Felicia's marriage. The girl had moved back home to raise her son, supported by her mother's job (Señor Hernandez's tiny life insurance payout was long gone) and the income from her own evening shifts at a local taqueria. There was durability here, Valerie thought, two harried women determined to keep life strong and bright for the kid. The apartment was flimsily furnished but spotlessly clean. Mother and daughter shared a vibe of hard work and willfully renewed energy.

"So," Valerie said, "I gather you and Mr. Grant didn't get along?"

She and Isabella were sitting at a small fold-out table under a plastic awning in the tiny backyard. A dusty lawn bordered by a little cactus garden with soil the color of paprika. A swing, a scatter of outdoor toys. Felicia was giving Gabriel his bath. The sounds of the kid's splashing and chatter came out of the window a few feet away.

"No, that's not right," Isabella said. "We got along fine, at first."

"I understood from Hester, his sister, that . . . ?"

Isabella tightened her lips and shook her head, not in denial, but in irritation. At herself, Valerie decided.

"I can't believe he's dead," Isabella said. "It's incredible."

Incredible, perhaps, Valerie thought, but not, to Isabella Hernandez, a great loss to the world.

"Could you tell me why you were dismissed?"

Isabella gave a slight snort. "You want the fake reason or the real one?"

"Both."

"The fake reason was that I 'stole' his gold cuff links."

"Which you did not."

Isabella laughed. Contempt. "He makes a big fuss in front of Mrs. Grant one morning after I've been cleaning in the bedroom. Insists on me emptying my bag. And what do you know? Cuff links! Eight months I'm working there. It's disgusting."

"Mrs. Grant believed him?"

"What's she going to believe? This is her husband. I'm the Mexican cleaner."

"I see. And the real reason?"

Isabella stood up. *"Momento,"* she said. She went into the kitchen and returned bearing a red plastic tray. A pitcher of iced tea and two glasses. Poured. Valerie knew better than to refuse Hispanic hospitality.

*"Muchas gracias,"* she said. In fact she was glad of it. The yard was dry and still. Isabella Hernandez regarded her, obviously weighing up her chances of being believed.

"A person could say it was nothing," she said. "A person could say this is a woman's imagination."

"I keep an open mind," Valerie said. "Always."

"Your job," Isabella said, with a tired smile. "Yes."

*"Qué dice el pato?"* Felicia said, in the bathroom.

"Quack quack!" Gabriel said.

*"Sí,* quack quack!"

Isabella laughed. Valerie smiled. Wondered about the household. Not easy, she decided, but there was warmth, determination, love. She spent her life so deep in horror sometimes these tiny reminders of people doing the right thing gave her a sad jolt. Isabella did what she had to do for her daughter. Felicia did what she had to do for her son. There was a liberation in this kind of motherhood along with all its constraints: Worrying about the kid meant you could stop worrying about yourself. Ask Rachel Grant.

"It was a few weeks before the cuff links," Isabella said. "A Saturday. Mrs. Grant was out shopping. Elspeth was home with Mr. Grant. I finished for the day, Felicia came in the car with the little one to pick me up. But we went a short way and I realized I left my phone charger plugged in upstairs. So we went back for it."

In spite of Valerie's attempt at a neutral demeanor, she suspected a little of what she already thought was evident.

"I called out when I went back in, but I guess they didn't hear. To be honest I thought they must be in the backyard."

"Right," Valerie said.

"Like I say," Isabella continued. "A person could say it was nothing. But when I was at the top of the stairs they came out of Elspeth's room. He was holding her arm and she kind of snatched it away from him."

No need, Isabella's look said, to waste time on the niceties. Valerie knew why she was being told this. By a mother with a daughter.

"Was she dressed?" she asked.

"Yes."

"Were they arguing?"

Isabella shrugged. "She looked upset. Kind of angry. I only heard him say something like 'That's not going to get you anywhere.' This is not exact words. It wasn't . . . It was the way she looked. And then *his* face when he saw me. I know that look. Like I'd caught him doing something bad."

"More than just embarrassment at being seen scolding his daughter?"

Isabella downturned her mouth and looked away. "All I can say is it didn't look right to me. But later I asked Elspeth if everything's okay and she says it's nothing. Laughed about it, even."

"But you weren't convinced?"

"He was different with me after that. Then this rubbish with the cuff links."

"Did he . . . Did they accuse you officially? To the agency?"

"No. *I* reported it, myself." A proud flaring of the Hernandez nostrils. "Twelve years I've been with this agency. They know me."

"And you never spoke with Mrs. Grant about it?"

"No."

"Nor about what you'd seen?"

"What did I see? How does it sound? He had ahold of her arm, that's all."

"Elspeth didn't look frightened?"

"No, like I say, she looked angry. She's not the type to be frightened."

Valerie made a note in her book. "And apart from this incident, you never saw anything to make you think anything was wrong?"

"Nothing. They were just a normal rich family."

Valerie nodded. "Everything seem all right to you between husband and wife?"

"Sure. I mean he was at work a lot of the time. They didn't seem to talk much, but . . ." Isabella made a dismissive gesture. "What do I know? That's what some people are like. I worked in a lot of fancy houses. Not much talking."

Valerie closed her notebook. "Okay, Mrs. Hernandez, I guess that's all. Thank you for your cooperation—"

"Is she okay? Elspeth?"

"She's having a hard time, as you'd expect," Valerie said, "but her mother's taking care of her." She got to her feet. "Thank you for the iced tea."

# 44

## *August 4, 2017*

Rachel got up at 7 A.M., showered, dressed, and went to look in on Elspeth. The girl was asleep in the fetal position, clutching a soft pillow. The fetal position. Memory of the womb's security asserted itself when you needed it, when the world outside the womb did its thing, hurt you beyond bearing. The body wanted so desperately to go back. Rachel had had a long, painful labor for her daughter. Adam had been there. Through the heat and weight of the pain she'd been aware of him trying to reassure her: You're doing great, honey . . . Breathe . . . Breathe. She'd felt the vast distance between his words and her agony. It had diminished him, made him genuinely pathetic. It was as if she'd become a god and was seeing the paltry dimensions of his humanity for the first time. She had always felt larger than him, but now his negligibility in the face of her pain made him tiny. They said they loved each other often enough, but the truth was her soul had always remained private. She knew him (she'd thought), but he didn't know her. And in labor, courtesy of the pain, she was further away from him than ever. He'd kept saying: That's it, baby, you're doing it . . . Breathe . . . He might as well have been tossing pancakes or doing the crossword. Eventually she'd said quietly: Stop talking. When it was over and Rachel had come back by degrees to the strangely shrunken and humbly detailed world, the midwife had given Elspeth to her to hold, still slick with blood, a whorl of mucus on the delicate head. Rachel's arms had been utterly without strength, but she'd held her, suffered a terrible mix of failure and fury when the doctor said: Careful, she's going to drop it—and the midwife had had to help keep the baby in Rachel's arms. Rachel had thought, through the blur and the dizzying warmth: I'm weak now, but I'll never be weak again. Not for you. I promise.

Now she went softly into Elspeth's room and sat on the edge of the bed, rested her hand on her daughter's back, felt the warmth of her sleep. She wondered if she was dreaming. Her dreams would be a curse now. Either they would be good, and waking would be a betrayal, or they would be bad, and waking would be a relief. A temporary relief, since the world into which she woke had itself become a crawling nightmare, filled with ordinary things.

Elspeth opened her eyes.

"What time is it?" she said.

"It's early. Go back to sleep. I didn't mean to wake you."

For a while Elspeth drifted, not quite yielding to sleep. For Rachel it was very peaceful in the room. The smell of patchouli and laundered denim and fabric-softened linen and the suede shoulder bag on the floor by the bed. Behind the drawn curtains was a soothing blue-opal light. She was tempted to lie down next to Elspeth. There was never enough holding her, now. She'd had to control herself. She was afraid she would destroy her with love, with her own failure to protect her.

"Do you hate me?" Elspeth asked quietly.

Rachel brushed the dark hair away from her daughter's face. Her heart hurt from the question. The irreversibility of what had happened. No matter what she did for Elspeth now it wouldn't erase the damage. Who knew that better than her? Here she was, all these years later, Larry's touch as close as if it had happened only moments ago. And though she understood her daughter's question she said: "Don't be insane. Why would you even ask that?"

"You were happy," Elspeth said. "If I hadn't . . ."

Of course she could think this way, Rachel knew. Now that Elspeth had been forced into knowledge, all the ugly logics were available to her.

"Don't waste a single second thinking that way," she said.

"But you're disappointed in me. For not . . . For not wanting to—"

"I told you: We do this whichever way you want. The only person who gets to decide what we do is you."

"But you think I should've told the police."

*I don't believe in the police. Larry was police. The law is nothing more than the people who get to enforce it.*

"I think you're the smartest, toughest person I know," Rachel said. "That's why you get to decide. And whatever you decide is right. That's all. I love you. I'll always love you. You know that, don't you?"

Elspeth nodded, closed her eyes. The little interlude of wakefulness had burgeoned, strangely. Now it was closing again.

"You haven't told anyone, have you, that he hasn't been living here?" Rachel asked.

"No."

"Good."

Rachel bent and kissed her. The softness of her skin, her hair smelling of sleep.

"I love you," she whispered. "I love you, I love you."

She waited until she was sure Elspeth was sleeping again, then went downstairs. Her hands were sweating. She tried to calm herself by going from room to room opening the curtains and blinds. In fact it did help, slightly, letting the big house fill with the early sunlight.

Still, it was procrastination. She took her phone and went into the study. It seemed right to make the call in here, in his room.

It rang four times. She pictured him seeing her name on the phone's screen: Rachel calling. Imagined the way his heart would race, wondering what new contortion her voice would demand. For a moment she thought—against all her expectations—that he might let it go to voice mail. That wouldn't work. There could be no record of what she was about to say.

"Hello?" he said. It really was a question. Either because he couldn't believe it was her—or because he dreaded that it was.

"Hey," she said. Gently. The way she would have before everything had changed. In the silence that followed she could sense him utterly incapable of guessing what would come next. He had long since passed the point of thinking anything he could say would make things better. Now he merely waited for the next infliction. A chained prisoner waiting for the next stroke of the lash.

"Listen to me," she said. "I need to see you." She left a pause. Softened and lowered her voice. "I've been so wrong. Adam, I was wrong. I'm so sorry."

His silence was a struggle between joy and suspicion. He was being faced with something so good it couldn't possibly be true. She imagined him seeing the gates of Hell opening: Light. Freedom. The impossible return. The miracle.

"I don't . . . What?"

"Don't say anything," she said. "Just listen. Come home. Tonight, after work. I know what happened. I know you were telling the truth. I don't expect you to forgive me."

More silence. She could all but hear his brain working. The impossibility of what she'd just said.

"I don't understand," he said.

"She told me the truth. I'm sorry. You can't imagine how sorry."

"She told you . . . ?"

"Oh, God, Adam . . ." She sighed. "I just . . . I just don't know why she did it."

And still he couldn't find the words. Of course he couldn't—since he knew the truth. She could feel him gearing up to clarify, to make sure he'd understood, the lawyer brain demanding no chink in the armor.

"Please," she said. "Don't let's do this on the phone."

"Jesus," he said.

"Just come home tonight. Please. We'll talk then."

"I'll come now."

"No"—(careful, Rachel)—"Don't come now. She's here. She can't be here. You can see that."

A much longer pause. All his calculations. Regardless of the truth—the truth he knew—he perceived righteousness making itself available to him. Naturally. Righteousness would be required if he was going to accept the role in the script she was offering. He would be unconvincing without it. He was working all this out at high speed, in shock.

"She's going to Julia's for a sleepover," Rachel said. "I don't know what happens next. I can't even begin to imagine—but I need to see you. Please come tonight. Will you?"

She had an image of a fox nosing the edge of a baited trap. Not *knowing* it was a trap, of course, but electric with hunger and tension. Her own voice in her head repeated: Come on . . . Just a bit further . . . Come on . . .

Adam exhaled, heavily. "Jesus fucking Christ," he said.

"I know. I *know*. Just come and we'll talk."

Come on . . . A little closer . . . Almost there . . .

"What made her . . . ?" He hesitated. "Why now?"

"I honestly don't know. I don't know what to do. I don't understand any of it. We need to help her. I know how much this has hurt you, but she's our daughter and one way or another she needs . . . We have to try to understand why she did this. I don't know how we get through it, but we have to."

"Maybe we don't get through it," he said. "I doubt *I* will." And there it was, the first tentative note of grievance. He was testing it out, the idea of his own victimhood.

"Please come tonight. You can hate me as much as you like but we still have to talk."

One more step. Just one more. You know you want it.

"All right," he said. "I'll come. I'll be there as soon as I finish."


Rachel dropped Elspeth at Julia's at 4 P.M. The half hour she spent having coffee with Dina Klein was a torment. The effort to keep living the old life while the new one raged inside her. She felt transparent, riddled with a disease anyone (certainly Dina, who didn't miss much) would see at a glance. But the universe not only allowed these dualities, it insisted on them. Therefore the horror footage ran while she confessed to having lost interest in *House of Cards*. She went to the bathroom for a few minutes just to get away from the absurdity. There were framed family holiday photos in there—as there were in her own bathroom. A copy of *Cosmopolitan: "Sex Tips for a Sinful Summer."* Sinful. Sin. Thou shalt not kill. Except that was wrong. At Berkeley someone had pointed it out. In Hebrew, the commandment was more specific: Thou shalt not do murder.

Not that that made any difference to her. She was guilty either way.

Back at home she tidied up, wiped down the kitchen worktops, put freshly laundered white linen on the bed. The rituals of domestic order. The good wife. Then she took her second shower of the day. Underwear. Nothing too overtly sexy. Nude lace briefs and bra. Forget the stockings. Overkill. Don't suggest premeditation. A seduction, yes, but it would have to come as if it were a surprise to her. Too blatant a reversal would back him off. His instincts were good. Let it emerge from sadness, regret, torment. Let the words run out so that the body must speak. If he even still wanted her. Perhaps he wouldn't. There was always the possibility he would want to exploit his newly acquired innocence, preserve the high ground to which she'd admitted him. She imagined him fending her off, saying, Really? This? Now—after what I've been through? In which case . . . In which case things would be difficult. Not impossible—but difficult. Don't think about it. Trust your skills. They're all still there. They'll always be there. Her legacy—Abigail's legacy, Sophia's legacy—whether she wanted it or not.

Eventually, after one last check in the mirror, there was nothing to do but wait. She stood in the big living room that looked out over the front yard and drive. The evening was coming in with a slow, comforting dimming of the sky's light. The lawn was already dusk blue, the maples Rorschach blots of darkness. The whole neighborhood was settling into a deeper gravity. Her face was warm, her hands sensitive. She felt perfectly suspended, looking neither forward nor back, her life without a past, without a future, just a moment-by-moment nowness from which it seemed nothing could follow.

And yet something extrasensory rose in her (the hairs on her bare forearms lifted) a couple of seconds before she actually heard the car, as if his approach had sent a tremor through the ether ahead of him and she knew before she could possibly know.

Then the seconds were gone and there was the car, nosing its way through the gate and turning with a sound of soft crunching onto the white gravel drive. She watched him get out. He looked up and saw her at the window. His face was drawn and blank. Not knowing what to hope. She didn't smile. Not a conscious decision. She was in the flow now, committed by something that demanded a dark spontaneity. Everything she could do beforehand had been done. Now she was back in the strange choreography, a subtle force that came from outside herself and to which there was nothing but surrender.

They met in the hallway, stood a few feet apart. He was still undecided, fundamentally. The gift on offer to him was huge. Premature acceptance could explode it. They stared at each other. Their bodies heated the cool space.

"What happened?" he said.

Rachel stood without answering immediately, shaking her head. It wasn't right to touch him. Not yet.

"Come into the kitchen," she said.

He followed her, took a seat at the white island. She opened the fridge, took the chilled bottle of Semillon chardonnay, poured them a glass each. Both of them felt the space where a toast, the clink of glasses, no matter how perfunctory, would normally be. Adam swallowed a large mouthful.

"I don't think I should be expected to do the talking here," he said.

"No. I know. Of course not."

Even in the flow she was amazed at him. Since he knew the truth, he knew Elspeth's alleged retraction was false. But he was subtle enough to imagine the psychology that would explain it, that she'd changed her story out of guilt, or fear, or both. He was considering—he was actually considering—living with that. Living with his wife and his daughter—and the lie he knew the girl had told out of suffering. Rachel knew she shouldn't be amazed that he was willing to accommodate this, but she was. There was no limit to him, to what he would dare to take for himself. It was, to the detached part of herself, impressive. Perhaps evil always was. Hence sympathy for the Devil. Lucifer.

"I didn't wring it out of her," she said. "I don't know what made her tell me. The truth is we were just here in the kitchen yesterday. We were talking about something else—about her doing a zip-wire at summer camp, in fact. She was . . . I don't know. She went quiet. I asked her what was the matter and the next minute she was in tears. She was . . . It was awful. My God, it was awful." Rachel put the wineglass down on the counter. Leaned on the heels of her hands. Again, not for effect. Her legs felt weak.

Adam was silent, absorbing, calculating. Willing himself not to speak too soon. He knew his words now had the potential to decimate his advantage. She could feel the mental care he was taking, measuring out the new dimensions, gently, gently.

"What, exactly, did she say?" he asked at last, quietly.

Rachel sat down on the island stool opposite him. She saw them as if from the viewpoint of someone looking in through the glass doors from the patio: a married couple having a serious conversation at the end of a long day. But not *this* serious conversation, not *this* long day.

"She said she made it up," Rachel said. Kept her voice flat, even. Let him infer the grueling hours she'd put in to assimilate this. Let him hear what it had cost her to accept the scale of the wreckage, the irreversibility of the damage done. The damage done to him.

He took another swallow of wine, with what looked like controlled aggression. The performance of suppressed outrage. He was letting her see him rising above it. The man was incredible. But she was incredible herself, she thought. Casually incredible, when it was demanded.

"Did she say why she did that?" he asked. Still the visible mastery of himself.

"I asked her. Obviously."

"And?"

Rachel rested her fingertips on the rim of her glass. Studied the pale golden liquid. Shook her head again. Weary incomprehension. "She said she didn't really know. I realize that sounds unbelievable, but that's what she said. She was angry with you."

"Angry? Jesus. Why?"

"I don't know, Adam. I talked with her for hours. It was a circle. There was nothing there for me to get hold of." She looked up at him. Brought distress into her face. "Don't you see? I don't know why she would do a thing like that. Which is bad enough, but what's worse is I'm not sure *she* knows. It's like she's going quietly crazy."

"She's not the only one."

Rachel looked away.

"Sorry," he said. "I know. But do you have any fucking idea what this has been like? For me?"

Her turn to exhibit self-control. "Well, I know what it's been like for me," she said. "It's been the worst thing that's ever happened to me." The self-control wasn't, entirely, fake. It was costing her a lot to play her part. Her amazement at him kept rising up, a hot nausea. "I'm sorry," she said. "Yes, I have an idea of what this has been like for you."

"There's literally nothing worse to be accused of," he said. "Not even murder. People can respect a murder. This?"

*People can respect a murder.* She hadn't thought of it that way—hadn't cared—but she saw he was right. It almost made her laugh. His astute ignorance.

"And I believed her," she said neutrally. "Don't think I don't know what that means to you."

Adam pursed his lips, breathed through his nose. Opened and closed his mouth. This was the performance of impasse. Of forcing himself through the impasse to see it from her side, from a *mother's* side.

"Yeah," he said, eventually. "But the world's not going to blame you for that."

"You do. You blame me. How can you not?"

He shook his head. Giant, resigned nobility. "You didn't have a choice. Why *wouldn't* you believe her. She's your daughter. I'm just one more fucking guy, in the last analysis. The world knows what fucking *guys* are like. Even fathers. Christ, especially fathers."

He swallowed the remainder of his wine. Rachel restrained herself. The Ambien was already crumbled. On a little piece of napkin behind the cookie jar. Wait. Not yet.

Adam put his head in his hands, ran them up through his dark hair, held it for a moment. Exhaled. He was still wearing his wedding band.

"I don't know what to say," he said. Truthfully, she thought. He was so full of lies his occasional truths were like little solar flares. "I just . . . Fuck. I can't believe this is happening. Why is this happening?"

"We have to find a way through with her," Rachel said. "Whatever the reason for what she did, it's nothing good. We have to talk to her." She left a pause. "She's going to have to know that you'll be able to forgive her."

Another facial performance: the wound inflicted on him—and the larger self grudgingly conceding that she was right.

"I don't know that there's a way forward." He hesitated. "For me, I mean."

"Don't you care about her? About us?"

"Jesus Christ, of course I fucking care!" He got to his feet, paced away to the big glass doors. His hands were clenched. "Of course I care. But . . . How, exactly, do you think it could possibly be between me and her now?"

Rachel went back to the fridge. Refilled his glass. Added the Ambien. Didn't touch her own. She took the glass to him. Relief when he took it and swallowed.

"This is going to sound insane," she said. "But I've made dinner."

The rest of the evening went as she'd imagined. There was nothing to talk about except the one thing. In spite of which they took occasional surreally ordinary detours: his work; Hester's marriage; his bizarre existence living secretly on the boat; even, for a few minutes, the president's latest gaffes. But always they returned to the same loop: that she wanted to heal what had happened and that they didn't understand why it had and that he didn't know how he could come back. The bottle of Semillon went, quickly, almost entirely to him. He ate only half his dinner, though it was his favorite, chicken in a wine and wild mushroom sauce, sautéed potatoes with paprika, asparagus. When she opened the second bottle and brought it to the table he said: I have to drive. She looked away from him. Didn't touch him. But said: No, you don't. Which shifted him into a new calculus. His goal was the same: to consolidate his gain. Now he was working out whether fucking his wife would help that. He was mentally busy, she knew, shuffling the necessities. But the wine had loosened him. As had the Ambien. In the lounge they sat at right angles to each other on the white corner suite. When he blinked, now, his eyelids met and parted slowly, like a failing mechanism.

She reached under her blouse, unhooked her bra, pulled it out, awkwardly.

He observed, struggled for alertness.

"It's new," she said. "Doesn't fit right."

They looked at each other. He was very uncertain. She had only a narrow window, she knew.

"I've missed you," she said quietly.


He was so groggy by the time they made it to the bedroom she had to pull his clothes off, albeit under the disguise of passion. She knew, in fact, that she didn't have to fuck him. He was close enough to sleep. He *would* sleep, and she would be at liberty to do what she had to do. She didn't need sex for her practical purposes.

She needed it to solidify her hatred.

When she straddled him (having applied lubricant in the bathroom) and took him inside her, she focused on his face and let the footage run. All of it. He and Elspeth had been at the Campbellville house alone. Elspeth had told her, between sobs, that he'd been in tears, after he'd done it. He'd got down on his knees and begged her to understand. He'd been taking medicines for depression, he said, and with the drink it had messed up his mind. It had made him crazy. He went to the kitchen and brought a knife. He said if she couldn't forgive him he'd kill himself right there, in front of her. Begged and begged and begged. For her silence, too. It'll kill your mother. It'll *kill* your mother. Please, angel. Either let me kill myself or let me get help.

The second time it happened he was different. There were, initially, the same tears. But there was anger, too: You've always known there's something special between us. And don't look so innocent. It takes two to tango. You know what that means?

Rachel thought of the courage it would have taken for her daughter to fight through that. Elspeth had walked around with it for months. Changed inside. Diseased. And in the end it was almost an accident that had brought it out. They—mother and daughter—had been arguing about Elspeth's falling grades. At some point Rachel had said: Your father's just as worried about this as I am. And Elspeth had said: He's not worried about *that*.

He's not worried about *that*.

The single emphasis. Even in that moment, seeing her daughter's face suddenly closing like a door too late to prevent the escape of a prisoner, Rachel had felt the world tilt. The world was nothing but a flat plane that could tip you without warning into the void. Elspeth hadn't clamped her hand to her mouth—but Rachel had seen the ghost of the gesture. They'd looked at each other. The kitchen bright and gleaming around them. The backyard's life of thick color and quiet breathing.

Then Elspeth's eyes had filled with tears.

*And don't look so innocent. It takes two to tango.*

Either because of the mix of booze and soporific or because he still harbored a lingering suspicion, he couldn't stay hard inside her. It was a disappointment to Rachel, that she couldn't sink low enough to accommodate her own disgust. She'd wanted the final ignominy. She couldn't think of another way of honoring her daughter's suffering.

In the end she rolled off him. They were past speech. Even his calculations had flailed, collapsed, dissipated.

He slept.

She waited five minutes. Ten. The house's silence gathered around her, rich with what it knew, what it was waiting for, since it had witnessed her preparations. There was a question in the quiet: Well? Are you going to do this or not? Bizarrely, the question was asked in his voice. Which gave her the necessary impetus.

She eased herself from the bed. Paused at the doorway to the landing. Listened. His breathing was deep and steady. She slipped into her nightdress and went into the reading room.

The larger hammer. The Indian-print throw. A pair of the vinyl gloves.

A quick glance out of the window above the box seat. Vincent was at his post in the Lyles' conservatory, book held up, reading lamp angled.

Back in the bedroom she stood over her husband. The hammer's rubber grip was solid, snug, perfectly designed. She had an image of it coming off a factory production line with thousands just like it. She wondered if anyone had ever written a novel from an inanimate object's point of view: *Autobiography of a Hammer.* Witness to all the ordinary domestic life: building a tree house; putting up pictures; refurbishing a bathroom. Conversations with other tools that did their other jobs. A novel with a cute device to observe human life. A novel you wouldn't really see the point of—until the end. Until a moment just like this one.

She raised her arm. Tightened her grip. Felt the hammer's weight of physics and innocence. Thor was the god of thunder. And here was the silence before it broke.

The sound of the first blow was distinct and intimate. A soft crack.

She stopped. No blood.

He groaned. She hadn't known what to expect. In all the planning this was the one blind spot.

She felt his body's alarm going off. A terrible biological awareness, red blood cells like firemen screamed awake by the Klaxon rushing, rushing to the site, consciousness scrambling—Jesus Christ . . . *Jesus Christ*—all the strands of his being hurrying to gather because this was death, death was here and they hadn't known, had never dreamed that it would come and it was too late, if they didn't run now, run now and gather and rise up against it—

His shoulders came alive. His arms. She could feel it. The comforter moved. His adrenaline sang madly in silence through the softness and warmth. His left knee bent—though his eyes didn't open. She hadn't seen this. Of course she hadn't been allowed to see this, to imagine it. Of course murder had demands, insisted on keeping certain secrets, to be revealed only in the full darkness of its flight. Murder gave itself to you, but not fully, not fully until it was sure of you, until you were in it, until there was no going back and it was guaranteed its delivery of blood.

The temptation was to watch. The temptation was to surrender to amazement—at yourself. But if his eyes opened . . . If he was *there*—

She lost herself after that.

There really was nothing.

The blows compressed time and space around her and dissolved her into a pure blind heat.

The world came back to her, or she came back to it, and she found herself slumped on the floor leaning against the side of the bed. She felt jet-lagged, tiredness upon her like a heavy second skin. What she wanted more than anything was to lie down and fall asleep.

She got to her feet. She must move very quickly now, do nothing except what needed to be done. The necessary actions lay ahead of her like pristine items in an immaculately clean and tidy house. Nothing must be allowed to invade the spaces between them.

The hammer lay next to him on the pillow. There wasn't much blood, but it was shocking on the white linen. His mouth was open. Each eye showed a sliver of white between the almost-shut lids. Eyes were like little boiled eggs. Revolting when you let yourself think that way.

*He's already dead. You don't need the knife.*

She had wondered about this. Equivocated. But in the end the knife was an irresistible insurance. The image of him coming to, in spite of everything. People survived all sorts of things, incredibly. But they didn't survive stab wounds to the heart. Or maybe they did? Biology was mischievous, either by cunning or caprice. Rasputin jumping up and attacking his assassins after God knows how much poison and how many bullets. There were no guarantees. All you could do was maximize the odds.

She went to the reading room and very delicately removed both the knife and the second hammer from their brown paper bags, taking great care not to touch the surfaces where she'd laid the prints. You hold the knife by the blade, the hammer by the claws.

It was an odd way to stab someone, even someone already dead. To hold the very tip of the handle between a thumb and forefinger, position the blade against the flesh—then press down with the flat of the palm against the top of the grip, putting your body weight into it. (It reminded her of Elspeth as a child, forcing cookie cutters into the dough with hilarious grim focus.) Perhaps no one in history had ever been stabbed in just this way. She imagined the bored universe that had seen everything now grudgingly conceding a novelty, though it was past caring. The blade went in as through raw meat. Of course it did: This *was* raw meat. It gave her a curious feeling of deflation, to have human corporeality so dully confirmed.

There was nothing from him, from the body, from the now plainly established corpse. No hiss of gas, no neural twitch. Just the yielding of the flesh to the puncture, the spurt and hurry of blood, as if the blood had been desperate to get out all these years.

Still, the heart. For an insane moment she thought to locate it by feeling for its beat. She did, actually, put her gloved palm where she thought it must be, if only to confirm it *wasn't* still beating. It wasn't. In spite of her paranoia she knew death was here, had taken up its place in him like a cat finding a warm spot. He was plain and solid with it.

Nonetheless, the heart mattered to her. A bit of whimsical consciousness said: symbolically—but she ignored it.

It took three failed attempts to pierce the breastbone before the solution offered itself to her. With a bonus: The force required oughtn't to be within the strength of a slender woman. She took up the first hammer. Put the point of the blade back in position, still holding only the tip of the handle, raised the hammer—then struck.

Tiredness came at her again when she heaved him from the bed onto the floor and rolled him over onto his back. It occurred to her that she might simply run out of fuel, faint, collapse, wake up to daylight and the whole thing ruined. She wanted a glass of water. Her mouth was terribly dry. Somewhere, in some glossy and redundant health magazine, she'd read: *Hydration is the most overlooked aspect of physical well-being.* Too bad. The machinations—a glass, the faucet, another set of gloves—were beyond her now.

She took the second hammer, as yet unsullied, and dabbed the metal head into his blood. Since there was no end to her imagination she saw a coroner in scrubs saying: *No fragments of bone on the hammer head, which is unusual, but not impossible.* Again, too bad. It wouldn't stand up against the rest of the evidence. It would pass because it had to.

In the wardrobe she found the new black joggers, sweatshirt and Lycra ski mask. She took off the gloves and pulled the clothes on. Hurried down the stairs. One by one she turned off the lights that had been left on when they'd gone up. Now, but for the lamp on the nightstand by their bed, the house was in darkness. In the kitchen she gave her eyes time to adjust. Then she put on fresh gloves and a pair of sneakers and went up to fetch the first hammer, the Murder Hammer, as she had begun referring to it, mentally, to keep things straight. Her breath was hot in her mouth and nose.

The yard's darkness was soothing. She kept to the shadows and moved quickly around the border to the shed, let herself in, and left the door open behind her. No flashlight. She couldn't risk it. Just the thin moonlight that came in through the door and windows. Again, it took her eyes a moment to find their landmarks.

Groping, softly, she found the bucket with the box and old tennis racket she'd set on top as a guide. She removed these and the smell of raw bleach came up to her. Rubber gardening gloves and an oily rag next to the bucket. She pulled the gloves on, scrubbed the hammer in the bleach, and put it back on the workbench with the other tools. With the bucket, she paused in the doorway and looked back at the house. Still and silent. Only the one buttery light from the bedroom. The lamp had been a wedding gift from one of his cousins. The wedding. The glint of the rings and the minister's steel-rimmed glasses. *Till death us do part.*

Well.

Stop that. Keep the spaces between the actions clear.

She emptied the bucket down the storm drain and returned it to the shed. Stuffed the used nylon gloves into an open bag of potting compost, put the gardening pair back on, and closed the door behind her. Then she went to the back of the yard.

There was black bamboo here, at the top of the border of mixed perennials, beyond which was the wooden fence that separated their property from the Lyles'. Green bamboo on the Lyles' side. Ferns, hostas, and fuchsia sloping down to their lawn. And if the security lights weren't working?

Pointless. You go ahead because there's nothing else to do. And if they're not working, fuck it. It's a subtraction from the scenario—but the scenario will hold.

At the same time she thought this the counter-thought rose up: The scenario won't hold. None of it will. There are probably less than two hours between you and your arrest. Somehow they'll know. They'll see and they'll know: *She did it.*

But she was already at the top of the fence, scrambling, dropping with a soft crash down on the other side.

She crawled through the plants, still moist from the sprinklers' last rinse. The good smell of earth and foliage. She got to her feet and strode out onto the Lyles' back lawn.

The lights didn't come on.

There was Vincent in his chair, *The Corrections* open on his lap. She waved her arms above her head.

The lights didn't come on.

She moved forward, toward the conservatory. Quickened her pace—and tripped over the edge of the lawn roller, concealed in the sycamore's shadow.

The lights came on just as she got to her feet.

She and Vincent stared at each other. The lights were painfully bright, it seemed to her. A ludicrous exposure. She should have bulked herself out with extra layers, flattened her breasts. Surely he'd know it was a woman? Surely he'd know it was her? In the few seconds when they were face-to-face it was as if she could hear him say: *Rachel?*

She turned and ran.

It took, of course, an age to wade through the bamboo and haul herself over the fence. Her composure was dreamily exploded. On the other side she landed badly and jarred her ankle. Heat flooded up around her like heavy water.

But now as never before she was at the mercy of the ticking clock. Optimistically she had perhaps twenty minutes. The deeper part of herself knew this was more insurance: Faced with this thing she had to do, this last, dreadful thing, she couldn't afford to give herself time to think. To think would be to give cowardice room. To think would be to fail.

She tossed the gardening gloves at the front of the shed and ran back across the lawn to the patio and the kitchen's glass doors.

Inside, she kicked off the sneakers, took a last (please God) pair of vinyl gloves from the box under the sink, and hurried to the utility room.

She stripped, stuffed the jogging gear into the bottom of the laundry hamper under the rest of the unwashed clothes, and went upstairs.

From a shelf in the walk-in wardrobe she took a cardboard box of photograph albums and opened it up. Not Adam's, these, but her own Polaroids and prints from the early years of their marriage, before his compulsive need to photograph everything properly did away with any inclination she had to pick up a camera herself. She folded the ski mask and put it underneath the albums. They will have no reason to look in here. They will have no reason to look in the laundry hamper, nor the shed, nor the greenhouse. When I come through the other side of this I will . . .

The thought was swallowed in an upsurge of fear. Ordinary fear, fear of pain, fear for her own body. In the religious depictions of Gethsemane, Christ was shown sweating blood. *Father, if thou be willing, remove this cup from me.* The memory of the image went through her, viscerally. Her own face felt studded with blood. She couldn't, for a moment, get to her feet. She stayed where she was, kneeling over the open box. The frail idea of Christ and salvation like a tiny cobweb the universe had long since blown casually to fluttering threads. The truth was an empty darkness, not even, the cosmologists said now, infinite. If there was an Intelligence it was as she'd felt it after killing Jenner, amoral, impassioned only by curiosity. It was neither for nor against her nor anyone else. Including Adam.

Including Elspeth.

The thought renewed her. The absence of natural justice. There was no justice beyond what we made. And here she was, making it.

She got up, replaced the box.

Almost, she didn't bother with the tiny parings of skin. There was enough without them, surely? And time, time was hemorrhaging.

But she had them, so it was foolish not to use them. She took the bag from the reading room, peeled off the gloves, used tweezers and the head of a pin to wedge them in as best she could under her nails, kept long enough for the purpose. If they fell out they fell out. They'd fall out near enough so that any CSI boffin worth his or her salt ought to find them.

She refitted the gloves, slacker after one use, but that hardly mattered now.

It was time. She put her bloodstained nightdress back on. Took her cell phone and set it by the French windows. Opened them. Lifted the photinia pot from its tray. As a late scene-setting precaution she took the lamp and smashed its amber glass shade against the nightstand. Tossed it to the floor. Some sign of a struggle, at least.

Then she picked up the knife—by its blade.

The knife was alive with physical innocence.

*If you prick us, do we not bleed?*

This is the last thing you must do. After this it's out of your control.

The amoral intelligence bristled, suddenly came close out of the remote constellations with a smile of calm fascination.

She placed the knife handle in the hinge of the French window and closed it until the grip was firm. The blade was pointed just under her ribs.

Then—trying to think and getting only a vast white terror like sheet lightning—she walked onto it.

The rest was a dream. She swam through soft heat and redness. Her heartbeat was outside her, a pulse in the room that pressed on her temples. The wounds spoke to her, though they had only one word: pain. The distress was terrible, as if her body couldn't believe her mind had forced it to perform this obscene act, this inversion of the most basic principle. Her body cried out in shock that it had been betrayed. She wasn't unsympathetic. She would have comforted it (as if it were a child) had she been able. Incapable as she was, there was still, in the red, soft-edged dream, some part of herself offering the silent equivalent of hush . . . *I know . . . I'm sorry . . . It'll be all right . . . I'm sorry, but I had to . . .*

She was unsure of her orientation. She was on her knees, she thought, but there were multiple sly gravities. The night outside the open windows was large and cool and open, scented by the green lawn and the neighborhood's dozing asphalt. She tossed the knife. Wondered as it left her hand what she would do if it didn't clear the balcony. She wasn't certain that it did, but the care was running out of her now. She hadn't known care would be such a precious resource, so easily spent.

It took an extraordinary, delicate, draining effort to remove the gloves and put them in the photinia's tray. Lifting the pot back into place to hide them took her for a while into starless darkness, her limbs distant things, unreliable. She lost a little time. Went again into darkness—then was hauled out by something, some part of herself she'd forbidden to shut down. Death—the curled-up cat—had left Adam's body and was walking near to her, intrigued. Was there more tonight? A feast!

The icons on her cell phone's screen danced and shivered. There was blood on her hands. She hadn't been able to override the impulse to hold her wounds, to try to stop what was inside from coming out.

The phone icon. White receiver on a green background. She was so very close to going out. It was a wonderful warmth being offered to her.

But she thought of her and Elspeth again, the image of the two of them driving Route 1 in ocean sunlight, Elspeth's bare sunlit feet on the dash and her long dark hair lifted by the wind.

She dialed 911.

# 45

## *September 18, 2017*

Valerie was wrapping up at the marina when Will called.

"They're back home," he said. For the last two hours Rachel and Elspeth had been at Élan, an upmarket beauty spa on Valencia. Will on surveillance. "The kid's got a nifty new haircut."

"Okay," Valerie said. "I'm done here. I'm heading over there now."

"We got what we need?"

"I doubt it."

"Shit."

For a few minutes Valerie stood on the dock watching the CSI team packing up their gear. Beyond the *Aqua Nova* the bay was golden-blue and sunlit, a fresh morning with a light breeze coming off the ocean. *Aqua Nova*. New water. She wondered if Adam Grant had renamed the boat when he'd bought it, little knowing that was precisely what his wife and daughter would be sailing into, figuratively, after his death. The world's insatiable appetite for irony. She imagined the phrase repeating itself in Rachel Grant's head, becoming the mantra that stiffened her resolve. New Water . . . New Water . . .

And her own new water? At least this time, postponement blame didn't rest with her. Yesterday evening—what should have been cards-on-the-table evening—Nick had gone to his mother's after work to assemble a new flat-pack wardrobe and had ended up staying over. It wasn't unusual: His mother loved having him under her roof for a night (it was terrible to Valerie, the ravenous maternity still there, starving, gnawing, grateful for crumbs) and he was a good enough son to indulge her, occasionally. But his voice had been cold on the phone when he'd called to let Valerie know. Her own fault, obviously, *obviously*. She was sick of it now, the untold truth—and the mess of feelings that surrounded it like a cocoon.

Which image turned her from the dock and headed her toward her car.


Rachel answered the door. She looked renewed; beautiful, in fact. Valerie had never seen her like this in the flesh, fully cosmeticized, coppery hair glowing. The green eyes were filled with feline life. She was wearing a deep red Lycra top that precisely matched her lipstick, tight white jeans, high-heeled sandals in pale gray suede. Beyond her, the big central hall looked freshly polished and cleaned. A sleepy odor of beeswax from the walnut floor.

"Hi," Valerie said. "I need to speak with you."

Not *quite* her imagination, she thought, that Rachel's face betrayed a flicker of something like recognition—of a dreaded moment come round at last. But she recovered in an instant.

"Of course," she said, stepping aside for Valerie to enter and ushering her into the kitchen.

"Is Elspeth here with you?"

"Yes, she's right there." Rachel gestured through the glass doors. Elspeth, in sawn-off denims and a white halter-top, was in a sun lounger on the travertine patio, headphones in, eyes closed, a glass of iced orange juice on the wrought-iron table next to her. "But I thought I made it clear—"

"We need to talk privately. Undisturbed. You might want to tell her."

Rachel adjusted, visibly, to Valerie's new tone. Some tension went out of her shoulders.

"Wait here," she said. Her tone was new, too. They understood each other. It had taken barely twenty seconds.

Valerie watched her go out to Elspeth. The girl (Will was right about the hairdo; it was still long, but had been given some layers and waves) looked up, removed her headphones, listened, looked back into the kitchen (nervous, nervous, *plainly* nervous), nodded. Valerie imagined Rachel's instructions: It's fine. Don't worry. She'll be gone in a minute.

Rachel came back inside and closed the door behind her.

"Let's go into the lounge," she said.

Valerie followed her back out across the hall and into the big room at the front of the house. No hospital bed now. Just the original minimalism, the vast white corner couch, the paintings, the discreet technology. Neither of them sat down.

"So?" Rachel said.

Well, yes, exactly: So? They were facing each other.

"I know you killed Dwight Jenner," Valerie said. "And I know you killed your husband."

Rachel didn't answer. But after a moment she lowered her eyes, turned, walked to the window and looked out. The green lawn, the maples, the high blue sky. She held her elbows. Valerie studied her from behind, the slender neck and wispily chopped red hair still smelling of the salon. She ran the footage, the only possible footage. This woman, here, now, in this house. What she'd found it in herself to do. The willpower that would have required.

"I have no idea what you're talking about," Rachel said.

Valerie crossed the room and stood alongside her, studying her profile. "Yes, you do," she said.

"Are you arresting me?"

"Not yet."

"Then I don't have anything else to say."

"That's quite an understated response to an accusation of murder. Double murder, in fact."

"I find I don't get easily overexcited these days."

"You use a timer for the photographs?" Valerie asked. "Or was that Jenner?"

Rachel smiled, sadly, didn't take her eyes from their glazed survey of her lawn.

"Why don't you say what you have to say and then leave?" she said. "You can come back when you're ready to arrest me."

Valerie felt her own tension leave her. "All right," she said. "Fine. You killed your husband because he sexually assaulted your daughter. Either she told you or you found out about it some other way."

Pause. No discernible change in Rachel. Then she very slightly shifted. Straightened her back, slowly released her grip on her elbows and let her arms hang loose. Valerie looked at Rachel's feet in the heels. No tremor.

"Coming to us wasn't an option. Maybe you didn't want to put Elspeth through it. Or maybe life with Lawrence Garner did away with any trust you might have had in the police."

Rachel closed her eyes. Breathed. Opened them again.

"You started an affair with Dwight Jenner. Incognito. Sophia. You knew he was out, because as the relevant prosecutor Adam would have been notified. The photographs were for us. To build the narrative that Adam and Jenner had a woman in common, as rivals. You point us to strip clubs and establish an independent witness, Gigi at X-quisite to confirm that Sophia was a real person. You called Jenner on Adam's phone, which as far as we're concerned is *Adam* calling Jenner. That's the link we're looking for so that's the link we find. The truth is Jenner was never anywhere near your husband. On July thirty-first you drove Jenner to the Campbellville house and killed him. We have you in the Volvo on camera with him, albeit as Sophia. You cut off his hands and feet, kept them, buried his body in the desert. I have to assume marking him with the Lucifer symbol was an insurance policy, since I can see no reason why you'd *want* the body found. And you knew about Lucifer because Adam had the case files here in the house. Or you saw them at the office. At any rate you saw them, and you knew the killer had never been caught. I guess you didn't need the feet, just the hands . . ."

Valerie shrugged. "You probably took the feet just to beef up the apparently ritualistic nature of the murder."

She paused again. She couldn't believe she was going to get through this without Rachel responding to something. But so far the composure was untouched.

"With Jenner dead and buried, you used his hands to lay the prints, the DNA, the all but incontrovertible physical evidence. What did you do—keep them on ice?"

Rachel lowered her eyes. Smiled. Said nothing.

"If you did, you kept them here. The big freezer in the utility room would do the job. And yes, there's a team on its way. We have the requisite warrant."

Rachel looked at her. Her eyes were calm.

"Oh, I don't imagine they'll find anything," Valerie said. "You've had weeks to get rid of the dead meat and scrub up. The props too. I'm not expecting to dig out a blond wig or a black ski mask. We know you took the boat out. It's a big ocean. We know Adam was living on the boat, too, after you kicked him out."

A young mother and her son walking a tan Labrador went past the driveway entrance, talking very seriously about something. The neighborhood was bright and still. Valerie didn't recall seeing a single scrap of litter anywhere, not even a cigarette butt. Pacific Heights.

"On August fourth you call Adam—as his phone proves—and persuade him to come home," she continued. "Easily enough done, I guess, since you had him pretty much by the balls. One way or another you get him in the bedroom. Which is where you killed him. Can't have been easy keeping the prints you planted clean. With Adam dead you get into the burglar gear and put in an appearance in the Lyles' backyard. You know you'll be seen because Vincent Lyle's your insomniac literary buddy. It all helps the narrative: crazy Jenner getting into your property from the rear. Obviously the burglar alarm's not armed. It's the kind of night where the standard domestic routine's suspended—or you just switch it off yourself. In the end we're looking for two ghosts: Jenner because he's already dead and Sophia because she never existed in the first place. The one person we're not looking for is you. Why would we be? As far as we're concerned you're collateral damage from the dirty side of your husband's life."

The smallest flicker. At the word "dirty." Valerie regretted using it. "I don't know how you found the guts to stab yourself, Rachel, but that's what you did. You have my admiration."

They were silent for a while.

Then Rachel turned and looked at her. "Come with me," she said.

"What?"

"Come with me."

Baffled, Valerie followed Rachel upstairs and into the master bedroom.

"Inside," Rachel said, pointing to the en suite.

Incredulous, Valerie reached for her gun.

"Don't be ridiculous," Rachel said. "Just show me you're not wearing a wire."

"I'm not wearing a wire."

"Show me. I have things to say to you. But not to a recording device. Take off your clothes. You can keep the gun."

"I'm not wearing a goddamned—"

"Fine, then get out."

Valerie laughed. "Are you serious?"

Rachel just waited, breathing through her nose.

Jesus Christ, Valerie thought. She was picturing the interrogation of Rachel Grant. Two realities: First, Rachel would do or say nothing that would concede her daughter's molestation. Second, she'd have the best lawyers money could buy. And there was plenty, *plenty* of money. Dan Kruger would probably do it for free. They could question Elspeth, of course. But even if Elspeth told them what had happened to her, it wouldn't convict her mother. They didn't have the evidence to prove Rachel killed Jenner, and if they couldn't prove that, they couldn't prove Jenner *didn't* kill Adam Grant. Not only beyond reasonable doubt, but nowhere near a point where doubt would face any kind of serious challenge. All there would *be* was doubt.

The physical evidence at the scene—right there in the bedroom—was overwhelming. Certainly more than a match for a handful of grainy images which might or might not be Rachel Grant in disguise.

Valerie got undressed, awkwardly, since she'd decided not to relinquish the Glock. She stopped at her underwear. Rachel unhooked a white toweling robe from the back of the door. "Everything," she said. "This is freshly washed."

There would be no negotiation, Valerie knew. Either she would comply or Rachel would simply tell her to get dressed and fuck off.

Rachel held out the robe and, not without a little absurd flicker on the ether between them, turned her back.

Valerie removed her underwear and put on the robe, which, she had to concede, smelled of nothing but floral fabric softener. She sat on the edge of the bathtub, still holding her firearm. This is going to make some story tonight, she thought. Hey, Nick, guess what: I got naked in front of a woman this afternoon. Except the thought reminded her that they weren't exactly in joking mode at the moment.

"Are you decent?" Rachel said.

"Yes."

Rachel turned, gathered up the clothes, and took them out across the landing to the reading room. Dumped them on the bed and returned. Closed the bathroom door behind her.

"Nothing's going to happen," she said to Valerie.

"By which you mean . . . ?"

"By which I mean you can't prove any of it."

"That's for us to—"

"I'm not stupid," Rachel said. "I know you'll try. But you won't find any of the things you need. You haven't a hope in hell."

Valerie found herself smiling. "Well, let's see," was all she said. She wasn't sure what Rachel expected her to say. "Tell me something," she said. "Do you have any doubts?"

"About what?"

"About Elspeth."

"Do you mean do I have any doubt that she told me the truth?"

"Yes."

"None whatsoever." They stared at each other.

"Did you suspect anything?" Valerie asked. "Before she told you?"

Rachel didn't (perhaps couldn't) answer immediately. There was another smile on the lovely mouth, now. Disappointment—in herself. The failure—of herself. Because obviously, she *hadn't* suspected anything. No matter what she'd done, now it would never be enough to atone for this sin of her own blindness.

"Are you married?" Rachel said.

"Yes." It was still a surprise to Valerie that she was, that they'd actually bothered with a ceremony (albeit a civic one) and a boozy party afterward. In the last two years she'd had to use the phrase "my husband" perhaps a dozen times. Always with a little mental dissonance, as if she were hiding under a fraudulent—and preposterous—identity.

Rachel opened her mouth to say something—then didn't bother. Valerie imagined the bitter cautionary lecture—*You think you know him? You don't.* But she saw too that Rachel Grant was past bothering, past caring. The predicaments of other women, other wives, other mothers, were of no interest to her. In fact, Valerie now realized, Rachel had always struck her as politically indifferent. Whatever had happened to her had made her singular, left no room for the extension of her identity into anything larger. She was a unique wild animal. Her world was the world of her own flesh and blood. What mattered was her daughter. Even her own survival was secondary.

"Adam rescued me," she said. "I never really knew why."

Valerie raised her eyebrows.

"Oh, sure, I was something at eighteen," Rachel said. "But that's nothing. He could've had his pick. At any rate, he wasn't under any illusions about me. He took the difficult case on purpose. Not just me. The job. The cloud of ethics with the nucleus of horror. Even if he didn't know himself, his soul did. It was all a compensation. Subconscious. Preemptive. His soul knew what was coming. I realize none of this makes sense to you. It didn't to me until after it had happened."

Valerie thought perhaps she did understand. Pour enough energy into the moral life and it might just turn out to be the antidote—to yourself.

Or not, depending on the strength of your nature, the ferocity of your needs. *The natural things are disgusting.*

"I haven't answered your question," Rachel said. "No, I had no idea. We weren't happy, but only in the unsurprising ways. We were bored, we got on each other's nerves. But we laughed, too. Last couple of years he was impatient with Elspeth, irritable. As if her adolescence was bringing his own back. I didn't make much of it. I didn't make *enough* of it, obviously."

Valerie sat with the Glock heavy in her hand. She was thinking of her own father, who had loved her and her sister without complication. She was thinking of Nick. Could she ever be wrong about him in that way? Intellectually you had to concede that you could. Other women's mistakenness entailed, by way of logical possibility, your own. Intellectually, yes, it had to be admitted. You could be willing to bet your life on how well you knew someone: There was always the possibility you would lose the bet.

That wasn't what mattered, she thought. What mattered was being willing to place the bet in the first place. In the absence of certainty there was only trust. The only way to avoid the betrayal of trust was to trust no one. And what kind of a life would that be?

"How did you find all this out?" Rachel asked.

"I didn't," Valerie said. "Not until right now. But I had the thoughts. Elspeth's behavior. The shoplifting, the attempted promiscuity. Adam's . . ." Leave that. Adam's *what*? Sexual nullity when she, Valerie, had him in bed? She shook her head. "Do you think Elspeth has any idea it was you?"

"Of course not."

"She doesn't wonder what you and Adam were doing in bed together the night he was killed?"

"She doesn't know we were. She won't, either, unless you tell her. In which case I'll say he forced me. She won't have any trouble believing *that*."

It was a curious relief to both of them to be speaking truthfully to each other. It allowed a mutual respect which had hitherto seemed irrational. Under different circumstances, Valerie knew, they could have been friends. Rachel Grant had a spartan strength that matched her own. They had both been formed by suffering. Valerie as a daily witness, Rachel as a victim.

"Did Lawrence Garner rape you?"

"What do you think?"

"I'm sorry."

Rachel leaned back against the door. Put her hands in her pockets. Sighed. "Jesus, I'm tired," she said.

"Yeah, I can imagine."

"Do you blame me?" Rachel said.

Valerie didn't know what to say. She didn't know what to say because she didn't know what she thought. If Adam Grant had raped his daughter, did she blame Rachel Grant for killing him? Well, did she?

"No," she said. "But my not blaming you doesn't make what you did legal."

"I notice you don't say it doesn't make it right."

Touché.

"There's nothing," Rachel began—then faltered, slightly. Recovered. "There's nothing I wouldn't do for her. I don't expect you to understand."

*Because you're not a mother,* Valerie added, in her head. Well, technically . . .

"I can't ask you what I'm about to ask you, but I'm going to anyway," Rachel said. She was a little dreamy now, as if whatever extraordinary fuel she'd been running on was, at long last, reaching its end.

"What's that?" Valerie said, though she knew.

"Don't make her suffer. You don't have to. You and I both know that even if she tells you what her father did it's not going to put me away."

"We don't have enough to arrest you," Valerie said. "Let alone get a conviction. It's not in my power to decide whether Elspeth will face questioning."

"Yes it is. Of course it is."

Yes, it was. That was the truth. There was absolutely nothing to stop Valerie letting the case go cold. If it had been just Adam Grant she might have been tempted. There was a temptation even now, in the soft robe and the clean bathroom, in the tiredness that seemed to spread out from Rachel to her, like warm, rising water. *Aqua Nova.*

"You shouldn't have killed Dwight," she said. "I don't blame you for killing your husband. I blame you for killing someone else to do it."

"A convicted felon."

"Who did his time. He has a family too." You should know, her inner voice said. You nearly fucked one of them. "That wasn't your decision to make," Valerie said.

"I know," Rachel said, still dreamily. "I know you'll do what you have to do. And if you succeed, a thirteen-year-old girl who was raped by her father will lose her mother. That's some moral math you deal in."

"Someone has to."

"I suppose they do. We all do. We just don't get the same answers."

Valerie got to her feet. "We're done here, I think," she said. "Get me my clothes, please."

# 46

The CSI team found, not surprisingly, nothing.

"We should have bugged the goddamned house," Will said, that evening at the station.

"We had no reason to," Valerie said.

"Or installed a camera. At least that way we'd have got to see you strip."

Valerie had, for the record, filed a report of her conversation, though it would count for nothing, since Rachel Grant would deny it ever took place. The fact remained: They had nothing except the traffic cam image of Jenner and a blonde they would never be able to prove conclusively was Rachel Grant. And even if they did, it wouldn't be enough for a jury. Valerie had told Rachel the truth: The evidence didn't justify an arrest, let alone a conviction.

"We're going to talk to the daughter though—right?" Will said.

"That's up to the cap. I know he thinks it's a waste of time, and he's probably right."

"What're you going to tell Jenner's brother?"

"Half brother. I don't know. Not the truth. I do that, he'll go after her himself and we've got another vigilante killing. Plus I don't think he's got the resources to get away with it. The truth would be his ticket to San Q. He doesn't deserve that."

———

And thus the imperfections of the law, Valerie thought, driving home through the darkening evening. Some people got away with murder. The question was: Weren't some people entitled to?

The truth was the law didn't work. It was nothing more than the best failure civilization had on offer.

Underneath or between or above the law was love—and all its distentions. In the face of love, the law was nothing.

*There's nothing I wouldn't do for her.*

Literally.

So far Valerie's love had been for her parents and her sister and Nick. Would she kill to save them? Undoubtedly. Would she kill to *avenge* them?

Not, she supposed, if she had impregnable faith in the law.

Which she did not. How could she? *She* was the law—and her faith in herself was ravaged, riddled, rotten with doubt.

Even her questionable love—precarious, unpredictable, incessantly compromised by selfishness—was already more than a match for the law. Imagine what it would become if a child claimed it. Would there be anything she wouldn't do for a daughter or son? The question was rhetorical to the point of comedy.

And that was what she was looking at, now: the promotion of motherhood to the top of the moral food chain. There was something vulgar and terrifying about it. Yet at the same time, through the swirl of these thoughts, a feeling of inevitability and relief. Almost the way Rachel had reacted to being found out earlier: the dreaded thing come round at last.


Nick was in the kitchen, cooking, when she entered the apartment. Smells of olive oil and garlic and chili. Her empty stomach—indifferent to the psyche's big moments—yowled, quietly, and with a reluctant yielding she knew he wanted to make peace. The willingness to make peace was like a palpable presence, in fact, in the yellow of the lamps and the softness of the couch and the dusk in the windows. Last of all, she realized with a kind of foolish surprise, it was in her, too. Love, like a boxer, slumped down on its stool at the end of a bruising round, knees weak, head reeling, piteously in need of the bucket and the sponge and the trainer's reality-defying optimism. Love went in and out of darkness, small bright stars flaunting their promise of oblivion. Then the bell rang, and all the world's horror stood up in the opposite corner, and in hopeless commitment Love wobbled to its feet and staggered back into the center of the ring, knowing there would be pain and wondering how long it could possibly last.

For a moment she stood in the kitchen doorway, watching him. His glasses were on his forehead. One shirttail was hanging out of his jeans. He was concentrating. Then he turned and saw her. He put the lid on a saucepan, lowered the heat, came over to her, and put his hands on her hips. She thought: If you touch him, it's a done deal, beyond recall. Back away now or you're screwed. This is your last warning.

"Listen to me," he said.

"What?"

"If you don't want a kid right now, it's fine. It's fine if you don't want one at all. I know that's what's going on with you. I know all of it."

She stood very still. His hands on her hips were warm weights. She thought about the feeling of cold space (and freedom) that would replace them if she backed away. She was close, so very close, to doing just that. Yet she found herself smiling.

"I'm pregnant," she said. "I have been for weeks."

Now it was his turn to go still. His hands remained where they were, but for the moment they'd lost their intelligence. The seconds of silence passed, one after another, each flatly surprised that no sound disturbed its transit. He looked away from her.

"And?" he said.

She knew what he was thinking: How *many* weeks? There were energies furiously at work in him, trying to calculate, not knowing. He was so completely suspended she almost laughed. Having someone utterly at your mercy was, whether you liked it or not, funny. Why torturers giggled, presumably, going about their dirty business. She suffered from the way her mind worked, its lawless associations. Still, she was stuck with it. She was stuck with herself.

*There's nothing I wouldn't do for her. The natural things are disgusting.*

*Intellectually, yes, it must be admitted you could be wrong.*

Valerie put her hands flat on his chest. Some layer of her being moved gently from her, like a veil being drawn off, slowly. It gave her a feeling of very slightly increased exposure.

"And if I'm wrong about you," she said, "I'll kill you."